AJA MINOR: GIFTED OR CURSED

A Psychic Crime Thriller Series Book 1

Chris Bliersbach

Smashwords

curiosity was far too expansive to be limited to the dictates of my grade school and now my junior high curriculum. Then, of course, there was the Internet, which only made it too easy to feed my voracious appetite for knowledge. Even if that knowledge shattered the whole story and foundation for my name.

Go ahead, search on Asia Minor. You don't need me to tell you. What you'll learn pretty quickly is that it's not a constellation. It's a part of the continent of Asia. The westernmost section. Most of Turkey, to be exact. This is ironic because I was born on Thanksgiving Day, which is my one and only connection to turkey. Asia Minor is also called Anatolia, which wouldn't necessarily have been a bad name, but people would have undoubtedly wanted to shorten it to Ana, and I wouldn't have liked that. In the scheme of things, I'd much prefer to correct people's pronunciation of Aja than sound presumptuous by saying my name is Anatolia, not Ana. Thank you very much.

Of course, it wasn't enough just to refute the myth of my name; I had to shatter it completely. So my next foray into the all-knowing Internet was to investigate the true identity of that diamond-shaped constellation with 5 stars. This took a little more work, and to tell you the truth, I wish I would have become frustrated and called off my search. But I didn't. Instead, to my horror, I learned its name is Scutum. Yes, I may only be 12, but I've had enough health classes to know that Scutum is painfully close to the name of something the boys in my class not only have but frequently also say as a taunt, usually to a boy that has done something stupid. Like "Billy, you're such a scutum!" That Scutum is Latin for shield and borders Sagittarius, which is my astrological sign, offered some redemption for the unfortunately named constellation. I don't think my father would have offered up Scutum Minor as my name if he knew what he was looking at that February evening on the beach.

In my Internet search, I also found the potential source

CHAPTER 1

What's In a Name?

I spent the first 12 years of my life under the mistaken notion that my parents had romantically named me after a constellation of stars. When I discovered the truth, it made me wish I had remained blissfully ignorant.

My name is Aja, pronounced like the largest continent on the planet - Asia. Not A-jay. Not Ah-zha. Not A-ya. And definitely not Aha, like someone just surprised themselves by discovering something. And believe me, I heard them all. Mostly from teachers on the first day of class when they took attendance. If I weren't so damned curious about how the next person would crucify my name, I might have come to resent those befuddling three letters in my name. Or become bitter towards humanity in general. But I didn't. Because up until what I call my enlightenment, I was not just a star. I was a whole constellation of stars supposedly named Asia Minor.

Yeah, that's my last name - Minor. Which was entirely accurate and descriptive of what I am at this so-called tender age of 12. I couldn't fault my parents, Trace and Cheryl Minor, for the deficiencies in their education on astronomy and geography. Their intentions naming me were pure. Ever since I could remember, my parents told me my name was based on two occurrences. One romantic and the other rather unfortunate but oddly related to the first.

We live in New Jersey, and before I was born, so the story goes, my parents went on a vacation to Florida in February to escape the frigid winter weather. One balmy evening, they decided to go to the beach and "lay out under the stars," as they would say. For the longest time, I was confused about how my parents laying out under the stars in Florida in February could result in my appearance in New Jersey on November 27th. I'm not so confused about it now, but I don't want to talk about it because it is my parents we're talking about here, ew! Apparently, while lying on the beach, a grouping of five stars in the shape of a diamond caught their eye. My father told my mom that the name of that grouping of stars was called Asia Minor.

This, in itself, was probably sufficient to earn me my name. But no, I needed to make damn sure to be sentenced to a lifetime of having my name mispronounced. Well, it was more the doctor's fault than mine. He failed to catch me when I arrived and dropped me on the floor. I don't know if it was on my descent or upon impact with the ground that I received a diamond-shaped laceration on my right cheek. Regardless, my parents saw the gash, which resulted in the diamond-shaped scar I sport today, as a sign from the heavens. A sign that Aja Minor was to be my name, not only written in the stars but now stamped indelibly on my face.

Before I tell you about my age of enlightenment, I must tell you about my age of ignorance, which in many ways, was much more appealing. Yes, I said ignorance, not innocence. I have my reasons which you will come to learn, as I eventually did. Anyway, everything seemed so much easier before I turned 12. Everyone seemed happier and more friendly. The operative word here being "seemed."

I have a sister, Misty, who is four years older than me. If there was a story behind her name, I have yet to hear it. She was and still is my best friend. Misty and I get along. I can't

ever remember a time when we fought. I didn't think that this was anything special until I saw other kids who seemed to get into fights with their siblings continually. We are so close that when Misty turned 12, she gave up her separate bedroom and asked if we could share a room. We still share a bedroom to this day.

Things that happened that are curious to me now never seemed odd to me before my enlightenment. I never questioned my Mom's story that my Dad was away on business, even though he was never home after I turned 7. His absence was now going on for five years. I also didn't question why my Uncle Phil, my mother's brother, stopped visiting. Or why I suddenly had to go to a different dentist. I also didn't care that many of the boys who used to talk and play with me started to defect and become friends with other girls rather than me. There was a whole parade of things that I didn't think anything about when I was little that concern me today and give me pause.

Then there is the whole looks and body image thing that really didn't become a thing for me until recently. My scar was never anything about which I thought or cared. The only time I'd think about it was when people would ask, and I would tell them the story of my name. It wasn't my scar that people talked about; it was my hair. People were forever commenting on how beautiful my hair was and how they loved my long dark hair. Some people, women mostly, couldn't just sit there. They had to touch it like my hair was some rare gem. Suffice to say, I never got the impression that I was hideous, quite the opposite now that I think and care about it.

Now, it seems strange and curious things happen to or around me on a more frequent basis. It's almost like discovering the truth about my name has made everything go haywire. I probably would have never found out the truth about my name had I not been somewhat of a nerd. You see, I was never satisfied with just what my teachers tried to teach me. My intellect

CHAPTER 1

What's In a Name?

I spent the first 12 years of my life under the mistaken notion that my parents had romantically named me after a constellation of stars. When I discovered the truth, it made me wish I had remained blissfully ignorant.

My name is Aja, pronounced like the largest continent on the planet - Asia. Not A-jay. Not Ah-zha. Not A-ya. And definitely not Aha, like someone just surprised themselves by discovering something. And believe me, I heard them all. Mostly from teachers on the first day of class when they took attendance. If I weren't so damned curious about how the next person would crucify my name, I might have come to resent those befuddling three letters in my name. Or become bitter towards humanity in general. But I didn't. Because up until what I call my enlightenment, I was not just a star. I was a whole constellation of stars supposedly named Asia Minor.

Yeah, that's my last name - Minor. Which was entirely accurate and descriptive of what I am at this so-called tender age of 12. I couldn't fault my parents, Trace and Cheryl Minor, for the deficiencies in their education on astronomy and geography. Their intentions naming me were pure. Ever since I could remember, my parents told me my name was based on two occurrences. One romantic and the other rather unfortunate but oddly related to the first.

We live in New Jersey, and before I was born, so the story goes, my parents went on a vacation to Florida in February to escape the frigid winter weather. One balmy evening, they decided to go to the beach and "lay out under the stars," as they would say. For the longest time, I was confused about how my parents laying out under the stars in Florida in February could result in my appearance in New Jersey on November 27th. I'm not so confused about it now, but I don't want to talk about it because it is my parents we're talking about here, ew! Apparently, while lying on the beach, a grouping of five stars in the shape of a diamond caught their eye. My father told my mom that the name of that grouping of stars was called Asia Minor.

This, in itself, was probably sufficient to earn me my name. But no, I needed to make damn sure to be sentenced to a lifetime of having my name mispronounced. Well, it was more the doctor's fault than mine. He failed to catch me when I arrived and dropped me on the floor. I don't know if it was on my descent or upon impact with the ground that I received a diamond-shaped laceration on my right cheek. Regardless, my parents saw the gash, which resulted in the diamond-shaped scar I sport today, as a sign from the heavens. A sign that Aja Minor was to be my name, not only written in the stars but now stamped indelibly on my face.

Before I tell you about my age of enlightenment, I must tell you about my age of ignorance, which in many ways, was much more appealing. Yes, I said ignorance, not innocence. I have my reasons which you will come to learn, as I eventually did. Anyway, everything seemed so much easier before I turned 12. Everyone seemed happier and more friendly. The operative word here being "seemed."

I have a sister, Misty, who is four years older than me. If there was a story behind her name, I have yet to hear it. She was and still is my best friend. Misty and I get along. I can't ever remember a time when we fought. I didn't think that this was anything special until I saw other kids who seemed to get into fights with their siblings continually. We are so close that when Misty turned 12, she gave up her separate bedroom and asked if we could share a room. We still share a bedroom to this day.

Things that happened that are curious to me now never seemed odd to me before my enlightenment. I never questioned my Mom's story that my Dad was away on business, even though he was never home after I turned 7. His absence was now going on for five years. I also didn't question why my Uncle Phil, my mother's brother, stopped visiting. Or why I suddenly had to go to a different dentist. I also didn't care that many of the boys who used to talk and play with me started to defect and become friends with other girls rather than me. There was a whole parade of things that I didn't think anything about when I was little that concern me today and give me pause.

Then there is the whole looks and body image thing that really didn't become a thing for me until recently. My scar was never anything about which I thought or cared. The only time I'd think about it was when people would ask, and I would tell them the story of my name. It wasn't my scar that people talked about; it was my hair. People were forever commenting on how beautiful my hair was and how they loved my long dark hair. Some people, women mostly, couldn't just stop there. They had to touch it like my hair was some rare gem. Suffice to say, I never got the impression that I was hideous, quite the opposite now that I think and care about it.

Now, it seems strange and curious things happen to or around me on a more frequent basis. It's almost like discovering the truth about my name has made everything go haywire. I probably would have never found out the truth about my name had I not been somewhat of a nerd. You see, I was never satisfied with just what my teachers tried to teach me. My intellectual curiosity was far too expansive to be limited to the dictates of my grade school and now my junior high curriculum. Then, of course, there was the Internet, which only made it too easy to feed my voracious appetite for knowledge. Even if that knowledge shattered the whole story and foundation for my name.

Go ahead, search on Asia Minor. You don't need me to tell you. What you'll learn pretty quickly is that it's not a constellation. It's a part of the continent of Asia. The westernmost section. Most of Turkey, to be exact. This is ironic because I was born on Thanksgiving Day, which is my one and only connection to turkey. Asia Minor is also called Anatolia, which wouldn't necessarily have been a bad name, but people would have undoubtedly wanted to shorten it to Ana, and I wouldn't have liked that. In the scheme of things, I'd much prefer to correct people's pronunciation of Aja than sound presumptuous by saying my name is Anatolia, not Ana. Thank you very much.

Of course, it wasn't enough just to refute the myth of my name; I had to shatter it completely. So my next foray into the all-knowing Internet was to investigate the true identity of that diamond-shaped constellation with 5 stars. This took a little more work, and to tell you the truth, I wish I would have become frustrated and called off my search. But I didn't. Instead, to my horror, I learned its name is Scutum. Yes, I may only be 12, but I've had enough health classes to know that Scutum is painfully close to the name of something the boys in my class not only have but frequently also say as a taunt, usually to a boy that has done something stupid. Like "Billy, you're such a scutum!" That Scutum is Latin for shield and borders Sagittarius, which is my astrological sign, offered some redemption for the unfortunately named constellation. I don't think my father would have offered up Scutum Minor as my name if he knew what he was looking at that February evening on the beach.

In my Internet search, I also found the potential source

of my father's confusion. While there is no star constellation called Asia Minor, there is one called Ursa Minor. A very popular constellation that most know as The Little Dipper. Seven stars, not five. And Ursa would have been a horrid name. All things considered, while the story of my name had taken a hit from the standpoint of accuracy, Aja and all of its various pronunciations still seemed better than Anatolia, Scutum, or Ursa. Good job, Dad! Wherever you may be.

As disturbing as it was to learn the truth about my name, it was another revelation that bothered me much more. That revelation would ultimately reveal that Scutum, a shield, may actually have more relevance to my life than I had at first thought. Indeed, it may have been the key that unlocked the mysteries of all the strange and curious things swirling around me.

CHAPTER 2

My Summer of Enlightenment

Yes, my enlightenment corresponded somewhat to those changes that girls go through at my age. I'll spare you the details, but let me just say that I think that the challenges of puberty are unfairly weighted against girls. Not that my protest will make any difference.

My enlightenment was really an incident that occurred that ultimately illuminated the cause of all the weird shit that had happened to me since day one. And it would continue to happen to me into the future. It was some kind of ironic poetry that this incident occurred on a beach.

It was summer, the only time the Jersey shore was hospitable enough to visit in a swimsuit rather than a parka. My mother, Misty, and I arrived at the beach, and after a swim, my Mom had gone off to get us some food, leaving Misty in charge. Misty, apparently, was more concerned about relieving her bladder than my supervision and went off to find the bathroom. Meanwhile, I decided to take another swim.

I'm not saying that I must have looked like a supermodel emerging from the water. But as I approached the shore, I distinctly remember feeling like I was being watched. For the first time that I could recall, I started to feel self-conscious about my body. Even the act of taming my hair, which now hung down to the small of my back, seemed embarrassing. Not to mention, my bikini, which now wet, seemed to cling, pucker, and protrude in ways I wished it wouldn't.

Just when I started to convince myself not to worry, I caught the eyes of three teenage boys staring at me. I guessed they were about Misty's age. As much as I tried to tell myself they were probably just friends of my sister's, I couldn't get over how they looked like three hungry wolves salivating over fresh meat. Then one of them walked up and talked to me.

"Hi, what's your name?" he said innocently enough from shore about 10 feet away.

"Aja," I replied, stopping short of the shore in knee-high water, hoping that despite his swimsuit, he wouldn't venture into the water.

"That's a pretty name," he said as he entered the water. "My name's Joey."

From the shore, one of his buddies yelled, "You going to tap that, Joey?"

I hadn't heard that term before, but I could tell by the fevered look in Joey's eyes and his menacing advance that I didn't want to find out. I started to back away into deeper water, but he kept closing the distance, finally lunging for me. One of his hands managed to touch my left thigh as he went underwater. I was about to scream when his head broke the surface, and he cried out in agony.

"Ahhhhhhhh," holding his hand up and dousing it repeatedly in the water like he was trying to put out a fire. His screams probably drew more attention than mine would have. It sounded like someone was killing him.

As I stood there in shock, he quickly made his way to shore, all the time holding his hand like it was burning and unleashing a stream of profanities in my direction. His cries started to subside as he and his friends got further up the beach and away from me. I was too afraid to leave the water and stood there until Misty came back.

Too freaked out to tell Misty what had transpired, I tried to act as though nothing had happened. I kept touching my left thigh, where Joey had touched it, wondering what could have caused his reaction. I even went as far as to ask Misty to touch my leg. When she looked at me like I was crazy for making such a request, I made up a reason.

"My leg felt hot. Does it feel hot to you?"

Buying my story, she touched my leg.

"Nope, feels normal to me. Maybe you're starting to get a sunburn. Put some sunscreen on?"

Although I knew it was definitely not the beginning stages of sunburn, I put some sunscreen on as Misty advised just to make it look good.

Mom came back with food, and she and Misty pigged out while I could hardly finish one French fry.

"What's a matter, honey?" my mom asked. "Aren't you hungry?"

"No," I replied, hoping that would suffice.

"You should eat something. Here, have a hot dog," she said, grabbing one and holding it out towards me.

"I'm really not hungry, Mom."

"She's probably just had too much sun," Misty interjected. "She said her leg felt hot."

"Well, put some sunscreen on," my Mom replied.

Between Misty and my Mom, you would have thought that sunscreen was some sort of miracle treatment. In truth, my stomach was churning from my close call with wolf Joey, and I couldn't make heads or tails out of what had happened. I started to wonder if Joey had all of a sudden contracted that flesh-eating bacteria that people sometimes get when swimming. That theory, however, didn't put my mind at ease since I had been right there in the same water as Joey. Before I knew it, I began imagining hot spots on my body and checking all over for signs of flesh-eating bacteria. When Misty suddenly put her hand on my shoulder, it startled me. Not just a little bit, but a lot.

"God, relax," she said as my heart was jumping out of my chest. "You're acting really weird, Aja. Is everything alright?"

Everything was definitely not alright, but I wasn't going to discuss it with Misty. At least not now with my Mom sitting right there. My only option at the time seemed to be to go with the over-exposure to the sun excuse.

"I think you were right. I've had a bit too much sun. Maybe I should go wait in the car or something," I suggested. Which I thought was brilliant because it gave the illusion I wasn't thinking straight and would force them to bring me home instead of just prescribing more sunscreen.

It worked. Although when we got home, I had to endure being put to bed and have fluids forced on me to counter my possible dehydration. Thank God my temperature was 98.6 when Mom took it, or I'm sure she would have packed me in ice. Eventually, my Mom declared me cured and let me get out of bed. It didn't matter if I was in or out of bed. I was still tortured by what happened at the beach.

Now, however, my thoughts around the whole incident started to evolve from a focus on what happened to cause Joey's pained reaction to what Joey's intention was in the first place. I was confused about being self-conscious about my body, even before I recognized that Joey and his friends were staring at me. I was confused by what Joey's friend had said. And I couldn't or didn't want to imagine what Joey would have done had he lunged and caught me.

Some of the mystery was solved when I searched on the phrase "tap that" and learned Joey's friend was probably not talking about opening a keg of beer at that particular moment. The alternate definition I found made me shudder. I was used to seeing boys ogle my sister and almost trip over themselves to get her attention. How do I put this delicately? Misty, even when she was 12, was endowed with more evident and desirable womanly features. People often thought Misty was older than she actually was. I, on the other hand, was the exact opposite. While my body was changing, I couldn't imagine anyone taking the kind of interest in me that Joey and his friends had. Not only couldn't I imagine it, but I also didn't like or want it.

More of the mystery was solved when Misty and I were preparing for bed that night. She asked me why I had acted so strangely at the beach. I then confessed, and the ensuing conversation opened my eyes to some realities I didn't necessarily enjoy.

"Remember when you were 8 years old, and I asked you if I could sleep in your room? Misty asked.

"Yes, of course," I said, my ignorance still firmly intact.

"Do you remember Uncle Phil?"

"Yes," I said, not so sure that I liked where this conversation was heading.

"Well, Uncle Phil came to my bedroom one night and started touching me."

Now I knew I didn't want to hear what Misty was saying, but she continued. I didn't stop her as the walls of my ignorance crumbled. And the dawn of my enlightenment broke over the horizon.

"I kept telling him to stop, but he didn't. When I told him I'd scream, he put his hand over my mouth and tore my pajama bottoms off and raped me," she said, disintegrating into tears.

That was bad enough, but after I consoled my sister, and she stopped crying, she continued to tell me more, whether I liked it or not. While nothing at the level of Uncle Phil's rape, Misty cataloged a series of traumatic events over the last 4 years. Being groped in a crowded subway in New York City. A man suddenly appeared in her dressing room at a department store and exposed himself. The dentist, who was caught by his hygienist, with his hand down Misty's pants while she was loopy from too much nitrous oxide. A High School teacher whose roaming eyes and compliments about her appearance got a little too personal and creepy. A date whose hand rode up her skirt at the movies. Even a female nurse in Junior High who fondled her breasts in the name of checking for swollen lymph nodes when Misty had complained of a sore throat. All left no doubt in my mind about two things. My sister was emotionally scarred, and Joey would have tried violating me had something mysterious not stopped him.

"Have you told Mom about any of this?" I asked.

"Well, the hygienist told her about the dentist," she replied, as I now understood the reason we had switched dentists.

"And the others?" I asked.

"No," she replied as my question renewed her tears. "I mean, he's her brother. And what could I do about the others? I didn't even know who grabbed me on the subway, and the guy in the dressing room just ran away," as her crying intensified.

As much as I love my sister, I didn't feel equipped to deal with the emotional tsunami that my questions seemed to be causing. So I stopped asking and just hugged her. All of the time, trying to hold it together as my insides roiled in fear that I could expect a similar fate.

But this was just the start of my enlightenment. I had opened the door, but much of my education still lay ahead. I didn't know this at the time, and even if I did, there would have been no way to go back and close that door and reclaim my ignorance.

CHAPTER 3

Thirteen and Suspicious

T he thing I feared most about starting 8th grade was what I'd write if my English teacher asked us to do an essay about what we did on our summer vacation. Sure, I did some fun things over the summer. Still, my Joey incident and the horrifying education I received from my sister had cast a pall over everything. There was also that niggling mystery about what happened to Joey's hand that frustrated me.

But frustration wasn't my predominant attitude. Suspicion was. I didn't like that my enlightenment had caused me to look at people differently. All people. I especially didn't want to go to the beach or the dentist, try clothes on in a department store dressing room, ride a subway in New York City, or go see the school nurse. Uncle Phil wasn't a concern, as my mother had told me he had moved to California.

I was also very conscious of when people would touch me. Not only because I was on high alert for sexual predators, but for any evidence that touching me would cause a "Joey reaction." That's the name I gave it. I didn't know how to refer to it otherwise.

Despite my suspicions and hypersensitivity to being touched, 8th grade was rather uneventful. I turned 13, and I filled out and became a little more curvey. Let's just say that my training bra now had something to train. The whole training bra thing amused me more than embarrassed me. Would they really wander off or behave erratically if not held in captivity by a flimsy cotton restraint? Whatever. I wasn't going to buck tradition and risk misbehaving boobs.

While no one who touched me ever had a "Joey reaction." I did notice that I would occasionally feel self-conscious about my body as I did at the beach, even though I wasn't in a wet clingy bikini. I also felt it when I was all bundled up in my winter coat sometimes. I couldn't understand the randomness of these feelings and eventually wrote them off as caused by the hormonal storms my Mom had warned me about during my age and stage of development.

I did notice that most boys in the 8th grade had an increased interest in girls. Their interest, however, did not necessarily mean they were comfortable or made themselves appealing to us girls. Most were incredibly awkward, and some just acted plain stupid.

I wasn't as popular with the boys as some of the girls. There were a few boys who tried to be my friend. All of them retreated almost as quickly as they had approached me. I wasn't surprised. I was not the most approachable person, all suspicious of their intentions and all.

One boy, Lyle, introduced himself to me during lunch one day. I was surprised to find myself comfortable with him, and we chatted up quite a storm. I remember thinking Lyle was cute and feeling that he showed some real promise. Then I started to feel that self-consciousness about my body and cursed the audacity of my hormones for interrupting my first potential foray into a boy-girl relationship. Despite being fully clothed, I felt embarrassingly naked. Lyle then asked me if I wanted to go to a movie with him that weekend. Before I could respond, Lyle's face contorted into a mask of pain, and he grabbed his stomach and ran to the boy's restroom. I thought it might be something he ate and waited for him to return. I kinda wanted to say yes to the movie. He never returned. When I saw him the next day at lunch, he steered clear of me and sat down next to another girl. Well fuck you very much, Lyle, I thought to myself, noticing that the girl he was sitting with had boobs that were long past their training stage.

But by far, the most important thing that happened when I was 13 didn't affect me as much as my mother and many other women who had Dr. Kent Schifflin as their baby doctor. I came home one afternoon after school and found my mother crying on the couch. Not only was it unusual for her to be home at that hour, but my mother rarely cried unless we were watching some sappy romance movie.

She tried to prop herself up and tell me it was nothing. I don't know if she decided to confide in me because of my persistence or because she realized I would eventually learn about it on TV or through the Internet. Dr. Kent Schifflin was the OBGYN that delivered me or perhaps dropped me would be more accurate. On this particular day, my mother told me that she had learned that Dr. Schifflin had been arrested on multiple counts of sexual assault. He had used his own sperm to impregnate 24 women who had sought fertility treatments in his clinic.

My mother sat on the couch with a letter in her hand and crumpled wads of tissue surrounding her. I was momentarily more concerned about my parentage than with what was causing my mother's distress. As if reading my mind, my mother quickly squelched the notion that I should be calling Dr. Schifflin daddy. She had been sexually assaulted by him, however. A fact she had never revealed and only now confessed prompted by a letter from the law firm trying to prosecute Dr. Schifflin and trolling for more of his victims. In the letter, it detailed some of Dr. Schifflin's unconventional "treatments" that he had used that had no foundation in medical science.

My mother had been the victim of several of these treatments. While my paternity was not in question, it only served to evolve my enlightenment to a new and disgusting level. You can't even trust doctors.

My mother, having unburdened herself of what she had been hiding, was uncharacteristically chatty as I sat and tried to console her. While she obviously felt comfortable opening up to me, I wasn't as comfortable being the recipient of the information. First, no 13-year-old wants to hear, let alone think about anything sexual involving their parent. Second, with both Misty and my mother sexually assaulted, could my sexual assault be far behind? I already had a preview, rescued only because of some unexplained occurrence.

My mother then launched into greater detail of my birth. While I obviously knew the story of being unceremoniously dropped, my mother confided that even in the hospital, as her contractions were getting stronger and more frequent, Dr. Schifflin had used what he called "stimulation therapy" to lessen the pain and speed up delivery. This "therapy," conveniently performed when no nurses were present, involved an ungloved hand and my mother's vagina because skin-to-skin contact was necessary. I could hardly listen to my mother anymore until she said that Dr. Schifflin had shrieked when I was delivered. My mother thought he had cried out because he dropped me, but she was more concerned about me than about him and initially didn't think anything of it. Then when instead of picking me up, he shouted to the nurse to pull his gloves off because it felt like his gloves were melting. My mother knew something was amiss. The nurse dutifully pulled the gloves off as he continued to scream. Despite no visible burns or indication that the gloves had been melting, he ran to the sink and doused his hands under cold running water. When Dr. Schifflin's pain or screams didn't subside, my mom said he ran out of the room. The delivery nurse not only rescued me from the floor but told my mom that Dr. Schifflin must have suffered an allergic reaction to his latex gloves. While this made sense to my mom, it sounded too much like a "Joey reaction" for me to dismiss. I asked my mom what Dr. Schifflin said about it when she next saw him, but she never saw Dr. Schifflin again. His partner visited the next day, and, by then, my mother was "basking in the glow of motherhood." No longer concerned about what had caused Dr. Schifflin's quick and dramatic exit. That glow was apparently bright enough to also make her blind to the damage Dr. Schifflin's fumble fingers had caused her little bundle of joy.

While my intervention seemed to help my mother regain her composure, I felt mine rapidly slipping away. I ran up the stairs and cloistered myself in my room. Never have I ever wished for greater salvation from an Internet search as when I typed in "symptoms of latex allergy." Unfortunately, nowhere in the bulleted list of 19 symptoms did I find anything remotely close to burning sensations. Undeterred, I searched six alternate sites and still came up empty.

Could it be that the first person who touched me when I entered this world and Joey had the same reactions? Was my skin so toxic to certain people that it caused the burning sensations? Powerful enough to cause the response even through latex gloves? Dr. Schifflin and Joey now formed odd bookends in my life. I tried to reason that causing two idiosyncratic reactions in 13 years shouldn't be something to concern myself over. Still, this logic did not seem to convince my brain to stop torturing me. I obsessed over the years in between, and whether in my age of ignorance, I may have missed something.

I wouldn't find the answers that evening and fell asleep more from emotional exhaustion than anything else.

CHAPTER 4

One Step Forward Two Steps Back

The summer before I started High School gave me hope that the storms of puberty and my fears of being toxic were things of the past.

I met a boy named Thomas at the mall one weekend when Misty and I were shopping. He was a year ahead of me in school. In addition to being a valuable source of information about what I could expect my first year at High School, he had an ease about him that I found comforting. Both Misty and I enjoyed his company that day at the mall. Not only did he have legendary patience with our frenetic shopping habits, but he actually seemed to enjoy it. We had so much fun that after shopping we went to see a movie together. I give some credit to Misty for making me more comfortable being with Thomas than if I had been alone with him. The next day, he invited us to go dancing, and unlike most boys, he was actually a good dancer. Thomas and I eventually went out without Misty in tow, and by mid-summer, we had become nearly inseparable.

I know what you're thinking. What about those raging teenage hormones? Well, at least with Thomas, they seemed to be quite tame. We would hold hands and hug, but it never ventured beyond that. Neither of us seemed to want or need more. Some girls might have wondered why their boyfriend wasn't pushing for greater intimacy. But after my recent and rude enlightenment, tame was just fine with me. Besides, I placed a higher value on the intimacy of communication. Thomas was a great listener and a great talker. Some of our "dates" were just sitting in the park and talking for hours on end. What greater intimacy is there than someone you can speak with on a profound intellectual, emotional, and spiritual level. Heck, sometimes we didn't even need to talk. Sometimes just getting a text from him would make me feel warm inside.

I arrived for my first day at High School optimistic, which was a far cry from the fears and suspicions I had when starting 8th grade. Nothing about my first two weeks of High School dimmed my positive outlook. Thomas and I got into a comfortable routine of having lunch together and meeting after school. I liked my classes and my teachers, and while other freshmen students complained of being taunted by upperclassmen, I seemed shielded from their insults. I attributed this to my relationship with Thomas.

Two things happened in the third week of my freshman year to shatter the calm contentment of my prior few months. I started to have more frequent episodes of body self-consciousness, specifically while I was in Gym class. This alone was not so shocking since we were learning gymnastics and made to wear skin-tight leotards rather than the usual frumpy shorts and t-shirts. Ms. Merkinson was our gym teacher, and the intel that I had received from other students was that she was easy on the girls and hard on the boys. As a girl, I didn't mind in the least this inequity and looked forward to the class.

On the first day of class, as we were all on the mats warming up and stretching, Ms. Merkinson, true to form, provided encouraging words to the girls but offered none to the boys. When she arrived at my mat, she told me that I had the perfect body for gymnastics. It was the first time anyone had said my body was perfect for anything, and I'll admit it made me feel much better about myself.

In the first two weeks of class, I was relegated to one of Ms. Merkinson's assistants on the balance beam, which, fortunately, was set on the floor. The skills we practiced on the beam were very basic, and I mastered them with ease. I was bored with the beam after two days and asked the teacher's assistant if she could raise the beam to the proper height. She denied my request saying it was against school policy. After two weeks and having survived the boredom of the balance beam, I was ready to move on to tumbling with Ms. Merkinson. I had watched other students with envy as she would instruct and spot them until they were tumbling on their own across the mat, some more graceful than others.

As I arrived at the tumbling station in the third week of my High School career, Ms. Merkinson's words about having a perfect body for gymnastics rang in my ears. Today's lesson was on the backbend kick over. After watching one of Ms. Merkinson's assistants demonstrate, Ms. Merkinson asked each student in turn to the mat where she would spot them. She would place her hand on the small of their back while they bent backward and tried to kick their legs over to complete the maneuver. I was third in line and began suffering another bout of self-consciousness about my body. I fought through it. When the first two students failed to execute the exercise, I approached determined to show Ms. Merkinson her perfect gymnast body comment hadn't been misplaced.

The good news is that I was able to complete the backbend kick over flawlessly, or so Ms. Merkinson's assistant told me later. The bad news is that when Ms. Merkinson placed her hand on the small of my back, she recoiled as though she had just touched a hot stove. Fortunately, her scream, which followed a second later, was just long enough for me to commence the exercise as if nothing had happened. Hearing her scream mid-flip confused me because I was hoping for an ovation of another kind. When I was standing upright again, I saw Ms. Merkinson high-tailing it towards the locker room, holding her hand and screaming. A classic "Joey reaction."

After Ms. Merkinson exited the gym, all of the students turned to look at me. I was mortified and started to cry. When one of Ms. Merkinson's assistants came to console me and put her arms around me, I thought I heard all the students simultaneously take in a breath. As if a fate similar to Ms. Merkinson's would befall her because she dared to touch me. When the assistant didn't get scalded, the students were instructed to take a seat in the bleachers. Another assistant went to check on Ms. Merkinson.

To make a long story short, Ms. Merkinson was fine when the assistant finally found her in her office with no evidence of what had caused her reaction. She refused to talk to anyone or let anyone examine her hand. Shortly after that, with a box of personal items in her arms, she left. Shockingly, Ms. Merkinson tendered her resignation and never taught another class at my High School. As we would come to learn, she not only left the school, but she left the State and moved to Michigan.

The manner of Ms. Merkinson's departure likely shielded me from any negative attention from the incident. Rumors that Ms. Merkinson had a mental or emotional breakdown started circulating, supported by her screaming, refusal to talk, and abrupt resignation without notice. While this may have spared me from the scrutiny by my peers, I was once again torturing myself with my fears of having toxic body syndrome. I went back and forth in my mind about whether I should talk to Thomas about it, quickly settling on not to. I was afraid it would just sound crazy, and I didn't want to risk driving him away. It was my personal cross to bear.

When I saw him after school, he hugged me, as was usual. Still somewhat traumatized, I apparently flinched a bit in the process, and he noticed.

"What's the matter, Aja?" he asked, a concerned look crossing his face.

"I guess I'm still a little shook up about what happened at the gym today," I said. Knowing the whole school had heard about Ms. Merkinson's outburst and mysterious departure.

"That happened in your class?" he asked with surprise.

"Yes," I replied, electing not to divulge my role in the whole fiasco.

"Wow, that must have been crazy."

He didn't know half of how crazy it was, and I was happy that my flinch was forgotten or forgiven without further explanation. That Thomas could touch me without having a "Schifflin Joey Merkinson reaction" was some consolation. But not enough to make me accept his invitation to get together that evening. I had too much on my mind, and I needed to work it out before my head exploded. I lied to him for the first time, saying I had too much homework. True to character, he accepted this with no evidence of suspicion or disappointment. That's one of the reasons I liked him, no pressure Thomas.

One of the downsides to sharing a bedroom with Misty was on those rare occasions when I wished to have some privacy. That evening was just one of those occasions, and I retreated to her former bedroom to try and reconcile the day's events and how they may be related to the previous two. Misty would not set foot in her old bedroom. I knew she would become suspicious of me if I secluded myself in there without giving her a compelling reason. I assembled an impressive stack of school books, a notepad, and my laptop for effect and lied to her as I had to Thomas.

Safely sheltered in Misty's old room, I shoved the books aside and proceeded to try to piece together what I knew about the three mystery events. Unfortunately, there was very little to piece together. The first problem was that I obviously had no recollection of Dr. Schifflin's reaction. The second problem was that other than the burning sensation, the events shared nothing else in common. It wasn't gender-specific. It happened in three different locations - two indoors and one outdoors. It wasn't age-specific. While two of the three events were preceded by my having body consciousness issues, I had already dismissed these as the scourge of puberty.

I briefly considered the commonality that in each case, I was not fully clothed, but that seemed to be a stretch. It also wasn't restricted to skin-on-skin contact. In Dr. Schifflin's case, he was wearing gloves. In Ms. Merkinson's case, she had touched my leotard. I also tried to make connections on what part of my body had caused the burns. My left thigh wasn't too far from my lower back, but I had no way of knowing what part of my body may have burned Dr. Schifflin. Presumably, his hands would have been large enough to touch a good portion of my body but apparently not large or adept enough to keep me from experiencing my little skydiving event.

It was an exercise in frustration. I realized that the thing that I probably needed to detect any trend or pattern was the thing I desperately didn't want, more cases of "Schifflin Joey Merkinson reactions."

CHAPTER 5

The Rollercoaster Ride Continues

Towards the end of my freshmen year, my relationship with Thomas evolved, but not necessarily in a good way. He started to spend more time with his male friends, and our lunches and time together after school became less frequent. It wasn't like things between us had changed. He was still the same old Thomas, and we still enjoyed each other's company. Then, one night, he texted me, saying he had something important to talk to me about. We agreed to get together after school the next day to chat.

I, of course, had a sleepless night trying to anticipate what he had to talk to me about. Did he want to escalate our physical intimacy? Did I say or do something that bothered him? Did he meet another girl? I racked my brain all night, and when we finally met the next day, nothing could have prepared me for what he said.

"Aja, I'm gay, and I'm in love with my friend Robert," he said while holding my hands and looking at me with a pained sincerity.

I wasn't angry. I wasn't even disappointed. I was numb. Other than telling him I was happy for him and the hug we shared, I don't remember anything that we talked about. It wasn't until well after our meeting that all the questions I had about his orientation and his relationship with Robert started to flood my brain. Guaranteeing another sleepless night.

In the end, it changed little about our relationship. We still remained friends, but we saw less and less of each other. What I had to come to grips with was the fact that I couldn't really claim that he had been my first boyfriend. I thought that our relationship was a normal, healthy, faithful, heterosexual relationship, but now I knew differently. This realization, combined with all the abusive experiences my mother and sister had, put me back to square one. Wondering not about when I would have such a relationship so much as rather whether such a relationship was even possible. I was 14 years old and disillusioned and doubtful.

Ironically, I decided to join my High School gymnastics team. With one flawless backbend kick over already on my athletic resume and Ms. Merkinson's words still echoing in my head, I said, why not? I didn't have a relationship with Thomas to occupy my time. I was afraid that if I didn't throw myself into something constructive, I would descend into a quagmire of cynicism, not just about people but about life in general.

The rigorous practice schedule was just what the doctor ordered. I had very little free time to perseverate on the mysteries of my life. What free time I had, was usually spent trying to relieve myself of the aches and pains I had from the pounding and contortions my body had to endure. Ms. Sylvester, who had replaced Ms. Merkinson, was a petite, fiery blond who had been a college gymnastics standout. She retained one of Ms. Merkinson's assistants but replaced the other assistant with Mr. Trahorn. He, like Ms. Sylvester, was a decorated college gymnast but also a degree in exercise science and kinesiology. I didn't even know there was such a thing.

Now, in my sophomore year and about to turn 15, my life was pretty much consumed by two things - school and gymnastics. While I was progressing nicely in gymnastics, I wasn't on the first team yet. My strongest routine was floor exercise with balance beam, my weakest. This described almost everyone on the team, so it was hard to break into the first team. One thing I had going for me on floor was my blazing fast tumbling and the height I could achieve at the end of my passes. Controlling my landing was another matter altogether, as I would frequently end up not just going out of bounds but entirely off the mat. Ms. Sylvester said if I could control my landings, not only would she put me in the first team rotation for floor, but I'd be the last one to perform in the rotation. A spot reserved for the best floor gymnast. That's all the motivation I needed, and when I wasn't required to be practicing other apparatus, you could find me trying to land my tumbling passes.

Gymnastics and my continuing march through puberty contributed to putting some muscle and fat on my body in just the right places. However, I still suffered frequent body self-consciousness, even in practice, when there wasn't a crowd of spectators. These feelings were even worse during meets, especially when we would first march out in a line past the bleachers to our first apparatus – the vault. At our first home meet, I not only felt that uneasiness come over me as we walked out, but shortly after, I was surprised when some boy in the audience called out.

"Nice ass, Aja,"

Other than Joey, whose attention I didn't want, and Thomas, whose attention I liked but no longer had, I was used to boys ignoring or avoiding me. And on those rare occasions in the past when they would yell something at me, it was usually about how my body was reminiscent of a two-by-four. This was unexpected and oddly welcome and unwelcome at the same time. Part of me wanted to be more like other girls, whose figures were more developed and attracted boys' attention. Another and much more significant part of me felt disgusted, insulted, and afraid by what I'm sure that boy in the audience thought was a compliment.

At our meets, whether home or away, I couldn't help but feel like I was naked and people were staring at me. Sometimes I would look around and feel stupid because absolutely no one was paying any attention to me. Other times I would catch someone, usually a boy or a man or Coach Sylvester or Assistant Coach Trahorn, looking in my direction. But then I'd realize I was standing with at least a half-dozen other girls and really didn't know who they were looking at and think I was just paranoid. Plus, in the case of my Coach and Assistant Coach, it was their job to lead the team, and it would be pretty hard to do that without looking at us.

I started to work on ignoring the feelings of self-consciousness. I knew that if I kept on being distracted by my concerns, I would never be able to concentrate and perform at the first-team level. Besides, if these feelings were caused by "the hormonal storms of adolescence," as my mother put it, I would eventually outgrow them. Ignoring these feelings proved to be as challenging as trying to stay in bounds on my tumbling passes.

As the gymnastics season progressed, I started to land my tumbling passes in bounds with greater frequency. I couldn't say I had the same success in ignoring my insecurities about my body. When one of our first team gymnasts went down with an injury late in the season, I got my chance at floor as Ms. Sylvester cobbled together a few of us to fill the void.

Mr. Trahorn, who worked exclusively with first-teamers, now took over the duties of prepping me. Prepping included a regimen of exercises and stretching, as well as applying kinesiology tape to areas of our bodies that suffered an injury or were vulnerable to injury. I also heard some of the girls say he was like a sports psychologist, helping them identify and remove thoughts that were blocking them from peak performance. As excited as I was to be on the first team, I wasn't particularly anxious to have Mr. Trahorn plumb the depths of my psyche. So I went into our first interaction with some trepidation.

It turned out that I had worried unnecessarily. He gave me pointers on how to improve my stretching, watched my floor routine, and let me know he would be applying tape to protect my knees. If he performed any psychological voodoo on me, I hadn't noticed. My body image issues were still safely locked away in my head.

The next day as I was warming up for practice, Mr. Trahorn complimented my improved stretching and asked me to report to the training table when I was finished. As I continued to stretch, my old familiar self-consciousness reared its ugly head. Instead of passing, as it usually did, it just got more intense as I made my way to the training table. Hopping up on the table and feeling like I wanted a blanket to cover myself, I thought about talking to Mr. Trahorn, the sports psychologist, about my self-consciousness. When he arrived, the first words out of his mouth changed my mind.

"You look like a hot pink girl."

"Excuse me?" I asked as my self-consciousness raged, and I started to look around in earnest for something to cover my perceived nakedness.

"Kinesiology tape," he replied matter of factly. "I have black, blue, and hot pink."

"Oh, OK," I said as blushing now joined my self-consciousness party. "Hot pink is fine."

As he rolled out and ripped strips of the tape and temporarily stuck them to the table on either side of my legs, Mr. Trahorn's face seemed to change. When he went to apply the first strip of tape to my right knee, he grabbed his stomach and looked like he was going to vomit. He looked at me briefly and, with bewildered eyes and a pained expression, turned and ran out of the gym. I could only presume he was headed to the restroom.

Two things happened immediately after Mr. Trahorn exited. My self-consciousness disappeared, and I was immediately reminded of the time Lyle had run out on me after asking me out to a movie. While I never learned what had come over Lyle, Ms. Sylvester informed the team that Mr. Trahorn had become sick and had gone home. While the rest of the team continued practice unaffected, I was distracted. Gymnastics had been my haven away from the intrusive thoughts I had about causing burning sensations in certain people who touched me. Now, I was starting to have disturbing thoughts about whether I was also causing certain people to become sick without even touching me. But how? Why?

As this was the last practice before our meet the next day, Ms. Sylvester took Mr. Trahorn's place and asked me to perform my floor routine. The only good thing that could be said about my performance was that I didn't go out of bounds. That was because I never fully completed any of my passes, missing or botching a skill each time. No amount of Ms. Sylvester's encouragement to concentrate helped, and she ultimately told me I wouldn't be competing on floor the next day. This news probably would have crushed my self-esteem any other day, but now I had too much on my mind that seemed to be more critical. I left practice and couldn't wait to get home and quarantine myself in Misty's old bedroom.

When I got home, I didn't even have to go to Misty's room to do my thinking because she was at a friends' house. After an hour, I decided that my situation demanded experimentation. And the key to any good experiment, as I had learned in Science class, was the ability to reproduce consistent results. What if I tried an experiment on Lyle and Mr. Trahorn? If I designed my research correctly, and I was indeed the cause of their reactions, I should be able to get them to run to the bathroom again. I formulated my plan for the next day at school and surprisingly got a good night's sleep.

CHAPTER 6

I Become a Research Scientist

Forgoing a lab coat and dressing in my usual school attire, I set off to school to find my first study subject - Lyle. I knew I wanted to control two variables in my experiment with him. He couldn't have his girlfriend with him, and I wanted to conduct the test before he ate lunch. I would occasionally see him at his locker between the second and third periods and hoped that might be my opportunity today.

As luck would have it, I spied Lyle at the appointed time alone at his locker.

"Hi, Lyle!" I said brightly.

Shocked to see me, he took a step back before replying.

"Oh, hi, Aja," he said as his eyes felt like they were starting to undress me.

"How are you feeling today? I asked, taking a step closer to him.

"I'm fine. Why do you ask?" he replied as his face grimaced, betraying his words and causing him to take another step back.

"I just never got the opportunity to talk with you after you ran out during our last conversation. I was worried about you," I replied, taking another step in his direction.

"Ahhh, thanks. Everything's alright, but I have to go, Aja," as the color left his face, and he started to turn to leave.

Taking another step forward, I placed my hand on his arm and said, "OK, I'm glad you're feeling alright, Lyle," which caused him to gag and run down the hall into the boy's restroom.

But a good investigator's job doesn't stop there. I ran down the hall after him, and while I was not bold enough to enter the bathroom, I stood close to the door. What I heard confirmed my theory. I made Lyle sick.

While I perversely reveled in my findings, poor Lyle apparently missed the rest of his classes that day. As promising as the results were, I still had another study subject - Mr. Trahorn. The two variables I wanted to control in my test with Mr. Trahorn were to conduct the study well before our gymnastics meet and to do so while he was alone. I had the perfect pretext to visit him that morning. Luckily, I found him in his office just before lunch.

"Hi, Mr. Trahorn," I greeted from his open office door.

"Oh, hi, Aja," he said, looking up and smiling. "I'm sorry about yesterday. I didn't mean to run out on you like that."

"That's OK. Ms. Sylvester told us you were sick. Do you feel better today?" I asked, taking a couple steps into his office.

"Much better, thanks. I'm sorry to hear you won't be competing tonight. I guess you had a pretty rough practice session."

"Yeah, I couldn't concentrate. I was too worried about you," I lied as I took a few more steps until I was standing at the side of his desk.

"You were worried about me?" he asked as something changed in the way he looked at me. Something that made me feel naked and gave me the urge to run out of his office. But I staved off my desire to run to complete the study.

"Yes. I was worried that I may have made you sick," I said

as I took another step closer and did my best to act coy.

"Oh, Aja, you don't make me sick. In fact, I," he began but couldn't finish. His eyes were now ablaze like the hungry wolf looks of those teenage boys at the beach.

"In fact, you what?" I asked, taking a step around the corner of his desk, now close enough to be within arms reach.

"In fact, I'm starting to feel sick again," as his eyes dimmed and his face twisted and grew pale. "I think you better go."

I had seen enough and mercifully retreated, stopping as I got to the office door.

"I hope you feel better by tonight, Mr. Trahorn," I called. He waved, and I could already see the color returning to his face and the hunger flashing in his eyes.

I had an abbreviated lunch, and although I went to my afternoon classes, I can't say that I remember anything about them. I was too busy wrestling with the reality of what I had learned. I confirmed that my self-consciousness was not entirely driven by hormones. Both Lyle and Mr. Trahorn had set it off. I also confirmed that in close enough proximity, I could produce an uncomfortable gastrointestinal response in both Lyle and Mr. Trahorn. What my research couldn't tell me was how and why. In both instances, I had felt like they were undressing me with their eyes. Could this really be what was going through their minds, or was it just my adolescent insecurities? Because God knew I had them in spades.

Not surprisingly, Mr. Trahorn steered clear of getting too close to me during the gymnastics meet that evening. On one occasion, when I was off in a corner by myself stretching, my body signaled to me. I looked up and caught him staring at me from afar with those wolf eyes. He didn't seem to mind that I had caught him. He just continued to stare as I wrestled with feeling suddenly naked. When he finally looked away, I felt clothed once again.

I don't know if Lyle was just good at avoiding me or if he transferred to another High School because I never saw him again during the last month of the school year. I can't say that I could blame him. I wouldn't want to be around someone that could make me puke at will.

My experiment complete, and my sophomore year ending, I realized that my enlightenment, which started years earlier, was only now coming into clearer view. I seemed to have a signaling device, but I wasn't quite sure what it signaled. All I know is that it made me feel naked. I also could have a very adverse physical effect on people. Still, I wasn't quite sure what kinds of people were susceptible to those effects. Or what differentiated those who got sick from those who felt like they had been set on fire. As a result, I wasn't sure if I had a gift or a curse.

CHAPTER 7

The Truth About My Father

My mother chose the summer before my junior year of high school to tell Misty and me the truth about our father. I guess she thought I was old enough. That Misty was going away to college in the fall also probably played into her decision.

Misty had always been the one more obsessed with his absence, now going on 8 years. It's not that I didn't care about or love him, it was just that Misty was 11 when he left, and I was 7. I remember the fights my sister used to have with my mother at the time. My sister pleading with mom to tell us the truth and then storming off to her room, calling her names. I could never understand why Misty couldn't accept Mom's explanation that he was away at work. Unlike Misty, I was blissfully ignorant at the time of the multitude of more typical and sordid reasons husbands and fathers left their families. Or how atypical and unbelievable my mother's story sounded. By the time I was old enough to recognize this, he had already been gone a few years. I guess I just didn't see any benefit in trying to unearth a different and potentially damning reason why he left. I wanted to believe my mother, and I wanted to believe that my father still loved me, even though I never saw him.

So when my mother told us she needed to have a chat with us that evening about Dad, Misty and I had very different reactions. Misty fully expected to learn that her doubt about Mom's original explanation would be vindicated. I, on the other hand, fully expected to have my belief in my Mom and Dad shattered. How could it be anything else? Mom wouldn't call a meeting just to reconfirm the same explanation she had been giving for 8 years. After Mom left and before Misty had to go to her work herself, she felt compelled to tell me her theory for the umpteenth time, but this time with greater confidence.

"See? Didn't I tell you?" she started. "I bet if it wasn't some woman at work, it was Gloria, that neighbor lady next door who used to go topless in her backyard in the summer. She was always trying to attract Dad's attention. And she moved out at about the same time as Dad left."

I had heard the Gloria's-boobs-and-move theory several times before. I had learned that trying to refute this theory only made Misty more vehement in her defense of it. I kept my mouth shut, so I didn't have to hear another rendition of how Gloria would come over and ask Dad if he would fix something at her house even though her husband was a fix-it guy. Or how Gloria would come to a party dressed in a mini-skirt and purposely sit across from Dad crossing and uncrossing her legs, playing peek-a-boo with her hoo-hoo.

In truth, it wasn't so much that I didn't want to hear all of these things again, but that I was now afraid Misty was right. Integrating this into my perception of my Dad's unblemished character was not something with which I wanted to wrestle.

While I usually enjoyed being home alone, I started to go stir-crazy after Misty left for work. I had to get out of the house. I also didn't want to have to deal with people. The only place that fit this description was the library.

My Mom used to bring Misty and me to the venerable old granite-hewn library downtown when we were young. In addition to story-telling and puppet shows, I always liked the smell and the feeling of being around books. Somehow it made me feel warm and secure.

Walking into the library after I don't know how many years away was magical. It didn't seem as big as I had remembered it, but it still had that smell. The mahogany tables and chairs on the main floor, stacks of books, and strategically placed comfy chairs transported me to my childhood. Temporarily away from my concerns about meeting with Mom that evening. I climbed the wrought-iron spiral stairs to the second level and found myself in the psychology section. The title "On Becoming a Person" by Carl R. Rogers caught my eye. When I saw it was originally published in the 1950s, I almost put it back on the shelf. It was ancient. But something just told me to read it, so I took it down from its place on the shelf to a comfy chair in a quiet corner.

I didn't know much about psychology or psychotherapy, but I was immediately captivated. I found Roger's concept of "unconditional positive regard" strangely foreign, even foolish at first. With what I already knew about the world and people, "unconditional negative suspicion" seemed more sensible. Yet, as I read on, it started to make more sense. I could see how it would be helpful in therapy but had a little harder time accepting how it could work in real-life situations. I thought about Joey and what I could only assume were his bad intentions toward me. How would unconditional positive regard have served me in that situation? Probably not well. However, if I was Joey's therapist, accepting him regardless of how broken or evil he was would be necessary if therapy were to be successful.

About two hours into reading the book, I started to feel that now all too familiar signal of self-consciousness about my body. I had learned to trust it and started to slowly look around for the source. It didn't take me long as I began to hear labored breathing coming from behind the closest row of books. The man had cleared a space on the shelf to be able to look at me and another area on a lower shelf so that I could, unfortunately, see a part of him. The part that he was furiously stroking with his hand. As my eyes met his, he groaned loudly, releasing a stream of seminal fluid, followed by more groans and several more spurts. I didn't know what to do, and before I knew it, he was around the corner of the stack, his manhood still in hand, approaching me. He didn't get too far when he started repeatedly screaming that his "dick was on fire," as he put it. The whole library was now alerted to his condition. As he made his retreat from me, his symptoms decreased, as did his manhood, I may add. He was quickly met by a Security guard who detained him and called the police. The librarian was elderly and had to take the elevator instead of the spiral stairs. When she arrived, she checked to see if I was alright. I was, or at least I told her I was.

A female police officer took my report, but when she saw the so-called "crime scene," she didn't need a lot of explanation from me. The big mystery to everyone but me was why he screamed that his dick was on fire. While I had obviously been the source of his arousal, I didn't let on that I was also the likely cause of the man's subsequent discomfort. I don't know how I could have explained that easily. To my great relief, I apparently could cause the burning sensation without the body part touching me. I would learn later that the man was a 50-year old sex offender. He had recently been paroled after serving time luring little girls into his car and molesting them when he had been in his 20's.

I knew libraries were supposed to be educational, but today's lesson had been a little too graphic. Despite that, it did confirm that sexual thoughts or acts prompted my signal. That I could cause the burning sensation from a distance, in this particular case, about 10 feet, was new. Could the nature of the sexual thoughts or acts by the person be what distinguishes who gets sick to their stomach versus who gets burned by touching or approaching me? The answer to that question was yet to be determined.

One thing I did know, whatever power I had, it had protected me from a known sexual predator. It had shielded me from harm. I couldn't help but think of Scutum, Latin for shield, the constellation of stars my father had mistakenly thought was Asia Minor. I reached up and touched the diamond-shaped scar on my cheek. I could no longer consider the signal of self-consciousness or my adverse effect on some people a curse. It was clearly a gift. I just didn't know how to tell anyone about it.

When I arrived home, I felt like taking a long, hot shower. It was weird. I felt dirty from what had happened at the library. As I didn't expect Mom or Misty for another hour or two, I started the shower and took off my clothes. Although I was only a few months away from my 16th birthday, I seemed perpetually stuck in a 13-year old body. I was 5 feet tall and weighed 100 pounds. Gymnastics had helped develop some muscle mass in my thighs, and based on the assessment of at least one boy in the bleachers, I had a pretty nice butt. My mother said my breasts were perfectly proportioned for my petite frame, which was kind but an injustice to the word perfect. I was now wearing a real bra, which seemed silly since I didn't have real boobs. I could jump up and down all day with nary a jiggle. Misty said they were cute, which she thought was a compliment. While I wouldn't call my face beautiful, it was at least pretty, even with the scar. I had full lips, not Anjelina Jolie-full, but passably pouty. If anything I have is cute, it would be my nose, but no one cares about noses as long as they don't take over your whole face. My skin also looked perpetually tanned, and that garnered some attention, especially in the dead of New Jersey winters when most everyone except me looked exceptionally pale. But my long dark hair was undoubtedly my most desirable feature. At least it's the feature that got the most compliments. I love my hair, but it takes a lot of work.

And on windy days, watch out. It flies all over the place.

As I stepped into the shower, the hot water doused my body and streamed off of me down the drain. I could feel whatever imaginary sliminess that man's actions had caused wash away. As usual, it was shampooing, conditioning, and rinsing my hair that took the longest. I poured the conditioner into my hand, and it looked too much like what the man had spurted out over the books and carpet in the library. I washed it off my hand quickly and made a mental note to try to find a different color conditioner the next time I went shopping. Drying and brushing my hair took nearly 45 minutes, and by the time I finished and put on fresh clothes, I could hear Mom and Misty talking downstairs.

As refreshing as my shower was, it could not lift the cloud that hung over me from what I expected to hear from my Mom. I descended the stairs reluctantly, feeling like my day had been too eventful already. I didn't need bad news about my father heaped on top of it.

"Hi, honey," my Mom greeted. "How was your day?"

"It was good," I replied, hoping that would suffice but knowing it probably wouldn't.

"What did you do?" she asked predictably.

"Oh, I went to the library and read a book," I responded, amusing myself by thinking about how I could have really livened up my response and our conversation.

"That's good. Did you learn anything new?"

Boy, was that a loaded question, I thought.

"Yes, I read a book by Carl Rogers on psychotherapy and unconditional positive regard," I replied. Once again, stopping short and avoiding the x-rated portion of my day.

"Did you have a good day?" I asked, hoping to move her off of my day.

"Oh, same old, same old," she replied, which I knew meant

it wasn't a good day, and she didn't want to talk about it.

"When are we going to have our little chat," Misty interjected impatiently.

"Relax, Misty. I just wanted to see how my little baby's day was."

I hated it when she called me her little baby.

"Well, she already told you. She went to the library and read a book. Done. We want to know about Dad." Misty adding me as sharing her sense of urgency even though I would have been happy to have Mom postpone our chat for another 40 or 50 years.

"OK, OK, well, this won't take long," she said.

I found this a curious thing to say about a topic that I fully anticipated would be quite emotional and, most likely bad news.

"First, you have to promise me that you will never tell anyone else what I am about to tell you."

"Mom, I think the whole world already probably knows about how Dad cheated on you," Misty blurted out.

"What? Where did you get that idea?" Mom exclaimed.

"He didn't run off with Gloria?" Misty replied.

"Gloria? Oh, heaven's no. Your Dad saw right through that floozy. Honey, Daddy and I are still married, and he loves us all very much."

"Then why haven't we seen him for like 10 years?" Misty replied.

"It's been 8 years, and the reason we haven't seen him is what I need to talk to you about. Now can you promise me that you will never tell anyone else what I am about to tell you?"

"Yes," I said, hoping that Misty would finally shut up and let Mom tell us.

"Yes, OK," Misty said reluctantly.

"Good. Because if you ever tell anyone, it could not only put us in danger but your father as well."

"OK, tell us already," Misty said impatiently.

"Your father works for the CIA."

"That's it?" Misty asked. "What does he do there?"

"I don't know, and he can't tell us."

"Well then, where does he live?"

"I don't know, and he can't tell us."

"Let me guess you don't know, and he can't tell us when he's coming home."

"Right."

"Well, this is bullshit. You don't know anything," Misty exclaimed in frustration.

"I can't know anything, honey. Your father has been away for 8 years for our protection."

"Well then, how do you know he still loves you?" Misty challenged.

"I don't think his salary would still get deposited into my bank account if he didn't love us."

"So, he's like a spy or something," Misty responded, prompting a non-committal look from her mother. "I know, I know, you don't know, and he can't tell us."

"I think you've got it," her mother smiled. "Aja, do you have any questions?"

"No, Mom," I smiled, unable to conceal my happiness that Misty's theories had been proven wrong.

That I still had a Dad who loved and cared for me was just what I needed, not only because of my day at the library. I needed my Dad because, for me, he represented everything pure and right in this world.

CHAPTER 8

My Junior Year

Shortly before I started my junior year at high school, Misty left home for college. She had worked for two years following high school but now wanted to pursue a degree and had saved up enough to go to a college in upstate New York. While I would miss her, she was going to miss me more. I know that sounds conceited, but I'm only saying this because she told me so herself and backed it up with the reason why on the night before she left.

Misty confided that Uncle Phil's rape was not the only such encounter she had with him. Two nights after she had moved into my room, Uncle Phil had entered our room while I was asleep and had tried to make her perform oral sex. I apparently stirred in bed at the same time as he was grabbing the back of Misty's head. Misty said he let out a whimper, released her head, grabbed his crotch as if in excruciating pain, and quickly left the room. Not only did Uncle Phil never try to enter our bedroom again, he never came back to visit. Shortly after, Mom told us he had moved to California.

Misty said that I was her "security blanket" and that she didn't know how she'd be able to sleep at college without me in the adjacent bed. I, of course, knew precisely what had caused Uncle Phil's reaction and retreat from our bedroom. My only surprise was that my protective powers apparently extended beyond me to Misty. I almost felt compelled to tell Misty about my gift but then thought better of it. When I thought about telling others about my powers, I couldn't think of a way of doing it without sounding crazy. In my mind, no good would come of telling Misty. She'd either not believe me and think I was a lunatic or believe me and decide never to leave my side.

One thing I learned about my junior year was that all the teachers seemed hellbent on getting us to make decisions about our futures after high school. It was like a more grown-up, kick-in-the-pants way of asking, "What do you want to be when you grow up?" I hadn't thought too much about it to tell you the truth, which might be precisely the reason the teachers were pushing this agenda so hard.

I had always been the youngest in my grade growing up. I started first grade when I was 5 years and 9 months old. My Mom told me that when she and Dad had discussed whether to enroll me or wait a year, they had "opposing views," which was Mom's way of saying they had an argument. My Mom thought that it might be too much pressure for me and hurt my self-esteem if I ultimately needed to be held back a year. My Dad reasoned that I had always been precocious as a child. I walked and talked early and was always trying to do things my older sister Misty was doing. And besides, he had been the youngest in his class and felt it had motivated him. My Dad's reasoning won out, not because my Mom finally agreed. It was more like he had worn her down, and she got tired of arguing and sur-rendered. It illustrated a fundamental difference between my Mom and Dad. While I love them both, Mom has always been more of the glass half empty type of person, while Dad has always been more the glass half full. Where Mom saw threats from which to retreat, Dad saw opportunities to charge ahead. I'm more like my Dad.

When it came time to do some serious thinking about a vocation and college, I was seriously stumped. I hadn't even turned 16 yet and wasn't even old enough to get a job in the real world. How was I supposed to decide my future?

That's when I was introduced to my guidance counselor. I didn't even know I had a guidance counselor. The way my homeroom teacher talked about it, I apparently had this guidance counselor at my beck and call since I was a freshman. Why didn't anyone ever tell me this? And shouldn't a guidance counselor notice and do something about it if one of their students hasn't shown up in the first two years?

The thing I first noticed when I walked into Mr. Mahovich's office was his garish plaid suit jacket. Then I was hit with the overwhelming smell of cigar smoke mixed with Brut cologne. I gagged and immediately abandoned any idea I may have had about engaging him in a lengthy conversation about my disappointment with his services, or lack thereof. I got straight to the point so that I could get out of there as fast as possible.

"Hi, Mr. Mahovich. I'm Aja Minor. I'm told you can help me decide what I might like to do in the future," I said. Trying not to breathe and realizing I was making myself dizzy from oxygen depletion.

"I'd be happy to help you, young lady. What grade are you in, 9th grade?"

"You know, Mr. Mahovich," I said, looking at my phone to sell the lie I was about to tell. "I apologize. I just realized that I'm going to be late for my class. Can we talk another time?"

"Anytime you'd like. I'm always here."

I was out of his office like a shot, but to my horror, the cloying smell followed me. Desperate, I ran to the nearest exit, burst through the door, and took in a deep breath of Northern New Jersey's finest fresh air. While I waited for the smell of Mr. Mahovich to mercifully dissipate, I scolded myself for thinking that someone who never met me could actually help me. I realized that unless I helped myself, I would be subjected to Mr. Mahovich again, and my teachers would continue to flog me with platitudes.

"Do something you love, and you'll never work a day in your life," my English teacher said.

"Follow your passion," said my Social Studies teacher.

I had two strengths that I knew of, plus my parent's careers as examples to draw upon. One strength was my gymnastics ability, but that didn't seem like a career choice. My other strength was the unique power I had. But here again, I didn't know how it could translate into a career. It's not like I'm going to go to college and major in sexual predator identification. I didn't even know if I could use this power outside of protecting myself and Misty. Would it work if I was in the presence of a sexual predator who was targeting someone other than me?

As for my parent's careers, I was definitely not interested in a career in healthcare. I am really proud of my mother, who worked her way up from a unit clerk to a nursing assistant and then to a nurse at our local hospital. But she comes home exhausted and disenchanted more often than she comes back happy and fulfilled. She regularly complains about how screwed up our healthcare system is and how her job has become 75% documenting in a computer and 25% caring for patients. That doesn't interest me. As for my Dad's job, I'm intrigued by the CIA, but I have no clue what it is he actually does. So, now, you see my dilemma.

Then it dawned on me. All I really need to do was tell the teachers that I wanted to become a lawyer, like about half of the rest of my classmates, and then they'd leave me alone! Meanwhile, I'd figure out my future on my own schedule.

You can't imagine the outpouring of support and glee my homeroom teacher experienced when I told her about wanting to become a lawyer. The next thing I knew, she was giving me pamphlets from Rutgers and Seton Hall. Both New Jersey schools that didn't cost an arm and a leg compared to the multitude of schools across the Hudson River in New York City.

I feigned excitement and gratitude the best I could. Anything to avoid Mr. Mahovich and more clichés about work!

That said, I was turning 16 in November. My mother was turning up the pressure on me to apply to the hospital for a housekeeping or food service job, and I desperately wanted to find an alternative. That alternative came from the last person I would have expected, Mr. Mahovich. Fortunately, I didn't need to report to Mr. Mahovich's office or even see him. In a follow-up to our abbreviated meeting, he had sent me a note. First apologizing that he had mistakenly thought I was a 9th grader, and second to make me aware of a unique job opportunity. The local Post Office had started a 20-hour per week work program exclusively for high school juniors and seniors. There were a limited number of Postal Aide jobs available that paid $15 per hour - 50% more than New Jersey's minimum wage. On top of this, a $2.50 an hour premium was paid for hours after 6pm.

I didn't need to do the math or weigh the pros and cons of the Post Office job versus the hospital opportunities. I applied immediately, and a week later, I was interviewed and offered one of the Postal Aide jobs, pending background check and fingerprinting. I hadn't anticipated this level of scrutiny, not that it was going to be an issue. I suddenly realized that, like my father, I was now an employee of the U.S. government. My mother was disappointed until she heard what I was going to be paid.

I almost decided to forego gymnastics. That is until I realized that Mr. Trahorn's likely fascination with underage girls allowed me to conduct additional studies on the breadth of my powers. It was a bit disingenuous to take up a spot on the team for this reason, I'll admit, but I needed to understand whether my gift could translate to others. I also still needed to know why some people, like Mr. Trahorn, got sick to their stomach while others felt a burning sensation. To do so, I would have to be in a position to get close to his potential targets. That meant

I had to make the first team.

I could tell Mr. Trahorn was nervous when I showed up at the first practice. We had lost two seniors from last year's first team, so he knew I was likely to advance and take one of the two available spots. I almost felt sorry for him, but not really.

Ms. Sylvester made first-team selections after the first two weeks of practice. That I made the team wasn't much of a surprise. But when a cute little blond freshman named Heather was selected to fill the final slot, everyone was shocked. Everyone but Mr. Trahorn who looked a little too happy when Ms. Sylvester made the announcement. When Mr. Trahorn saw I was looking at him, reacting with pleasure, his attempt to transition to a more neutral expression just made him look more guilty.

My being on the first team presented a dilemma for Mr. Trahorn. He obviously still had a fascination for me. I know because I would still get signals and catch him staring at me longingly from time to time. And there was no way he could have ever stomached, taping my knees, pun intended. To Mr. Trahorn's credit, he trained the other Assistant Coach how to tape, so I was still given first-team treatment.

One thing I started to notice about Mr. Trahorn is that he only used black or blue tape, except for Heather, who had hot pink. Off the cuff one day, I asked one of my teammates who was wearing black tape why she selected black tape. Her response was interesting.

"Oh, I didn't select it. Mr. Trahorn said for my body type, black worked the best. I wanted hot pink, but I guess you have to be a little pixie, like you or Heather, to get hot pink."

When I subsequently consulted the trusty Internet, I learned that the kinesiology tape colors were purely for aesthetics and did not denote any difference in function or strength. Busted. Mr. Trahorn was just marking his territory. He was making it easier to find his targets in a crowd and ogle their nubile bodies to his heart's content.

The next day I asked for the black tape, and the look on Mr. Trahorn's face when he saw I wasn't wearing hot pink was priceless. Almost as if I was cheating on him.

Now my concern turned to whether Mr. Trahorn's ogling was the full extent of his fascination. My working theory was that those that get sick to their stomach are just the creepers. The ones that may stare and fantasize, but that never act, or haven't yet acted, upon those fantasies. I knew I was safe from Mr. Trahorn, but naïve little Heather, I wasn't so sure about. I made plans to become Heather's BFF and continue my research into the twisted and likely perverted mind of Mr. Trahorn.

CHAPTER 9

Minding Mail and Malevolent Males

I started my job at the post office the week after my 16th birthday. Anyone who thinks that the U.S. Post Office is obsolete and dying hasn't worked there. I couldn't believe the shit-ton of mail that went through that place. Of course, it was December, so I arrived at the height of the busy season.

While many of the tasks at the post office's processing center are automated, they still require some human intervention and oversight. Some jobs are still fully manual, like sorting boxes into large canvas mailbags in zip code order. Then there are the crazy things that some people send through the mail that defy standard treatment and your belief in the superiority of the human intellect.

I was able to customize my work schedule so that it didn't conflict with gymnastics, which ran from November through March. Usually, three other postal aides like myself would report to work each day, and we'd be assigned to a task. Some tasks required us to work together, which was fun but didn't always guarantee our full attention or highest productivity. Other times we worked alone or with a seasoned postal employee that we came to be known as "Zombie Lifers." It wasn't meant to be derogatory. We were just talking one day about how they all shuffled along mindlessly doing their jobs with blank expressions on their faces. One of the postal aides said, "Ya, like zombies," while another added the embellishment, "Zombie Lifer." The name stuck and eventually morphed into ZL, pronounced "zeal." Which ironically sounded positive but was the absolute last word you'd think of to describe how they went about their jobs.

When I wasn't working, I was trying to become Heather's best friend. This was challenging. In order not to arouse Mr. Trahorn's suspicions, maybe not the best verb to use in this case, I had to become her confidante without him knowing. In short, to conduct my study, I was the variable that needed to be controlled. If he knew we were best friends, he would likely change his behavior.

Another challenge was the lack of time I had available to invest in my relationship with Heather. Sunday was the only day when I wasn't either working, going to school, or at a gymnastics practice or meet. The only other time I could talk with Heather out of view and earshot of Mr. Trahorn was in the locker room. The locker room turned out to be a surprisingly effective place to accomplish my mission. While some girls kept to themselves or waited to shower at home, others saw it as an opportunity to bare their souls while in various states of undress.

Heather, being a freshman on the first team, had an uphill climb to acceptance, let alone friendship with the other girls. Those passed over for first-team resented her, and most of the more seasoned first-teamers felt threatened by her. She didn't help her cause by being vocal about her accomplishments. What with all the trophies and medals she had accumulated and being taught by former Olympians at summer gymnastics camps.

So when I made an effort to spend time with her and talk with her, she ate it up. We'd yak on and on until we'd be the only ones left in the locker room. While my original reason for befriending her may have been less than genuine, I actually came to like her. And despite her youth, she knew a lot more about gymnastics than I did. While most of my teammates wrote her off as some self-centered hotshot, I saw an accomplished athlete who was hungry for acceptance. Even if her interpersonal skills and humility may have taken a backseat to her sole lifelong focus of honing her gymnastic skills. Not only did I want to be her friend, but I knew I could also learn a lot from her. When I finally asked her if she wanted to come over to my house on Sunday, she was ecstatic.

Before Heather's visit, we had our first gymnastics meet on Thursday. While Heather and the rest of my teammates looked confident and calm, I had the biggest case of butterfly stomach ever. Ms. Sylvester recognized this and put her arm around me, and uttered what I'm sure were words designed to prop me up and calm me down, but I didn't hear any of them. I had been alerted by my signal and was watching as Mr. Trahorn finished taping Heather's knees and started rubbing and kneading Heather's thighs, presumably to loosen up her quadriceps. That he would do this at all, let alone with a gym full of spectators, was unbelievable. Perhaps he thought it wouldn't be perceived as inappropriate in public view and in the context of a gymnastics meet, but my signal told me otherwise. Just as I was about to interrupt Ms. Sylvester and call it to her attention, Mr. Trahorn happened to look over, and our eyes met. That he immediately stopped Heather's massage at that moment didn't seem like a coincidence. And although he tried to hide it, I thought I detected a slight tenting in the front of his gym pants.

We won the meet. Heather was fabulous while I struggled. It wasn't a complete bust for me as I landed all my tumbling passes and had the third-highest score on floor exercise. I wasn't as concerned about my performance as I was for Heather. If Mr. Trahorn was bold enough to massage her thighs in the middle of a crowded gym, what would he do if he ever got her alone? I was determined to protect Heather, and if Mr. Trahorn was what I think he was, I needed to find a way to stop him.

Unfortunately, I didn't have a lot of time between the meet and Sunday to think about how to best approach Heather with my concerns about Mr. Trahorn. I hadn't been comfortable talking about my powers with Misty, so that was definitely not an option when I got together with Heather. The best I could hope for was to get her talking about him, see what she thought about him, and take it from there. We really hadn't talked about anything but gymnastics, so I had no idea about how savvy Heather was when it came to boys or men.

Sunday morning broke, and I was still exhausted even after almost 10 hours of sleep. I still wasn't used to the additional 20 hours of work tacked on to my school and gymnastics schedule. I hadn't made any definitive plans for what we'd do when we got together. I hoped Heather wasn't planning on anything too strenuous.

The doorbell rang 10 minutes before noon, and I opened the door to see Heather in winter jogging gear, red-faced and out of breath.

"Hi, Aja," she panted. "I'm a little early. I misjudged how long it would take me to get here. Hope you don't mind," she said, gulping in a big breath of air.

"You ran here? Where do you live?" I asked incredulously.

"Oh, a little under 3 miles," she said as I motioned for her to come in.

"Wow, how long did it take you?" I said as she started to unzip her vest jacket and take off her running shoes.

"Twenty minutes and ten seconds," she replied after consulting the smartwatch on her wrist. "That's a 7 minute and 12-second pace per mile. Twenty-eight seconds faster than my usual pace. I guess I was excited about getting here."

"Well, I'm excited you're here, but I hope you don't want me to go running with you. I'm still tired from working all day yesterday."

Thankfully, Heather didn't want me to run with her, and we went up to my room, where I joined her doing some cooldown stretches on the floor. I didn't need to prompt her to talk about gymnastics or Mr. Trahorn.

"Wasn't that a great meet Thursday?" she began.

"Well, you did great, and I'm glad we won, but I pretty much sucked."

"No, you didn't. You got third on floor. That was an awesome routine. I hope I can tumble and fly like you someday."

"Well, thanks, but the rest of my routines sucked. Especially beam and vault."

"Those are the two hardest events. I've been doing gymnastics practically my whole life, and you just started last year. Don't you know how incredible it is that you're performing at the level you're at? I had to work my butt off for years to get where I'm at."

She made a good point, and I really hadn't thought of it from that perspective. It made me feel better about myself, if not a little guilty, that I had initially befriended her for research purposes. I tried shifting the conversation.

"So, what do you think of Ms. Sylvester and Mr. Trahorn?" I asked, not wanting to sound too obvious about who I was trying to target our conversation on.

"Well, when you've been trained by former Olympians, it's probably not fair to hold them to that standard. Ms. Sylvester is good. She seems to know how to keep us focused and relaxed. Which is really 90% of a coach's job. You can have the best gymnasts in the world, but if they're distracted or uptight, a mediocre team that's focused and relaxed will beat them every time."

Heather's vast experience and understanding of leadership were truly remarkable for her age. She looked like a little naïve and vulnerable waif, but she spoke like a seasoned professional. I agreed with her assessment of Ms. Sylvester and was anxious to hear what she had to say about Mr. Trahorn.

"And what about Mr. Trahorn?" I prompted.

"Mr. Trahorn might be able to be a good coach if he focused on coaching," she replied.

"What do you mean by that?" I asked

"He's not there to coach, Aja. He's there to troll for little girls."

I couldn't believe what I just heard come out of Heather's mouth. My first thought was that my unique powers may not be so unusual. Maybe Heather shared the same abilities.

"Why do you think that?" I asked.

"Haven't you noticed? The signs are obvious. Besides how he drools over me, I've watched him watching you. He has a real hard-on for you. You better keep an eye on him. I'm surprised he hasn't insisted on taping you up yet," she said.

I tried to keep my composure while inside I was reeling from the cognitive dissonance between Heather's naïve and innocent appearance and her sophisticated skills of observation and knowledge of predatory behavior.

"I hadn't noticed," I lied, more interested in trying to learn how she knew all this than confirming her observations and letting her know about my history with Mr. Trahorn.

"Well, you better start noticing. I had to learn the hard way," she said as tears rimmed her eyes.

"What happened?" I said, not sure that I really wanted to hear what came next.

"When I was 8, one of the coaches I had at summer gymnastics camp molested me. He told me he knew a secret training technique that would make me a great gymnast, but I had to promise not to tell anyone."

Now I knew I didn't want to hear more, but Heather was now tearfully committed to telling her horrific story.

"I didn't know any better, so I agreed to meet him in his office. At first, he just helped stretch out my legs. Then he started to massage my legs. He said the secret technique would hurt the first time but that it didn't hurt after the first time. He made it clear that to work, I would need at least 4 treatments. Then he started to massage between my legs, and before I knew it, one of his fingers was inside of me. It hurt bad, and I started crying, but he wouldn't stop."

Heather's face was a mask of pain and awash in tears. I had started crying and told her to stop, but she shook her head and continued in torturous detail how he continued to abuse her. So determined to be a great gymnast, she said she would have gone back for more, but that night a female camp counselor was alerted by Heather's screams. She was having a nightmare. After Heather calmed down, she thought she had wet the bed, but when the counselor pulled back the covers, they found Heather's pajama bottoms soaked in blood. Heather, afraid she was going to die, told the counselor about the "secret training technique" the counselor had performed. The counselor notified the police and Heather's parents and accompanied Heather to the hospital, where a rape kit exam was performed and her lacerations treated. The male counselor had disappeared but was found two days later in a wooded area near his home, dead from a self-inflicted gunshot wound.

All I could think to do was hug Heather until her tears subsided. When Heather regained her composure and pulled away from my embrace, she chuckled, which struck me as odd.

"You want to hear something funny? The next year I went to a different gymnastics camp, and the first day they had a class on how to keep yourself safe and how to recognize sexual predators."

I didn't find that funny. I found it sad. I felt lame when all I could think to say was, "I'm sorry you had to go through that."

"You're the first person I've ever told. Well, my parents know, but you're the first person outside of my parents. You're the first person who has ever wanted to be my friend."

Now that made me even sadder, and my sadness prompted two things. I hugged her again, and then I told her about my signal and the unusual effect I had on some people, including Mr. Trahorn. She had bared her soul, and now I was baring mine. I worried about how it sounded and how she might take it. When I said she was the first person I ever told and paused anxiously awaiting her reaction, she hugged me. I broke into tears, and Heather held me like I had held her. When my tears stopped and we released our embrace, I felt a bond between us, unlike any other connection I'd ever had.

After conspiring on a plan to get Mr. Trahorn removed from his Assistant Coaching post, we had lunch and watched a movie. As Heather geared up for her trek back home, I found myself agreeing to join her for a run the following weekend. We hugged at the door, and as she gracefully strode down the walkway, turned down the street, and picked up her pace, I realized that Heather was my BFF, and Mr. Trahorn was toast.

CHAPTER 10

Heather and I Go to War

I woke up Monday morning thinking about Heather and our plan to ensnare Mr. Trahorn. Heather's horrific abuse kept playing in my head, making it hard for me not to generalize my anger and disgust to all men. I knew this wasn't rational, but emotions, especially anger, rarely are. At least I knew we could rid the school of one perverted man who was posing as an upstanding member of our school's faculty. He had an upstanding member alright, but we were about to chop it off figuratively since doing it literally was, unfortunately, not a viable option.

When I arrived at school, the cheerleaders were selling single roses to help fund their travel to the national cheerleader competition in Florida coming up in January. The table was mobbed by guys who were either buying roses for their girlfriends or more likely just trying to score points with the cheerleaders and ogle their pom-poms. I stood in line and bought a red rose, ignoring a boy who made a snide comment that I had to buy a rose for myself because I didn't have a boyfriend to buy me one. His remark didn't help the downward spiral of my already low opinion of males. Not that it was any of his business, but I bought the rose for Heather. It wasn't a part of our devious plan for Mr. Trahorn. I bought it because

I cared about her and wanted to let her know how much it meant to me that she confided in me.

Heather cried when I gave her the rose. I cried too. We made quite a scene in the hallway, with those around us probably wondering who had died. We didn't care. We were united in a common purpose, and tomorrow would be a happy day - Mr. Trahorn's last day.

At work that night, I was paired with a 60-something Zeal who incredibly had started out as a postal aide when he was in high school almost 50 years earlier. Unlike many of the Zeals, who shuffled around silently, he was a talker, which I appreciated because I needed a distraction from my brain that was working overtime on Heather and our plan for Mr. Trahorn.

The Zeal told me all about his experiences as a postal aide. At that time, they had employed more high school students because almost all of the tasks were manual. It was not uncommon for him to work with 8-10 classmates, and by the sounds of it, it was a wonder anyone received their mail in the 70s! Their favorite workstation was sorting letters into the pigeonhole cases that were situated in such a way that you could see your co-worker in the next row over when certain pigeonholes were empty. These cases were equipped to accommodate a tray of mail with canvas pouches filled with rubber bands situated for easy access when you needed to bundle a stack of mail from a full pigeonhole.

Putting teenagers in proximity to one another with unlimited numbers of rubber bands was not a recipe for productivity. My Zeal's eyes sparkled as he described the creative ways they found to shoot each other with the rubber bands and how intense the rubber band wars would get. Shooting a co-worker across from you through empty pigeon-holes took a fair amount of skill but ultimately was banned as too easy. This ban introduced a wide array of ricochet shots. Other rules were introduced, like you couldn't shoot a co-worker on your side of the row. Co-workers on the opposite side were the enemy and fair game. One time, he and three others in his row linked a string of rubber bands together that spanned 6-feet. He and another co-worker then snuck around, flanking the enemy combatants on the other side. When they had stretched their atomic rubber band to its maximum length, they yelled, "Bombs away!" alerting the four enemies, who turned and saw their impending doom. The rubber band bomb fell short, but the effort was applauded and became part of post office lore.

My Zeal's story was apt because the next day was our D-Day. The day Heather and I would storm the beach and launch an assault on Mr. Trahorn. One battle in our war against those who prey on kids. Our plan was simple. Heather would go to Mr. Trahorn's office around lunchtime and tell him that she wouldn't be able to be at practice because she had strained her lower back and was going to see a chiropractor. That would be Mr. Trahorn's moment of truth. If he thanked her for letting him know and wished her a speedy recovery, he'd be off the hook, but we were betting on that he'd see it as an opportunity.

When I saw Heather first thing Tuesday morning, I was even more confident that Mr. Trahorn would succumb to his perverted and baser instincts. Heather was dressed in skin-tight jeans and a flattering top that emphasized her perkiness, if you know what I mean. Her make-up and radiant, long blond hair only made her more stunning. I didn't have to say anything. The boy's reactions around us told the story. Heather looked hot.

The more complicated part of our plan was how to capture evidence of Mr. Trahorn's depravity. Step one was to have Heather audio record their interaction using her phone. Step two, if Mr. Trahorn did as we expected, was for me to go to Ms. Sylvester and tell her that I was worried about Heather. I'd tell her that Heather had gone to Mr. Trahorn's office to tell him about needing to miss practice but that she hadn't returned from his office. Just being behind closed doors with a female student would likely be sufficient grounds for at least a suspension. If he was found giving Heather a massage or attempting anything beyond that, his goose was cooked. Timing was of the essence as we needed to wait long enough to capture sufficient evidence but not so long as to put Heather in danger.

I had a moment of doubt and asked Heather if we should reconsider our plan.

"Why don't we just tell Ms. Sylvester our concerns about him and let her deal with it?" I said, not comfortable putting Heather in a vulnerable position with Mr. Trahorn.

"What could she do? Talk to him? If she does that, he'll just be more careful or go underground for a while until another girl comes along. And who knows what he's doing outside of school. We need to do this. Not only for us but also for all the other girls he might be stalking or taking advantage of."

I couldn't argue against Heather's rationale and found myself in awe of her maturity and bravery. The plan was on. T minus 3 hours.

I accompanied Heather just far enough to watch her enter Mr. Trahorn's office. When the door closed 30 seconds later, I knew that Mr. Trahorn had failed the test. When I couldn't find Ms. Sylvester and realized that I hadn't developed a contingency plan, I started to panic. I considered going to find my homeroom teacher, but I was receiving an overwhelming signal that told me time was running short. I decided I had to go to Mr. Trahorn's office, not sure what I was going to do when I got there. I didn't have to worry. As I stood outside his office, I heard Mr. Trahorn start to scream. All of a sudden, he came bolting out of his office, still screaming and holding both hands up like they were on fire. He ran past me and into the men's room down the hall while I went to his office to check on Heather. She was just zipping and buttoning her jeans. When she saw me, a look of relief crossed her face, and she grabbed her phone and stopped the audio recording.

"Thank God for tight jeans," she said. "You got here just as he was trying to pull them down. Pretty impressive that power of yours."

"Oh my God, Heather. I couldn't find Ms. Sylvester and didn't know what to do," I said, entering the office and giving her a hug.

"Let's get out of here. I got enough evidence on this audio recording to burn him even more than you just did."

As we walked by the men's room, we could hear running water and Mr. Trahorn's echoing whimpers. We held our laughter just long enough to be out of earshot of Mr. Trahorn and fortuitously ran into Ms. Sylvester on our way to the Principal's office. There, Heather played the audio recording of the encounter for Ms. Sylvester and the Principal. I wasn't allowed to join them, but Heather played the audio for me later. Suffice to say, the police were called, and in addition to losing his job, Mr. Trahorn was arrested and charged with Aggravated Criminal Sexual Assault in the Third Degree. One mystery on the recording was the source of Mr. Trahorn's screams. The principal, Ms. Sylvester, and the police all asked Heather what happened, but she pled ignorance. My secret was safe with her.

Gymnastics practice was canceled that afternoon, so Heather and I got together at her house after school. Her parents had been notified, and as you can imagine, they were very concerned about what was now the second assault of their daughter. Perhaps not surprisingly, their initial reaction was to prohibit her from participating in gymnastics ever again, which caused a meltdown I, unfortunately, got to witness. Later, her parents relented, realizing that they had over-reacted. This, of course, was a couple of hours after I had tried to put Heather back together again while we were cloistered in her room. We hadn't thought about or planned for Heather's parents' potential reaction, and as a result, their unexpected response was more traumatic for Heather than Mr. Trahorn's expected actions.

I'm not going to disgust you with the specific things Mr. Trahorn said on the audio Heather played for me. Suffice to say, he didn't waste much time moving from massaging her lower back to her nether region. When Heather refused to voluntarily pull her jeans down so he could supposedly access her sciatic nerve, he forcibly tried to remove them, succeeding in uncovering half of her butt when the pain of the invisible flames consumed his hands. While his actions were bad enough, it was the things he said in the process of his "treatment" that revealed his depravity. Let's just say that Mr. Trahorn wasn't planning on eating his lunch in the cafeteria, and he said many things that made Heather sound like a plate of hor d'oeuvres into which he intended to plunge his cocktail stick.

The good news was that he was no longer at our high school, was staring at a minimum of 3-5 years of jail time, and would never work in a job with children again. The bad news was that we knew he was just one of many predators.

I had dinner with Heather and her parents, and by the time I left that evening, I truly felt like we would be friends forever. Fighting in a war, having each other's back, and surviving adversity together do that.

CHAPTER 11

My Summer Internship Jinx

I woke up the following morning not only with the realization that my signaling and protective powers could be extended beyond Misty and me but that they had a more extensive range than I had previously experienced. I had received my signal when I was on a completely different floor from Mr. Trahorn's office. And as for causing the burning sensation, I was in the hallway outside the office, perhaps thirty feet from where he was trying to depants Heather.

I began to wonder if my powers were something I could cultivate or refine, like how practicing my tumbling repeatedly eventually resulted in improved reliability to stay inbounds. I also began to wonder if my powers would ever allow me to be intimate beyond the hand-holding and hugs that I shared with Thomas, my one and only relationship with a boy. Were my powers triggered by all sexual thoughts and actions, or just those that were exploitive?

I was starting to become overwhelmed with the questions I had about my supposed "gift" again. And frankly, I was starting to freak out a bit. What if my powers evolved to such an extent that all sexual thoughts and actions of everyone within a certain proximity to me started to signal me? Or if people en masse began to get sick to their stomachs or flail around as if on fire when within a specific range? My gift was starting to sound like a potential horror story. All I could imagine was the Centers for Disease Control identifying me as the source of people's sickness and imaginary immolation and a small army of men in lime-green hazmat suits taking me away and quarantining me in some dark, dank, secure facility in a remote place where my powers no longer could menace society.

No, the day after Heather and my victory to remove Mr. Trahorn did not start out well. I was almost afraid to go to school but forced myself to go. I'm glad I did because it ended up being a typical, rather boring day at high school. No mass gastrointestinal fireworks. No throngs of people erupting in flames. And no men in lime-green hazmat suits. As a matter of fact, I went a few months without getting a signal and was beginning to wonder if I had lost my powers.

Heather and I continued our friendship and spent any available free time together, which wasn't much. As I had promised, I started to go on runs with her. The first few weeks felt like torture, but then it got easier and, at times, even exhilarating. I began to believe Heather's claims about the existence of a runner's high.

The gymnastics team not only survived but thrived in the absence of Mr. Trahorn. My skills improved, primarily due to Heather's influence and guidance. Heather began to establish herself as the team's best gymnast, which still didn't earn her any respect or acceptance from her teammates. They couldn't get over that she was a freshman, and they wouldn't accept that her consistently superior performance proved that their perception of her as a self-absorbed hotshot with an over-inflated opinion of herself was categorically wrong. Our team just missed out on going to the State tournament, but Ms. Sylvester liked our chances for next year, as we were only losing one senior from the first team.

One of the things I didn't count on when I had appeased my

teachers and Mr. Mahovich by telling them I wanted to become an attorney is just how vigorously they would work to support my supposed career choice. Giving me pamphlets from Rutgers and Seton Hall was one thing, but offering me a summer internship at a law office was quite another. I was about to reject the notion out of hand when Mr. Mahovich mentioned that it would give me high school and college credit. The opportunity to finish high school early and get a jumpstart on college was too attractive to pass up.

So, in the summer before my senior year, I started my internship at Lowe, Hartford, Smith, and Westin. Their name was amusing to me. They sounded like a big box store that sold insurance, groceries, and guns, not legal services. My internship was 24-hours per week for 8 weeks. I was able to adjust my schedule at the post office so that I had weekends off.

In the first couple of weeks at the law office, I shadowed a law clerk, a paralegal, a court runner, and a few other non-attorney employees to gain an appreciation for the inner workings of a law office. In the third week, I met with some of the partners and junior partners. While I couldn't say that my internship was igniting a torch to become an attorney, it was interesting enough to hold my attention.

It got infinitely more interesting when I walked into the office of Hugh Jinks, JD, a junior partner in the firm. When I first saw Attorney Jinks' name on my schedule, I had what I suspect was a typical reaction. What an unfortunate name. One letter away from high jinks. That might be a good name for a clown, but an attorney? And wouldn't you be concerned and want to avoid the bad luck a lawyer named Jinks may bring you? Being somewhat an expert on unique names, I suspected that for Mr. Jinks to aspire to his station in life and succeed, he must have a very strong backbone, a great sense of humor, or both.

The transition between my enthusiasm for meeting Mr.

Jinks and my dread occurred the moment I opened his office door. Although I was dressed in a conservative pants suit with equally conservative footwear, I could swear that I was naked. The office chair that sat beside him at the desk, a plain chair, looked to me like it had wrist and ankle restraints, suitable for allowing him to lecherously explore my body. What's more, Mr. Jinks appeared naked and way too happy to see me as he stood up erect in more than one way to salute my arrival. It had been a few months since my last signal, and I had never had one quite this graphic. It threw me, and I think he detected my hesitation as I stopped in my tracks just two steps into his office.

Instead of canceling our meeting, which is what I hoped he would do, he started to walk towards me. He was still 15 feet away when I felt his hands all over me and an intense pressure between my legs as if he was penetrating me. I opened my mouth to scream, but before I could, he clutched his chest and collapsed on the floor, not 10 feet in front of me. I ran out of his office and alerted his secretary, who in turn called 911. A couple of his colleagues entered his office to try to rescue him, but their efforts failed. By the time the paramedics arrived, Hugh Jinks, the 48-year old junior partner was dead, from an apparent heart attack. I wasn't so sure.

I was traumatized, which all the law firm staff reasonably thought was due to my witnessing him collapse and die. Little did they know that I was fairly certain that I had killed him. I went to the one and only person I could confide in, Heather, who tried to reassure me that I wasn't lethal.

"People die of heart attacks all the time. Especially people with high-stress jobs like lawyers who sit on their butts all day and don't get enough exercise," she said, trying to convince me.

"Maybe you're right," I replied, which was a bald-faced lie designed to make Heather feel like she helped me when I still wasn't persuaded.

"Let's go for a run," I suggested, knowing this would further convince Heather that her intervention had worked because I would never ever propose a run unless I was feeling unusually energetic or happy.

Even though Heather couldn't convince me that I didn't kill Mr. Jinks, I still valued being able to bare my soul to her. While Misty and I had always been close, and I definitely missed her being away at college, my relationship with Heather had grown to take a very prominent place in my life. I was acutely aware that I, unlike most of the girls my age, neither had a steady boyfriend nor was I steadily fielding opportunities to go on dates to potentially land a boyfriend. While I didn't necessarily feel the need to have a boyfriend, I couldn't help but think that my powers were to blame. Sadly, that boy that teased me when I was waiting in line to buy that rose was right. Of course, if he knew that I could kill him by imagining he had bad intentions towards me, he would have thought twice about opening his big mouth.

A week later, while I was interning at the law office, a news report broke about Hugh Jinks that not only rocked the law firm and the community but freaked my mother out and confirmed my deepest fear. I did kill Hugh Jinks. Not that anyone other than Heather would ever know or care. I lied to my mother and told her that I didn't know or ever see Mr. Jinks when I was there. This only had a marginal impact on her hysteria, which, at its height, demanded I quit my internship immediately. While I didn't really care that much about the internship, with only two weeks left, I didn't want to forfeit the high school and college credits. She eventually calmed down and allowed me to continue my internship.

Mr. Jinks' autopsy showed that he didn't die of a heart attack. He didn't even have a history of a heart condition. Instead, when the coroner opened him up, he found that his heart and several other internal organs had been cooked. The coroner had never seen anything like it but surmised that it was most likely caused by a "thyroid storm," a rare and acute case of hyperthyroidism that raised his heart rate, blood pressure, and internal body temperature quickly and significantly enough to kill him. I knew better. The only storm Hugh Jinks experienced was Hurricane Aja. But no one was asking me, and I wasn't about to confess.

If that wasn't proof enough, what they found in Mr. Jink's home only made my guilt in his death irrefutable and oddly heroic. The bodies of six teenage girls age 13 to 16, missing over the last two years, were found buried in his basement. Videos of what he had done to them before their horrific deaths and a collection of souvenir lingerie were found telling the gruesome story. As frightening as it was to realize that you have the power to kill someone without laying a hand on them, I felt vindicated. No one was going to grieve Hugh Jinks' death, quite the opposite. It was a blessing. A blessing that I had conferred upon society. Ironically, my internship for a career I never had any interest in pursuing helped me to decide not just a career but a calling that ignited a passion and a drive I had never experienced and could no longer ignore.

When you finally realize what you want to be and what you want to do, you can't wait to get there and do it. I knew exactly the person I needed to talk to, but the problem was I didn't know how to find him, let alone speak to him.

CHAPTER 12

My Search for Dad Begins

W hile most of my classmates were flush with the excitement of their last year in high school and had definite plans for the future, as well as the sense of independence that being 18 years old conferred, I was once again the anomaly.

Don't get me wrong, I was excited to graduate, but my future after that was more than a little bit fuzzy. Also, I wouldn't be turning 18 until five months after I graduated, and physically I still looked 13. I recognized my unique powers and had a better idea of their capabilities, but it wasn't something I could put on a resume or a college application. Could you imagine seeing "Summer internship: Fried internal organs of a serial sexual predator and murderer."

I wanted to use my powers to bring people who exploit and abuse children to justice. My problem was that, except for Heather, I couldn't talk about my unique talent. I didn't know the educational track to make my goal a reality, and I really didn't want to sit in college for 4 years, majoring in something like criminal justice when I had already brought two monsters to justice. To me, that would feel more like a prison sentence where my powers would only be used for the random Joeys, Lyles, Mr. Trahorns, and Mr. Jinks's I might come across. I wanted to have a more significant and more immediate impact on those that preyed on children. I wanted to talk to my Dad because I knew he'd understand and be able to help me, even though I hadn't seen or talked to him in 9 years.

So, in between classes, gymnastics, and my job at the post office, I tried to find a way to communicate with my Dad. I first tried to get some intel from my Mom without arousing her suspicions.

"Mom, if you absolutely had to communicate with Dad, would there be a way to do it? Say I had a terminal illness and was going to die in 3 months."

"That's an absolutely horrible thought, Aja. Where do you come up with these things?" she replied, missing entirely the question I really wanted her to answer.

"I'm just curious. I know Dad wants to keep us safe, but what if we had to contact him for some reason? An emergency."

"Well, I'm sure if it was an emergency, I could probably call someone at the CIA, and they could advise me on how we could get him a message. Why? Is there something you're not telling me? You're not pregnant, are you?"

"No, Mom. I'm not pregnant, and if I were, I'd be in good company with the Virgin Mary. You'd have to pray to me. Maybe they'd even make a prayer in my name."

"Don't be blasphemous, Aja. It happens, you know," my mother replied, stating the obvious and then launching into stories about all the young girls she sees in the hospital with babies they didn't want.

I had eeked out all of the information I dared get out of my mother. As you can see, even when I try to make a question sound innocent, my mother immediately jumps to conclusions. Any further discussion on the topic of communicating with my Dad would only heighten her suspicions.

I considered my mother's response and even thought about calling the CIA myself, but then realized my dilemma. What if I wasn't supposed to know that my Dad worked for the CIA? My mother had told Misty and me very clearly not to speak to anyone about Dad. Would I endanger my Dad in some way by calling them? Would alarms sound at the CIA, and they'd contact my mother and get me in trouble? And even if I posed as my mother on the call, they wouldn't be prone to believe my identity over the phone. CIA Headquarters in Langley, Virginia, was over 200 miles away, so going there was out of the question.

I was stuck until I had a revelation. My mother must know more. There must be a way she could contact someone through some secure means. She just wasn't telling me. If my Dad was a spy, I hoped he had given me some of his spy genes because I needed to do a little investigating. My first target, the locked file cabinet in my mother's bedroom.

My opportunities to accomplish my mission were limited. My schedule had me out of the house during the same hours my mother was away. There was only one solution - play hooky. I had considered feigning illness to stay home but feared my doting mother might elect to stay home from work to minister to my fake malady. Instead, I left for school, as usual, only to return home an hour later when I knew my mother would be gone.

I searched high and low for the key to the file cabinet. I even braved going through the junk drawer, and amidst the crazy collection of miscellany, found a whole ring of keys that I was sure must include the file cabinet key. Three of the keys slide into the lock, but none of them opened it. Three hours later, after exhausting all the potential places Mom might hide a key, I tried my lock-picking skills. I had watched enough TV shows to understand the general principle, and with two modified paperclips, I futzed with the lock in every conceivable way, to no avail. Short of prying the drawers open or finding the key, I wasn't getting in. I needed a Plan B.

That evening, after my Mom got home and I creatively responded to her interrogation about my day, I noticed her key ring laying out in its usual place on the counter. When she went to take a shower, I examined the keys on her key ring, finding one similar to the three that had fit the file cabinet lock. I weighed the risks of trying the key and rifling through the file cabinet while my mother was in the shower or just taking the key off the ring and hoping she wouldn't notice so that I could inventory the file cabinet at my leisure when she wasn't home. I chose the latter strategy.

Luck was on my side. Not only did my Mom not notice the key was missing, but she needed to leave early to work the next morning, allowing me to do my exploring without compromising my school attendance. The top drawer of the 2-drawer file cabinet contained old tax returns, warranty information on our household appliances, insurance documents, bank statements, and other uninteresting paperwork. I hit the jackpot when I opened the bottom drawer. There lay a satellite phone under which was a manila folder containing all the information for how to use the phone to contact my Dad. The folder also had a very prominent warning taped to the inside cover in bold red letters, "Use Only in Case of an Emergency." If this was not clear enough, below the warning was a list of things they apparently thought fit the definition of emergency, including a death in the family, the kidnapping of a family member, the receipt of death threats, or repeated instances of being followed.

I could hardly claim that any of these circumstances existed. I toiled over whether to make a call but eventually settled on putting the folder and phone back and locking the cabinet. Instead, I would make a copy of the key, return the original to my Mom's keyring, and give some more thought as to if and when to call my Dad.

That evening, I successfully returned the file cabinet key to my Mom's keyring. I hid my copy by taping it to a part of my desk that was only visible if you were sitting under the desk with the center drawer fully open. I hadn't made any headway on whether to call Dad and restlessly tossed and turned in bed until well past midnight. Just as I was starting to think I might finally fade off to sleep, I felt a signal. On the intensity meter, it wasn't quite as intense and graphic as when I had walked into Mr. Jinks' office, but definitely stronger than most. I couldn't immediately understand the source, because as far as I knew, my mother and I were safely locked in the house. I hazarded a glance outside my bedroom window but saw nothing of concern. I was about to leave my room to check on Mom when my cellphone sprang to life, suddenly piercing the dark with an eerie glow, burring loudly on my nightstand, nearly scaring the life out of me. When I saw that it was Misty calling, I immediately knew the source of my signal.

"Is this Aja?" the female voice on the other end of the line asked, pronouncing it as Ah-zha.

"This is Aja," I replied, pronouncing my name correctly. "Who is this?"

"This is Tina. I'm a friend of your sister Misty," she slurred, confirming that what I heard in the background was a party.

"Is everything alright?" I asked, looking at the clock on my nightstand, which read 2:37 am, and thinking immediately how stupid my question was. I steeled myself for the bad news I was sure would next spill from Tina's mouth.

"Yeah, Misty is awright now, she's jus a li'l drunk and wanded me to call you. Some guys jus tried to gang bang her," she blurted. "She wants to talk to you. Here, led me give er the phone," she added, as I could hear her fumbling with the phone and trying to rouse Misty, who babbled something incoherent in response.

"Wake up, Misty, Ahzha's on the phone," Tina said insistently in the background.

Misty finally mumbled something into the phone. I had never known Misty to drink and didn't have any experience with someone as inebriated as my sister sounded.

"Misty, what happened?" I asked, which sounded like a perfectly clear and easy question to comprehend.

Unfortunately, what Misty said in response sounded like some foreign language interspersed with an occasional slurred English word that didn't add up to anything resembling coherent communication. After several attempts to have her clarify what she was saying, I asked her to give the phone back to Tina. I heard some more jostling of the phone and mumbled communications, which seemed to go on interminably before Tina returned to the line.

"Tina, can you tell me what happened," I asked in frustration.

"She tol me these three guys pulled her in here and said they were gonna gang bang her," she replied, adding marginally to what I already knew.

"Where's here?" I asked. "And what guys?"

"We're at a frat house, and they pulled her into this bedroom. I don't know the guys. I think they might live here, though," Tina replied.

"What did they do?" I asked, ignoring the fact that I didn't know what a frat house was.

"She said they took her clothes off, but they all started screaming in pain when they tried to make her suck their dicks and fuck her. I wouldn't have believed her if I hadn't heard their screams myself. They ran past me, still screaming when I got to the room. I helped her put her clothes back on. She's passed out now."

"Are you going to stay with her?" I asked.

"I'm gonna call for a ride back to our dorm. I'm her roommate. I'll make sure she gets home safely."

I thanked Tina, who sounded like our conversation had started to sober her up. I asked her to call me when they got back to the dorm. Thirty minutes later, Tina called to confirm they were safely back in their room but that Misty had puked on the ride home.

There was no hope for sleep for me after Tina's call. Not only was it approaching 4 am, but my mind was reeling with the knowledge that I had shielded Misty from being assaulted from several hundred miles away. Part of me was grateful for the extensive range of my powers, while another part of me revisited the concern about what kind of life I would have if those powers continued to evolve to shield more people. I already knew they also extended to Heather. How many more could I possibly accommodate?

Unfortunately, it was too easy for me to imagine what it would be like if my signal regularly tripped or, worse, always stayed on. My gift would quickly become a curse, and I would eventually die from a lack of sleep as my signal perpetually bombarded me with horrific images and feelings of nakedness, penetration, and violation. Like multiple Mr. Jinks' signals on steroids. My own imaginary yet ultimately fatal gang bang.

Misty called me just before I was about to leave the house for school. She hadn't had much sleep, spending most of her night in the bathroom. She introduced me to the experience and phrase "worshipping the porcelain god," which quickly dispensed with any of the glamour I may have associated with drinking. She didn't remember talking to me and only vaguely remembered the incident. Her roommate, Tina, had refreshed her memory, and when Tina told her about the boys screaming and running from the room, it had immediately reminded her of Uncle Phil's reaction. I wasn't expecting to hear what Misty said next.

"Do you think I have some special power that is protecting

me? Maybe I developed it after all those experiences I had when I was younger. I mean, the same thing happened to Uncle Phil," she reasoned. "I know that sounds crazy, but what else could have caused it? Tina just thinks something must have scared them off."

"That does sound crazy, Misty," I replied, not divulging that I had plenty of experience not telling people about my powers precisely for that reason. "But what do I know?" I added, figuring there was no harm in Misty believing she was the source of her defense against being assaulted.

"Whatever you do, Aja, don't tell Mom. Promise?"

"I won't."

"And don't drink," Misty added.

"I don't, and I won't," I replied, realizing that I was starting to talk in rhymes.

"Good. I'm sorry I had Tina call you in the middle of the night. I don't want you to worry about me. I'll be fine."

"I know," I said, even though I knew the only reason I could say that was that it was my powers that were protecting her. If I were normal, I would have been very worried about Misty. But I'm not, so I wasn't.

One thing my sleepless night resolved for me, though, was that Trace Minor's daughters had both been attacked and threatened. Never mind that my unique powers may have thwarted the fulfillment of the assailant's ultimate intentions. Any way I looked at it. This was an emergency. When the next opportunity presented itself, I was going to call my Dad.

CHAPTER 13

A Surprise Awakening

Heather could read me like a book. So despite make-up, eye drops, coffee, and my best acting job, she knew something was amiss immediately when she saw me at school.

"What happened?" she asked right out of the gate as her face adopted a look of concern.

"What do you mean? What happened?" I replied, hoping my words and a feigned look of confusion would convince her that she had misread me.

"Nice try, Aja, but have you forgotten I'm your soul sister?"

"OK, OK, but I can't tell you about it now. I have to get to class. I'll tell you later," I responded, as her face turned from concern to self-satisfaction that her radar was still alive and well.

"Good. I'm not going to forget, so don't think I'm going to let this go," she said as if she could see that exact thought going through my head at that very moment.

I should have known better. Our connection to one another was uncanny. Rarely did a day pass when one of us didn't complete the other's thought or supply just the right word of encouragement when it was desperately needed. It was scary and incredibly comforting all at the same time.

My problem now was just how much to tell Heather. I didn't have a problem telling her about Misty's incident. She already knew about my powers, and other than the surprise she might have at the range of my abilities, everything else wouldn't shock her. The problem emerged when it came to telling her about my Dad. She had asked about him once early in our friendship, and observing my promise to my mother, I just said to her that he had left when I was 7. At the time, she hadn't pressed me for details, but I knew that wasn't going to hold her forever. It was the last piece of uncharted territory between us in a relationship that didn't seem to tolerate uncharted territory.

It didn't help that I felt as if I was losing my mind. My fear that my evolving powers would make me a host to more and more people, draining me until I was dead, seemed like a very real possibility. My only safe harbor was Heather, at least until I got a chance to talk with my Dad. I know what you're thinking. How could I be so sure that my Dad would magically calm the turbulent seas I was trying to navigate after being away for 9 years? I didn't have a good answer except to say that I felt like he would help, a feeling that seemed as reliable as my signal.

Heather and I lingered in the locker room after gymnastics practice until we had the place to ourselves. It had become our haven, our confessional. It was pointless for me to script my story when it came to Heather. She'd see through anything rehearsed. I also knew that she wouldn't accept anything less than a complete baring of my soul. She'd know as surely as if I were standing in the shower wearing my bra and panties that I wasn't revealing everything.

In reality, this made it easier for me. I didn't have to overthink things and devise a communication strategy. I just needed to say what I'd say and feel what I'd feel with no filters. In return, I'd get no judgment, just acceptance. Like I was talking to my external self. In many ways, Heather was my mirror image, except she had long blond hair and no facial scar.

As the locker room started to empty out, I caught Heather's eye, and any nervousness I may have felt about our ensuing conversation melted away. We were safe in our little corner of the locker room, Heather taking her seat at the end of her bench as I took mine on the bench perpendicular to hers. The diagonal divide seemed perfectly suited for meaningful and private conversations, with just the right amount of physical space to feel comfortable yet still close.

"Ready, Aja?" Heather asked, knowing that I would understand she was referencing the talk I owed her from that morning.

"Ready, Heather," I confirmed as we sat half-dressed in our respective places.

Telling Heather about Misty, as I predicted, did not surprise her. Oh, of course, she was concerned about my sister and amazed at the range of my powers, but she was also sure that that was not the whole story.

"And what else is on your mind, Aja? I can tell there is something bigger. Something you're afraid to tell me," she said. Convincing me yet again that she not only had a finger on my pulse but probably knew every vital sign, lab value, and molecule in my body.

I started to cry. Not because I feared what I had to say but from the relief of having her as a friend. Friend being a totally inadequate designation for what Heather meant to me at that particular moment.

I wasn't surprised when Heather came over and hugged me. I felt like I was crumbling apart, and she was holding me together. Then she kissed me. Softly, on my star-shaped scar, as if saying she loved all of me, even my imperfections. It felt like much more than a kiss, and I returned one to her lips, which accepted mine with a mutual hunger. Our hands gently traced and caressed each other's bodies as we continued to kiss. It felt natural and exhilarating beyond my wildest imagination. All my fears about a lifelong sentence of having intimacy cause my signal and retaliatory pain to melt away.

The few clothes we had on were now an affront to our need to bare ourselves entirely to one another. We needed to feel each other's skin as both of us gently liberated the other from any offensive attire. We wouldn't be satisfied until our flesh was fused together without even the sheerest barrier. Despite this inaugural introduction, nothing seemed unfamiliar, forced, or fumbling. We knew the where, when, what, and how of each other's need for our touch. It felt right. It felt like I was finally home. That a vital and missing part of me had finally been found. Silently, tenderly, our actions filled us up and emptied us out. Leaving only contentment and a new place and space neither of us had ever been and would never want to relinquish.

"I love you, Heather," I whispered when I finally came down to earth from whatever dimension to which she had transported me.

"I love you, Aja," she replied, looking into my eyes but clearly seeing well beyond them to my soul.

We continued to hold each other. More words would have only interfered with the pleasant waves of satisfaction passing through our bodies. There would be time for talking about my Dad. I still wanted to talk to him, but the desperation I had felt previously was gone. Even Heather seemed satisfied that we had communed sufficiently and didn't press me, even though she knew that something still loomed deep and dark inside me. We got dressed and exited the locker room, content in knowing we were now more together than apart. More complete than incomplete.

CHAPTER 14

Twelve Minutes

Some of my feelings of desperation faded after our "talk" in the locker room. A huge puzzle piece in my life had been found and connected, eliminating the concerns I had about living a life without love and intimacy. But like everything in life, it seems, any good thing almost always raises another thing about which to be concerned.

I'm not talking about society's still lukewarm at best acceptance of same-sex relationships. However, I fully anticipated that Heather and I would get our fair share of grief. What I was concerned about was what would become of our relationship when I graduated in just a few months. Our relationship introduced a whole new wrinkle into my planning. Heather would still have 2 years left of high school when I was expected to become "the hope for our future." As someone would inevitably ascribe to our class at our graduation ceremony. No pressure there. I still didn't know what I would be doing after graduation. Let alone have any clear sense of how to fulfill other graduation expectations like "striking out on my own" and "making my mark on society." I could always get a full-time job at the post office and aspire to become a Zombie Lifer. Now wouldn't that lend a whole other meaning to "striking out" and "making a mark?" So while I was delighted with my blossoming relationship with Heather, I still had to reconcile my powers and passion with a plausible plan I could execute after graduation.

I unexpectedly got my opportunity to call my Dad that afternoon. My homeroom teacher reminded us that we just had a half-day of school because of parent-teacher conferences. Seniors were exempt from these meetings, so I was able to go home at lunchtime. I retrieved my copy of the file cabinet key and secured the phone and folder with instructions. Then I tried to make myself comfortable in a bean bag chair that I inherited from Misty but rarely sat in.

My heart was beating so hard it felt as if it was punching me, telling me I was about to do something very wrong. I paused and took several slow, deep breaths to try to calm myself. My heart ignored these attempts and only seemed to beat harder. Then my brain started flogging me with doubts. What if my Dad really didn't care about us anymore? What if he cared, but calling him put him in danger? Or calling him put us in danger? Or got my Mom in trouble? I was a wreck, and something about sitting in the bean bag chair made me feel trapped. I rolled out of the chair, which was the only way I could have extracted myself from its death grip. Now I know why Misty left it for me. It was possessed and hungrily consumed any who dared to put their derriere in its quicksand-like maw. I picked it up and threw it out in the hall to be dispatched later with the garbage.

Pacing back and forth in my room was the only way I would be able to initiate this call. I punched in the numbers and heard a series of unfamiliar sounds, presumably signaling that connections were being made. I had paced the length of my room three times before I heard a click followed by a groggy voice.

"Cheryl, are you alright?" the sleepy voice rattled, followed by a clearing of the throat sound.

"Dad, it's Aja," I said, my heart now pounding so hard I feared it might explode.

"Aja, how did you," he began to ask a question and then shifted mid-sentence. "Is your mother alright? What about Misty?"

"Yes, they're alright. I called you because I needed to talk to you. I'm sorry."

"Oh, superstar, don't be sorry," he said, as his use of my nickname caused a flood of memories from my childhood when he was a normal Dad that came home after work at night. "What do you need to talk about?"

His response opened the floodgates, and I started to cry and wonder where to begin. I began at a place he could not go.

"Where are you?" I asked.

"I can't tell you that superstar. I can tell you it's almost 2 am here. Now, what's on your mind?"

"Dad, I don't know where to begin. I have so much to tell you, and I'm afraid you'll think I'm crazy," I blurted out.

"Relax, honey, take a breath and start at the beginning," he said, which sounded so cliché but somehow also seemed to work.

I told him about all the incidents that had convinced me of my powers and how they not only protected me but protected Misty and my friend Heather. I told him how confused I was about what to do after high school. How I wanted to use my powers to help eliminate abuse and exploitation but had no earthly clue as to how to go about it. When I finally paused, I felt sure that he was already thinking about how to get me committed to a psychiatric hospital. His response, however, surprised me.

"Aja, I'm sorry I haven't been there for you, and I'm glad you called me. I'm not surprised by your gift. I always knew you were special. I think I know someone who can help you."

"You don't mean help, like my daughter's crazy kind of help, do you?"

"No, Aja, I don't think you're crazy. I believe you. Some day I will have the time to tell you why I believe you, but for now, you're going to have to trust me. I can't tell who will contact you, but when they do, they will use your nickname as code, so you know I sent them and that you can trust them. OK?"

"OK, thanks, Dad."

"I love you, superstar."

"I love you too, Dad," as tears fell once again, and we ended the call.

Twelve minutes is all it took to take me from hopeless confusion to hope. That my optimism rested on some mysterious someone who would have to communicate with me in code was novel but sufficient to calm the concerns that had been plaguing me.

I had just returned the satellite phone and folder to my mother's filing cabinet when the doorbell rang. To my surprise, it was Heather, fresh from her parent-teacher conference. We had three hours before my Mom would be home and much to talk about. I bared my soul, and eventually, we bared even more and found a use for that bean bag chair. It redeemed itself, saving it from a trip to the local landfill.

CHAPTER 15

My Mom the Matchmaker

I t's amazing what my brief call with my Dad did for my outlook and my ability to deal with stressful things, like my
Mom.

She had now gotten into the act of regularly asking about
my plans for after high school and offering up her suggestions.
I knew she was just trying to be a good parent. Still, with my
Mom, it always seemed she was trying to control my decisions
versus helping me make the right decision for myself.

Mom also started quizzing me on why I didn't have a boyfriend and, worst of all, began suggesting the sons of friends
of hers who were all "very nice boys" by her assessment. This
was a startling new development given how militant she had
previously been about boys and men. She had apparently gotten over the anger and trauma of Dr. Schifflin's abuse and now
seemed to sound like she wanted to pimp me off to her friend's
sons.

The height of Mom's devious plans to control both my career choice and love life occurred one evening. I came home
from gymnastics practice to find my mother and two people
I didn't recognize in our house. One a woman about my
mother's age, and the other a boy who was presumably her
son and my age. The woman, I learned, was the Director of

Radiology at the hospital where my mother worked, and her son was Ethan, a junior at a high school two towns away. You probably don't need me to tell you how that dinner and evening went, but let me get it off my chest anyway.

My first reaction, which I tamped down, was to explode in a fit of rage for being hijacked. This evolved into a slightly more socially acceptable plan to play along with the game. However, to do so in such a way that my Mom would never consider springing such a surprise on me again. Let me add here that my mother had obviously been chatting me up to them before my arrival and had also shared some photos of me. When a complete stranger says, "Oh, you look even prettier than in your pictures," you know my mother had a hand in prepping and coaching them. Their interest in me was as fake as my response to the Director of Radiology's suggestion that I become a Radiological Technologist.

"Oh, I don't think I'd like working in Radiology. I'm afraid of the dark. Now I'd love to work in Pathology," I lied, hoping to set the Director of Radiology and my mother up for my coup de grace.

"Oh, the Lab & Pathology Director and I are very good friends," she replied. "What interests you about Pathology? Maybe I can get you a job in the Lab."

"I like dead bodies. I especially like it when the pathologist cuts people open for autopsies," I responded. Trying desperately to keep a straight face as my mother's and our two guest's faces looked at me like I was some kind of freak.

I thought that would put them off their efforts, but I guess it wasn't gruesome enough for them. They insisted on continuing to suggest other hospital jobs, like becoming a surgical tech so that I could help surgeons who opened up people who were still alive. It was all quite pathetic, and I didn't know if I was ever going to be able to forgive my mother. Poor Ethan wouldn't leave unscathed from this melee, either.

I couldn't believe it when, after dinner, my Mom suggested I take Ethan upstairs to show him my room. I think Ethan sprang a woody just at my mother's suggestion. Little did he know how I was going to torture him, starting with my ascent up the stairs. He was like a puppy following me, his face inches away from my ass, which I made sure swayed tantalizingly in front of him.

I should have stopped there because if Ethan had any bad intentions towards me, I would have received my signal. By all accounts, Ethan probably was a "very nice boy," and I was about to punish him for our mother's indiscretion at setting up this ruse.

When we got to my room, I feigned feeling hot and asked him if he minded that I change into something else. He indicated he didn't care, and I grabbed a pair of gym shorts and went to the bathroom to put them on. When I returned, I made sure to drop my jeans and panties on the floor in plain sight. I had purposely selected a pair of loose-fitting shorts and a crop top t-shirt. Guaranteeing that when I sat down cross-legged in front of him or raised my arms, he could get a glimpse of parts of my anatomy that fueled every adolescent boy's wet dreams.

I engaged Ethan in conversation, asking him about his school and what he liked to do. It was clear his mind and his eyes were elsewhere as I had intended. The bulge in his pants was my barometer of success. I should have stopped there, but I didn't. I acted like I was mindlessly doing stretches, purposely letting my shorts and my t-shirt strategically ride up, working him into a real lather.

At some earlier time and place, perhaps I would have tried to actually have a meaningful relationship with Ethan. However, I was in love with Heather and angry at my mother. I wasn't going to stop until Ethan broke.

Eventually, my peek-a-boo party with various body parts

was too much for Ethan, and he suggested we continue our conversation in my bed. He actually used slightly more descriptive terms, involving the insertion of something of his into a variety of openings of mine. I acted disgusted and outraged at his suggestion. Just what kind of girl did he think I was? And how I had half a mind to go tell his mother about the wicked things her little boy wanted to do to me.

I couldn't blame him for being angry as he stormed out of my room, but I also couldn't have cared less. Shortly after, I heard our guests leave, followed by my mother's footsteps on the stairs. She had the courtesy to knock, which I hadn't expected, and I welcomed her to come in. Before she said a word, she saw my jeans and panties on the floor and the loose shorts and crop top t-shirt I was wearing.

"You purposely sabotaged this evening Aja, and I'm angry and embarrassed."

"You're angry and embarrassed? What do you think I am? How dare you spring this little plot on me that I'm sure you're going to try to convince me was all done in the name of my own good."

"Well, someone had to light a fire under you because you certainly weren't making any plans for your future."

"What do you know about what I have and haven't done?"

"Every time I've asked, you haven't told me anything. How am I supposed to know if you don't tell me?"

She had a point. I didn't talk to her. Mostly because I never felt like it was a talk, but more like a test. A test I invariably failed, and then my mother would tell me what I should do. Then there was that whole glass half empty, glass half full thing. She seemed to always see the downside of my ideas or plans. How things can't or won't work instead of how they could succeed. I couldn't talk to her about my relationship with Heather. I couldn't talk to her about my powers and how I wanted to help rid the world of people who prey on others.

They would just be two more things she would reject out of hand. Not talking to my mother was the only way for me to preserve any semblance of a relationship with her.

As my mother stood there impatiently waiting for a response to her question, I elected to smooth the waters rather than having this chat swirl into a Category 5 hurricane.

"I'm sorry, Mom. I'm just not good with surprises. I appreciate what you're trying to do, but I need you to trust me. I am figuring things out, and when I finally do, I'll tell you."

"OK, well, I'm sorry about the surprise. I won't do it again," she said, looking at my jeans and panties on the floor and deciding it best not to ask me the questions I knew she had about what may have transpired with Ethan.

And just like that, Mom left my room. And I knew we would be good for a few more weeks until the next time she felt the impulse to control my life.

CHAPTER 16

Smile, You're on Candid Camera

Our gymnastics team finished second in Sectionals, and we all thought we had lost our opportunity to compete in the State Tournament. When we were subsequently informed that our team's Sectional score was amongst the best of the non-winners, we were one of the 10 teams invited to compete at the State Tournament. This was a first for our High School gymnastics program, and with it came a surprising amount of attention and recognition.

I had medaled in Floor at our Section meet, which I was satisfied to think would be my one accomplishment in my high school gymnastics career. But now we were going to be on "the big stage," as Ms. Sylvester put it.

Heather, in the meantime, was bejeweled with medals as Section champ in vault and beam and a second-place finish in the individual all-around competition. These are all unheard of for a sophomore. Consequently, most of the attention we were getting was focused on her. It won her many new fans but galled the few remaining teammates who still couldn't get over their envy.

Truthfully, I was excited to go to the State tournament for two reasons. To support Heather's dream to become New Jersey's all-around champ and to room with her at the hotel the night before the meet. Heather's ultimate dream was to be in the Olympics, a goal few disputed as realistic.

The week before the State tournament was a blur. Between pep rallies, practices, and my school and work schedule, I was looking forward to traveling and competing in the tournament, which sounded comparatively relaxing.

My mother, who had never been to one of my meets, made the surprising decision to take time off from work to watch me compete at State. I confess that I was somewhat conflicted over this, despite feigning joy and appreciation when she told me. It was hard to feel like her interest and support were genuine when she hadn't taken the time to watch me practice or compete before. I don't mean to sound catty, but it's hard not to notice your parent's absence when you've seen all of your teammates' parents at meets over the years. In reality, it was my Dad that I wished could come and see me compete, but I knew that wasn't happening.

When I finally sat down next to Heather on the team bus for the 2-hour trip to the hotel, it was the first time in days we had been able to see each other outside of practices. I had missed her, and when she clandestinely squeezed my hand and looked at me intensely with those dreamy blue eyes, I knew she had missed me too. I didn't anticipate how hard it was going to be to sit next to her for 2 hours and modulate our conversation and actions. While virtually everyone knew we were friends and were often seen in each's company, the extent of our friendship was not known, and we wanted to keep it that way. There was enough drama in high school in general and enough pressure the day before the State tournament specifically to be found out or to come out now. As they say, there is a time and a place for everything.

We arrived at the hotel at dinner time. Ms. Sylvester had arranged for a team dinner followed by time for us to enjoy the pool and hot tub before 9 pm lights out. Ms. Sylvester was no fool. As disciplined as we were as gymnasts, we were still teenage girls untethered from home and parents. Hence, she made sure to tightly supervise and schedule our free time to discourage any potential "incidents."

The hotel was nicer than I expected, but something about our room gave me a queasy feeling from the moment I stepped into it. I didn't have time to worry about it, as we were expected at dinner shortly after we checked in. I felt it again when we went to change into our swimsuits, but this time it was unmistakably my signal. I hesitated after removing my t-shirt and prompted Heather to put some clothes on as she was nearly naked.

"What's the matter?" Heather asked.

"I don't know. I'm being signaled," as I put my t-shirt back on.

"But we're in our room. Could it be a signal that Misty's in trouble?" Heather surmised.

"No, there's a difference. This one feels like we're being watched," I replied as I started to look around for the source of my signal.

There is something to be said for watching TV spy and crime shows, as I started to canvas likely places in the room for planting listening devices or cameras. Anyone other than Heather would have thought I was crazy, but she knew to trust my instincts and started to help me look.

"What's this?" she announced. Pointing at something in the vent grate near the top of the wall adjacent to the bed.

Pulling the desk chair over to the wall, I climbed up and still couldn't quite make out what it was. Our suspicions now on screech, we went to the bathroom to inspect the vent in there. Sure enough, we saw something similar in that vent, which was not placed nearly as high. This time, when I climbed up on the chair, I could clearly see it was a camera. We were being watched and maybe even listened to.

I'm sorry to say that our discovery spoiled Ms. Sylvester's and the team's plans for swimming and hot tubbing. Not wanting to alert whoever might be watching and listening, I pulled Heather out into the hallway before telling her my plan. We subsequently went to Ms. Sylvester's room, and she answered the door in her swimsuit. She gave us a quizzical look when we asked her to step out of her room so we could talk. Retrieving her door key, she stepped out into the hall, and we informed her of our discovery. Consequently, she went back into her room and covertly inspected to see if her room had the same devices in the vents. Ms. Sylvester came out of her room, a distressed look on her face. She was already on her phone with the police.

When the police arrived, they found video surveillance equipment and a wireless router in a back office concealed above the drop ceiling. Cameras were found in 8 rooms that were used for block booking of groups. The hotel management was stunned. Ms. Sylvester and our teammates were apoplectic as all had disrobed to get into their swimsuits and now feared that the images would show up on the Internet. We were moved to other rooms after police confirmed they weren't equipped with cameras. Thank you very much. Of course, before any of us were comfortable enough in our replacement rooms to think about sleeping, it was well past Ms. Sylvester's lights-out time.

The police would subsequently trace the IP address to which the router was transmitting to the home computer of a hotel night shift employee. Management would admit that they knew their night shift desk clerk was a bit strange but had written it off as typical for the kind of person who takes a night shift job. Besides, what could it hurt when most of the guests would never see or interact with him? What could it hurt indeed? His home computer had two years and over one thousand video clips of what he must have considered the most titillating recordings of hotel guests. That his stash of recordings showed an affinity for young girls and couples with more adventurous sexual proclivities was no shock. To their knowledge, the police did not think he had shared these video clips on the Internet. To say that our relief was somewhat dubious would be an understatement.

It probably won't surprise you that we were all a bit distracted by the incident, which made competing in the State meet an after-thought. This ironically served to our advantage as we were too distracted to think about or get nervous about how we'd perform. Performance in gymnastics, and perhaps any athletic endeavor, seems to improve when you just let your body do what it has repeatedly been trained to do without the intrusion of your brain. Consequently, we far exceeded anyone's expectations, including Ms. Sylvester's. We had entered the competition ranked 9th out of the 10 teams but finished 4th in the tournament. Virtually everyone on the team set personal bests, and Heather narrowly missed first-place in the coveted All-Around category. I got 3rd place on both floor and bars.

Our performance at State was a big deal to many, but for most of the girls on the team, it was just a temporary distraction from feeling violated and the challenge of dealing with the corrosive anxiety that accompanies it in the aftermath. The Internet and social media was your friend until it wasn't, and then it could destroy you. Heather and I had discovered the surveillance and dodged a bullet. Our teammates, however, now lived in perpetual fear that images of their naked bodies would be found and forever memorialized by the unforgiving Internet. A few girls were so paralyzed and anxious in the intervening days that they had to seek professional help. Some were prescribed anti-anxiety medications just to feel comfortable enough to leave their homes. A picture may be worth a thousand words, but we learned firsthand how it can also damage someone, perhaps for life. There is nothing innocent or inconsequential about taking pictures.

Unfortunately, an even bigger news story than our performance at State was the media attention given to our discovery at the hotel. This only added to the damage that had already been done. While the media tried to spin it as heroic and something we should be proud to have uncovered, we knew better. We knew that while some would genuinely appreciate and thank us, others would see it as an opportunity to make jokes and be cruel.

And that is what happened one day when three boys ran into Jaylyn in the hall. Jaylyn was a member of the gymnastics team and a senior, like me. The boys said they had watched a video of her on the Internet and made some crude comments about her anatomy. They asked her if she would strip for them so they could make another video. They would later confess that it was all in fun, and they had never seen any video of her on the Internet. But by then, it was too late. Jaylyn had hung herself that evening, leaving a note about the boys' comments and not wanting to suffer further embarrassment. In a final insult, Jaylyn's parents couldn't find an attorney that would bring criminal charges against the boys. Essentially, they were told boys will be boys and that one interaction was insufficient grounds to prosecute the case.

All this heavy, heavy stuff dwarfed the fact that my mother came to the State tournament and had witnessed my personal best performance. Not that this earned me any recognition. She seemed more concerned about why my coach would even accept alternate rooms in that hotel and let us compete the following day instead of bringing us home. As if we should maximize the damage and punish ourselves for bringing a pervert to justice rather than try to carry on and persevere. Or, in our case, excel. I couldn't believe how she went on and on, with not even the faintest hint of praise for me discovering the cameras or my subsequent performance at State. As I said, I was conflicted about my mother coming to watch me, and now you can see why.

Not lost in the flurry of all this was the comfort and peace Heather and I experienced sleeping together when we finally got to our room without a view, so to speak. Before we went to sleep, we talked and found out that neither one of us had ever imagined falling in love with another girl. After Heather's gymnastics camp experience, she was understandably hesitant to have any kind of relationship, least of all with a male. But she always knew she would probably need to get back on the horse again. Probably not the best analogy to use, but she said it, not me.

She got back on that horse the summer before freshman year. While nothing about the boy bore any resemblance to a stallion's anatomy, I'll torture the analogy further and say he was too quick out of the gate. Or should I say the horse finished the race well before the finish line? Whatever. You get the point. It was, as the David Bowie song lyrics go, a "wham, bam, thank you ma'am" experience, and Heather had had enough. She focused on school and gymnastics and didn't worry about boys, romantic relationships, or love. That is until she met me.

For both of us, it was the emotional connection that kindled the fire. In other words, instead of an outside-in relationship where you have an immediate physical attraction and later develop an emotional connection or not, ours was an inside-out relationship. I never found another female's appearance to be the least bit enthralling. Other than the occasional envy of some girls' endowments in the boob department, the thought of being with a girl never crossed my mind. Had anyone ever suggested it, I'm quite sure I would have found the idea inane if not bordering on gross. Once Heather and I established our intense emotional connection, my perception changed quite quickly and quite radically. I felt not just an emotional connection to her but also a physical attraction. Never mind that our bodies are so similar that we could probably swap them if that were possible, and no one would probably notice. The simple fact was we wanted each other, and we had the patience and the insider's knowledge of how to satisfy each other. Sometimes it was as simple as a look or just holding each other. Other times, well other times, it got pretty hot up in here y'all. Let's leave it at that, shall we?

CHAPTER 17

Meeting Roy Roger's Horse

Gymnastics behind me and graduation fast-approaching, my teachers' and my mothers' crescendoing pleas to finalize my life plans reached their zenith.

By virtue of my summer internship at the law office, I technically had enough credits to graduate 3 months early. A fact many of my classmates knew and envied. I elected, however, to take a couple advanced placement courses those final months so I could graduate with my classmates. My reasoning was two-fold. I hadn't heard from my father's mysterious source yet, and I wanted to continue to see Heather each morning and have lunch with her after my two classes.

I signed up for AP U.S. Government and AP Psychology on the strength that both my father and I were employed by the U.S. Government and Psychology because Carl Rogers' book "On Becoming a Person" had piqued my curiosity on that fateful, somewhat disturbing day at the library.

I lobbied my boss at the Post Office to extend my hours to full-time and succeeded. This, more as a backup plan, should my father's source be further delayed or worse never appear. I reasoned that this would also help shield me from accusations of being lazy or that I was dragging my feet on my future. I began to realize that I was tired of having to do things to win certain people's approval. Or, conversely, avoid their disapproval and the raft of shit that came with it. Yes, I'm talking about my Mom and my teachers primarily. Though, it's incredible how many people you run into that feel compelled to share an opinion on what it is you should do with your life. Would there ever come a time when I became what I was to become, and people would just shut up and mind their own business? Somehow I doubted it, but hope springs eternal, as they say.

A couple of weeks into my last semester, Heather and I had settled into a comfortable routine, meeting at a coffee shop on our way to school, having lunch at the school cafeteria, and spending any other free time together, which was usually Friday evenings and Sundays.

In terms of future plans, Heather never doubted what it was she wanted to become. She was well on her way to becoming classified as "elite," which was a prerequisite to be considered for the U.S. Women's Gymnastics team. But Heather's dreams didn't end at becoming an Olympian. She had goals for a career in gymnastics. The only decision she toiled over was whether she wanted to coach a top collegiate team, say UCLA, LSU, Oklahoma, or Utah. Or open up a private gymnastics school to train the next generation of top gymnasts. What was amazing to me is that she had set these goals for herself when she was 10. Fueled in equal parts by her love of and proficiency in the sport and the abuse she had suffered at that summer gymnastics camp when she was 8. Heather was proof positive that adversity is a powerful motivator, and it doesn't have to defeat you.

One day, as Heather and I were walking to school armed with our customary hot chocolates, a man pulled up next to us in a car asking for directions.

"Excuse me. I'm sorry to bother you, but I'm supposed to meet someone at Mugs coffee shop in the next 10 minutes. Can you give me directions there?" said the man who was dressed in a suit and looked to be about my Dad's age.

Heather was suspicious and hesitant, but I wasn't getting any signal, so I obliged and told him how to get to the coffee shop.

"Thanks, young lady, you're a superstar!" he replied, winking at me and then driving away.

"Jeez, Aja!" Heather exclaimed. "Did you see that? He winked at you. And he called you a superstar. I think he wants to get into your pants. Did you get a signal because I sure did?"

"No, Heather, I didn't get a signal. And superstar is the code word that my Dad said the guy who is supposed to help me would use. I have to go back to the coffee shop."

"Are you crazy? What if he just used that randomly?"

"Trust me, Heather. If he were a creeper, I would have known the moment he rolled down his car window. Go to school, and I'll text you after I've met with him," I said, hugging her and giving her a quick kiss on the cheek.

The fact that I risked even the briefest public display of affection probably helped to convince her not to worry about me. It also, as I would learn later, really turned her on, but that's a story for another time.

I returned to the coffee shop and found the gentleman sitting in a corner booth with a coffee in his hand. He gave me a little smile and a wave of recognition. The fact that I didn't suddenly feel naked to the world told me I could trust him.

"Good morning, Aja. I'm Special Agent Trig Halvorsen. Thanks for the directions."

"Good morning. So my Dad talked to you?" I asked, even though I thought it was a stupid question the moment I said it.

"Yes, and I think we can help you. Have a seat. Do you need another coffee?"

"It's hot chocolate, and no thanks, I'm good. Whose we?" I

asked as I slid into the seat across from him.

"The Federal Bureau of Investigation."

"But my Dad's in the CIA. How does he know you?" I asked, immediately conscious that perhaps I shouldn't have divulged that I knew my father was with the CIA. If Special Agent Trig was concerned, he didn't let on.

"Your Dad and I trained together. He started in the FBI and then transferred to the CIA. And if you tell anyone that, I'll have to kill you," he said deadpan, waiting for a beat until my face told him I had bought his threat, and then he broke into laughter. "I'm kidding."

Trig Halvorsen had Nordic good looks, and when he laughed, his steel-blue eyes twinkled, making it virtually impossible not to laugh with him.

"You have a funny way of trying to put me at ease, Special Agent Halvorsen," I said after laughing with him.

"Please, call me Trig."

"Trig, that's an interesting name. Don't tell me your parents named you after Roy Roger's horse."

"Wow, I'm surprised you even know about Roy Rogers, let alone his horse Trigger, but no. It's short for Trygve, which my parents tell me is Old Nordic for "trusty.""

"Interesting, and are you?"

"Am I what?"

"Trusty?"

"I think so. Why? Doesn't the girl named after a constellation of stars trust me?"

"Oh, so you know that story?"

"Yes, how couldn't I? Your Dad never stopped talking about you."

"And do you know that my name really isn't a constellation of stars?"

"Oh, so you know that too, huh? I never had the heart to tell your Dad."

"Yes, the romantic notion of my name was shattered by the so-called wonders of the Internet."

"My condolences, but if it's any constellation, you're just as pretty as the stars like your Daddy said you were."

"Nice play on words. You're quite the comedian Trig, but my AP Psychology class starts in 30 minutes, so perhaps we should get to what it is you think the FBI can offer me."

"No problem. I'll tell you what we have in mind, and if you trust me, I can give you a ride to school and make sure you don't miss your class."

"I trust you. I have secret powers."

"That's what I hear, so I'm afraid they're not so secret."

"Yeah, well, if you tell anyone about them, I'll just have to kill you," I parried.

"Touche," he replied, laughing. "OK, let me tell you what we're thinking about. Your Dad obviously told me about your powers and some of your experiences. We're interested in learning about how we might be able to best use them, but there's a problem."

"What's that?"

"The FBI generally requires that applicants for jobs have a bachelor's degree and be at least 23 years old."

"So, are you saying I have to go to college, and in five and a half years, I can apply?"

"No, that's not what I was going to say. What we'd like to do is bring you in as an intern. We'd pay you a stipend and pay for your room and board. You'd go through the regular 20-week new agent training. In addition, we'd conduct some assessments to determine the extent of your powers and how they might be applied. Depending on how you do in training and what we learn from our assessments, we may be able to get an exemption to hire you."

"So, no guarantees?"

"No guarantees, but understand that what I'm offering is highly unusual. We're doing this because of your unusual talents. In other words, we're making an exception for someone exceptional."

"You certainly have a way with words, Trig. Flattery will get you everywhere. I'm sold. When do I start?"

"Well, first, I'll have to get you the Internship agreement, and you'll have to have your mother co-sign it as you're still a minor."

"I'll always be a minor," I shot back, causing Trig's face to wrinkle with confusion briefly.

"Oh, I get it," he replied as his face brightened. "Your last name is Minor. You're sharp. I think you'll do just fine at Quantico."

"Can you get my Dad to co-sign the agreement?" I asked, certain that my mother would veto the opportunity as being too dangerous.

"Well, that will be a bit difficult, but I'm sure we can figure it out. Mom, not a fan of the FBI?"

"Mom doesn't know about my talents and is, how shall I say this, a wee bit overprotective."

"Gotcha. I'll get Trace to co-sign the form. Do you want that ride to school now?"

"I guess I can trust you, sure," I said, smiling.

As I hopped in his car, we talked about a start date. Because I was enrolled in classes and executing the agreement would take time, he suggested I complete the school year and begin my FBI internship in the summer. That out of the way, Special Agent Trig asked me about how I knew about Roy Rogers.

"It was one of my grandpa's favorite shows, and we'd watch it together when I visited him. We also watched Hogan's Heroes."

"So you'd also get any Colonel Klink and Sergeant Schultz references then," he replied.

"I see nothing! I hear nothing! I know nothing!" I parroted in my best Schultz imitation.

"Good, that will actually come in handy when you're in the FBI!" he exclaimed, causing me to laugh.

"Have you seen my Dad recently?" I asked, suddenly getting serious.

"Well, if by recently you mean in the last year, yes. But I can't really tell you where, when, how, or why."

"That's OK. If I get through FBI training, will I get an opportunity to see him?" I asked, feeling tears welling up in my eyes.

"I can't make any promises, Aja, but I can say that you'd have a much better chance of seeing him as an FBI agent than not. I'm sorry, that's the best answer I can give you," he replied, pulling the pocket-square out of his suit and handing it to me to stop the river of tears that had overflowed their banks.

I took it, pausing as it was linen with a decorative pattern.

"Go ahead, use it. I don't have a handkerchief or any tissues. Besides, who am I trying to fool? I'm just an ordinary old G-man, not some GQ model."

That made me chuckle, and I daubed my cheeks, halting my tears path towards my chin. Special Agent Trig may not have been a GQ model, but he was handsome, made even more so by his sense of humor. I liked him. He reminded me of my Dad, and I could see why they had become buddies.

"Will I see you again?" I asked as he pulled up to my school.

"Absolutely. As a matter of fact, I'll be your boss, Probie. So you better not screw up." he said in an exaggerated authoritative manner.

"I won't," I laughed. "Thank you, Trig," I said as I opened the door to get out.

"Don't thank me, thank your Dad. And watch your 6, Aja."

"I will, boss," I said with a smile as I bounced out of his car, ecstatic to finally have some direction to my life.

I got to my AP Psychology class just in time, but if you tested me on what the lesson was that day, I'd fail miserably. My mind was in Quantico, Virginia, imagining what it would be like to be training to be an FBI agent.

CHAPTER 18

True Confessions

I had been so in my own little world after meeting with Special Agent Trig that I had forgotten entirely to text Heather. I remembered as soon as I saw a flustered blond waif approaching me at warp speed.

"What the hell, Aja," she yelled when she was still 20 feet from me, attracting the attention of all the students within earshot.

"I'm sorry," I said, knowing that was not going to be sufficient to calm the anger and hurt I saw on Heather's face.

Fortunately, the girl's bathroom was close by, and I pulled her into it to try to limit drawing any additional attention from the unwelcome audience in the hallway. Heather started to go off on me, and her voice echoed loudly off the tile walls. Seeing no one was in the bathroom with us and not able to fit a word in edgewise, I did the only thing I could think to do. I kissed her with a full-on tongue assault. She struggled at first, trying to pull away from me and wanting to give me a different kind of tongue-lashing for my oversight, but I refused to let her go. I pinned her up against a wall and continued to kiss her deeply. Eventually, she relaxed and started to reciprocate. My hands moved down her back, grabbing her butt and pulling her hips into mine. Her hands began to fondle me, and whatever anger she had when she entered the bathroom was magically converted to an unquenchable hunger. There was no stopping this runaway freight train now, and I pulled her into one of the stalls. I knew that I owed her answers, and I fully intended to supply them, but right now, my words weren't what she wanted or needed.

When we finally left the bathroom, the hallways were empty, and we were late for our next class. Rather than go to class late, we decided to go to my house and continue our reconciliation. Eventually, while lying naked and sated in my bed, I told her about my meeting with Trig. I had not thought about the consequences that accepting Trig's offer would have on my relationship with Heather, but now it hit me full force. It was even more of a gut-punch for Heather. This was a practical problem that couldn't just be dispatched over another hot and heavy session in a high school bathroom. The real work of our relationship was beginning. After she recovered from the initial shock and flood of tears, we were determined to find a solution.

One option we discussed was called our "wait and see" option. Since my internship didn't guarantee I'd be employed by the FBI at the end of 20-weeks of training or where I might be stationed, for that matter, Heather would stay put and go to high school. We'd just have to suck it up and live with the fact we wouldn't see each other for a while.

Another option was the "go for broke" option. Heather would find an elite gymnastics training facility near Quantico and get a tutor to continue her education. This was not unusual for elite gymnasts with aspirations for the Olympics, but it wasn't inexpensive. I didn't know if Heather would be allowed to room with me, but if she could, that would obviously help defray the cost of this option. Heather was also not sure whether her parents would support such a move. There was probably at least a handful of elite training centers much closer to where we lived in New Jersey that her parents might reasonably support. Rather than sending her 200 miles away from home. The training center in Virginia would need to offer something very compelling that centers closer to her home could not, other than proximity to me.

The third option was the "be happy where we are" option. This involved me postponing or rejecting the FBI's offer altogether and going to college nearby so we could continue to be together.

We ultimately decided on a combination of the first two options. I'd go for my 20-week training, and Heather would stay back. If I happened to become employed by the FBI, she'd consider moving to wherever I would be stationed. If I didn't get the job, I'd come back to New Jersey and apply to college. Since I was starting my training in the summer, we also hoped Heather might be able to visit before the start of her junior year. So as not to have to endure being apart for 5 months.

We also discussed if and when to come out to our family and friends and reached the conclusion that the concept of "coming out" was unnatural and unnecessary. I mean, you don't see people making a production about getting into a heterosexual relationship or a mixed-race relationship. Sure, your selection of a partner may shock some people, and you may have to field some questions or tolerate people's opinions about your choice, but that's after the fact. If we live in a country that values acceptance and equality, why should the rules of choosing a same-sex partner be any different? Coming out perpetuates the notion that same-sex relationships are different. That they require some additional notice or permission that you never see and are not in the least expected to give or get in any other loving relationship. So collectively, I guess Heather and I were saying, "fuck that" to coming out. And no, we weren't going to ask anyone to excuse our French!

We settled a lot that day, and while it served to strengthen our relationship and clear up much of the fogginess of our future plans, we also knew it would probably just hasten the collision course we were on with our parents.

I didn't have great optimism that my Mom would survive the quintuple-whammy I was about to give her. Whammy one, informing her that I was moving to Quantico to train to be an FBI agent. Whammy two, Dad's permission trumping any attempt she might make to try and veto my decision. Whammy three, finding out that I contacted Dad by breaking into her file cabinet. Whammy four, telling my Mom about my powers and my aspirations to fight abuse and exploitation of children. Whammy five, finding out about my relationship with Heather. Not to mention the potential for whammy two driving a wedge into my mother's relationship with Dad. That could be whammy number six. And that one concerned me more than the others. I could accept and tolerate the grief my mother would give me for the decisions that may adversely affect our relationship. I couldn't say the same for my actions adversely affecting my parent's relationship. That was just wrong, and I knew it. I would have to talk with her before Dad signed the consent, recognizing that this could throw a wrench into my plans, if not doom them to failure. I would have to be strategic about when I had this conversation with Mom. The problem was I had no clue about how and when best to approach her so that she'd be receptive. The only time we ever had a heart-to-heart that ended favorably was when she had spilled her guts after being notified of Dr. Schifflin's arrest. There was no way for me to be strategic. I decided to rip the bandaid off, strike while the iron is hot, whatever idiom you like. Or are those adages, aphorisms, or proverbs? Whatever they are, I was going to do it sooner rather than later. Come hell or high water. Which I think is an idiom.

Heather left shortly before my mother came home. I suddenly realized I could be strategic and prepare dinner for my Mom. I wasn't the most skilled chef, but I knew she liked Italian food, and linguine and white clam sauce was one thing I knew how to cook. I also made a salad and toasted garlic bread in the oven. I even put a bottle of white wine on ice. I didn't care that she'd immediately be suspicious of my motives, given the rarity of extending myself to make her dinner. What I hoped was that she would ultimately appreciate my effort and cut me some slack when I confessed all my sins and plans.

Mom arrived home in her usual condition – beat after a long day of taking care of patients. I was happy to see her face brighten when she saw the table set and detected the garlic, basil, oregano, and parsley smell permeating the house.

"My, my, what's the occasion?" she said predictably.

"I got home early and decided to make dinner," I replied matter-of-factly, not wanting to sound like it was a big deal even though it was.

"And wine too? I hope you know you can't have any of that."

"I know. That's for you."

"Do I have time for a quick shower? I want to wash the day off of me and get into something comfortable?"

"Yeah, dinner will be ready in about 15 or 20 minutes," I replied.

Happy to be given a little more time to rehearse in my head what I was going to say to her, and more importantly, HOW I was going to say it. I planned to ease my way into it. I'd ask about her day, possibly commiserate with her if her day sucked, or act impressed and proud if she did something the least bit heroic. I know the way I said that makes me sound as if I had to force myself to be empathetic or congratulatory, but that's not the case. Despite my issues being open and communicating with my Mom, I loved her. I knew that what she did for people on a daily basis as a nurse was far more purposeful and essential in the context of contributions to humanity than many other jobs. I just thought that if I could connect with my Mom on an emotional level with something other than the shocking news I planned to share, it might go over better.

Mom came down the steps just as I was putting the dish of linguine with clam sauce on the table. All I needed was to find the corkscrew for the wine. Then perform as brilliantly as the rehearsal in my head had gone.

"Feeling better?" I asked as I fired my first "connect with compassion" salvo.

"Much. And I'm delighted not to have to cook after the day I had today."

"Why? What happened?" I asked as everything so far was going as rehearsed.

"I took care of four patients today, and the circumstances of two of them just tore my heart apart. One was an elderly woman with dementia who had broken her hip in a fall at home, whose three adult children couldn't agree on what to do with Mom. Meanwhile, the orthopedic surgeon, who is neither very patient nor diplomatic, inserted himself into the fray and just made things worse. I eventually had to get involved, and it worked out in the end, but only after a lot of unnecessary heartache and delay. Not to mention, pain for their mother."

"What did you do that made it better?"

"I went into the room and told the doctor there was an emergency, and I needed him elsewhere. When I got him outside the room, I told him I didn't want him wasting his precious time arguing with the family and that I would get them to agree to the best course of action. The doctor isn't a bad guy. He just wanted to get the patient to surgery because the sooner you get a hip fracture patient to surgery, the better."

"So, did you get them to agree?"

"Yes."

"And how did you do that?"

"I just went in there and asked them to stop arguing. Then

I asked them what their mother would want and need if she could express her wishes. When they looked at the situation from their mother's perspective versus their own, they made the right choice. They knew their mother wouldn't want them fighting, and they knew she wouldn't want to be in pain. They had all been thinking about the situation from their own perspectives."

"So, she went to surgery?"

"Yep, about an hour later and within the 24 hours of admission, which is what the doctor was concerned about."

"What about the other patient?"

"The other patient had been raped by her cousin, and she wasn't much older than you. Her physical care wasn't complex, but the emotional trauma she was feeling and expressing was way too close for comfort. She reminded me of you, and after what Dr. Schifflin had done to me, I didn't feel at all equipped to help her."

"So, what did you do?"

"I pushed my thoughts aside about Dr. Schifflin as best I could and imagined what I would do if the girl in that bed was you. That made all the difference, and I knew exactly what I needed to do. She really just needed someone she could trust to be with her, to listen, and to show they cared. And when I could do that without freaking out myself, she felt better."

"That's great, Mom. So, everything worked out in the end. Because of you."

"Well, the elderly lady is still going to have dementia, and the young girl is going to continue to fight her demons. But yes, today ended up being pretty good. I think I'm just more emotionally exhausted today than physically exhausted."

Mom's last sentence almost discouraged me from proceeding with my plan. Here I was about to unleash an emotional atomic bomb after she tells me her emotional reserves have been depleted. I did the first thing that came to mind. I opened the wine and poured her a glass.

"Thanks," my mother said with a sigh. "I guess it wouldn't hurt you to have a little wine if you want. I hear the French let their children drink it at dinner."

I didn't need any further encouragement and got myself a wine glass. After pouring a small amount into my glass, I proposed a toast.

"To my Mom. The best nurse and Mom in the world," I said, raising my glass.

I know what you're thinking. You're thinking I was laying it on maybe a little too thick. But at that moment, I really did believe what I said. I had never taken the time or allowed my Mom to tell me about what she did every day. And now that I had, I felt I had truly missed a big, important piece of who my mother was as a person.

"Tell me about your day," Mom asked, which was not a question I had rehearsed an answer for, surprisingly.

"Oh, it was the usual. Nothing special," I replied while accepting the pasta bowl from my mother.

"This looks delicious," my mother exclaimed as she stabbed a forkful of salad.

Meanwhile, I took a long sip of wine. Almost as if I was one of those TV characters that needed a shot of alcohol before proceeding with a difficult or potentially painful task. My liquid courage, so to speak.

"Mom, I have something to confess," I began, thinking that admitting to my failings may shield me from the full measure of her wrath.

"And what's that?" she replied after taking a bite of the linguini and clam sauce.

I proceeded to tell her everything while she disturbingly continued to eat her meal. Her facial expression was so neutral that it didn't give me any clues as to how she was processing the information. I told her about the day on the beach with Joey, how I made Lyle sick, Ms. Merkinson's reaction after touching me. I even told her about being in Hugh Jinks' office and causing his organs to fry. That made her stop eating for a bit.

I was surprised but also happy that she was content to let me just spill my guts without interruption. I felt pretty sure that when I got to the part about breaking into her file cabinet and calling Dad, that would change. I was wrong. I got through all of that, with her only response being to pour herself another glass of wine. I wanted to take another gulp of wine myself, but I feared the pause would cause my Mom to finally explode after showing such restraint this whole time.

I transitioned to telling her about how Dad helped connect me to Special Agent Trig Halverson and the FBI's training and internship offer. My mother had finished her meal by the time I was done, while my dinner had gone cold and remained untouched. I ended with the only words I could think of, even though I felt they were hopelessly inadequate. I didn't think they would prevent my mother from dropping the bombs I definitely deserved.

"I'm sorry, Mom."

While her response came seconds later, it felt like the most uncomfortable hour or two of my life.

"Well, Aja, I must say that I am very proud of you," she began, and I thought I must have misheard her.

"Proud?"

"Yes. I was beginning to worry that you didn't feel you could come to me and talk to me about things that were important to you or that concerned you. I'm glad you finally did."

"So you're not mad?"

"No, I'm not mad now. I was when your Dad called and told

me everything that you just told me."

"He called you?"

"Yes, of course, he did. The same day that you called him."

"Then why aren't you mad now?"

"Because, honey, your father helped me understand that it didn't matter who you told, just that you told one of us. He also helped me realize that sometimes I don't make it easy for you to come to me. I know you are more like your father and that I tend to be a little more critical and controlling. I just want what's best for you, and that's how I express it."

"Why didn't you tell me you spoke to him?"

"He told me not to. He said I should wait to see if I eventually talked with you. We even made a bet."

"A bet?"

"Yes. He said you'd come and talk to me within a week of speaking to Special Agent Halvorsen."

"So, he won the bet."

"Yes, he did. And frankly, I'm happier to have lost. I'd rather have a daughter who can come to me with her concerns than win a bet and have a daughter who avoids talking to me. I've learned a lot about you and myself in this process. Now, do you want to see the FBI agreement?"

"You have the agreement?"

"I do. Special Agent Halvorsen sent it to me yesterday. All you have to do is sign it above where I signed."

None of my rehearsals of this conversation ended anywhere close to where this one ended. By the time I got around to Mom's side of the table, I was awash in tears, and we hugged for a long time. I had lived most of my life feeling like I only had one over-controlling parent. Now I knew I had two parents that both loved and supported me. It was a transcendent moment.

CHAPTER 19

Stumbling Towards the Finish Line

I have never been so torn between wanting time to leap ahead and have it slow to a crawl as in the last few months of my high school career. On the one hand, I was ready to start my internship, while on the other, I was ill-prepared to leave Heather. She was really the only person on earth who knew everything about me - the full, unvarnished truth. And the only person who I could transparently confide in.

With everyone else, I had to either hide a part of my life or be deceptive. I couldn't even tell my teachers about my opportunity with the FBI; instead, I had to maintain my lie about going to college to study law. But now, it wasn't good enough just to say I was going to college. Kids were now getting their college acceptance letters and enrolling. I was expected to tell them what college I was going to attend and make sure it would hold up under some scrutiny if they bothered to check. I could have easily just said I was going to go to Rutgers. It was a fine school, just an hour's drive away, but I couldn't be certain my teachers didn't have connections there or a way to check student enrollment there. I could have also said I was going to work for a year to be able to pay for college. Though that may lead Mr. Mahovich to contact my mother about financial aid and grant programs.

In some ways, this was a pain. But I guess it was a good primer for what I'd probably have to do for the rest of my life if I did become an FBI agent. So my teachers all believed I was going to become a Sun Devil at Arizona State University. Apparently, I had chosen my fake university wisely. No one called me on it, and most just envied that I'd be basking in the sun the following winter.

Meanwhile, Heather was making her plans for the summer, which involved researching the best elite gymnastics training camps. I couldn't believe it when Heather informed me that New Jersey actually had a gymnastics academy that had qualified the most junior Olympians in the country. So her decision was a no-brainer. She enrolled and was promptly accepted into the academy. I was happy for her, though it didn't bode well for our plan should I become an FBI agent. Why would her parents ever agree to let her move to Virginia? The highest-ranked academy in Virginia was 6th in developing Olympians. Heather had checked, and she now shared my concern about our original plan. Rather than wring our hands about our impending separation and the status of our long-term plan, we tried to make the most of the time we had together.

Heather and I could always be found at the same table at the same time each day for lunch. So, I guess I shouldn't have been shocked when a group of boys at school came by our lunch table one day and asked us if we wanted to go hang out at the bleachers. Now sitting on the bleachers wasn't an issue, but what frequently happened under the bleachers was and my radar had gone off immediately when they had approached. What's more, this time, my signal was accompanied by a foreshadowing of what they intended to do. How do I put this delicately? Let's just say that neither Heather nor I were interested in consuming cream-filled cannolis for dessert. The boys took our declination better than I expected, and I foolishly thought we were done with them. That they didn't get sick or have their innards fried at close proximity told me they didn't intend any real harm. However, the next day, they approached us again. I got the same signal about the same "dessert" offering. This time they weren't quite as patient or understanding. When we declined again, they launched into a loud tirade calling us every derogatory term for lesbians you can think of. Some that just were frankly antiquated, like rug muncher. How 1970's, I thought. I was amused until I realized how people started to look at Heather and me afterward. It was like our associating with one another was now somehow wrong or disgusting. Of course, there were some boys who also found the idea of us being lovers a huge turn-on, allowing them to voice their fantasies as they passed our table. We could no longer have lunch together without the disapproving stares or lesbian fantasy-fueled comments, so Heather and I started to go out to lunch instead. This worked for a while. Though apparently, when people see two girls enjoying each other's company and having fun to the exclusion of boys, they immediately think they must be lesbians. Eventually, no matter where we went to lunch, the climate around us would change.

Those few months gave us a taste of what we would face when we lived together, didn't hide our affection, or came right out and admitted our orientation. I was used to the isolation one feels when you are different in some way. In some cases, you're isolated because you don't dare talk about your differences, like my ability to detect sexual predators. In other circumstances, you wear them for the world to see, like my star-shaped facial scar. Growing up, I couldn't help but notice those people who stared at my face just a beat too long, knowing they were looking at what they probably thought was an imperfection. I was less prepared for the ridicule that came with having a lifestyle perceived as unconventional, abnormal, or immoral.

If I was unprepared for the ridicule, Heather was even more ill-equipped. She was so used to performing and striving for that perfect 10 in the eyes of the judges that when people looked at her funny or judged her harshly, she internalized it as a flaw she needed to fix in herself. Not as a defect in the judge's perception or their fucked up sense of what was right and wrong. It was the first crack I saw in Heather's armor, and I have to admit that it scared me. People who place too much value on the opinions of others tend to abandon their true selves. They favor fitting in rather than standing out. Eventually, they feel like their lives are a constant performance. Marginalizing themselves to such a degree that whoever they could or should be is irretrievably lost to the mediocrity of the masses.

To Heather's credit, as much as people's disapproving looks and cruel comments bothered her, she didn't let it compromise our relationship. At least not yet while I was still here. I worried about when I was gone and what the combination of being apart and the overwhelming social expectation of being "normal" may cause.

I also worried about the reliability of my being able to keep her safe from a distance. While I had evidence that I could provide long-distance protection for Misty, I wasn't sure this would hold true for Heather. I had learned to trust that my gift reliably protected me. I just didn't have enough experience with protecting others from a distance to have that same level of confidence. I would be devastated if my decision to leave resulted in harm to Heather. While Heather was certainly savvy to predation, that did not protect her from it. She might be a fierce little pixie, but size matters when it comes to self-defense, and nearly everyone was bigger than Heather.

CHAPTER 20

Graduation and Good-Byes

For almost a year and a half, I had gone along believing everyone's stories of the glorious moment of graduation, the sense of accomplishment and purpose, and the unfettered freedom it conferred. But here I was, weeks shy of that event, my excitement about my FBI training overshadowed by worry. I felt mislead.

I was beginning to wonder if this was how life was. You dream about reaching some idyllic point in your life only to realize when you get there that it doesn't quite sync up with how you imagined it. That there would always be some reality you hadn't accounted for that sneaks in and spoils things. Like hopping in a Ferrari only to learn that it has a governor prohibiting it from exceeding 55 mph. Or me going out and buying a push-up bra only to realize that you need something to push up to achieve its advertised benefits. Maybe that's why my grandpa always seemed to be listening to that Rolling Stones song (I Can't Get No) Satisfaction when I used to visit him. Maybe it wasn't just a song about some guy down on his luck. Perhaps it was an anthem about life itself. God, I hoped not.

Graduation day arrived, and while I may have had a more jaundiced view of the occasion than most, I was nonetheless excited. Misty was home from college for the summer and joined Mom and Heather at the ceremony.

As predicted, the teachers and students who gave graduation speeches all reminded us of the lofty expectations they had for us. Not to mention the anticipated impact we'd all have on the future and on society in general. There were the typical shenanigans that briefly disrupted the ceremony by the usual suspects that had reputations as class clowns. It was all very much to script. Even though some of those participating probably thought our graduation was somehow unique, unlike the millions of graduation ceremonies that had preceded ours. I saw it for what it was, the marking of a transition, for those that needed it, a celebration of an achievement or a reason to have an audacious after-party.

Yes, you may say I sound cynical, but I had reason to be. I knew the sick and twisted minds out there that plotted their devious plans for sexual violence. I could even feel some deviants sitting in the audience at our graduation ceremony. My senses seemed to be getting more acute. Better able to discriminate between pure fantasizers from those who would act if given the opportunity. And detect those that had already committed crimes against kids and would act again out of sheer compulsion. As I had feared, my gift was evolving well beyond me, and nary a day passed anymore when I didn't feel some signal alerting me to someone.

Unlike my personal signal, which made me feel naked and, in some cases, violated, this more advanced indicator was more like a feeling of anxiety. I called it my uneasiness meter. A general sense I would get in a crowd that registered what I presumed was the proportion of individuals that had less than wholesome thoughts or desires. I couldn't be sure exactly what my vacillating anxiety levels were. All I knew is that some groups of people only set off mild uneasiness, while others made me very uneasy. You'd think a graduation crowd made up mostly of families, relatives, and close friends would be quite tame, but you'd be wrong. My uneasiness meter was high. All I could think about was how many Uncle Phils must have been in the room and how many of my high school class-mates were silently suffering behind fake smiles, too ashamed, embarrassed, or fearful to come forward and identify their abusers.

I didn't expect to see a Subaru Outback in our driveway when we arrived home – a graduation gift from Mom and Dad. My joy was only exceeded by Misty's anger. Misty's graduation gift had been Mom's hand-me-down Honda Civic. It didn't seem to matter to Misty that my Subaru was 2 years older than her car and looked like a glorified station wagon. It was just the fact that she received a hand-me-down and I received a "new" old car. I even offered to trade with her, to which she said, "No fucking way, I'm not going to drive that ugly thing!" Proving that this was less about car envy and more about Mom showing preferential treatment to her baby Aja. I didn't think my car was ugly. Perhaps somewhat stylistically challenged, but not ugly. In honor of my sister's slight, I named my car "Mugly," combining my sister's first initial with her slur.

What Mugly lacked in looks, she made up for in terms of space for moving my stuff to Virginia. It's not that I had a lot of stuff. It was just that some things, like my bean bag chair, took up a lot of room. Yes, I know I had once threatened to throw that chair out, but now it held the memory of Heather and our first time. OK, maybe the locker room was our first time. Re-gardless, throwing it out or leaving it behind would have felt sacrilegious.

Heather and I had arranged to go to dinner and a movie the night before I was to leave for FBI training. She had started at the elite training academy the day after my graduation, which was pretty much like having a full-time job. When I picked Heather up that evening, she had just finished her first week of training.

"You look tired. You sure you still want to do this?" I said after watching her trudge to the car and fall into the passenger seat.

"Yes, I'm sure. It's our last time to be together for who knows how long," she said, leaning over towards me, which automatically caused me to lean over and kiss her. "Now I feel better," she said, falling back into her seat.

We went to one of our favorite Italian restaurants. Unlike me, who pigged out on bread, lasagna, and dessert, Heather was on her gymnastics diet, which consisted of water, salad, grilled chicken, and vegetables. I couldn't even interest her in a bite of my dessert, which ironically was a cannoli with a traditional chocolate chip ricotta cream filling.

After dinner, we nixed the movie in favor of taking a circuitous and scenic drive through a State Park on the New Jersey-New York border. It ended at a secluded turn-out where we made out. Mugly was packed to the gills, so making out required some front-seat gymnastics, which, as you can imagine, wasn't a problem for either of us. We had considered pulling the bean bag out of the car. However, urgency won out over digging through my packed car and being butt-naked in a dark, wooded area home to who knows what kinds of animals.

For two hours, we exhausted our bodies and any thoughts and words we had to share with one another. We left the park, and Heather was asleep within 5 minutes. I drove home listening to her rhythmic breathing. Parking in front of Heather's home, I watched her angelic face illuminated by the dashboard light and her chest as it rose and fell. I missed her already and wished we could have an encore performance of our front-seat gymnastics. I caressed her awake. With a hunger that only the recognition of our impending separation could fuel, we locked in a desperate embrace abbreviated only when car lights approached. The car passed, and after one final kiss, Heather forced herself out of the vehicle. I watched her walk away slowly, wanting her more than ever. Knowing the next few months could be the hardest time not only in our relationship but in my life.

Saying goodbye to my mother and sister the following morning was easier but still tearful. Misty apologized for her tirade about my car. Mom subjected me to a dozen questions about whether I had everything I needed. One look at Mugly should have told her I probably had too much. And before I knew it, I was on my way. The nearly 300-mile, four and half hour journey would take me through Philadelphia, Baltimore, and Washington D.C. to my home for at least the next five months – FBI Academy in Quantico, Virginia.

CHAPTER 21

Smoked Sausage & Pizza

My trek to get to Quantico would likely have convinced any sane person to turn back and come home. I, on the other hand, found it to be the perfect motivator.

The four and a half-hour drive took six and a half hours due to accidents in Philly and Wilmington and road construction outside of Baltimore. I stopped for gas outside Washington D.C. and went into the station to go to the bathroom and get some snacks. As soon as I walked in, I felt that unmistakable feeling, but nature called, and I thought I would be safe in the ladies' room. Never underestimate the power of predatory desires. While taking care of business, my signal continued and crescendoed when I heard the door open and a male voice called out.

"I'm glad you were so accommodating as to come in here and pull those tight little jeans down, darlin'. It will save me some trouble."

I didn't dare say anything. Despite total faith in my protective shield, I began to have inklings of doubt as I heard him approach my stall, where I indeed had my tight little jeans down.

"Come on now, don't be shy. Daddy's got a big surprise for that tight little pussy of yours," as I saw large work boots move into place in front of my stall and heard him undoing his pants.

Now would not be a good time for my powers to fail me, I started to think. Then, I heard a thud as his body hit the floor, followed by a crack as his head bounced off the tiles, his face ending up under my stall door, as his glazed eyes stared up at me. I didn't worry that he could see me stand up and pull up my panties and jeans. I knew he was dead. I had to step over him to get out of the stall. The sight of his smoldering penis, black against his otherwise white skin, was more than I cared to see. Even though it was an entirely fitting end to his sorry and depraved existence. I knew upon exiting the restroom that I would later read about a serial rapist found dead in a Washington D.C. gas station restroom. I felt somewhat ashamed about not telling the gas station attendant and leaving some other poor woman to walk in on the scene. However, I was already overdue for my arrival at Quantico. Needless to say, I had lost my appetite and didn't get any snacks opting to high-tail it out of there instead.

I finally arrived at the base, and after being checked in, I was given a temporary ID badge, a map of the campus, and a hefty packet of information. A uniformed and armed Marine escorted me to my dorm and led me to my serviceable but spartan room. Famished, I asked my escort where I could get some dinner. He showed me on my map where I could find "the chow hall," as he put it, helpfully pointing in the direction I needed to head from the one window in my room.

I got to the chow hall ten minutes before closing, and as they were out of the chicken chow mein, I settled for the last two lonely pieces of pepperoni pizza. I don't know if it was because I was hungry or if the pizza was really that good, but I wolfed it down. Chow hall doesn't conjure up images of gourmet-quality meals, but I can honestly say I was thoroughly satisfied. Re-energized, I unloaded Mugly and decorated my new "home" as best I could.

Finished unpacking, I lay down on my bed and started to go through the packet of information. The first thing in the packet was a welcome letter from Trig. It was a generic welcome letter to all new trainees, but on the bottom, he had scrawled a personalized greeting,

"Schultz, your days of hearing nothing, seeing nothing, and knowing nothing are about to end! Colonel Klink P.S. See you at 7 am in the Chow Hall."

I laughed, remembering our first conversation and how his sense of humor had put me at ease. The next thing in the packet was my daily schedule for the first week, followed by additional pages describing various aspects of the training program. All I can say is that it was a good thing that I had set my alarm right after reading Trig's letter because I fell asleep in the middle of going through the packet. My alarm clock jolted me out of deep sleep the next morning. Despite a firmer bed than I preferred and sleeping with the light still on, I had the best night of sleep that I could recall.

Forgoing the hour-long process of washing and drying my hair, I was ready for the day well before my appointed meeting with Trig. With time to spare, I fired up my computer. Sure enough, there on my newsfeed was a story of the pervert found in a gas station restroom with his smoked sausage. A disturbingly accurate police sketch of the man accompanied the article. I learned that he had been responsible for a string of unsolved incidents where women had been terrorized or raped in gas station bathrooms across the D.C. metro area. Police were at a loss as to the cause of his death, but I suspect that virtually everyone who read about how he was found thought he got what he deserved. Then I got to the last few lines in the article and grew concerned. "The Medical Examiner is conducting an autopsy to determine the cause of death. Police have confiscated the store's video surveillance to collect additional information on what occurred and who may have been involved." A closing statement encouraged people to contact the police if they had any information related to the case. All I could think about was how leaving the scene of a crime would not be an impressive way to start my training as an FBI agent. I realized that I would have to fess up to Trig and hope that it wouldn't end my FBI career before it even began.

I forced a smile as I approached Trig, who was seated in a booth, a cup of coffee in his hand, and another cup in the place adjacent to him, presumably for me.

"Good morning, Aja," he said, standing up and extending his hand.

"Good morning, Special Agent Halvorsen," I returned, placing my hand in his and giving a firm shake.

"I took the liberty of getting you a hot chocolate," he said, pointing to the cup as we both took our seats. "If you'd like something else, I won't be offended."

"No, this is great. Thanks," I replied. Wondering how and when to broach the topic that would likely put an end to my internship and aspirations.

"I see you were busy on your trip down here yesterday," he said, smiling.

I'm sure he saw confusion in my facial expression. While internally, I was wrestling with whether it was even possible for him to know about my involvement at the gas station. Could the police have already identified me on the video and learned that I was an FBI trainee? It didn't seem possible, and my mental processing was too slow to formulate a response to his comment before he spoke again.

"If I'm not mistaken, you're the only FBI trainee to ever solve a case and to do so on their first day on the job."

"I don't understand," I said, even though I was beginning to.

"Come on, Schultz, don't hold out on me. You ran into the Gas Station Rapist yesterday, didn't you?"

"Yes, but how could you know that? Did the police contact you?"

"No, I contacted them. We were working on the case with the DC police. The Gas Station Rapist didn't confine himself just to the D.C. area. He committed similar attacks in Maryland, Delaware, and Virginia. I told them not to release any information on what they may have found on the video."

"Why?"

"Because I was afraid it would compromise an important FBI asset."

"What does that mean?"

"I'm sorry, I forget that you're not trained in FBI lingo yet. I was afraid that if they revealed your identity, it would limit your opportunity to solve other cases in the future. It would also put a big target on your back."

"So, I didn't screw up?"

"No, quite the opposite. You got a very dangerous criminal off the streets and preserved your anonymity. Now you can look forward to never being able to take credit for it. At least not publically."

"Wow, and I thought I'd be packing up and going back to New Jersey after our meeting."

"Nope, you're stuck here. Of course, you've set a pretty high bar for yourself. How many crimes are you going to solve today?" he laughed.

Recognition of what I had accomplished and relief washed over me, finally making me comfortable enough to laugh with him and take a sip of my hot chocolate.

"So, what's the next case you want me to solve?"

"Not so fast, superstar," he replied, invoking my father's nickname for me. "You still need to go through agent training and, more importantly, an assessment on the range of your abilities and to what degree you can control your responses."

"Control my responses?"

"Yes, like could you have only disabled that guy yesterday instead of frying him?"

"Why would you want me to do that?"

"Oh, don't get me wrong, you saved us a lot of time and money by sending him directly to hell. The reality is that most of these sexual predators are part of a larger network of like-minded scum. If he had survived, we probably would have been able to get him to roll over on a few of his associates."

"That makes sense. I'm just not sure if I can control it. It just seems to happen. It doesn't even seem to be something that comes from me."

"And that is exactly why we need to do an assessment. We need to see if your skills can be honed, just like any other skill."

"Like how I had to practice controlling my tumbling in gymnastics."

"Now, you've got it."

"But I don't understand how you're going to be able to do the assessment. Finding a sexual predator to experiment on is a lot different than finding a tumbling mat to practice on. And is experimenting on sexual predators even ethical?"

"Oh, finding sexual predators is not a problem, but your question about ethics is a good one. You'd be amazed at what criminals will agree to do. I can assure you that anyone who participates in your assessment has fully consented to it."

"In exchange for what? Reduced sentences?"

"No, we never reduce their sentences. All they get is the knowledge that they are contributing to our efforts to understand and eradicate predatory sexual behavior and abuse. You'd be surprised how many of them just seek some peace of mind."

"You're kidding, right?"

"No, I'm not. OK, sure, some get involved in these experiments in hopes of feeding their depraved fantasies. Still, many feel tortured by their compulsions and have remorse and a desire to give back in some way."

"But doesn't that remorse and desire to give back confound the experiment then?"

"Oh, I can see you know a little something about research then. Any chance you've conducted experiments of your own in the past?" he asked with a knowing smile on his face.

"Ahh, maybe," I replied, confident that I was failing the poker face test.

"Good. You'll want to tell us everything you've learned about your abilities and how you learned about them. It will help us design additional experiments. None of what we just discussed had anything to do with what I originally wanted to talk to you about. Still, I can see you're going to be a precocious student, so we'll skip ahead. I trust you got your first-week schedule?"

"I did."

"Good. Follow that and get comfortable with your new home. We'll start assessing your abilities next week. If you need anything, here is my cell phone number. By the way, you'll get a secure cell phone later today. Only use that phone for FBI business, including any communications with me. You can continue to use your personal phone for personal business. Understood?"

"You don't call me Schultz for nothing," I replied, smiling.

"Oh, one last thing, here," he said, handing me an envelope.

"What's this?"

"A letter from your father. Read it and then destroy it."

"Destroy it?" I asked, unable to believe I couldn't keep the one thing my father had given me in the last 10 years.

"Yes. Sorry, FBI regulations. There's a shred room in every building. Use one of them to dispose of it. Don't worry, if you play your cards right, you might get a chance to see him before the year is out."

I almost felt like a little kid who believed in Santa again after he said that. I thanked him for the letter and confirmed that I would dispose of it as he requested. He offered to escort me to my first class, which I gratefully accepted. Along the way, Trig told me about the course I was about to attend and how brilliant the instructor was. Dropping me off at class, he wished me well and went on his way.

Fueled by Trig's enthusiasm about the class, I waited in great anticipation for the instructor's arrival. I thought about opening my Dad's letter but feared I would start to cry, and as difficult as it was, I decided to wait until I got back to my room. Other trainees filtered in and took seats, all at least 6 to 8 years my senior. Some couldn't help doing a double-take when they saw me. I was a few months shy of 18 years old but knew I looked even younger. My enthusiasm started to wane as my self-consciousness about being an anomaly waxed. I kept hoping for the class to begin to draw people's attention away from me.

Finally, the door at the front of the classroom opened, and Special Agent Trig Halvorsen walked through it, smiling like a cat that just ate a mouse. I had fallen for his ruse. He was the brilliant instructor of the class. Any concerns and self-consciousness I was feeling disintegrated into a smile as he caught my eye and winked. He had my back, and I had already solved a case for the FBI. I was where I was supposed to be.

When I finally got back to my room after a full day of classes, I opened the envelope and pulled out the letter from my Dad, and read:

"Dear Aja,

I am so proud of you. Proud that you talked with your mother and proud that you are putting your abilities to good use.

I'm sorry that I haven't been able to see you or stay in touch over the last 10 years. Someday soon, I hope to be able to see you and help you understand why I had to do what I have done.

I never doubted that you would grow up and contribute significantly to the betterment of the world. I know now how hard your journey must have been while I've been away. And it will likely get harder before it gets easier. Just remember that despite my absence, I have always been with you, and I have always believed in you. Don't get discouraged. Your FBI training and assessment may be the hardest thing you ever do, but once you're through it, you'll never regret it. Lean on Trig. He's a good man.

I love you, superstar!

Dad"

My tears were soaking the letter before I even finished it. I was crying not only over the sentiments shared but also because I knew I had to dispose of the message. I couldn't think of anything else that was more valuable to me at the moment. Having to shred the letter felt like cruel and unusual punishment.

I cycled through all the stages of grief as I thought about disposing of my Dad's letter. I almost convinced myself that Trig had never instructed me to destroy the message – almost. Then I got angry at Trig for being so insensitive, even though I knew better. Followed by considering taking a picture of the letter, because what would the chances be that anyone would ever find out. Trailed quickly by the sad realization that I had no choice, which spurred another round of tears. Eventually, my tears morphed into acceptance that I had to shred the letter. However, I could still cling tenaciously to the thoughts and feelings my Dad had expressed. Nothing and no one could ever take that away from me.

CHAPTER 22

Guilty Until Proven Innocent

I don't know if it was my law and legal system class, or Trig's comment about trying to learn to control my responses, or just my damn introspective nature that was causing me to feel guilty over being judge, jury, and executioner.

Up until now, I had somehow divorced the unpleasant and sometimes fatal reactions people had to me from something I did or had any control over. When Hugh Jinks dropped dead from fried internal organs, I didn't associate it with anything I did. I was just standing there, being bombarded by self-consciousness and graphic imagery of what he presumably wanted to do to me. His death, and the death of the guy at the gas station, had felt like some higher power had smitten them, not me. But now, I wasn't so sure, and it was really starting to bother me.

Don't get me wrong, I didn't feel one iota of remorse that those sick bastards died. If anything, I wished that their deaths would have been more painful and protracted. However, if I was the one causing the reaction, and I could modulate the intensity of my response, I had to take ownership of that power. I could no longer write it off as some magical "Hand of God" and go merrily on my way. If it was my hand that could dial up the punishment from a minor tummy ache to cataclysmic immolation, then I had to use that power responsibly.

After losing a few nights of sleep over this, I texted Trig and asked him if we could meet. We met over coffee and hot chocolate on Saturday morning after my first week of training.

"What's up, Superstar?" he asked as I slid into the booth across from him.

"I'm not feeling so super," I responded.

"Are you sick? Do you need to see a doctor?"

"No, I'm fine physically, except for lack of sleep. I guess I've been mentally torturing myself over whether I can control the intensity of my powers."

"I'm sorry."

"Why are you, sorry?" I asked.

"Well, I feel responsible because I know I may have helped plant that seed when we met last week."

"Well, thanks, I appreciate that, but you were right to suggest it. I guess I was just being blissfully ignorant and shielding myself from feeling responsible for what was happening."

"Don't beat yourself up. You have unique powers that I've never heard of or seen before. It's not like there's an instruction manual. Who knows, you may not be able to control it. Maybe the punishment fits the crime."

"Yeah, that's a theory I had considered. I just don't have enough proof."

"Which brings us to our assessment of your powers. I have your schedule for the next 6 weeks that combines your FBI Agent training and your assessment sessions. I'm afraid you're going to be pretty busy," he said. Handing me six pages stapled together, each page outlining my weekly schedule.

"Busy is good. Less time for me to torture myself through

introspection."

"Well, let me suggest we add something to your schedule. Something that may help you channel and manage your introspection so that it's less torturous."

"Like seeing a psychiatrist?" I said, interrupting him and anticipating what I thought he was dancing around.

"What? You're a mind-reader now, too?" he replied.

"No, but you might say that psychiatry and psychotherapy are interests of mine."

"So, you wouldn't be opposed to seeing a psychiatrist?"

"No. In fact, I'd welcome it."

"Good. I'll get you on her schedule. I think you'll like her. Her name is Dr. Leslie Ledbrinker."

I thanked Trig, and we briefly discussed how my first week of FBI Agent training had gone. My training was divided into four different areas of concentration, academics, case exercises, firearms training, and operational skills. The only area foreign to me was firearms training. I had never held, let alone shot a gun before, and I was pretty nervous my first day at the range. After some instruction on how to stand, how to hold and aim the weapon, and surprisingly how to breathe, I not only liked shooting, but I was pretty good at it.

My previous summer internship, no thanks to Hugh Jinks, was useful preparation for my law class. My gymnastics training and runs with Heather made the physical fitness portion of my training a relative breeze. Case exercises reminded me of the planning that Heather and I had done and then executed to nab Mr. Trahorn and send him packing.

While I didn't have any significant concerns about the training program, the age gap between the other trainees was an issue – more for them than for me. I couldn't help but think about Heather and how she must have felt when she made the first team as a freshman. All the upper-class first-teamers didn't accept her and had a jaded opinion of her worthiness and talent. Now I was in that position, and let me tell you, it didn't feel warm and fuzzy. It also made me miss Heather more than I already did. Sure, we texted each other frequently. However, between my having to be cautious about what I texted and not being able to be together, texting just increased my frustration and loneliness.

Just flipping through my schedule over the next 6 weeks was exhausting. Besides the 40 hours of FBI Agent training, I had 16 hours of assessment sessions each week. This didn't even include the sessions with Dr. Ledbrinker or the home-work that went along with my training. Sunday was the only day on the calendar where nothing was scheduled. I laughed when the only thing I saw on Sundays was the word "Rest." Damn right, I thought to myself. And on the seventh day, Aja rested, I said under my breath, hearing my mother's voice in the back of my head telling me not to blaspheme.

Recognizing that this was going to be my last free weekend for the foreseeable future, I hopped into my car. I drove off base to act like a tourist and visit Washington, D.C. The one-hour drive and my need to focus on navigating the city traffic helped clear my head of the concerns that had consumed me. I had intended to start at the Lincoln Memorial and then take a walking tour of all the various memorials, monuments, and a tour of the White House. It was summer, and the heat and the humidity were oppressive. After visiting the Lincoln Memorial, I spied a bike rideshare station and quickly abandoned the walking tour idea. I zipped around on two wheels for about an hour, taking in an admittedly abbreviated visual tour. Ultimately deciding to take up shelter in the cool Smithsonian National Museum of Natural History – cool in temperature and in content. The few hours I had left before the museum closed were not nearly enough to get to all the exhibits and interactive displays. I then had the brilliant idea of staying in DC overnight and continuing a more leisurely tourist crawl on

Sunday. One thing stopped me from following through on this idea. You guessed it. My so-called "gift." The gift that just keeps on giving whether I wanted it to or not.

I had walked back to Mugly and drove to a hotel where I was happy to learn that my Quantico ID badge entitled me to a discount on the room rate. As I was walking to my room, I started to get a unique signal that was more like a visual hallucination than my usual feeling of self-consciousness. While I was actually walking and looking down an empty hotel hallway. I was seeing a little blond girl in a red bikini being dragged into a supply closet by a guy dressed in coveralls. He looked like a janitor and had his hand over her mouth. She looked terrified, and her eyes were so real to me that I yelled, "No, stop," even though no one was there to hear it. My hallucination faded, but I was overwhelmed by the need to find the supply closet.

As the little girl in my vision was in a swimsuit, I made my way towards the pool area. As I drew closer to the pool, the smell of chlorine grew stronger, as did my hallucinations. Snippets of horrific visual images started inundating me. The little girl was now naked with her mouth and wrists duct-taped. She was on her back, and he was starting to duct tape one leg to a shelving stanchion. I had to hurry and started to run. I ultimately found a supply closet adjacent to the restrooms near the pool. When I found the door was locked, I began to scream for him to stop and banged on the door with both my fists. If he was actually doing what my visual hallucinations were indicating, she was already in excruciating pain. She was already scarred for life. Now, I was just hoping to save her from permanent physical damage and possibly death. My screaming quickly attracted a housekeeper in the area who looked at me like I was crazy.

"He's raping a little girl in there," I screamed, which caused the housekeeper to change her opinion about my sanity. She approached rapidly while reaching for her keys.

Before she got there, however, the supply closet door burst open, hitting me in the face and knocking me down. The man in the coveralls ran down an opposite hall and disappeared. The housekeeper arrived, stopping to help me up before peering into the closet. The housekeepers' scream told me all I needed to know. I went to look for myself, knowing that what I would see would test my ability to keep the contents of my stomach down. The man had impaled the little girl with two broomsticks, and blood was pooling between her spindly legs spread-eagle and taped to adjacent shelving posts. Her terrified eyes were the same eyes I had seen in my hallucination. I went to console her. Only to have chaos erupt outside the closet when a woman, who I presumed was her mother, appeared outside the closet door and saw her daughter. The mother's piercing screams tore my heart out, and I moved aside as she rushed in. She went to pull the broomsticks out, but I discouraged her from doing this for fear her daughter would bleed out. By this time, her screams and the commotion had attracted others. I told the mother to stay with her daughter and that I would call the police and an ambulance. I exited the closet, closed the door to prevent any looky-loos, asked the housekeeper to stand guard, and made the calls I had promised the girls' mother.

When the ambulance arrived, one of the EMTs approached me.

"Ma'am, let me take you back to the rig, so I can treat that nose."

"I'm not the one who needs treatment. It's the little girl in the supply closet," I said, pointing to where the housekeeper was standing guard.

"But, you're bleeding, and your nose is obviously broken."

"I'll be fine. I'm not so sure about the little girl. Now go," I commanded forcefully.

A police officer then came over to interview me. I didn't tell him about my visual hallucinations but told him I had heard a scream from the closet. As I was giving him a description of the man, another image flashed in my head. All I saw was a door numbered 117. When he asked me if I saw where the man had fled to, I suggested they look in Room 117. He radioed his partner and the backup officers that had arrived. Sure enough, they found him hiding in Room 117 behind the shower curtain in the bathroom.

I saw the EMTs transporting the little girl on a gurney with her mother in tow while I was talking to the police officer. The broomsticks had been removed, and I imagine they had packed her injuries to staunch the bleeding. The little girls' eyes met mine briefly as they wheeled her out. I thought I saw a brief glimmer of gratitude before her eyes transitioned back to a forlorn, long-distance stare. I desperately wanted to go to her side, but I didn't know what I would have done or said if I had been able to. I don't think the mother ever really saw me at any point, even when I was crouched by her daughter's side in the supply closet. It was just as well. Her daughter needed her now. Which got me to thinking about where her mother had been when the man had grabbed her daughter. Unfortunately, my visual hallucinations weren't like a DVR that I could rewind to see how the opportunity had presented itself. All I had seen were the despicable acts – in other words, the lowlights.

The hotel manager was also on scene and, from what I could see, was spending most of her time trying to reassure guests of their safety. She even offered to comp me my room, but there was no way I was going to stay. I had been in two hotels in the last six months and, in both cases, had collared a sexual predator. I'll take my too firm bed at Quantico, thank you very much.

When I hopped into Mugly to drive back to the base, I was shocked to see the condition of my face in the rearview mirror. My nose was pointed towards the scar on my right cheek. Dried blood looked like I had a maroon Fu Manchu mustache, and swelling and bruising under my eyes gave me a raccoon-like appearance. No wonder the EMT had approached me.

While I had seen plenty of movies where heroic characters would set their broken noses themselves with a resounding and nauseating crunch, I wasn't feeling that heroic. Nor did I trust Hollywood to be my definitive source of recommended treatment for broken noses. I decided to call Trig since I wasn't sure what medical facilities were available on base. After telling him about my escapade, he advised me to go to a hospital in a town a few miles from Quantico. The one clinic on base was not open on weekends, and he feared that going to an Emergency Room in a DC hospital would sentence me to an interminable wait.

When I arrived at the hospital emergency department, I was surprised to see Trig. I was even more amazed when his presence caused a flood of emotions from feeling after the traumatic episode I had just witnessed. Witnessed, in this case, probably doesn't accurately capture my involvement. Had I been physically present to witness what I saw in my visions, I could have prevented it. Instead, my visions made me feel like a helpless bystander, watching it unfold with no way to stop it. In the end, I felt guilty, like I was more an accomplice than a rescuer. Questions racked my brain. Why didn't my powers to cause the perpetrator to recoil in pain work this time? Why had they failed that poor little girl?

I disintegrated into tears, and Trig wrapped me in a fatherly embrace. My crying caused my nose to start to bleed again, and before long, it turned into a real gusher. Fortunately, the emergency room was not crowded, and I was quickly taken back to a room accompanied by Trig. A nurse and a doctor worked to set my nose, pack it with gauze to stop the bleeding, and prescribed some pain medication.

By the time I got back to my room on the base, I was exhausted – more emotionally than physically. I felt like I was about to lose my sanity. My unique powers were evolving, and I wasn't sure that I would be able to adapt to or survive the immense responsibility they placed on me. On top of that, I missed Heather, my one true confidant, and Misty. I even missed my Mom, and of course, my Dad. If not for Trig, I don't know what even darker place I may have descended to. All I knew is that I needed to see Dr. Leslie Ledbrinker sooner rather than later.

CHAPTER 23

No Pain No Gain

I woke up Sunday morning with black eyes in full bloom and a straight but swollen and painful nose that undoubtedly contributed to my dull but radiating headache. My first order of business was to pop open the bottle of pain pills. So much for my bragging to the doctor about my high pain tolerance!

My main concern, however, wasn't about my appearance or my pain. I couldn't get the look that little girl gave me out of my head. I was kicking myself for not getting her mother's name and contact information so that I could check on how the little girl was doing. I doubted the hotel manager would share this information with me. Here I was, working for the FBI, and I felt at a loss for how to get information. I didn't want to bother Trig. I had already inconvenienced him enough this weekend. Despite my headache, I searched high and low on the Internet for a news story or police report, to no avail. Frustrated but starting to feel the effects of the pain medicine, I lay down and was soon fast asleep.

I awoke with a start as my FBI phone rang.

"Hello?" I answered groggily.

"Hi, Aja. It sounds like I woke you. I'm sorry," Trig apologized.

"I took some pain medication. I must have fallen asleep. What time is it?"

"One o'clock. I was just calling to see how you were doing and if you need anything?"

"Thanks, I'll be fine. There is one thing you can do for me, though."

"What's that?"

"I never got that little girl's name or how to contact her mother. I want to see how she's doing?"

"I think I can probably help you with that. Why don't you go back to sleep, and I'll call you in a few hours with any information I'm able to find."

"Thanks, Trig. And thanks for being there at the hospital last night."

"No problem, Aja. I'm glad you called me. By the way, I spoke to Dr. Ledbrinker, and she's going to fit you into her schedule tomorrow."

"I'm sorry I'm such a mess and keep getting into trouble."

"Stop that. I can't imagine the stress your powers and your experiences have caused. Don't ever forget that what you have already done in your life has saved countless numbers of kids from physical and emotional harm. We will get through this together, OK?"

"Thanks, Trig. I needed to hear that. I wish I could hug you right now."

"Consider your hug received and mine given in return. Now go back to sleep. I'll call you later."

With the hope to learn about the little girl's health and psychiatric salvation for me on the horizon, I rolled over in bed, hugged my pillow, and returned to la-la land.

I woke up a couple of hours later and took a shower. That and the diminishing effect of the pain medication helped to make me feel somewhat back to normal. I hadn't eaten all day, and while it was mid-afternoon and between meal services, I padded down to the chow hall. With only limited options, I grabbed a sandwich, a salad, a cookie, and a bottle of peach iced tea. I wondered why people were staring at me but then remembered what my face looked like. That's all I needed, something to call even more attention to myself. I just wanted to be like everyone else and fit in. But anonymously normal had never described me, and now to make it even worse, my face looked like a conspicuous billboard sign saying, "Look at me. Look at me!" I nixed the idea of eating my lunch in the chow hall and returned to my room.

I had just taken my first bite of the sandwich when my FBI phone sprang to life. It was Trig, so I had to chew double-time to answer the call without breaking my mother's rule of not talking with my mouth full.

"Hi, Trig," I answered brightly.

"Hi, Aja. You sound much better."

"I am, but I'm afraid my face looks like Amanda Nunes just used it as a punching bag."

Trig laughed, getting my reference to the women's mixed martial arts champion.

"Well, get used to it. It won't be the last time."

"Why do you say that?"

"The only FBI trainees that escape bumps, breaks, bruises, and lacerations are the ones that quit before the self-defense and hand-to-hand combat courses in the last half of the training."

"OK, but how do I explain this to the other trainees? They already look at me like I'm some kind of freak."

"Well, I don't know why you would feel the need to explain it to them, but you have several options. I'd go with the truth, though."

"Tell them I had visions of a little girl being abducted and raped? Oh yeah, that would really confirm their assessment of me."

"No, you tell them you saved a little girl who had been abducted, and because of your actions, you saved the little girls' life."

"Yeah, but that would be an exaggeration. I don't know that."

"But I do. I spoke to the girls' doctor and the mother."

"You spoke to them?"

"Yep. And they were both happy that I tracked them down, especially the mother. She wants you to come over to their house sometime so they can thank you properly."

"Why did they think I saved her life?"

"Because you told the mother not to remove the broomsticks. If she had done that before paramedics were on the scene, the girl would have likely bled out and died. Your intervention saved the girl from irreparable damage to her reproductory organs."

"I can't believe it. What a relief."

"Well, believe it. I know you probably wished you had prevented the attack before it even began. If you hadn't been there, the girls' mother would be preparing to attend a funeral."

"What's the girls' name? How old is she?"

"Her name is Amber. Amber Lane, and she's seven years old."

"And the guy? What will happen to him?"

"He will be in jail for a long time, assuming that he recovers."

"Recovers?"

"Yes. A group of inmates attacked him last night. He had

been bragging about what he had done, and I guess some took offense. They administered their own brand of justice, which ironically involved broomsticks. He's in intensive care right now and may not survive."

"How poetic. Am I a bad person for finding some satisfaction in that?"

"I'd worry about you if you didn't find some satisfaction in that. He deserved whatever he got."

"What possesses a person to do things like that to a child? To anyone for that matter?"

"I wish we knew, and I wish it was something we could detect and prevent before they ever acted on what motivates them. You may not like hearing this, but right now, the closest thing to having such a solution is you."

"Me?"

"Yes, you. You told me yourself that your signals vary based on what you think is the person's likelihood to act. I think you said fantasizers get tummy aches, and serial rapists get fried."

"I did, but I can't prove that. Plus, I'm going a little crazy now that my powers seem to be expanding. I'm afraid I'll eventually just end up in a psychiatric hospital being bombarded by all the depraved thoughts and acts occurring in the world."

"And that is exactly why we want to conduct our assessment and have Dr. Ledbrinker provide her support. Don't forget this, Aja. I care more about your health and well-being than I do about your special powers. I want to help you harness those powers so that you can live with them, and then, and only then, do I want you to apply them so we can prevent abuse and exploitation. Understand?"

"Yes, sir. Thank you, sir."

"I know we're on a military base Aja, but you can call me Trig."

"I'm sorry, Trig. I guess I hear it so much around here that it rubbed off on me."

"Understandable. I was stationed in Texas when I was younger, and within two weeks, I had incorporated y'all into my vocabulary. It didn't sound quite genuine when paired with my New York accent."

I laughed and realized once again how fortunate I was that Trig had taken me under his wing. We completed our call, and I went back to eating my dunch. Or was it my lunner? When I got to my cookie, I realized I was staring at my bean bag chair, daydreaming about Heather. I picked up my phone and sent her a text. I didn't think anything of it when I didn't receive a response. Heather couldn't text when she was training or when she was in the midst of a long run, which she typically did on Sundays. I finished my meal and took another dose of medication as my pain was returning. Despite my physical pain, knowing that Amber was going to be alright provided something more important to me – emotional relief and some semblance of sanity. I plopped into my bean bag chair, turned on the TV, and started to watch a movie, only to succumb to sleep when the pain meds kicked in thirty minutes later.

CHAPTER 24

On the Brink of Losing It

I woke up in the early morning hours still in my bean bag chair with some overly enthusiastic TV pitchman trying to sell something. I found the remote and silenced him. I extracted myself from my bean bag chair and padded to the bathroom. My black eyes, which had formerly been a uniform dark purple, had faded to a light purple with green and yellowish highlights. How lovely, I thought. Who needs eye shadow? I felt hungover from the effects of the pain medications and hoped a shower would clear some of the cobwebs from my head.

Marginally better from my shower, I postponed getting dressed and doing my hair, lingering in a towel with another for my hair. I picked up my phone from beside the bean bag chair, fully expecting to see a series of missed calls and texts from Heather. Seeing none, I began to worry. Although it was only 5 am, I called Heather, only to have my call go to voicemail. I hung up and didn't leave a message.

Restless and growing more anxious by the minute, I decided to occupy myself with the mindless task of drying and brushing my hair. Hoping that during the 45 minutes it took, I would hear from Heather and stop worrying. If anything, this only raised my anxiety level, glancing down at my phone every few moments. Midway through drying my hair, I even shut my phone off and restarted it. Thinking that maybe I hadn't been receiving calls or texts for some technological reason or glitch. My phone remained stubbornly dark, with no missed calls or texts.

Once my hair was done, I got dressed and started putting on my make-up, knowing there was very little I could do to conceal my multicolored eye shadow. I couldn't bother. My mind was elsewhere, and I didn't care what my trainee classmates would think. Too restless to sit in my room for another 90 minutes before my first class, I decided to go to the chow hall and have breakfast. I had to stay busy with something, so I didn't go crazy waiting for Heather to return my call or texts.

When I got to the chow hall, I realized I was famished. The server looked at me in disbelief, trying to reconcile my 5-foot, 100-pound frame with the plate of cheesy scrambled eggs, 3 strips of bacon, hashbrowns, and a short stack of pancakes.

I took my loaded tray to my customary booth, trying unsuccessfully not to continually look at my phone as I dug into my breakfast bounty.

"Mind if I sit with you?" a male voice asked as I looked up to see one of my trainee classmates holding a tray as burdened with food as mine.

Caught by surprise, I welcomed him to join me more as a reflex than due to my sincere desire to have him join me. I just wasn't able to think of a gentle way to tell him to leave me the fuck alone. As he slid into the seat across from me, I was already starting to regret my response. I didn't want to answer his inevitable questions about what happened to my face. Hell, I didn't even really want to talk and started to formulate plans for how to deftly abbreviate our breakfast together.

"Thanks, I'm Travis. I'm in the trainee program with you."

"I know. I'm Aja," I replied curtly, sounding less friendly than I had intended.

"I hope you don't mind me crashing your breakfast. I don't know anyone here, and I guess that over the last week, I've learned I'm not a fan of eating alone."

Although I was presently feeling on the opposite end of the need for company spectrum, I could relate to his sense of loneliness. I was also surprised that he chose to sit with me, throwing a wrench into my assumption that my classmates were loath to accept me. If nothing else, Travis was a diversion from my obsessive worrying over Heather. Most importantly, Travis wasn't triggering any signals that would make me wary of his intentions.

"Yeah, I hear ya. This hasn't been the easiest place to feel welcome or get to know people," I said, purposely softening my response so he didn't think I was a total bitch. "Where are you from?" I asked, hoping to preempt his inevitable questions about my face.

"I'm from Cumberland, Wisconsin, originally. I went to college in Minnesota, and I was working in law enforcement in Minneapolis before enrolling here. What about you? Where are you from?"

Here we go, I thought. The moment Travis finds out I'm just out of high school is the moment he decides eating breakfast alone isn't so bad.

"I'm from New Jersey. I worked in a law office and at the Post Office before coming here," I replied. Enhancing my law internship experience slightly and totally avoiding any reference to my educational background.

"What made you want to enroll in FBI agent training?" I asked, kicking myself for asking a question that I couldn't answer myself if and when he asked me.

"My supervisor suggested I apply. I guess he thought I'd make a good agent. It really wasn't on my radar."

"Well, we have something in common then," I replied, seeing an opportunity for a quick and easy way out of answering the same question.

I didn't offer a follow-up question recognizing that if I probed too deeply into his life, he would expect me to share my life story as well. Fortunately, he seemed content to wolf down his breakfast. What conversation we did have was focused on our respective perceptions of the first week of training. He never asked me about my face, which actually started to bother me. Didn't he notice? Did he notice but not care, or was he too gentlemanly to ask? He also had to know that I was much younger than all the other trainees, yet he never mentioned it. Sometimes you can't win with me. If he had asked about my face and my age, I would have resented it. And if he didn't ask, then I'd cast aspersions on his lack of perceptiveness or compassion. Despite this, I liked him. As long as we kept the conversation on the surface, he was easy to talk to. Not to mention, 30 minutes passed without me having to look at my phone.

We polished off our breakfasts and walked to our first class of the day. I was somewhat surprised when he elected to sit next to me. Of course, had he chosen not to sit next to me, I probably would have thought he regretted ever associating with me in the first place. As I said, sometimes it's hard to win with me.

The only good thing about my busy class schedule was that I didn't have the opportunity to check my phone constantly. However, I was definitely aware that I still hadn't received a response from Heather. When my phone finally rang late in the afternoon, just before my first session with Dr. Leslie Led-brinker, I was sure it was going to be Heather.

I was wrong. It was my mother, and to my disappointment, I almost didn't pick up her call. Thinking better of it, I answered.

"Hi, Mom," I said in a tone I knew probably telegraphed my

lack of enthusiasm.

"Hi, Aja. I'm sorry to bother you, but Heather's mother just called me. She's wondering if Heather is with you."

"With me? Why would Heather be with me?" I asked.

"Well, you are her best friend, and Heather didn't come home from her run yesterday. Her mother said Heather had been talking about missing you. So, you haven't heard from her?"

"No, I haven't," I said as my mind started to reel. I couldn't understand how Heather could be missing. I hadn't experienced any signals. There had to be a logical and innocent explanation. Otherwise, I would have had ominous signals by now. Wouldn't I have?

"Do you have any idea where she might go? Another friend's house, maybe?"

"No, Mom, this is totally not like Heather. I'm scared."

"I'm sorry, honey, I didn't want to upset you. I have to get back to Heather's mother. She's been trying to file a missing person report. The police won't honor it until it has been 24-hours, and they know she's checked and exhausted all possible places Heather might go. You'll call Heather's mother or me if she contacts you, won't you?"

"Of course, Mom," I said, exasperated not so much by her stupid question but by my concern for Heather's welfare. "Did someone check the routes Heather usually runs? I know she liked to run the park trail on Sundays. There's a 5-mile loop there that we'd run."

"I'm not sure, but I'll ask her mother. Are you going to be alright?"

"I don't know, Mom. It depends on whether Heather is alright? The only thing holding me together right now is that I'm not getting any signals to be concerned."

"Well, that's a relief."

"Yeah, but my signals have been changing, Mom. I can't count on them being the same as they have been in the past."

"Let's try not to get too worked up. I have to call Heather's mother. I'll let you know the moment I know anything, OK?"

"OK, Mom."

Suffice to say that by the time I walked into Dr. Leslie Ledbrinker's office, I was the poster child for someone who needed psychiatric intervention.

If you were trying to find a woman who represented the opposite end of the body type spectrum to me, you couldn't do much better than Dr. Ledbrinker. At nearly 6-feet tall, she towered over me. She had dizzying womanly curves that immediately conjured up words like zaftig, lustful, and envy. Dark auburn hair, piercing, uncommonly bright green eyes, and full, to-die-for lips completed the picture. Undoubtedly, Dr. Ledbrinker could have a successful career in modeling if her psychiatrist gig didn't work out for her.

But none of that really mattered to me as I entered her office, or as I fell apart in her office would be more accurate. I didn't even have to say anything for Dr. Ledbrinker to diagnose and begin my treatment.

"Come over here and sit down," she said, grasping my elbow in one hand and grabbing a box of kleenex with the other.

I was sobbing uncontrollably. Once seated, she kept a hand on my shoulder while offering words that, in any other context, would have sounded cliché, but in this context, were just what I needed to hear.

"You're safe here, Aja. We're going to get you through this. Just feel what you need to feel and when you're ready, I'm here, ready to listen."

With the aid of a handful of tissues, her words, and her hand on my shoulder, I finally got to a point where uttering words seemed possible.

"Thank you," I said but then disintegrated into tears again.

"That's OK. Take your time. Let it out," she coached, never removing her reassuring hand from my shoulder.

I attempted again to compose myself, recognizing that my grip on self-control was extremely tenuous.

"I think I can talk now," I offered as I looked up at Dr. Ledbrinker's face that somehow conveyed acceptance, under-standing, and determination all at once. Perhaps it was just my need to see these things, or maybe Dr. Ledbrinker was really very good at her job. I didn't know, and I didn't care. I blurted out what was foremost on my mind – my relationship with Heather and my fear for her welfare. Dr. Ledbrinker lis-tened, and something about how she attended to what I was saying just made me want to continue until every last detail had been shared. I didn't know what to expect when I finally paused long enough to allow Dr. Ledbrinker to say something.

"Is there anything else you want to share?" she asked. As if the last 20 minutes of tear-filled, heart-wrenching narrative about my relationship with Heather was not enough. But it worked. I then proceeded to share the history of learning about my powers and the experiences and concerns I had about their evolution. I felt myself rushing to tell her my story, conscious that my appointment time was approaching its end. I was worried she wouldn't have enough time to do whatever voo-doo psychiatrists do to make you feel better.

"Don't worry about the time. You're my last appointment today," Dr. Ledbrinker interjected as if she could read my mind.

An hour and a half into my hour-long appointment, I felt satisfied that I had brought Dr. Ledbrinker up to speed on all my concerns. I paused, anticipating Dr. Ledbrinker to spring into action and work her magic.

"Thank you for sharing all that, Aja. What are you feeling

now?"

I hadn't anticipated that question and had to consciously transition from thinking-mode to feeling-mode. Oddly, while I had no more answers to my concerns than when I walked in, I felt a sense of relief. Talking about my concerns had somehow made them more manageable, more contained, and controllable than the chaos and despair I felt walking into her office.

"Ah, I feel better," I offered.

"Good, but what are you feeling?"

I didn't understand at first, and I'm sure my face telegraphed it as she followed up with a clarification.

"Better is not a feeling. It's a statement of comparison. While I'm happy you're feeling better, I'm curious to know what you're feeling?" she stated. Offering me a couple of feeling words in her response as if to prompt me.

This time I got it.

"I feel relief. I still feel concerned, but it seems more manageable now that I've talked about it. Is it really that simple?"

"Is what really that simple?" Dr. Ledbrinker asked.

"This therapy stuff. Talking about it makes it better. Provides relief, I mean?"

"I'm afraid not. Talking about things can provide temporary relief, but therapy also focuses on developing insights into your stressors and more effective methods for dealing with them in the future. I usually cover the goals of therapy in my first session with clients, but I think you needed to get things off your chest today. If you're in a good place right now, I'd like to suggest we meet daily for the rest of the week."

"Daily? You think I'm really that screwed up?"

"No, I don't think you're screwed up at all, Aja. I think you've been dealing with some unique and very significant stressors without the support to understand and deal with them."

"But what about my scheduled assessment sessions? Trig said I'd be starting those this week."

"I'll talk to Special Agent Halvorsen, and we'll work out the details of how to coordinate our sessions and your assessment sessions. I think they're both important to the work we need to do."

"Alright. Thank you for putting me back together again, Dr. Ledbrinker."

"You're welcome, but you put yourself back together. I just offered you the opportunity and the environment in which to do it."

I left Dr. Ledbrinker's office, surprised. Not only by the results of the session but that I had just shared the most intimate details of my life with someone I didn't even really know. I would have never done that if I hadn't been as emotionally distraught and vulnerable as I was when I got to her office. I guess timing is everything.

CHAPTER 25

A Very, Very Dark Place

D r. Ledbrinker was right. Talking about your fears and concerns offered only temporary relief. As a matter of fact, by the time I arrived back to my room, the therapeutic effects were already starting to diminish. Each minute my phone sat dark and idle chipped away at my sanity. My therapy session now felt like a band-aid applied to a crack in a dam. My sanity was destined to be overwhelmed by the flood of raging emotions I was experiencing.

While not hearing from Heather in the last two days was bad enough, what really was eating away at me was the total absence of any signals. Every time I tried to convince myself that this was an indication that I shouldn't worry about Heather, the thoughts that I had lost my powers crept back in.

I was a master at over-thinking things, even though it rarely helped the situation I was perseverating on. I started thinking that maybe I still had my powers, but they had changed or, God-forbid, my powers had a range, and Heather was outside the scope of their effectiveness. My thinking got so far off the rails at one point that I considered going to some seedy neighborhood. Just to walk around in the hopes of running into someone that would trigger my signal to confirm I still had my powers. Then vetoed that as foolish, considering what could happen if, in fact, my powers had left me. After what felt like a couple hours of this mental agony, my phone jumped to life, announcing that my mother was calling. Hers was not the name on my phone that I had hoped for.

"Hi, Mom. Please tell me some good news," I pleaded, knowing that if there was good news, it would have more likely been Heather who would have called me.

"I'm sorry, Aja. They found Heather in a wooded area of the park."

"Is she alright?" I asked despite tears immediately falling from my eyes, my lacrimal glands accepting the horrific truth before my brain would allow me to.

"No, honey. She's dead. I hate that I have to tell you this over the phone."

I know my mother said more to me, but I didn't hear or comprehend anything she said after she said the word "dead." Any semblance of sanity I had been clinging to crumbled. I don't even know if I hung up on my mother or whether we had completed our call.

One thought and two questions emerged. Why didn't I get a signal? And how do I kill myself most expediently?

It was fortuitous that I hadn't yet been issued a gun, but I did have a few days worth of pain pills. I took them all and lay down on my bed, hoping that they would stop everything - my pain, my thoughts, my heart, my life.

I woke up in a hospital bed with the worst sore throat and tubes seemingly coming out of every part of my body as equipment beeped all around me. Glaring lights blinded me, distorting the figure in front of me that looked vaguely like my mother. Someone placed a straw in my mouth and urged me to drink. Thinking this might help my sore throat, I complied, only to feel like I was swallowing acid and multiplying my pain. I choked, spit out the straw, and coughed, which only made the pain in my throat worse. If they were trying to kill me, they were certainly trying to make it as painful as possible.

I slowly regained my senses and learned that I was in the Intensive Care Unit of the hospital that had treated my broken nose a few days earlier. My sore throat was from being intubated and on a respirator. It was my mother that was standing in front of me with a look of concern.

Then the realization of what had brought me to this place flooded in. Heather was dead, and I had failed in my attempt to kill myself. All I know is that I got very agitated and teary. Then some elixir was squirted into the intravenous line running into my arm that quickly and magically made everything seem better. I didn't even care what the magic potion was. I was floating on air and half expecting to see rainbows, unicorns, and puppy dogs.

I woke up sometime later in the same bed but had forgotten where I was or why I was there until my mother reoriented me to the harsh reality. Shortly after my mother's review, Dr. Ledbrinker and Trig visited me. I felt sure that they were going to tell me that my FBI internship was over, but they didn't. They expressed their condolences for my loss and their wish to support me in getting better. They also told me not to worry about my training or assessment. I may have appreciated these thoughts and gestures if I had any will to live, but I didn't. Unless, of course, that nurse would come around and spritz that happy juice in my IV line again.

The next time I woke up, I actually thought I was dreaming. My father was giving me a hug and telling me how much he loved me. It wasn't until he was holding my hand and calling my name repeatedly that I realized I was awake, and he was standing there. That snapped me out of my fog, and for the first time in days, I made an effort to sit up in my bed. I didn't get far as the room started to spin. He grabbed my shoulders and gently helped me return to my former position.

"Dad, what are you doing here?"

"I was going to ask you the same question, superstar," he replied. "I'm here because I was afraid I was going to lose you."

"I'm sorry. I was just so lost and depressed, I didn't know what to do," I replied, realizing that I couldn't yet verbalize the words death and Heather in proximity to each other. I also realized that I didn't know the circumstances of her death and wasn't sure I wanted to know at this point.

"I'm here to help you see that you have lots of reasons to live, Aja. Your mother and I need you, but it's more than just us, honey."

"I don't know that I'm ready for this conversation, Dad," I said, wanting to wallow a little longer in my fatalistic, woe-is-me thoughts and feelings.

"Sometimes, we need to do things we're not ready for, Aja. It helps us grow. Otherwise, we stagnate and roll over and die. Heather needs you."

That last sentence woke something up in me.

"Heather's dead. What could she possibly need from me?" I asked him, somehow both angry and happy that he had pulled me out of the dark place in which I had been residing.

"She would want you there at her funeral. You were the most important person in her life, Aja. When her mother was trying to find out where she was, she found Heather's diary. It's filled with entries about how much she loved you and how you gave her life happiness and meaning."

"Really?"

"Yes, really. Her funeral is in two days. But there is more."

"More?"

"Yes, but for now, I just want you to concentrate on getting out of this bed and going with us to Heather's funeral. After that, we will talk about what else you can do for Heather. Can you do that?"

My father's presence and his challenge sparked a flame in me. A flame that had almost been snuffed out by my own hand after Heather's death. Only my Dad could have ignited the kindling that I had so thoroughly doused with despair and self-loathing. His intervention was even more magical than the hospital's happy juice. I felt like I had a reason to persevere, a reason to live again.

Unfortunately, just telling the doctor that I felt better and didn't want to kill myself anymore wasn't enough to earn myself a discharge from the hospital. For that, I needed a psychiatrist to assess my mental state. Thankfully, since I had what the doctor called a "therapeutic relationship" with Dr. Ledbrinker, he agreed to accept her assessment of my suitability for discharge. Before she could come to assess me, I had to endure another night in the hospital. They transferred me from the ICU to a semi-private room, which, thankfully, was for all practical purposes private as no one was occupying the other bed.

Nevertheless, being awake and cognizant in a hospital does not necessarily promote relaxation, comfort, or confidence. Overhead paging, the incessant and varied bells, and alarms, and the echoing voices of patients, visitors, and hospital staff in the hallway created a din that I would hardly classify as healing. A nurse also came into my room and scanned a few things on her cart and then proceeded to hand me medications she was convinced I needed to take. Thank God I questioned her about it as she then scanned my wristband and realized she had the wrong patient. Something told me that perhaps she should have scanned my wristband first, but what did I know? The food was surprisingly good. However, I didn't trust my gastronomic judgment as I was so hungry that I could have probably convinced myself that cardboard was filet mignon.

Dr. Ledbrinker arrived mid-morning the next day to conduct my assessment. It started off with some weird questions like who was I, where was I, what was today's date, and who was the President of the United States. It then proceeded to more reasonable queries, more befitting the assessment of my sanity and suicidality. Despite Dr. Ledbrinker's favorable assessment, I still had to wait nearly 6 hours before I was discharged. Despite the rationale for this interminable wait my mother provided, I couldn't help think it was the hospital's last test of my emotional stability. Could I endure waiting nonsensically in their god-awful environment for 6 hours without succumbing to the desire to off myself? Either that, or they were just plain inefficient. Regardless, I passed their test or survived their inefficiency.

It was weird getting into the backseat of my mother's car and seeing my Dad in the driver's seat. It made me feel like I was 7 again, which is probably the last time I had been in a car with both of them. Before we set off for home in New Jersey, we had to stop at the base so I could pack some clothes. Trig met us there and reassured me that my good standing in the FBI was still intact and that he was working with Dr. Ledbrinker to recalibrate my schedule. I knew Trig and my Dad were buddies, but it was odd seeing them chummy. It was even more strange when my mother hugged Trig.

On the drive back to New Jersey, my mother informed me that she had contacted Trig after she had called me about Heather's death. She had tried calling to check on me, and when I didn't answer, she became worried. Good thing she did because Trig found me alive but unresponsive and had me transported immediately to the hospital. Thanks to the quick work of the paramedics and emergency room staff, they were able to counter the adverse effects of my overdose.

My mother tried her best to give me a layperson's description of what the medical personnel did in response to my overdose. Because I was unconscious and my breathing was shallow, the paramedics gave me a drug that reversed the effects of the pain medication. The emergency room personnel pumped my stomach to remove any pain medications that I hadn't fully absorbed. They also gave me something to reduce acetaminophen levels in my blood to protect my liver from potential damage. I'm sure my mother told me the other things they did. However, my capacity to retain all of that medical mumbo-jumbo was limited. What I could retain was scary enough, now that I had the will to live.

Thanks to the hospital's glacial speed of discharge, we had gotten off to a late start for our 4+ hour trek home. Despite this, Dad elected to stop for dinner along the way. And when I say dinner, I don't mean one of those just off-the highway fast food options. He took us to a proper restaurant on Baltimore's Harbor. I had to completely recalibrate my culinary rating scale after eating there. Dad suggested that I get the Crab Stuffed Lobster. He knew I loved lobster, and I guess he also knew I wouldn't order it just based on price. At his insistence, I splurged, but not before asking what Haricots Verts were, which I pronounced just as it looks – Harry Cots Verts. Actually, when I first looked at it, I couldn't help but see Harlots Perverts. My mother informed me that it was pronounced "Airy Corvair" and that they were thin French green beans. Leave it to the French to name mundane green beans to look and sound like prostitutes driving in a convertible from the 1960s! They were quite tasty, and ultimately, I had to agree. Just naming them "green beans" would have been a gross injustice. Give me prostitutes in a convertible, please. Viva la France!

Back on the road, darkness and an overly full belly had me snoring in the backseat before we crossed into Delaware. Magically, when I awoke, we were pulling into our driveway in northern New Jersey. It was near midnight, and after hugging my parents, I crawled into my bed, too tired to undress.

CHAPTER 26

Ashes to Ashes

I woke up fully clothed and oddly disoriented to find myself in my bedroom at home. The sudden realization that it was the day of Heather's funeral then hit me hard, reminding me as subtlely as a gut-punch of the reason I was home.

I turned on the shower, peeled off my clothes, and took inventory of my body in the mirror. The bruising on my face was almost gone. Replaced by bruising on my left arm from the IV and on my right arm from blood draws. I stepped on the bathroom scale, and at 92 pounds, I was 8 pounds lighter than when I had entered the hospital. My ribs were more prominent, and I realized that I hadn't had my period in nearly two months. My eyes seemed dull, and my skin pallid. Even my hair didn't look as healthy. I stepped in the shower and washed and conditioned my hair, hoping to restore its sheen.

After a luxuriously long shower, I stepped out, dried off, and hoped I could work a miracle on my face with my make-up. There is only so much a shower, shampoo, conditioner, and make-up can do, however. Any way you cut it, the stress of my FBI training, Heather's death, and my overdose and hospitalization had taken its toll. What had once been a form-fitting and flattering black dress that I chose to wear for the funeral hung loosely off of me without a hint of its former body-hugging qualities. My hair looked better after my conditioning treatment. Some make-up helped give my face some color, but the lack of sparkle in my eyes, gaunt appearance, and bruises on my arms made me look like some anorexic, drug-addled tweaker.

I finally descended the stairs to join my parents, who were having coffee and a light breakfast in the kitchen. Both of them commented on how nice I looked, proving that parents can actually see a silk purse in their sow's ear child. I poured myself a cup of coffee. Or should I say I added some coffee to my mug, three-quarters full of milk with two spoonfuls of sugar? I wasn't hungry and twice rejected my mother's offer to prepare me a plate of food. Platitudes about the importance of the first meal of the day, be damned.

We got into the car, and I realized I didn't even know anything about Heather's funeral. Where was it being held, or who was going to be there? I don't know why I assumed her parents would have a church service and burial ceremony. I guess I thought I was the only one who knew about Heather's preferences in death. Unfortunately, growing old together and scattering our ashes in our home's backyard garden, as we had discussed and imagined, wasn't going to become a reality.

So I was surprised when my Dad drove to Heather's house. We joined a small gathering in the backyard consisting of Heather's parents, several relatives, Ms. Sylvester, and a few girls and her coach from her summer gymnastics academy. Three tables sat near the garden – one with framed photos of Heather through the years, another with her gymnastics trophies, medals, and ribbons, and a third filled with flowers surrounding a wooden box laser engraved with a poem likening Heather's life and death to that of a caterpillar's conversion to a butterfly. It was just as she would have wanted it, except about 70 years premature.

It was all too real, too much for me to assimilate, and I decompensated. My Dad caught me just as my knees buckled, and I almost went to the ground. My face was an agonized mask awash in tears, snot, and drool, as if they were toxic substances that needed to be expelled. Heather's mother, of all people, helped me into the house, laid me down on a bed, and tried to clean me up and console me. My inconsolable grief eventually evolved into guilt-ridden embarrassment as Heather's mother stroked my hair and offered lovingly supportive words. Here I was, so incapacitated by my sorrow, that Heather's mom had to attend to me. If anything, I should have been the one consoling her.

I then realized that I was lying in Heather's bed in Heather's bedroom. Her mother seemed oddly comforted, sitting on the edge of the bed and caring for me. As if I were her surrogate daughter. I knew she knew about the nature of my relationship with her daughter. Perhaps it was her selfless acceptance of me and her boundless compassion that served to restore my composure. Or maybe it was being in Heather's room and feeling her still present in me. Whatever it was, it worked. I hugged her mother, got off the bed, and as we exited Heather's bedroom, she put her arm around my shoulders. She didn't remove her arm from my shoulders until we were in the backyard, and I was safely in the presence of my parents again.

Shortly after my return, a brief ceremony was held in which a priest offered prayers and led the group in the recitation of Psalm 23. It wasn't until I learned the details of Heather's death that I would see the irony and the truth in the oft-recited psalm. Both Ms. Sylvester and Heather's coach from her summer academy spoke mostly about her gymnastics talents and accomplishments, which is how they knew her. Missing was the Heather I knew and the Heather I'm sure her parents knew, but maybe everything didn't have to be said. Perhaps holding that unique and unstated part of Heather in your heart was what we needed.

I cried during the ceremony, of course, but standing between Heather's Mom and my Dad made me feel like I was being propped up by two strong pillars. After the ceremony, the group was invited into the house for some appetizers. I wasn't hungry, but when I saw the snack Heather had always raved about, something she called Devil's on Horseback, I had to try one. I ended up eating four of the sinfully delicious bacon-wrapped dates with goat cheese morsels. I stopped more out of concern that if I didn't, I'd finish the entire plate. God knows I could have used the caloric intake!

After about an hour, most of the guests had left. Heather's parents pulled me aside, and we returned to Heather's bedroom. There, they handed me Heather's diary and a small, gift-wrapped box.

"We want you to have Heather's diary," her mother stated with tears in her eyes.

I couldn't formulate any words in response, and her tears prompted mine.

"We are so happy that Heather found a true friend and true love in her brief time," her mother continued tearfully. "We know she would have wanted you to have it, and we know that you will cherish it."

"Thank you," I managed to say, sobbing and having to wipe a couple of tears off the diary cover in the process.

"Open the gift," Heather's Dad prompted.

I unwrapped the small box, opened it, and saw a necklace with a silver butterfly pendant. I took it out of the box, and Heather's mother's offered to help me put it on.

"Some of Heather's ashes are contained in the pendant," Heather's mother said as she clasped the necklace around my neck.

I had to sit down on the bed as my knees once again threatened to fail me. Both of Heather's parents hugged me, and I managed to thank them, my emotions barring anything more eloquent.

"We're going to leave now and get to our guests, but you take the time you need here. OK?"

I nodded, wiped away my tears, and gave them both another hug.

I sat alone in Heather's room, with her diary in hand and the butterfly pendant with her ashes next to my heart. I didn't need these things to feel Heather's presence in my life, but something about having something tangible, something I could hold or feel on my skin, made her feel closer. I cried until I couldn't anymore.

For the first time since learning of Heather's death, I wanted to know how it happened. But today was not the day to ask. Heather deserved her day in the backyard, next to the garden, surrounded by loved ones, flowers, and the symbols of her athletic accomplishments. Even at the tender age of sixteen, no ceremony could adequately capture her life. Her essence and her meaning to the few people who really knew and loved her defied words or rituals. Unfortunately, I think a lot of people misunderstood or envied her, missing entirely the person she really was.

Heather would have been happy to know her funeral wishes in death had been granted. But to me, any human and earthly ceremony felt incomplete, inadequate. When Heather died, her spirit didn't just leave her. It left me. Something vital in my world was gone, never to be reclaimed, replaced, or experienced again. And I didn't quite know what to do about the chasm that occupied the space where my heart used to be.

CHAPTER 27

Shock Treatment

I woke up the day after the funeral feeling more empty than I had the day before. The delicate butterfly pendant on a chain around my neck felt unusually heavy. More for what it symbolized than its actual weight. If not for having my Dad home, I would have had very little to cling to in this thing called life. The questions I had about how Heather died, which seemed urgent yesterday, seemed less so today. You only want to know and care about things when you have some investment in the world around you, and I was having a severe investment crisis.

I have to credit both my parents for detecting my downward spiral, despite never uttering a word to them about how empty I felt. I imagine my actions, or more accurately, inactions, spoke louder than words. If I wasn't isolating myself in my room, I trudged around aimlessly. I didn't want to eat, didn't want to talk, didn't even get out of my pajamas, or take a shower. After nearly two days of living this zombie-like existence, my parents had seen enough and descended upon me in my bedroom hideout.

"I'm concerned about you, Superstar," my Dad began. As my parents took seats next to my bed, signaling this was not just going to be a hit-and-run interaction.

"We love you, honey," my Mom added. "And your Dad and I can't imagine how difficult it must be for you."

Meanwhile, I was staring vacantly at them from my bed, more content to let their words bounce off of me than allow them to penetrate the prison walls I had erected. I wasn't even sure they were actually talking to me. Perhaps I was sleeping, and this was all just a dream. I was beginning to believe this until my Dad got up, sat on my bed, moved my greasy, unkempt hair from my face, stroked my cheek gently, and dropped a bomb.

"Heather was brutally raped and murdered in the woods. She was stabbed 25 times. The person who did this hasn't been found, Aja."

Tears breached the banks of my eyes, and part of me just wanted to die right then and there. Another part of me felt the beginnings of anger that quickly grew, dousing my suicidal ideation and replacing them with feelings of rage and vengeance. Another part of me questioned why I hadn't felt any signal before, during, or after Heather's rape and murder. All of these feelings were more than enough to breathe life back into me. I sat up, and having reclaimed the purpose that had fueled my desire to join the FBI in the first place, I spoke.

"I need to find him. I need to get that fucking bastard before he does it again."

"There's my little, Superstar," my father replied, as my Mom looked shocked in the background. I imagine my salty vocabulary, combined with my desire to find and take down Heather's murderer, may have had something to do with my mother's concern.

"I want to go back to the base right now," I demanded, swinging my feet past my Dad and joining him in a seated position on the side of my bed.

"Slow down, now. We can get you to the base," my Dad replied.

"Yes, dear. You might want to wash up and eat something before we go," my Mom added.

She had a point. I was feeling and probably smelling a little ripe. And for the first time in days, the word "eat" stimulated my stomach to growl and a desire to sate my ravenous hunger. I took a shower, put on a fresh set of clothes, and packed up. After dinner, in which I think I ate enough to regain almost half my 8 pounds back, we hit the road. Along the way, I called Trig to inform him that I was returning to base.

"Are you sure you're ready? You know you can take more time if you need it." Trig offered.

"I'm absolutely sure I'm ready, Trig. I don't need more downtime. I need to find and stop the person who raped and murdered my friend Heather. But I'm going to need your help to do it."

"I'm glad to hear that, Aja. Over the last few days, I started to investigate Heather's case. It appears that Heather is the perpetrator's sixth victim in the last year. We can discuss this in greater detail tomorrow, but as long as you're willing, Dr. Ledbrinker and I are more than happy to support you in our effort to track the perp down."

"I'm more than ready and willing, Trig."

"Good. Then let's meet for breakfast tomorrow."

"Our booth at 7 am?" I asked.

"I'll be there," Trig replied.

I hung up and finally felt like I was back on track. I settled into the backseat, not at all expecting or prepared for what my Dad would tell me next. If you haven't gathered yet, my Dad has a penchant for saying things that tend to shock or challenge me, usually to inspire me. This was just another one of his unique motivational speeches.

"Ms. Merkinson was arrested in Michigan last year as part of an international child porn ring," he said bluntly.

"How do you know about that?" I asked. I had told him about my former high school gymnastics coach and how she had recoiled in pain after touching me, but I didn't recall telling him her name.

"My work in the CIA is focused on international crime, specifically sexual abuse, exploitation, and trafficking of children. Ms. Merkinson was part of a network of teachers in grade schools and high schools that were identifying little girls and boys for sexual exploitation by the rich and the famous."

"Really? No wonder I burned her. So, do you have special powers too? Is that the reason I have them?"

My father laughed, "No, but I wish I had your powers. I have good intuition, and my training and experience help, but I don't have the powers you have. So I can't take credit for them."

"Or the blame," I laughed. "My powers don't necessarily feel like a gift sometimes."

"I suppose not."

"And then when I wish I had them, they fail me. I'm sure I could have prevented Heather's death if I had been signaled. I can't understand why I didn't get any signals," I said.

Conscious of the butterfly pendant necklace that hung around my neck as a constant reminder of my failure.

"I'm sure Trig and his team will help you figure out your powers. Trig and I have worked together for years. We still do, but it's different now. Now we just hand each other cases that we become aware of."

"Do you know about the perp that killed Heather?"

"No. All I know is what Trig told me. Heather was his sixth victim, each one in a different state. He leaves a unique signature on his victims. He's also a souvenir collector apparently, but Trig didn't tell me the details."

"A souvenir collector?"

"Yeah, I don't know what Heather's perp collects, but some serial killers take something from their victims, like a piece of clothing or jewelry or a body part."

"That's sick," I said, as my mind immediately kicked into overdrive, wondering what the perp had taken from Heather.

"You have no idea. I've been doing this work for 10 years now, and all the wickedness I've seen makes it hard to believe in the benevolence of people."

"Oh, I have more than an idea. I have 5 years of experience getting signals, and I've already seen and felt more than enough wickedness."

"I guess I keep forgetting you're not my innocent little girl anymore," my Dad replied.

"I'll always be your little girl, Dad. But innocence? That went out the window a long time ago."

I could tell that my mother was uncomfortable with the path of our conversation and had heard more than she cared to hear from both of us. Remember? My mother is a glass-half-empty person, and we were threatening to make her a glass three-quarters empty person. Especially if we continued to talk about the devious and despicable nature of humanity. I fell silent. For the remainder of our trip, we all made small talk. Never venturing anywhere near topics that would further drain my mother's already pessimistic worldview.

Saying goodbye to my parents, in particular, my Dad, was difficult. The circumstances around seeing my Dad for the first time in a decade were far from ideal. Regardless, I was happy that the mysteries around who he was and what he did had been solved. He also seemed to know how to inspire and motivate me, even at the lowest point in my life. That our talents and missions working for the FBI and CIA were so similar only endeared me to him even more. I didn't want to stop hugging him, knowing that when I did, he would be gone again. The downside of spending a few days with my Dad was that I now saw what I lost from not growing up with normal parents in a typical family. There was a cost to not having my Dad come home every night during the most formative years of my life. What I had gained over the past few days being with him only made what I lost by his absence the preceding decade that much more devastating. There was no way to reclaim that time with him. It was gone, passed, just like Heather.

CHAPTER 28

The Assessment Begins

Even though I arrived at the chow hall a few minutes early, Trig looked like he had been sitting in our booth for a long time. He was studiously examining several papers laid out in front of a nearly empty cup of coffee as I approached.

"Hard at work already, I see," I announced as I slid into the booth.

"Aja, good morning. I was just going over your revised schedule," he replied as he gathered up the pages and smiled. "How are you doing?"

"I'm good, and thanks to you, alive. So, thank you."

"I think your mother, the paramedics, and the hospital staff deserve the credit for that, but you're welcome. Why don't you grab yourself some breakfast while I get a refill on my coffee."

"Why? Do I look that emaciated?"

"That wasn't why I suggested breakfast, but now that you ask, yes. You look like you could use a hearty breakfast or four."

"I'll get your refill," I said, grabbing his empty coffee cup and leaving to get breakfast.

When I returned, he was once again reviewing my schedule.

"So, what am I going to be doing today?" I asked as I put down my over-full breakfast tray and handed him his coffee.

"Thanks for the coffee, but I didn't mean for you to literally eat four breakfasts," he replied, looking at my breakfast tray. "As for your schedule today, we'll get to it."

"I'm not going to be running 10 miles or anything this morning, am I? Because if I am, I will rethink my breakfast choices."

"No, you won't be running today unless you choose to. I can see you're raring to go, so eat, and I will tell you what Dr. Ledbrinker and I have worked out for you."

I dug into my cheesy egg scramble while Trig rifled through the papers he had been reviewing. While Trig was searching for what he was looking for, I heard someone greet me.

"Welcome back, Aja. It's good to see you," he said as I looked up from my breakfast to see Travis making his way to a table with some of my other trainee classmates.

"Thanks, Travis. It's good to be back," I replied. Genuinely impressed that Travis not only noticed my absence but wasn't concerned about being friendly to me in front of the other trainees.

"Well, well, I see you have a fan club," Trig said after Travis had passed and I had returned to my breakfast.

"A fan, maybe. A club, hardly," I replied.

"I wouldn't be so sure about that, Aja. Travis wasn't the only one who was asking about you last week."

"Well, I'm sure that most of them were probably asking in the hopes that I had dropped out or I was invited to leave the program."

"You know, you don't look good in negativity. I much

prefer how you look when you wear your confidence and positivity."

"I'm sorry, I guess except for Travis, my classmates didn't seem to be all that happy that I was in the program."

"Let me tell you something. Most of your classmates admire you but don't feel like they can measure up to you. They don't approach you because they lack confidence or think they're deficient in some way."

"Do I come across as though I'm superior or as a bitch?"

"Hardly. And that's part of the issue. You make it look easy."

"Easy? I almost killed myself. It's been anything but easy."

"Yes, but whatever crisis is going on inside you is rarely reflected on the outside. You would make a great poker player. Outside you usually appear calm, cool, collected, and confident."

"Wow, it sounds like you're talking about someone else, not me."

"And that is a perfect segue to what Dr. Ledbrinker and I have done in revising your schedule. What you need is not so much the practical FBI training but self-knowledge and insight into the nature of your unique skills. Once you have more of a handle on that, you can go back and complete the basic FBI training. You're still going to join your FBI trainees from time to time. However, there will be a much greater emphasis on your assessment and your therapy sessions with Dr. Ledbrinker."

"That sounds good," I replied, knowing that what kept me up at night the most was trying to understand, trust, and control my unique powers.

As I wolfed down the rest of my breakfast, Trig reviewed my schedule for the week. Mornings were reserved for the assessment of my powers. Afternoons were split between attending a couple of FBI training classes and therapy sessions with Dr. Ledbrinker. Evenings and weekends were free. The reduced hours concerned me at first. Trig warned me that the assessment and therapy work I would be doing would probably be more taxing than I expected. He and Dr. Ledbrinker were open to revising my schedule as I could tolerate it. For now, they wanted to error on the side of being too conservative. Only a couple of weeks removed from trying to commit suicide, I saw the prudence in their approach.

"Are you ready for your first assessment session?" Trig asked after I had polished off breakfast.

"Lead the way," I responded.

We exited the chow hall and went to a different building from where my FBI Academy training classes were held. There, Trig introduced me to Dr. Lara Winsted, who would be coordinating my assessment process.

Dr. Lara Winsted, an internal medicine physician, had joined the FBI five years ago after practicing medicine for 20 years at Walter Reed Army Medical Center. Dr. Winsted was the Chief Research Officer at the FBI Academy and, in addition to an uncommon eye for detail, was known for a disciplined thoroughness. A thoroughness, as I was to learn, that could be exhausting, not for her, but for her research subjects.

My first impression of Dr. Winsted was her intensity. Everything about her physically and behaviorally screamed a no-nonsense, don't bother me, let's get down to business approach to her work. Even the limited amount of time Trig took to greet Dr. Winsted and introduce us seemed to strain her limits for chit-chat. Before I knew it, Dr. Winsted had whisked me into a room, sat me in a comfortable recliner, and left the room. Leaving her assistant to apologize for her less than cordial bedside manner, or should I say recliner-side manner?

"Don't take it personally. Dr. Winsted is always like that. She's a brilliant physician and researcher. You're in good hands with her, but she's about as sociable as that chair you're sitting in. I'm Amanda, Dr. Winsted's assistant."

"Nice to meet you, Amanda. And thanks, I was beginning to wonder what I did to piss her off."

"Believe me, it has nothing to do with you and everything to do with her single-minded focus on your assessment. I have worked for Dr. Winsted for 10 years and came over here with her from Walter Reed. I'm a Nurse Practitioner. Let's just say that what Dr. Winsted may lack in sociability, I have in spades. So, you will be seeing and dealing with me most of the time."

"So, how are you and Dr. Winsted going to assess me?"

"Well, first, I am going to do a full history and physical on you. We want to get a baseline of your physical health and vitals before we begin any tests. After that, you're going to tell me all about your unique powers. I've been briefed on them by Special Agent Halvorsen, but I need to understand them from your perspective and experiences. Then, Dr. Winsted and I will design tests to better understand your powers and your ability to control them."

After completing a health history form, Amanda examined me from head to toe. She had me strip and put on a hospital gown for her exam. When she saw I was still wearing my butterfly pendant necklace, she asked me to remove it.

"That's really a pretty necklace, but I'm afraid I'm going to have to ask you to take it off."

I hadn't had the necklace off since Heather's mother had put it on me, and something about the thought of removing it felt wrong. Amanda recognized my hesitation.

"I'm sorry, Aja. I can see that the necklace is important to you. I guess I can work around it. Just don't tell Dr. Winsted. OK?"

"OK," I said, relieved.

After Amanda completed my physical exam, a lab technician drew blood and had me provide a urine sample. Amanda subsequently hooked me up to a couple of different devices that produced a bunch of numbers and squiggly lines that seemed to make sense to her. Since she wasn't reacting in shock, I took it to mean there was nothing seriously amiss. I have had physicals before and obstetric exams as well, but I never felt as thoroughly poked, prodded, and hooked up to machinery as with this exam.

"Do all trainees get such a thorough exam?" I asked.

"Honey, this is the basic exam. A thorough exam would take 2 to 3 days to complete. And yes, all trainees get a basic exam before they start the more rigorous physical training in the last half of their academy training. So you're ahead of the game."

For the last two hours, Amanda asked me to tell her about every instance of experiencing my signal and powers that I could remember. From Joey to the man that had brutalized Amber Lane in the hotel supply closet. What was different about this retelling was that Amanda was taking notes and asking questions about each one. Questions that I didn't necessarily understand the purpose of and many I couldn't answer, like what I had to eat or drink before experiencing the signal. Was I having my period when I experienced the signal? What other significant events may I have experienced the 24-hours before the signal? What was I thinking about just before I experienced the signal? She also tried to plumb my thoughts and feelings immediately after each signal. Here I thought I was a master in over-thinking, and Amanda was quickly proving that my thinking about my signal and powers had been overly narrow. I also never thought of recording any of my experiences or thoughts afterward. If only I had kept a diary as Heather did, perhaps then I would have been able to answer more of Amanda's questions.

I left my first assessment session feeling like I had been

turned inside out. I had just enough time to grab lunch and then get to trainee classes for the next two hours. Seeing an empty seat next to Travis, I claimed it just as the instructor entered to begin class. I could tell he wanted to talk to me, and knowing he was probably wondering where I had been all morning, I wrote a message in my notebook and turned it toward him so he could read it.

"Training program changed. Only with this group 2 hours a day. TTYL"

After he had read my message, he looked at me, smiled, and seemed to relax. A few minutes later, I saw him writing something in his notebook, and he turned it towards me so I could read it.

"Thanks. I missed you. I hope everything is OK. BTW nice necklace."

I smiled at him in response, and as I thought about hazarding a quiet verbal reply, I realized that we had held our gaze a bit longer than perhaps I had intended. We both looked away at the same time towards the instructor, which is where our attention should have been. Seconds later, and in unison, we turned our heads towards each other and shared a brief glance and smile. I don't know why it felt like we had just gotten away with something wrong. It wasn't like other boys, and men hadn't expressed an appropriate affinity and concern for me. Travis's attention just felt oddly exhilarating. A feeling I had only previously experienced with Heather. Perhaps that is why it felt out of place – it felt more intimate than I expected.

After class, I found myself accepting Travis's offer to have pizza and a beer at Tony's Inn for dinner. I didn't have the heart or the time to tell him that I wasn't old enough to drink beer. One of the unofficial components of trainee orientation was sharing intel about where to go off base for food, drinks, and entertainment. From what I had learned, Tony's was the preferred restaurant/bar in town specializing in pub food and fair-priced adult beverages. The restaurant's military décor was not only appropriate for the clientele who frequented the establishment but fitting for Tony, the owner, who was a retired Marine. However, we were cautioned never to call Tony retired. To Tony and many Marines I had met, they subscribed to the once a Marine, always a Marine credo. Semper Fi, oorah!

Before I could worry about meeting Travis at Tony's Inn, I was expected for my therapy session with Dr. Ledbrinker.

"Welcome back, Aja. It's good to see you."

"Thanks, it's good to be back," I replied, taking a seat in her office.

"I thought today I would go back and catch you up on my more traditional first-day therapy topics. But before I do that, I need to know how you're doing? Have you had any more thoughts about hurting yourself?"

"No. Quite the opposite. Although last week was hard emotionally, I've come out of it feeling a renewed energy and purpose."

"That's good to hear. Just know, however, that grief has a way of sneaking back in and relapses into feelings of anger and depression are not uncommon. If and when that happens, and you don't feel you can handle it, I want you to call me, OK?"

"OK, thanks."

The rest of our session was mostly listening to Dr. Ledbrinker tell me a little about herself, the type of therapy she practices, and the goals of treatment.

"I was the first American-born in my family. The rest of my family were all born in Germany. The name Ledbrinker was thought to be bastardized from "lied," which means "song," and "brinc," which means "raised meadow" in Middle Low German. This proves that only Germans could make something as beautiful and poetic as "Song of the Meadow" sound ugly."

I laughed. After Dr. Winsted's anti-social, no-nonsense

approach that morning, I appreciated Dr. Ledbrinker's transparency and sense of humor. I subsequently learned that her classmates in medical school called her Dr. Headshrinker after she had done her psychiatry rotation. Ledbrinker, headshrinker, now that was even funnier.

Although my session with Dr. Ledbrinker had not demanded much of me in the way of sharing, it nonetheless felt therapeutic.

I had two hours to kill before I was to meet Travis for dinner and decided to take a shower. I realized halfway through putting on my makeup and selecting what I wanted to wear that I was suffering from a combination of nervous excitement and dread. When I tried on my fourth different outfit, I realized that I was inordinately concerned about my appearance. I had never experienced this clothes-changing affliction before. I had certainly seen it and been called into such decision-making dilemmas when Misty was toiling over and preparing for her dates. As a young woman whose only romantic relationship had been with another young woman, I was treading in foreign territory. On top of this, I had no idea what I should say to Travis about what I was doing in the FBI training program. Do I lie about my age? Do I avoid talking about the unique talents and experiences that brought me here? And if so, what does that leave me to talk about? Maybe I should just call Travis and tell him I can't make it tonight. With the clock now seeming to be working against me, I called Trig.

"Hi, Aja. How was your first day back?" Trig answered.

"It was good, but it's not over, and I don't know what to do."

"What to do about what?" Trig asked, confused by my cryptic comment.

"I'm kinda embarrassed to have to call you about this."

"Well, is it something someone else can give you advice on? Dr. Ledbrinker, for example?"

"No. Well, yes, I'd be comfortable talking with her, but I really need to talk to you. It's about what I can and cannot say to my classmates."

"Let me guess. Travis has asked you out."

"How in the hell did you know that?" I blurted out and then felt embarrassed even more.

"Because after I dropped you off at Dr. Winsted's this morning, I ran into him, and he asked me if it was alright if he asked you out to dinner."

"Oh, so you haven't implanted surveillance chips in all of us."

"No, but that's a good idea. Thanks, I'll start working on that," he joked.

"And what did you tell him about me?" I asked, now nervous about what he may have divulged to Travis.

"Nothing. I just told him it was fine to ask you out. So I'm assuming you must have accepted his invitation?"

"I did, but now I don't know what I can and cannot say to him."

"I would definitely recommend not talking about any sensitive intel you might have on North Korea," he said in a serious tone.

"I don't have any sensitive intel on North Korea," I replied, wondering why he would think that I did.

"That's good. I see you've already practiced your responses," he replied, laughing to tip me off that he was pulling my leg.

"Always the comedian," I replied. "But I'm serious, Trig."

"I'm sorry. I know you are, and you should feel free to tell Travis whatever you're comfortable telling him. Once you're assigned to specific cases, then it is best to avoid talking about them, but for now, you're both FBI trainees. You both have special skills, and you both need some normalcy in your lives. Go out and have fun, but not too much fun."

"Thanks, Trig. I feel better now."

"Happy to be of assistance. Oh, and get the Cajun Fries. They're awesome."

I felt significantly more comfortable after my call with Trig. Finally, I decided that anything other than casual jeans and a t-shirt combo would probably be overkill. I also didn't want to have Travis think I was trying to attract anything beyond just a friendly dinner together. Not that I could really flaunt my womanly qualities. Even if I wore a blouse, I didn't have cleavage to speak of. And judging by how loosely my jeans fit me from my recent weight loss, that nice ass bleacher boy said I had, was no longer tantalizingly straining the denim as it had in the past. Hell, I wasn't even comfortable yet with the idea that I was going out with a guy.

As I was making my way to Tony's, I started feeling anxious. What if I made Travis sick or worse, he touches me and runs from me in pain? He had never triggered my signal before, but I was at a point where my signals and powers felt less consistent, less reliable. It wasn't long before I got the answer.

Travis was waiting for me outside of Tony's. As we greeted each other, he opened the door with one hand and instinctively or purposefully put his other hand on my upper back as if I needed guidance to navigate the entryway. I realize this was probably just a quaint gentlemanly behavior that might have irritated me, given other circumstances. However, I was more concerned about whether I'd prove toxic to him. So far, so good. He touched me and made it into the restaurant unscathed. When he pulled my chair out at the table, I knew he had probably been conditioned to be a gentleman by his parents. I liked it because I knew I would rather tolerate someone's overly proper behavior than endure or try to change some slob's boorish behavior.

I didn't like Lydia, our server, from the outset. It wasn't her impressive bosom or the way she chose to give them room to breathe by failing to button the top two buttons of her blouse. It wasn't even her overdone make-up that made her look like she was trying to channel a Kabuki mask. It was the way she looked at me like I had no business being there, and least of all, being there with Travis.

Travis was a handsome guy. At 5 foot 8, he wasn't tall, but next to me, he was plenty tall enough. His brown hair always looked messy but somehow perfectly coiffed. But it was his warm brown eyes and boyish grin bracketed by parenthetical dimples that seemed to automatically coax from me a war between maternal and carnal responses. Something in his face seemed to hint that he was deviously cooking up something wonderfully mischievous that you wouldn't want to miss or may even want to participate in.

Lydia gladly took Travis' order for a beer and bearly tolerated having to take my request for an iced tea.

"Is that a Long Island Iced Tea?" she asked in response to my order. I could almost see her salivating to ask for my ID so she could blow the lid off of the fact I was not of drinking age.

"No, thanks. Just a regular iced tea," I replied to Lydia's chagrin.

"I'll be right back with your beer, hun," she said to Travis in such a sugary sweet tone I feared it might cause him tooth decay.

He either didn't notice Lydia's obvious flirtatious response or was too much of a gentleman to respond.

"I hear the Cajun Fries are good here," Travis stated as we both picked up the menus Lydia had left us.

"Mmm, that sounds good. Let's get some," I replied while chuckling silently inside, knowing the source of his information.

After we perused the menu and chit-chatted about what looked good, Travis put down his menu and asked the inevitable question. A question that I was now prepared to answer, thanks to Trig's advice.

"So we missed you last week," he started making it sound like he was talking for the whole class even though I knew that wasn't the case. "Your note said they changed your training program. Was that why you were gone?"

"No, a close friend of mine died last week. I went back to New Jersey for her funeral," I replied, which was only half the truth. I wasn't prepared to hit him with my suicide attempt right out of the box.

"Oh, I'm sorry to hear that. How did she die? If you don't mind my asking."

"She was raped and murdered," I replied as I fought back the tears.

"Oh my God, that's horrible. We don't have to talk about it. I can see I've upset you. I'm sorry."

"No, that's OK. It's good for me to talk about it," I replied, which I said more on faith than from practical experience in dealing with grief. "That's where I got this necklace," I said, touching the butterfly pendant reflexively.

"Yeah, I noticed that. It's beautiful. How did you know each other?" he asked, opening the door for me to continue to talk about Heather even though I could feel a lump forming in my throat.

Fortunately, or unfortunately, I don't know which, Lydia reappeared with our drinks, short-circuiting our conversation.

"Here you go, hun," she cooed. Putting Travis' beer down in front of him and then unceremoniously setting my glass of iced tea down in my general vicinity without a word.

"Are you ready to order?" she said, pointing in his direction in more ways than one.

Instead of responding to Lydia, Travis looked up at me and asked me a question.

"Are you ready to order, babe?" he said matter-of-factly, which threw me until I realized what he was doing.

"I am, thanks, hun," I replied.

The look on Lydia's face was priceless. A mixture of indignation and embarrassment. Travis' intervention magically transformed me from unwanted ugly duckling to royalty in Lydia's eyes.

"What can I get you, hun?" Lydia asked, turning her syrupy and fake sweetness on me.

"I'll take the bacon cheeseburger, cooked medium, please. We'd also like to share an order of Cajun Fries. And I'd like a Garden Salad with Ranch on the side, please. Thank you," I finished and handed her my menu.

"Good choices. I'll be happy to get that for you," she said through a fake smile that may have fooled some people but not me.

Lydia then took Travis's order without any flirtatious accompaniments. Walking off in a manner befitting a dog that slinks away with its tail between its legs.

When she was out of sight and earshot, Travis and I shared a good laugh.

"How did you know to do that?" I asked.

"It's not the first time I've run into a catty female server. Let's just say I've learned through trial and error. I'm glad you picked up on what I was doing. I was worried you might think I was presumptuous."

"Well, there was a second there when I was thinking about throwing my iced tea at you, but then I saw the expression on Lydia's face and couldn't resist rubbing it in even more."

"You did great. I especially liked it when you said we

wanted to share the Cajun Fries. Nice touch."

"Thanks, but I couldn't have done it without you, hun," which set us off on another round of laughter.

We never did get back to discussing how I had met Heather and all the reasons for my week-long absence, but we did talk about the change in my program. I told him that I was being groomed to focus on child abuse and exploitation, and that is why I was on a different track from the typical FBI Agent Training. I didn't divulge my unique aptitude and powers, thinking that, like my suicide attempt, that might be a bit too much for Travis to digest. He asked about my name, and I obliged by telling him the story. I didn't ask, but he volunteered that his parents had given him his name because they were fans of country-western singers Randy Travis and Travis Tritt.

I voluntarily told him my age. He had made a point of telling me he was 26, and I knew he was too much of a gentleman to ask me my age. It would have felt awkward withholding the information.

"I'll be 18 in November," I said, looking intently at his face for any sign of an adverse reaction. There was none.

"I knew there was something special about you. Other than your stunning looks, I mean," he said and then blushed.

He looked so cute and vulnerable at that moment. I felt a shiver work its way through me, triggering a physical response I hadn't felt since Heather and my first intimate encounter. Given my insecurities, I did what I usually did when people complimented my appearance. I tried to say something funny and self-deprecating.

"I see they accepted you into the FBI Training program even with the obvious deficits in your vision."

Travis laughed, recovered from his embarrassment, and then seemed to be worried that he may have made me feel uncomfortable.

"I'm sorry if I embarrassed you by what I said, but my vision happens to be 20/20. Don't get me wrong, Aja. I'm not so shallow as to call you special just because of your looks. I saw how special you were in the first week of training. You were killing it, and I knew you couldn't have been anywhere near the FBI's minimum age requirement."

"Thanks, Travis," I replied as it was now my turn to blush.

Lydia interrupted to give Travis the bill. I couldn't fault her. We had given her the impression that we were a couple, and there was still a male bias when it came to paying for a date. I offered to pay half, but Travis wouldn't hear of it. He deferred to the "I-asked-you-out-so-I-pay" rationale, and I wasn't about to argue with him.

We got up from our table, and he once again opened the door for me upon our exit. But this time, his hand on my back made me tingle. If it made him feel anything, I didn't notice. We had arrived in separate vehicles, which at the time felt comfortable and appropriate. Having to take different cars now, however, felt unnatural, at least to me. I didn't dare voice my desires. Frankly, I couldn't even remember ever having such desires for a boy or, in this case, a man.

He walked me to my car, and I thanked him for dinner. The moment was pregnant with unanswered questions. What was each of us was feeling, what did each of us expect, and what was the appropriate farewell gesture. Travis saved the moment from awkwardness, took the initiative, and enveloped me in a hug. While holding me, he thanked me for the fun time and completed the hug with a sweet, simple kiss on my cheek. A kiss on my star-shaped scar, to be exact. And then he was on his way, and I stood there fumbling for my keys and feeling somehow like my whole world had just changed.

CHAPTER 29

Riding an Emotional Rollercoaster

L et me be the first to attest that you can feel hungover without having had a drop of alcohol the previous night. That's how I felt the morning after my dinner date with Travis.

No, not the kind of hangover from love-drunk giddiness about a new relationship. You know what I'm talking about. That unrealistic perception of the flawless partner in a perfect relationship, and you drive your friends crazy talking about him and posting on your social media page ad nauseam. "In a Relationship with fill in the blank." Gag me. We've all seen that before. And then you wait two or three weeks for the inevitable transformation of that Mr. or Ms. Perfect into some execrable spawn that doesn't deserve to breathe on this earth.

No, that wasn't my hangover. My hangover was more like, "Who the fuck am I?" Sorry for the vulgarity, but using any other term would fail to convey the total sense of wonderment I had about my identity as a person. Here I was on the dawn of my adulthood, and everything about me seemed to be all catawampus. My powers had changed to the point that I couldn't rightfully know what they were or whether I could rely on them. And here I was, a young, presumably gay woman, now having romantic notions about Travis. To say I was feeling at loose ends would have been an understatement. I guess my only salvation was that I now had daily therapy sessions with a psychiatrist.

I skipped breakfast, not ready for that day after the first-date interaction with Travis. I would see him soon enough in class, an environment that gave us limited opportunities to interact. Amanda greeted me as I arrived for the second day of my assessment. After telling me that my lab results looked good, she took me to the same room I had been in the day before. Once again, she hooked me up to all the monitoring equipment.

"How are you feeling today, Aja?" Amanda asked after she had confirmed the monitoring equipment was transmitting my squiggly lines.

"I'm good," I lied, thinking I'd save my identity crisis conversation for Dr. Headshrinker.

"Hmm, that's funny," Amanda commented. "My machines are telling me a different story. It appears you may be feeling some stress."

Shit. I may have a poker face, but I guess my squiggly lines gave me away.

"Yeah, I guess I'm a little nervous about this whole assessment process," I lied again, but with what I thought was a perfectly reasonable excuse.

"That's understandable, but you really have nothing to worry about. This assessment process is going to help you understand yourself and your powers better. And that's a good thing. Right?"

"Yeah, I guess so," I answered. Not wanting to agree emphatically, just in case my squiggly lines told her I was still experiencing some stress, which I was, only not as a result of the assessment process.

Amanda proceeded to tell me that I would undergo two

tests. The first would be a test to see if visual cues produced any signal or response. The second, a test she said she couldn't tell me about without potentially biasing me and the results.

For the first test, Amanda had me scroll through images of mug shots on a computer. My job was to note any image that triggered any signal and write down the details of my response. Twenty minutes and about 200 images into the test, I was convinced that looking at mug shots was not going to trigger anything. I actually felt like I had lost my powers because not even the images of the most ominous and depraved-looking individuals produced any signal.

Just when I was almost convinced this test was a failure, I clicked to another image. I was immediately transported to a dark, dank basement where a young girl was bound naked to a chair. She was blindfolded, and her mouth was held open with one of those devices dentists use. Similarly, I felt like my arms and legs felt bound and an ache in both sides of my jaw, as if I had been forced to hold my mouth open too long. Then I saw the man from the mug shot come into the picture, and he started to fondle the girl. I felt his hands and fingers on and in me as he continued to caress and probe the little girl. Then he unzipped his pants, straddled the chair, and, while stroking his swollen member, inserted it into the girl's mouth, which promptly made me feel like I was gagging. I started breathing desperately through my nose only to have the image and the feelings fade, returning to the assessment room to see Amanda standing by the computer. She had advanced the picture on the computer to the next image.

"What happened?" I said, surprised to see her in the room.

"That's what I want to know," she replied. "All your vitals went off-the-charts, and when I called your name, you didn't respond. I thought I was going to have to call the medical team."

I told her what I had experienced, and she recorded the details on the paper she had given me.

"How are you feeling now?" Amanda asked.

"I'm fine. Now that I know what I was experiencing wasn't real."

"Was what you were experiencing like any of your previous incidents?"

"I guess it was most similar to when I walked into Hugh Jinks' office."

"Any differences?"

"Yes. When I was in Hugh Jinks' office, it only felt like he was assaulting me. I didn't see anyone else. This was like watching a movie and feeling everything he did to that girl at the same time. I also fried Mr. Jinks' organs. I don't know what I did, if anything, to this guy."

If Amanda was concerned about the guy's welfare, she didn't let on. Instead, she just asked me if I was up to looking at about 150 more mug shots.

"I guess," I said noncommittedly.

"What's your concern, Aja,"

"No concerns. I just don't feel like I'm very good at this. One signal after all of those pictures?"

"Try not to think of this as a pass/fail exam, Aja. Just try to relax and let what happens happen. I'll be here if you have another experience like you just had, OK?"

"OK."

Amanda left the room, and I started to scroll through the images again. After a few minutes of nothing, I was surprised to see a familiar face – Ms. Merkinson. I once again experienced a vision, but this time, all I could see was a well-dressed man in a business suit sitting in the back of a limousine perusing a laminated menu card from a restaurant that looked to have a French name. Although I didn't see anything other than this,

I felt sick beyond anything I had ever felt in real life. It was the flu or food poisoning on steroids. My stomach was about to give up its contents, my head actually felt like it was splitting in two, and I wasn't just feverish. I was burning up. Once again, I came back to reality to find Amanda standing next to me with a different image on the computer screen. Once again, she religiously recorded the details of my experience. This time, however, Amanda announced that the test was over.

"How did I do?" I asked. Still wondering what it all meant and somewhat worried that having only two signals when I had looked at over 300 mug shots was a disappointing performance.

"I'll review the results with Dr. Winsted, and we will let you know later. I know that may be frustrating, but we don't want to bias you with any findings at this point."

"I understand, and you're right. It is frustrating," I remarked, forcing a smile.

"Ready for test number two?"

"Do I have a choice?"

"Well, yes, you actually do. This is all voluntary. If you're not feeling up to it, that's fine. We can postpone the test until a time you're feeling ready."

"No, I'm ready," I responded, not wanting to delay the assessment process.

"Alright, this test will be easy. All you need to do is sit in your chair and relax. The computer will periodically show a TV program or play music. When it does, all you need to do is watch the show or listen to music. When there's no TV program or music, all I ask is that you stay seated."

"That's it?"

"That's it. This test will take up to an hour."

Amanda checked that all my monitoring equipment was still transmitting and left the room. For the first 5 minutes, I just sat in the chair, staring at the computer monitor, wondering when the TV program or music would come on. Then my mind began to wander, and I revisited my night with Travis at Tony's. How he deftly put Lydia in her place. How much we laughed. How knowing my age hadn't deterred him from treating me as an equal. I had smiled so much at dinner that my cheeks actually hurt when I got home. And, of course, I thought about the hug and his tender kiss.

My reverie was unceremoniously interrupted when the computer monitor came to life. I wasn't prepared for what happened next, but I knew that Trig must have had a hand in it. The familiar theme song that opens with a snare drum march transported me almost immediately to my grandfather's house, where we would watch Hogan's Heroes. When the theme song got to John Banner, the actor who played Schultz, I couldn't help but smile and then got a bit weepy. I missed my grandfather, who was now in a locked memory care unit. He no longer recognized any of his family members, let alone me. As a tear fell from my cheek, my sadness was suddenly interrupted by a horrific vision. Stopping my tears in their tracks.

I couldn't and didn't want to comprehend what I saw. Even though I closed my eyes and turned my head away from what I was seeing, I kept on seeing it. Worse, I started to feel the cold and suffocating discomfort that the dozens of shivering, scantily clad Asian girls must have felt. They appeared trapped in some kind of metal container, freezing and gasping for oxygen. Several girls were obviously dead and had literally been stacked in a corner to afford the remaining girls some space. It smelled like death, and I wasn't getting enough air. I clutched desperately at my throat. As if the reason for my asphyxiation was that I had forgotten how to breathe. Then, as quickly as the vision had come on, it was gone, and I was staring up at Amanda again.

"Are you back?" she asked, placing her hand gently on my

arm.

"I think so," I responded less than convincingly as I was still trying to evacuate the sight and smell of that gruesome tomb from my senses. Feeling Amanda's warm hand on my arm only prolonged the feeling that I was still cold.

"Take your time," Amanda said reassuringly.

After a minute, I felt back to normal. Even if someone who is obviously not normal has such a state of being.

"Aren't you worried I'm going to start associating all these events with you?" I asked, now having "woken up" from my visions to see Amanda looking at me with concern.

"I'm counting on it," she laughed. "Better it's me you imagine seeing after such horrifying experiences rather than me causing you to have terrifying experiences. I'm not the trigger for your events."

"What is then?"

"That is what we are trying to understand, and today's sessions have been fascinating."

"When are you going to tell me what you've learned? I'm more than a little interested in figuring this out." I asked impatiently.

"I know you are, and we will talk to you in time. Drawing any conclusions from this small sample would be unscientific. Telling you what we think we've found could change how you respond to future stimuli we present in our assessment."

"Science sucks."

"Only until it doesn't, Aja. I promise we will talk with you as soon as we are reasonably certain that our conclusions are sound. The last thing we want to do is mislead you. That would not only delay your understanding of your powers but cause you to mistrust us. You did good work today."

"Aren't we going to finish this test? You said it was going to take an hour."

"It's finished, and I said it would take up to an hour."

"Sneaky," I said.

"Science," Amanda replied, smiling.

I couldn't help but smile back.

My assessment session may have ended a bit early. However, having experienced three rather head-splitting, stomach-churning, soul-sucking visions had exhausted me emotionally. More out of habit than hunger, I went to the chow hall for lunch. I put a few things on my tray and sat at what I now considered "my booth," picking at more than eating the food.

"Mind if I join you?" a familiar voice asked, surprising me out of a trance. I looked up to see Travis standing there with a full lunch tray.

"Be my guest," I replied after a beat as I refocused my brain to the present.

"Sorry to interrupt you. You looked deep in thought," Travis responded as he slid into the booth across from me.

"Oh, no problem. I just had a very interesting morning."

"Oh, yeah? That's more than I can say about mine. Tell me about it."

"Umm, I'd rather not. I have nothing against you, but I'm just not up for reliving it right now. Maybe some other time?" I replied, not wanting to convey I didn't trust confiding in him.

"That's fair," he responded as he dug into his lunch with vigor while I kept moving my food around on my plate.

After a minute, Travis stopped eating long enough to address my continued silence.

"Is everything OK, Aja? Is it something I did or didn't do?"

"No, Travis. Yesterday was great, but this morning was pretty exhausting. Don't take it personally."

"OK, I'll try not to. I really enjoyed our time together last night. Thank you."

"I did too, Travis. And thank you for inviting me out," I replied, seeing that he still needed additional affirmation that he wasn't the cause of my current mood.

"If you're not too tired later today, do you want to go for a run?" he asked.

His questions made me think about Heather. I paused, and the memory caused me to delay my response long enough to prompt Travis to fill the void and make a follow-up statement.

"It's OK if you don't want to. I just need to build my endurance. Our last timed training run kicked my ass."

"That sounds good," I replied, recognizing that I was banking on finding the will to do it over the next few hours. "What time were you thinking?"

"I'm done with classes at 4, so maybe 4:30?"

My therapy session with Dr. Ledbrinker ended at 4:30, so I proposed a friendly amendment.

"How about 5? I'm not done until 4:30."

"Five it is. Meet you at the trailhead?"

"It's a date," I replied, trying to sound enthusiastic and throwing him a bone as I felt I had been less than a pleasant lunch companion to that point.

"Thanks, Aja," he said and went back to eating, finishing the remains of his lunch.

After lunch, we walked to class and sat next to each other. Midway through the two-hour class, I realized that the cloud I felt that morning had lifted. Now I felt pent-up energy that begged for the release of a run.

I entered Dr. Ledbrinker's office more focused on getting to my run with Travis than doing the work of therapy. Dr. Ledbrinker didn't let me slide as I had hoped. She immediately attacked a soft spot – my feelings about not being able to save Heather. This had been the impetus for my suicide attempt, and she correctly determined that I needed to deal with those feelings more definitively than just trying to suppress them.

I was ill-prepared for her probing questions, and before long, instead of visions of running energetically through the woods with Travis dancing through my head, I felt like I was crumbling like a skyscraper imploding from a thousand dynamite explosions. Unlike a building, however, mine was not a controlled demolition. My demolition felt very out of control. I didn't have any answers to Dr. Ledbrinker's questions, and if she had any answers, she wasn't giving them up. I seemed to only have two options: curl up and die or blow up in anger and frustration. I chose the latter, and what came out shocked me more than it apparently did Dr. Ledbrinker.

"Stop asking me your stupid, fucking questions," I screamed. "You're always trying to control me and tell me what to do. It's my life, not yours. Just leave me the fuck alone."

I was expecting shock, indignation, or a reprimand in response, but instead, I got something unexpected.

"Who are you yelling at right now, Aja?" Dr. Ledbrinker asked in an infuriatingly calm voice and demeanor.

"You, you fuck," I said, pissed off that I hadn't succeeded in pissing her off.

"Are you sure?" she responded.

I was about to jump out of my seat and throttle her. However, her insistence caused me to pause just long enough to realize that I wasn't yelling at her. I surrendered to her question.

"No, I'm not," I said as I felt tears about to replace my anger. "I think I'm yelling at my mother, not you."

"And why do you think that?"

"Because nothing I ever did was good enough. She was always trying to get me to do things I didn't want to do. Every time I took the initiative to do something or had an idea, she would have a negative comeback. A reason why my initiative or idea might fail."

"What does that have to do with your feelings about not saving Heather?"

That one stopped me in my tracks as I searched for an answer. Then, in horror, I had to wrestle with a possible explanation.

"Because maybe my mother was right. I failed. Heather's dead, and it's all my fault," I sobbed.

After allowing me to cry for a minute in silence, Dr. Ledbrinker intervened.

"We all fail, Aja. And you didn't kill Heather."

"But I didn't save her," I blurted, as renewed tears filled my eyes, and I completely ignored her comment about everyone failing. "If I had been there, she wouldn't have died. I was too far away."

"Do you really know that, Aja?"

"No, but," I started but couldn't find words beyond that.

"I know Heather was very special to you. If she could, do you think she would be blaming you right now?"

"No."

"What would she want you to do?"

"She'd want me to find the person that killed her. She'd want me to avenge her death."

"And?"

I looked at her, confused.

"What else would she want you to do?" Dr. Ledbrinker clarified.

"She'd want me to be strong and believe in myself."

"And what about your mother? What do you think she wants for you?" Dr. Ledbrinker shifted gears on me.

At first, the question threw me, and I wasn't sure. Then, as I thought about it, I realized that I knew precisely what my mother would want.

"She would want exactly the same. She'd just deliver the message differently."

"How so?" Dr. Ledbrinker prompted me to go on.

"She'd probably couch her wish for me to be strong and believe in myself. In between warnings about the dangers of being too over-confident or going off on my own crusade without proper support or back-up."

I suddenly realized that what I had perceived as my mother's effort to control me was not that at all. Instead, out of an abundance of love and concern, my mother had always presented me with alternatives. She knew that my nature was to go after the bright, shiny object that was foremost in my view and not necessarily take time to consider and weigh all my options. I was brash and spontaneous, while she was cautious and deliberate. She was the yin to my yang. No wonder there was always some tension between us in the balance. I had gained a whole new perspective and now felt ashamed that I had misjudged my mother.

"So, what are you going to do?" Dr. Ledbrinker asked.

"Call my mother tonight and apologize to her," I replied.

Before Dr. Ledbrinker could ask me to elaborate, I told her about the insight I had gained from her questions. How I had misjudged my mother's communications and intentions.

"You've done some good work today, Aja. How are you feeling now?"

"Other than anxious to speak to my mother and embarrassed by how I yelled at you, I'm feeling more together than I did 15 or 20 minutes ago."

"That's great. Don't be embarrassed about yelling at me. That's part of the therapeutic process. Aiming your emotions or thoughts at me is called transference. It frequently happens in therapy, and as you just experienced, it can lead to great insights."

"OK, but I'm still sorry."

"Apology accepted. Anything else you'd like to talk about before we end our session?"

"No, I'm good, Dr. Ledbrinker. Thank you."

I left her office with a definitive plan for the rest of my day - run with Travis, grab dinner, call my mother. Well, you know what they say about best-laid plans.

When I got back to my room and was in the process of changing into my running gear, I received a text from Travis.

"Can't make our run. Sorry. Will explain later."

I responded with a sad face emoji but didn't receive a text in response. Knowing my mother wouldn't be off of work for about an hour, I decided to go on a run without Travis. I had run on the 7-mile Quantico trail before but had only made a short loop. I don't know if it was Travis' cancellation or the emotional roller-coaster ride I had experienced that day. I felt like I needed to run myself into the ground. Just blow it out until I was exhausted. I started off slow to warm up but was soon pushing a pace well beyond my comfort zone.

The trail was moderately challenging, with a few elevations that got my lungs and legs burning. I wanted to feel that pain and discomfort, and instead of slowing down or stopping, I pressed on. At one point, I felt tears mix with the sweat rolling down my face. I felt Heather with me. Perhaps it was the butterfly pendant that was gently bouncing off my chest to the rhythm of my footfalls. Maybe it was that I was in a wooded area, probably similar to the area in which Heather was found.

Or perhaps it was that I missed her striding next to me. Whatever it was, I reached the end of the 7-mile loop well before I expected. Part of it was my torrid pace. Another part of it was that my mind had distracted me from my physical pain and any concept of time.

I had accomplished my mission – utter exhaustion. I was hard-pressed just to walk back to the dorm. I showered on wobbly legs, a combination of my run and not having had a substantial meal all day. Drying myself off was the last thing I had sufficient energy to accomplish. Naked, I laid down on my bed for a minute with the intent of getting dressed, getting something to eat, and calling my mother. That minute turned into 10 hours as I didn't wake up until the next morning.

CHAPTER 30

Road Trip and Road Work

Waking up famished and having little time before my assessment session to grab breakfast, I had to make choices. I skipped a shower as I had taken one the night before and did the best I could with my hair. Then I threw on just enough make-up so as not to scare anyone and was out the door.

I sat at my customary chow hall booth and expected that Travis might join me, but he never showed. I hadn't received any additional texts from him after he backed out of our run. I began wondering if maybe he was having second thoughts. Or perhaps I had read too much into our "date." I mean, he was almost 9 years older than me. Maybe he felt more like an older brother who needed to protect me. But then there was that kiss on my cheek. What did that mean? I didn't have time to torture myself very long with these thoughts. While I expected I would see him in class, I decided to shoot him a friendly text before I headed off to my assessment session.

My assessment session ended up being more like a road trip than sitting in a room connected to monitoring equipment. Amanda led me to a couple places on base and a few places off base and asked me to describe any thoughts or feelings these places spurred. For the most part, nothing of any great significance struck me. I did report feeling some uneasiness when we walked through a food storage room at a local high school. It was nothing specific, just a claustrophobic feeling. It could have been entirely due to the room, which in actuality was quite cramped with narrow rows between shelving and food-stuffs stacked from floor to ceiling and no windows. I fought off feelings about not performing well in the assessment. I also was thinking about what findings of significance Amanda could have gleaned from our session. Still, I knew better than to ask her, knowing she would pull out the trump card of pre-serving scientific objectivity.

Amanda and I grabbed lunch at a pizza place in town be-fore she drove me back to base for my afternoon class. When I entered the classroom, Travis wasn't in his customary seat. Thinking that maybe he was running late, I took the seat next to where he usually sat.

When the instructor strolled in, I began to worry. I checked my phone, but there were no texts from Travis. I quickly shot him a text, asking if he was coming to class. When I didn't get a response, it only amped up my concern. I found it hard to concentrate on what the instructor was say-ing, as my mind whirred around all the potential causes of Travis' absence. Was he sick? Did his program get changed as mine had? Did he drop out of the program? Was he dead? It's amazing how my mind could so quickly go to the worst pos-sible outcomes and hold me there without a shred of evidence. I mean, why couldn't my brain go to reasons like his phone died or he lost it. Maybe he had a perfectly innocent reason for missing class. And would I have necessarily felt obligated to tell him if I were going to miss a class? Probably, but that's be-cause I thought that maybe there was a thing between us. Per-haps he didn't feel that we had a "thing."

Long story short, I didn't get much out of class that day. However, my concerns about Travis certainly provided fodder for my therapy session. I didn't divulge Travis's name to Dr.

Ledbrinker. I just told her I was worried about a friend from class. She did drag out of me that it was a male friend and that he had taken me out to dinner. Our whole session revolved around communication and expectations in relationships and how these two things either build or destroy trust. It was good from a theoretical standpoint, but it didn't get me any closer to what the hell happened with Travis over the last 24 hours. I left therapy and, failing yet again by text to get a response from Travis, considered going to Trig to convey my concerns. Instead, I decided to go on a run. Not a race to exhaustion like the day before, just a nice, comfortable stride through the woods to hopefully gain some perspective. Or maybe just to get a shot of endorphins to make me feel better for the moment.

I succeeded in getting my runner's high but failed to push my concerns about Travis from the forefront of my brain. Cooling down on my walk back to the dorm, I fortuitously ran into Trig.

"Hi there, superstar. How was your run?" he greeted, correctly guessing my previous activity by my attire and sweat.

"Hi, Trig. It was good, but I have something that's bothering me."

"What's that?"

"I haven't heard from or seen Travis in the last 24 hours."

"He didn't tell you?" Trig asked, sounding somewhat shocked.

"No, he didn't," I replied, sounding more hurt and irritated than I had meant to convey.

"Well, I think he'll be OK with me telling you. He had a family emergency and had to go back to Wisconsin."

"Do you know what kind of an emergency?"

"Apparently, his Dad is in the hospital, but I don't know any more than that."

"Thanks, I wish he had told me. I've texted him like a half-dozen times."

"All I know is that he was in a rush to catch a flight last night. I'm sure he'll be in touch with you. He cares about you."

I looked at him, disbelievingly, "How do you know that?" I asked.

"He told me."

"When?" I blurted.

"Before he left."

"So, after our dinner together."

"Yes. Why do you sound like you doubt me?"

"I'm sorry, my mind has been bouncing all over the place since that night. I didn't know what to think."

"Well, he likes you, and hopefully, he'll be in touch soon. Relax."

"Easier said than done for me!" I exclaimed.

"I see that. Maybe you need to make another loop on the trail."

"No, I'll be alright. Now that I know why he's not here."

"I know it's only been a few days, but how do you feel your new program is going?"

"It's fine. I like Amanda, and my sessions with Dr. Ledbrinker have given me some insight. Still, it's frustrating not knowing how I'm doing in the assessment portion."

"Well, stick to it. In a month or two, I hope to assign you to work on a case with an experienced field agent."

"Really?"

"Really. The ability to translate what you learn here into practical skills in the field is not something every trainee can do. We've had trainees who have been excellent in the academic and simulated portions of training only to fail miserably when they got into real-world situations. I don't expect it will be a problem for you."

"That's sounds great. I'm looking forward to it."

"Not as much as I am, Aja. You doing alright otherwise?" he asked. Which I presumed was a veiled way of asking me whether I had moved on from the state of mind that prompted my depression and suicide attempt.

"Yes, life is good otherwise," I replied and then recalled something from one of my prior assessment sessions.

"I especially like that I get to watch episodes of Hogan's Heroes during my assessment."

"Huh, I wonder who approved that?"

"Yeah, I wonder," I said facetiously as he broke into a broad grin.

We parted ways, and I had a little extra spring in my step from our interaction. Not only did Trig help me solve the mystery of Travis's absence, but he had dangled a carrot in front of me – the promise of doing real fieldwork.

CHAPTER 31

Hurry Up and Wait

It was a few days after running into Trig when I finally received a text from Travis in response to the half-dozen I had sent him. By then, I had pretty much conceded that my level of concern for his welfare far exceeded his need to provide me with reassurance. In short, I had ceased to expend emotional capital on him and transferred that energy into my training. Nonetheless, when I received his text, I felt for him.

"Sorry, Aja. My father died. I'm needed at home and won't be back. I hope we can still stay in touch."

The proper thing, an easier thing to do in retrospect, would have been just to call him. Some things really require more than the immediacy but impersonal nature of a text. For a variety of reasons, I chose not to call him. Instead, I toiled for twenty or thirty minutes over what to text back, finally settling on the following.

"Sorry about your Dad and that you won't be back. Take care, Travis."

In addition to the half a dozen versions I revised, I toiled over whether to include a version of a sad or crying face emoji. Finally deciding to forego one altogether. I wanted to convey an appropriate amount of sadness for his loss. But not express too much personal pain for either his delayed response or his not coming back to the program. I also wrestled with how to convey I would miss him without coming right out and saying it. "I'll miss you," was too much. "We will miss you," or "you'll be missed," was too impersonal. Being sorry he wasn't coming back was the best I could come up with. I didn't know how to deftly respond to his hope to stay in touch. I figured that by sending him a response, it automatically meant I was open to future communication should he so desire. The other conflict I had was whether to thank him again for our "date." I decided that doing that would make the text sound too final. As if I had to get in one last expression of gratitude before we went our separate ways forever. For better or worse, I sent it.

I didn't know how to interpret it when I didn't receive a response to my text. In the past, I could have easily lost sleep over such an event. But I had turned over a new leaf. I was focused on myself. How I felt about myself. Not based on how others might see me or think about me. I needed to be the best version of myself. I needed to find the version of me that I could live with, not the version that other people might need or want me to be. It felt selfish at first, but being true to myself, being true to what I wanted and needed, made a world of difference. I wasn't wasting time, emotional energy, or sleep on things I couldn't change or didn't need or want in the first place.

As my assessment process had progressed, more of my time was spent taking field trips than being wired up in a room. On these trips, I would wear a wireless biosensor device that monitored my vitals and transmitted them to Amanda's laptop. My job on these trips was simply to note when I felt any signals or saw any visions and then describe them so Amanda could document them for the record. Sometimes we would just drive through neighborhoods. Other times we would get out and walk through a park, a mall, or random stores. Although there were trips where I didn't get any signals, on most trips, I would experience at least one episode. On one occasion, we drove through a neighborhood in Alexandria. I received so many signals that I had difficulty distinguishing when one signal would end and another would start. It was like trying to comprehend a movie that was playing in fast forward. I was bombarded by images, and I'm sure my vitals were off the charts. It literally felt like I was being mobbed and molested by a pack of hungry sexual predators. I was overwhelmed. I couldn't even speak. Amanda must have realized it because, at the same time that I started to tap her leg in submission, she was giving the driver instructions to book it out of there. It was intense. All I wanted to do when the barrage finally stopped was sleep, which Amanda let me do after I had given her a description of what I had experienced.

The most frustrating thing about my training was waiting for Trig to meet with me about my case assignment. This frustration was followed closely by my growing ire with Amanda's continued silence about what she was learning from my assessment sessions. I woke up every day, anticipating that today would be the day Trig would speak with me about the case or my assessment findings. Only to have nothing happen. By week nine in my training, I was fit to be tied. I was sure that Trig had said he'd be assigning me to a case and an experienced field agent in a month or two, yet here I was past the two-month mark and still waiting. I was sure this could only mean something bad.

Halfway through my twenty-week training and assessment program, Trig finally met with me. We met in his office instead of our usual breakfast spot. Given this formality, my frustration level, and the anticipation of bad news, I went into the meeting fully expecting the worst. Instead, all Trig told me was that he had met with Dr. Winsted, Dr. Ledbrinker, and Amanda to review my progress, and they needed a few more weeks before they could meet with me. I think he thought that telling me this would provide me with some anticipatory excitement. It only annoyed and frustrated me more. He noticed.

"What's the matter, Aja?"

"You told me you'd be assigning me to a case in a month or two. It's been two and a half months. Why don't you tell me what I'm doing wrong now and spare me having to wait longer," I said in a tone of anger tinged with despair.

"You haven't done anything wrong, Aja. And I'm sorry, I should have talked with you earlier. The reason there's been a delay in assigning you the case is because of the complexity of the abilities you possess. Dr. Winsted and Amanda need more time to assess your powers before I put you out in the field."

"Why can't I do both? Work a case and continue my assessment."

"Because the case I want to put you on will require you to be off-base for an extended period."

"So, you already know what case I'll be working on?"

"Yes, I do. And the agent who will be mentoring you."

"Can you tell me about it?" I asked as a spark of excitement started to make inroads towards diminishing my frustration.

"I think I've learned my lesson about telling you things before I'm confident of a definitive date they'll occur," he replied with a smile.

"Oh, I promise not to get upset if it doesn't happen right away," I pleaded, now sorry that I had expressed my frustration about having to wait.

"And I promise I will tell you as soon as I can, Aja. For the next few weeks, we want you to attend assessment sessions full-time. No more training classes for now. And Dr. Ledbrinker will see you once a week unless you want or need to see her more frequently. This will accelerate getting you out in the field. OK?"

"OK," I said enthusiastically.

My frustration level, momentarily alleviated by the promise of an accelerated assessment process, I bounced out of Trig's office. Had I known how taxing full-day assessment sessions would be, I wouldn't have been so eager.

Not only did the length of my assessment sessions expand, but their intensity seemed to increase. We periodically went back to that neighborhood in Alexandria, and Amanda would press me to try to unbundle the mash-up of signals I would get. She had me in tears more than once as I repeatedly failed at what seemed to be an impossible task. By the fourth visit, the signals seemed to start cooperating, and I was able to pick out a few specific visions. By the sixth visit, I had identified twelve separate signals. I was happy that Amanda had pushed me and that I had persevered. However, all I could think about was how depressing it was that one small neighborhood could have such a concentration of depraved individuals. I even started calling it "Predatorville" when we'd pile into the car for another trip.

I also had intense sessions at the base where a mannequin was placed in the room with me, and they would darken the room and project different faces onto the dummy. When a face would trigger a signal, Amanda would pipe in different instructions to me through an earpiece I was wearing. After each episode in which I had a signal, she would debrief me as to whether I heard her instructions and what I had experienced. At first, I wasn't even conscious of Amanda's instructions. Slowly, I began hearing them amid my visual and physical signals. It was unsettling the first few times she would say, "burn him." Most of the time, she would say things like, "stop him without hurting him" or "cause him temporary disabling pain." I recognized that these tests were aimed at seeing if I could control my response towards the perpetrator. Unfortunately, I couldn't tell if I was being successful or not. Like me, the dummy was apparently rigged up with its own monitoring devices. Unlike a real perpetrator, the dummy obviously couldn't express the effect I may have been having on it. So if

I was having any impact on the dummy, only Amanda and Dr. Winsted knew. Eventually, these tests graduated to Amanda, just telling me before we started what level of response she wanted me to take if and when I experienced a signal.

My weekly sessions with Dr. Ledbrinker, unlike my assessment sessions, were an opportunity to decompress. To learn new strategies to dispense with the frustration of being involved so intensely in something yet not having a clue about whether I was successful. Almost all human endeavors have feedback systems that give you evidence as to whether your efforts are effective or not. You take a class, and you get grades on homework, quizzes, and for the class itself. You practice your tumbling run in gymnastics, and you stay in bounds or not and get a score from the judges. I had been living in a vacuum, bereft of any substantive feedback for nearly four months. Oh sure, Amanda would usually say, "you did good work today." But after you hear that every day for a couple of weeks, it ceases to register as something genuine. It's almost like when you ask someone how they're doing, and they answer, "fine." Neither the question nor the answer really means anything. It's a social ritual or a habit with absolutely no connection to how anyone is really feeling.

Dr. Ledbrinker had a way of helping me filter out my frustrations and circumvent my cynicism. Our sessions could probably be best described as cerebral celebrations of self. In other words, thought exercises that made me feel better about myself. Somehow, she would direct my thoughts down new and different paths instead of the old familiar ones, familiar and occasionally toxic ones. These new and different paths led to some interesting insights.

For example, when I complained about the lack of feedback I received on my performance, she asked me why I disavowed my evaluation of how I was doing. That question threw me for two reasons. First, the only previous use of the word "disavow" that I had heard was in the Mission Impossible movies, so I immediately started thinking about Tom Cruise. While he may be therapeutic to some, I didn't think it was what Dr. Ledbrinker had in mind. More to the point, her question made me realize that I wasn't even trying to evaluate myself. I was waiting for everyone else to tell me how I was doing and blaming them for feeling aggravated because they were withholding the results. Ironically, while I complained about people always trying to tell me what to do, I was overly bound to and reliant on their assessment of me. Dr. Ledbrinker said it wasn't uncommon for psychological hurdles to manifest themselves as dichotomous thoughts or feelings. Which, to me, sounded like a psychiatrist's nice way of saying, "you're really fucking screwed up." Suffice to say, Dr. Ledbrinker and I worked for several sessions on why I over-valued other's perceptions of me and under-valued my own. As with most things in psychiatry and in life, apparently, it all went back to my childhood.

I wouldn't learn for another few months the disruption and controversy my powers and my assessment findings were causing. Battles not only over how my powers defied what science had previously thought possible. But epic confrontations about the legality and ethics of employing my skills at any level within the government. This, I would come to find out, was the major reason for the delay in learning the results of my assessment. Trig, Dr. Ledbrinker, Dr. Winsted, and Amanda had gone to bat for me multiple times to convince the upper echelons of the FBI and the Department of Justice to continue their work with me. If I had known this when I was all bitchy with everyone about having to wait for the results and my field assignment, I would have been grateful and kept my big mouth shut. Instead, my big mouth and selfish self-interest only guaranteed I would have a moment of mortified embarrassment.

CHAPTER 32

Judgment Day

J udgment day finally arrived, and Trig, Dr. Ledbrinker, Dr. Winsted, Amanda, and I convened in a conference room. Little did I know that my actual judgment day had occurred a week earlier when Trig finally received approval from the Office of the Attorney General to continue my engagement with the FBI.

Dr. Winsted and Amanda introduced the types of assessments performed and welcomed me to ask questions during their presentation. A condensed timeline showing spikes in my vitals across the continuum was used to illustrate the episodes when I had received a signal. Or, in the case of my trips to Alexandria, multiple signals causing my vitals to trace a pattern that easily could have passed as a representation of the entire range of the Rocky Mountains. All in all, Dr. Winsted indicated that I had received an estimated 127 signals. Estimated because, like me, even the vital signs monitoring equipment couldn't accurately distinguish the number of signals I received in Predatorville.

While Dr. Winsted and Amanda couldn't possibly report on all 127 signals, they highlighted several of the episodes which they said supported the conclusions of their assessment.

"Aja's insights revealed themselves in her first session," Dr. Winsted began. "Our first test asked her to view hundreds of mugshots and to tell us if and when she had any reactions indicative of her reported powers. The test included only two individuals convicted of abusive crimes against minors, which she correctly identified," she said. Pointing to the first two peaks along the timeline and asking Amanda to elaborate.

"Not only did she get signaled and correctly identify these individuals, but she reported experiencing or seeing the crimes they perpetrated," Amanda added. In the first case, a man abducted a young girl and bound her naked to a chair with her mouth forced open using a bite block. The second being a woman who was Aja's former high school gymnastics coach. Later convicted as part of a network of teachers that identified girls for a child prostitution service offered to the rich and famous."

I remembered both episodes vividly and was happy that Amanda had avoided going into detail about what the naked girl in the chair had experienced. I was curious, however, about the menu that the man in the limousine had been perusing.

"What was the significance of the menu that guy was reading in the limousine? Why did I get so sick?"

What Trig said in response, I already knew. What Amanda said after Trig was more than enough to convince me why I had become so ill. Trig said that my Dad had been involved in first identifying Ms. Merkinson's involvement in an international child porn scheme. I did my best to react with surprise, not wanting to get my Dad in trouble for telling me something he shouldn't have divulged. My feigned shock was passable, if not Oscar-worthy.

Amanda then elaborated on the significance of the menu, which was from a restaurant named La Fontaine de la Jeunesse. Amanda helpfully translated this as the Fountain of

Youth, correctly assuming that French wasn't in my wheel-house. With a restaurant name like that, I probably could have guessed that it wasn't food or aging remedies that the propri-etors were selling, but Amanda obliged me anyway. Handing me a copy of the menu I had seen in my vision, I started read-ing.

"Fine dining specializing in dishes guaranteed to restore the vim and vigor of your youth," read the tagline under the res-taurant's name. Then came what looked like a fairly standard restaurant menu.

Appetizers

Jalapeno Poppers - Mexican jalapeno peppers stuffed with cream cheese (8 to 16 count)

Poutine – Imported Russian potato steak fries smothered in hot gravy and cheese

Tater Tots - A favorite. Tender potato minis. Pop them in your mouth (6-10 per plate)

Dumplings - Plump doughy goodness served with white or brown gravy

Salads, Soups & Stews

Paella - Traditional Spanish recipe with tender meat, fresh seafood, and some heat

Shrimp Etouffee - Petite, hot and spicy shrimp stew from the bayou

Asian Chicken Salad – Tender strips of chicken on a bed of greens with succulent mandarin bits bathed in a sweet soy and sesame dressing

Entrees

Baby Back Ribs - Fall off the bone goodness slathered in our special BBQ sauce (8 to 16 oz)

Filet Mignon - petite, regular, or jumbo cut served naked or with a sauce of your choice

Poke Bowl - Fresh pieces of raw marinated tuna and salmon, just begging to be eaten

Desserts

Chocolate Lava Cake - Dark and moist with a hot chocolate ganache filling waiting to erupt

S'Mores - Imported Mexican graham crackers filled with dark African chocolate and creamy white marshmallow ganache (serves 4)

Premium Ice Creams – Choose from vanilla, dark chocolate, mocha, or a scoop of each

By the time I reached the end of the menu, I was already anticipating how some of the dishes and descriptions were more innuendo than fact. Amanda confirmed some of my suspicions and elaborated on some I hadn't even caught. References to countries were the child's country of origin. Any numbers were references to available ages, not portion sizes. And portion sizes alluded to the child's body type. Flavors like vanilla, chocolate, and mocha were references to skin color. Amanda also noted the significance of and distinction between what you were allowed to do with the child based on whether the description included gravy, sauce, or dressing. I can't remember or didn't want to remember what depraved acts each term allowed.

"What would make anyone be involved in such a thing?" I asked, feeling my stomach churn as it did when I had the vision of the businessman in the limo.

"Big money," Trig replied. "Ms. Merkinson made $200,000 per child. That's more than four times her annual teacher's salary in Michigan."

"Well, I'm glad she was caught, and it's not a thing anymore."

"Oh, it's still a thing," Trig said, correcting me. "Ms. Merkinson was a very small fish in a very large pond. We have yet to identify and catch the organizers. They're the ones that are making out like bandits. Executives pay up to 1 million dollars for some of those "dishes." According to Ms. Merkinson, the organizers have operations in multiple cities, not only in the U.S. but across the globe. If that's the case, thousands of children are being exploited. We've only scratched the surface, unfortunately."

Trig's information did nothing to calm the turbulence in my stomach, and I asked if we could change topics. Dr. Winsted obliged.

"The second test on that first day was designed not to provide Aja with any sensory cues. Moreover, we had her direct her attention to a TV program. As soon as we brought the child trafficking kingpin into a room next to where Aja was, she had a pronounced physical reaction. She reported with uncanny accuracy the horrific scene that we ultimately discovered."

Once again, Amanda filled in the details.

"Aja reported feeling like she was in a metal container with a group of Asian girls, some of whom were dead and stacked in a corner. As we know, only three of the twenty abducted girls ultimately survived the trans-pacific journey. And they were subsequently instrumental in helping us find the individuals involved in that child trafficking operation."

I could see that the meeting I had so impatiently waited for was going to continue to make me sick to my stomach. It was at times like these when I wished I didn't have special powers and accurate visions. The truth was just too appalling. I was about to ask if we could take a break when Trig spoke up.

"Did any of the criminals presented to Aja experience any ill-effects?" Trig asked, which was also on my mind, and a welcome transition from the horrors that the victims endured.

"Yes. The guy we brought into the room next to Aja's started to complain of pain, and his vitals were off the charts. We rushed him out of the room, and his pain subsided by the time we got him outside of the building. To our knowledge, he didn't suffer any lasting effects."

"Too bad," Trig responded, echoing what I was thinking. "To what do you attribute the pain?"

"I address that in detail later in my presentation concerning the mannequin studies we conducted. It appears that Aja can produce an effect that is similar to the Department of Defense's Active Denial System," Dr. Winsted replied.

Although Amanda and Trig seemed to know what Dr. Winsted was talking about, I was clueless. Once again, Amanda obliged by bringing me up to speed on what Dr. Winsted had referenced.

"Aja, the military has developed a non-lethal weapon called their Active Denial System. It directs heat waves that are painful enough to cause humans to retreat, but that does not cause permanent injury. The heat rays are produced by microwave technology and calibrated to deliver a short burst of energy that heats human skin to a range of 112 to 120 degrees. Hot enough to produce pain but not hot enough to cause actual burns. It's called the Active Denial System because it is most often used for crowd control and for keeping people away from top-secret areas."

"Thanks," I said simply, hiding my shock that such technology existed and that I seemed to have the ability to produce a similar effect.

"Did any other subjects that you presented to Aja have adverse effects?" Trig prompted.

"No. None of the other incarcerated subjects that we had access to that were involved in this first phase of assessment experienced any ill effects. I can't speak for the registered sex offenders who aren't incarcerated and whose homes we drove by in several of our field trips."

"What about my ability to protect people from attacks?" I asked, concerned that Heather's death was due to the degradation of my powers or that I had been out of range.

"Unfortunately, we haven't been able to figure out how to test this aspect of your abilities," Dr. Winsted replied. "Foremost, it presents an ethical challenge. To test it, we would have to put someone you know and care about in harm's way. We can't do that. We do have another series of tests that we want to do, however."

"What's that?" I asked.

"We want to test how your powers are affected by different levels of consciousness and alertness."

"OK, but how will that test whether my powers can protect someone remotely?"

"It won't prove or disprove your remote powers directly, but it may provide a clue. You were taking pain medications for your broken nose on the weekend that your friend Heather died, correct?" Dr. Winsted asked.

Her question surprised me, and I had to pause to search my memory bank to supply a response. I couldn't recall specifically but knew that my broken nose incident and Heather's death had occurred around the same time. I wasn't surprised when I couldn't come up with a definitive memory to confirm or refute Dr. Winsted's statement. Everything for about a week after learning of Heather's death was kind of a blur. The thought that Dr. Winsted might be correct only dredged up old painful feelings that I was responsible for Heather's death.

"Aja, did you hear Dr. Winsted's question?" Dr. Ledbrinker asked, pulling me out of the trance-like state I had fallen into.

"Oh, I'm sorry. I guess I didn't remember that or connect

the two," I replied as the realization brought tears to my eyes.

"We'd like to test you under a variety of conditions," Dr. Winsted continued, impervious to the emotional storm she had created in me.

Thankfully, Dr. Ledbrinker could see the darkening clouds and the approaching conflagration and recommended we take a short break. She hustled me out of the conference room and into an empty exam room across the hall, where I promptly fell apart. Ten minutes later, Dr. Ledbrinker helped me sufficiently patch up the emotional wounds Dr. Winsted's revelation had opened. After which, we returned to the conference room and continued the meeting.

Trig looked at me with compassion and gave me a reassuring pat on the shoulder as I sat down. Dr. Winsted looked at me like nothing had happened and forged ahead with her report. I didn't hear the first few things she said because I was lost in thoughts and concerns about the welfare of her kids, if she had any. God help them if she did, I thought. If nothing else, Dr. Winsted helped me gain a whole new perspective and appreciation for my mother.

"An interesting finding was that Aja's ability to discern is very accurate when not overloaded," Dr. Winsted was saying when I finally refocused my attention. "On our field trip to Quantico, she correctly and with great detail identified areas where sex crimes had been committed. We were even surprised when she had a visceral reaction to a high school food storage room where a sex crime had been committed ten years earlier. However, on our field trip through one particular neighborhood in Alexandria, where there is an especially high concentration of registered sex offenders. Her ability to identify specific, unique areas, individuals, or occurrences was severely compromised. This suggests that there is an upper limit to her abilities that can be jammed or overwhelmed. That said, repeated visits to that area demonstrated that she can adapt to and overcome this limitation. By the sixth visit, she was able to discern the homes of all twelve registered sex offenders."

"What about Aja's ability to control the impact of her response on perpetrators?" Trig asked, seemingly as impatient as I was to hear about my internal Active Denial System.

"OK, I guess I can jump ahead," replied Dr. Winsted, a bit perturbed to have to divert from her intended course. As soon as she started talking about my powers, however, you could see the excitement in her eyes and hear it in her voice. For the first time, she actually seemed to have feelings.

"At first, it didn't appear that Aja had any control over this aspect of her abilities. In the control phase of this test, we just had her respond to the images we projected onto a mannequin equipped with monitoring devices with no intervention. We purposely selected images of individuals who had a wide range of offenses representing each of the five major types of crime, including personal, property, inchoate, statutory, and financial crimes."

Amanda, seeing the quizzical look on my face, risked interrupting Dr. Winsted to provide me with examples of each type of crime. Personal, property, and financial crimes were pretty straightforward and not the source of my confusion. Inchoate crimes, Amanda explained, were crimes that were initiated but not necessarily completed or crimes in which someone conspires with or aids someone else in committing a crime. Statutory crimes, she explained, were typically alcohol, drug, or traffic-related offenses. I thanked Amanda for the clarification, and Dr. Winsted, whose face registered her displeasure at being interrupted, continued.

"Interestingly, Aja's responses, as measured by her vitals and the mannequin's monitoring equipment, were triggered almost exclusively by crimes that specifically involved abuse, kidnapping, rape, or assault of minors. Similar crimes committed against adults or different types of crimes involving minors, like statutory crimes, generally failed to trigger her response."

"Dr. Winsted," Trig interjected, "you said her responses were triggered almost exclusively by crimes involving abuse, kidnapping, rape, or assault of minors. What anomalies did you discover where this was not the case?"

"I'm glad you asked," Dr. Winsted replied happily. Making it appear as though she only took offense at being interrupted when it was someone who was not her peer or superior.

"The exceptions to this rule were cases like Ms. Merkinson, who aided in supplying minors for exploitation by others, or cases involving supplying drugs or alcohol to minors. My working theory is that some of the perpetrators charged with supplying alcohol or drugs may have also abused, raped, or otherwise assaulted the minors. However, for some reason, either the minor didn't recall the abuse or failed to report it. We'd have to conduct additional tests to determine if my theory holds water."

"And what about the intensity of Aja's responses? Did they vary based on the severity of the offense as Aja reported to us?" Trig asked once again, anticipating a question that was burning in my head but hesitated to ask, fearing a disapproving reaction from Dr. Winsted.

"I'm going to answer that with a conditional yes," Dr. Winsted replied. "Conditional because I am not convinced we have a sufficient sample of cases to be more definitive. In short, there is definitely a pattern of the intensity of her response, fitting the severity of the crime. However, I am more excited and more certain about Aja's ability to control her response. She failed to do so in the control phase and in the intra-test phase. That is, when Amanda would prompt her in the midst of one of her episodes, it did not change the intensity of her response. However, when Amanda provided a pre-episode prompt regarding the intensity that was desired, Aja ultimately reached an 80% rate of success at modifying her response. I am optimistic that with additional training, Aja will be able to improve on her ability to control her response."

While I was delighted to hear this, I wasn't as optimistic as Dr. Winsted. For the simple reason that it still felt like magic to me. While the results may have changed when Amanda prompted me before an episode, I didn't know that I felt any differently during the episode. And how would pre-episode prompts work in real life when I never knew when an episode would occur? Fortunately, I had Trig, Amanda, and Dr. Ledbrinker, who seemed to have a window into my mind. This time, it was Dr. Ledbrinker who asked the questions swirling in my head.

"Dr. Winsted," Dr. Ledbrinker interjected. "I am familiar with how pre-sleep suggestions can modify dream content. Are Aja's episodes like dreams? And have you tested whether she can prompt herself on the degree of her response?"

"Great questions, Dr. Ledbrinker. Her episodes are very much like dream states. While her eyes remain open and she blinks at normal rates during these episodes, she exhibits the rapid eye movement we see in people who are dreaming. Her brain activity, heart rate, body temperature, respiration, blood pressure all indicate that she is experiencing something during these episodes. We have not tested asking Aja to prompt herself, but that is clearly something we need to do in the next phase of our assessment."

"It sounds like she definitely has retrocognition, Dr. Winsted. What about precognition or remote viewing?" Dr. Ledbrinker asked, leaving me temporarily befuddled until Amanda stepped in once again to be my translator.

"What Dr. Ledbrinker just said is that you have demonstrated the ability to see past events or what is called retrocognition. Now she's asking whether you can see future events, which is called precognition. Or if you can see events without any sensory stimuli, which is called remote viewing. These three things, precognition, retrocognition, and remote viewing, are all abilities that fall under the wider classification of clairvoyance."

Dr. Ledbrinker apologized to me for not explaining her question, which was nice, but what I was stuck on was Amanda's use of the term "clairvoyance." That was a term I had heard before and not generally in a favorable or reputable way. People who claimed to be clairvoyant were considered wackos. They stood on street corners claiming they could see the end of the world or the second coming of Jesus or, conversely, appear on TV talent shows claiming someone's dead grandmother had a message for them. But no one really believed them or that they genuinely could divine the past or the future with some so-called sixth sense. I couldn't help but blurt out my concern.

"Isn't all that clairvoyant stuff bullshit?" I said, immediately embarrassed by my profane response. "I'm sorry. I mean fake?"

"Yes, things like extrasensory perception and clairvoyance have long been thought to be what we call a pseudoscience," Dr. Ledbrinker replied. "However, if we discounted everything that we couldn't necessarily immediately prove via the scientific method, we'd probably still think the world was flat, the sun revolved around the earth, and lobotomies were the only treatment for schizophrenia. In short, we try to keep an open mind even though it may be hard to prove with current evidence or technology."

Meanwhile, Dr. Winsted was more than a little antsy to respond to Dr. Ledbrinker's original question about precognition and remote viewing and put an end to my mini-education session with Amanda and Dr. Ledbrinker.

"If I may, I'd like to answer Dr. Ledbrinker's question now," Dr. Winsted interjected. "As for precognition, we haven't specifically tested for this, and doing so presents some logistical and ethical challenges. On the other hand, Aja's identification of the girls that were transported in the shipping container was an example of remote viewing. She independently reported this event without any sensory input other than the perpetrator's proximity in an adjoining room. But one example of remote viewing is hardly sufficient to reverse decades of skepticism about the existence of such an ability."

"I had a vision of that man abducting Amber Lane and taking her into a supply closet at that hotel in D.C. when I was walking down the hotel hallway. Was that remote viewing?" I asked, hoping that Dr. Winsted didn't take offense.

"Yes, that would be another example of remote viewing. However, since it wasn't experienced under scientifically controlled conditions, we couldn't use it to prove the case for the existence of remote viewing. Someone could just as easily claim you made up the story after hearing a commotion in the supply closet."

"Yes, but I also was correct in telling the police to check Room 117 for the perpetrator," I replied.

"And someone could just as easily claim you saw him go in there," Dr. Winsted countered, seeming to enjoy our little back and forth. "That's why it has been so hard to prove that these abilities exist. For every Aja, there are dozens of crackpots who have made claims to have such powers that were subsequently refuted, or at the very least, unsubstantiated."

"Trying to prove clairvoyance and any of the abilities associated with it is like swimming upstream against a raging torrent," Dr. Ledbrinker added. "I'm afraid we're fighting a long history of charlatans."

"Yes, but that won't deter us from continuing to assess your abilities," Dr. Winsted chimed in.

"So, does that mean another delay in assigning me a case and putting me in the field?" I said, looking at Trig with a forlorn face that I'm sure telegraphed my frustration.

"Well, you'll be happy to hear that it doesn't delay it," Trig replied. "Dr. Winsted and Amanda will work with you for the next week to try to improve your ability to control your responses. If all goes well, you'll be joining a field agent next week."

Sweeter words could not have been uttered, and I'm sure I shocked Trig and the audience when I leaped up and gave him a big hug. I didn't care. Receiving my assessment results had given me confidence and certainty about the abilities that I had never had before. And the promise of being able to apply my powers under the auspices of the FBI was quite a head trip for someone still a couple months shy of their 18th birthday. I boiled over with eagerness.

"What case will I be working on? Who is the agent I will be working with? Where am I going to be stationed?" I rattled off excitedly.

"We'll discuss your assignment tomorrow at breakfast, OK?" Trig replied. "Same booth, same time?"

I didn't like having to wait, but I didn't want to spoil the joyous moment.

"OK. I understand. Same booth, same time," I replied with as big a smile as I could manage.

"Good. We're done here. You get the rest of the day off, superstar. The rest of us have places to be and things to do."

I thanked everyone effusively, and it felt like I was walking on air as I left the conference room. Getting the rest of the day off was an unexpected gift that turned into a curse when I got back to my room. The meeting had energized me, and feeling restless, I had nothing to occupy my time. There was only one solution – I needed to run.

Fifteen minutes later, I was striding comfortably on the Quantico trails. After completing the 7-mile loop, my mind and my motor were still running, and I decided to take another lap. There is something to be said for mind over matter. My mind was working so hard, and my mood so elevated that I didn't even notice the strain of the run on my body. It was like one long runner's high aided at some point with an infusion of endorphins. I ceased to feel my legs pumping, my lungs heaving, and my heart pounding. I felt like I was just a head floating merrily along without a care in the world. I had Heather to thank for introducing me to this running thing, the most powerful and healthy hallucinogenic on earth. That and always feeling closer to her when I ran were reason enough, I guess.

CHAPTER 33

I Finally Get My Assignment

I love the mornings when you wake up and realize it's a day when something you've long been waiting for has finally arrived. It makes the transition from that groggy, sleepy apathy to that purposeful enthusiasm to jump out of bed almost instantaneous and seamless. It transforms the drudgery of your morning routine into a purposeful and energizing series of steps designed to properly prepare you for whatever it is you're looking forward to. That's how I felt when I woke up and realized that I would soon be meeting with Trig to learn about my first case as an FBI trainee.

The one downside to this productive energy is I was too efficient in my morning preparations. I was done well before I needed to leave for my breakfast meeting. After pacing around the room aimlessly in search of something to occupy my time, I turned on the TV. That I had to wipe a generous build-up of dust off the screen should give you some idea how much time I spent watching it. As the TV came to life, a newscaster was just finishing a story about a local business lost to a fire overnight. However, it is what he said just before cutting to a commercial that caught my attention.

"When Channel 9 News returns from commercial break, a gruesome discovery at a waterfront park just outside of DC."

Commercials are bad enough, but they're even more irritating and seem much longer after someone prefaces them with a tantalizing piece of information. After tolerating what detergent I should use, which fast food place I should go to for breakfast, which lawyer to call if I were injured, and what reality show I shouldn't dare miss, the newscaster returned.

"Let me caution viewers that this next story is accompanied by video footage that may be disturbing or inappropriate for some viewers," the newscaster announced. "The search for Maryland teen Madison Miles who was reported missing a few days ago, ended in tragedy yesterday afternoon. Police were called to Riverfront Park in Bladensburg, where Madison's body was found just off a hiking trail."

The TV screen cut to video footage that must have been shot from above, showing a white sheet covering all but Madison's two bare feet and an area cordoned off with crime scene tape on the riverbank beside a walking bridge. The camera operator zoomed in on the scene despite the efforts of one of the crime scene investigators to wave the helicopter away. For the camera operator's and the TV news executive's lack of decorum for allowing the footage to be shown, Madison's dignity and the feelings of her family members were thoroughly trampled on. Viewers were treated not only to Madison's pale white feet but bloodstains on the white sheet and articles of her clothing that lay in evidence around her.

"Police confirmed that the body was that of Madison Miles. They did not give a cause of death, only saying that they were treating this as a murder investigation. The police asked that anyone having knowledge or information about this tragic case contact their local law enforcement officials immediately."

Mercifully, the video finally cut away from the crime scene to a picture of a smiling Madison in a cheerleading outfit. Something about her face seemed familiar, and before I knew it, I was transported to a dark and marshy place, which I immediately recognized from the video even though in my vision, it was nighttime. I saw a figure dressed in dark clothing crouching in a shadow just outside the range of a dim light near the end of the bridge. I noticed someone running on the other side of the river but headed toward the bridge. As the runner approached each light stanchion along the trail, the light would go from dim to bright. Watching the runner sequentially trigger the motion-activated lights and start to cross the bridge, I could see the crouching figure poised to spring. When he did, I screamed, "Watch out!" and tried to get up from my vantage point to try to stop what I knew was coming.

Instead, I returned to reality and found that I had jumped up from my chair. I was standing in front of the TV with my heart beating wildly and feeling out of breath. The newscaster had been replaced by a shapely young woman providing the day's weather forecast. She spoke in a babydoll voice that was irritating but that I'm sure some men probably found appealing. I had to sit down and calm down. I had likely just seen the perpetrator of Madison's assault and murder. Yet, somehow I had short-circuited the vision before I could get a good look at him. I tried to will myself back into the trance-like state I must have been in, to no avail. Then I browsed my phone for a picture of Madison, thinking that seeing her face may trigger a vision. I found one, but it wasn't the cheerleader picture, and for whatever reason, staring at it did not return me to the scene of the crime in my mind.

I was shocked when I looked at the time and saw I only had 5 minutes to get to my breakfast with Trig. I shut the TV off and bolted out of my room, committed to telling Trig about my vision. Arriving at the chow hall at precisely the appointed time, I quickly slid into the booth and let out a huge sigh of relief.

"What? Were you racing to get here?" Trig asked, noticing how I had rushed in and sat down.

"I didn't want to be late. I got distracted by a morning news story, and it triggered a vision."

"So you saw that they found Madison Miles," he said matter-of-factly.

"How did you know that?" I asked, almost irritated by his uncanny ability to guess what I was thinking or experiencing.

"I got a call last night from the Bladensburg Police and figured the story would get out. The media has no shame when it comes to stories like hers. Especially when they end tragically."

"Yeah, but why would you think that case was what triggered my vision?"

"Because it involves a 15-year old girl who it appears is the seventh victim of rape and murder by the animal who raped and murdered your friend. At least, that is what the evidence is pointing to."

Trig's words knocked the wind out of me, and I struggled to respond verbally. There wasn't anything wrong with the functioning of my lacrimal glands, however, which quickly produced a flood of tears that I stanched with a napkin that Trig handed me.

"I didn't know that," I snuffled, finally regaining my ability to speak.

"I gathered by your reaction. Sorry for being so blunt. I should have been a little more gentle in breaking the news to you."

"No, that's alright. I'm more upset that my vision ended before I got a chance to identify the guy. All I saw was a guy dressed in dark clothing crouching in a shadow."

I proceeded to tell Trig how her cheerleader picture triggered my vision and what I saw that prefaced Madison Miles' attack.

"Why don't you grab breakfast, and I will tell you about

what I have in mind for your first case assignment."

"I'm not really hungry," I replied.

"OK, well then. How would you feel about trying to catch that guy who was crouching in the shadows?"

I was rendered temporarily speechless once again. Not because of feelings of loss and despair but a combination of excitement mixed with trepidation.

"Earth to Aja," I heard Trig say, pulling me out of my silence.

"Yes!" I blurted out. "Sorry. Oh my God, I absolutely want to find him."

"Good. Let me introduce you to the agent you'll be working with," he said, looking across the room, raising his hand, and motioning to someone that I couldn't see.

This was all happening too quickly, and I wasn't sure I was ready to meet the agent to whom Trig assigned me. I found myself wishing that he had prepped me first. Perhaps tell me a little bit about the agent before I had to meet them. Trig got up out of his seat as if readying himself to welcome the agent, but I still didn't see anyone approaching the booth. Then he sat down again in the booth.

"Hi, I'm Special Agent Trig Halvorsen," he said, extending his hand towards me. "I'm the agent who will be working with you to bring the Peace Sign Killer to justice."

I was ecstatic, and his irrepressible sense of humor pulled me out of any apprehension that I may have been feeling about the case.

"Hi, I'm very Special Trainee, Aja Schultz Minor. Happy to meet you?" I said, shaking his hand and playing along.

"Very special, indeed," he replied.

"Why is he called the Peace Sign Killer?" I asked.

"Because he carves a peace sign into the lower abdomen of

all of his victims. It's his signature. But don't refer to him as the Peace Sign Killer outside of the agency."

"Why not?"

"Because it's one of the ways we can distinguish him from other serial killers. If the world knew his signature, it could attract copycats."

"That makes sense," I said as a sick feeling came over me, realizing what Heather must have had to endure.

"He also collects a finger from each victim."

"That's sick."

"Yes, and he is removing the fingers sequentially, it appears. His first victim was minus her right thumb. His next victim was missing her right index finger. And so on."

"So, Heather was missing her left thumb?" I asked, knowing she had been his sixth victim.

"Yes. And Madison was missing her left index finger."

"What's he going to do if he gets to his eleventh victim?" I asked.

"I'm hoping he doesn't. Frankly, I'm hoping that the next middle finger he gets is from us as he gets carted away to prison," he said. A grin on his face, which caused me to laugh even though the morbid topic was the furthermost thing from funny.

"So, where do we begin?" I asked.

"We hit the road starting next week."

"Next week?" I asked, surprised that we were delaying the investigation.

"Yes. I want you to work with Dr. Winsted and Amanda this week to refine the control over your response to perpetrators. I'm sure you and I would both like to see this guy fry. However, I'd rather our judicial system levy that punishment. We need to interrogate him and learn if there are any victims we don't know about. He also may be able to give us leads to other criminals that share his sickness."

While I was disappointed not to be hitting the road immediately, I understood his rationale. The pit in my stomach had transitioned from a feeling of illness to one of hunger. I excused myself and went to get some breakfast. Upon my return, Trig began to brief me on what he knew of the Peace Sign Killer and his victims. This made me appreciate that another part of my training was getting comfortable eating a meal while hearing horrific and grotesque details of what sick human beings are capable of doing to others.

"All his victims have been petite, athletic, teenage girls. All died from multiple stab wounds. All have been found in a remote area that provides some cover from discovery. All had evidence of trauma from vaginal and anal intercourse but no ejaculate. He's meticulous. Neither the crime scenes nor the victims have produced any traceable evidence, DNA or otherwise. To date, there has been one victim per State with a frequency averaging about one every 3 to 4 months. He started in Maine two years ago and since has been traveling in a southern direction with victims in New Hampshire, Massachusetts, Connecticut, New York, New Jersey, and now Maryland."

"What about Rhode Island and Delaware? Did he skip those states?"

"It looks like it. Up until Madison in Maryland, each victim was from a state that shared a border with the prior victim's state. His pattern has just enough variability to make us uncertain about his next victim. It could be Virginia, but we're not discounting the possibility of Delaware or West Virginia. Both share borders with Maryland, but if he jumps contiguous borders again, it could be North Carolina."

"You said we're going to hit the road. Where are we going?"

"First, we're going to visit the site where Madison Miles was found. Then we'll visit Amber Lane and her mother," he replied.

Rekindling the sickening memory from my trip to Washington, DC, the first weekend after my arrival to Quantico.

"Then, we'll go to the crime scenes in New Jersey, New York, and Connecticut and see if they generate any of your signals," he said, consulting his watch.

"But for now, you better gobble down that breakfast. Dr. Winsted and Amanda are expecting you in 10 minutes, and I have to get to an appointment."

After Trig left, I forced myself to shovel a few forkfuls of eggs and hashbrowns into my mouth before heading off to my session with Dr. Winsted and Amanda.

"I'm going to find your killer, Heather," I said under my breath as I was disposing of my breakfast tray. "He's toast," I said to myself as I dumped my plate containing a half-eaten piece of toast in a garbage bin. Apparently, Trig's brand of humor was rubbing off on me.

CHAPTER 34

To Hell and Back Again

The week-long process of training myself to control the intensity of my response to sexual predators was entirely different than my previous assessment sessions. Instead of the tightly controlled and blinded studies used to determine that I possessed retrocognitive and remote viewing abilities, my sessions were now much more transparent. We were still using the mannequin upon which images of criminals would be projected. The difference was that I knew, going in, what the individual had done, and what the goal was. Amanda would tell me about the crimes the individual had committed. Then I would spend a moment telling myself the response I wished to have towards the perpetrator.

Dr. Winsted and Amanda had assembled images of the 50 most notorious sexual predators on file with the FBI. My job was to try to improve upon the 80% success rate I had previously achieved of disabling the individual versus killing them with my own brand of Hell's fire. Dr. Winsted and Amanda had identified temperature and duration ranges for my responses that could distinguish between having no impact, disabling temporary pain, or what was considered a fatal response. The plan was for me to look at 10 criminals per day and record what impact I had on the mannequin's monitoring equipment after my remote viewing response. I would then get immediate feedback on the results after each test. The only variation was what I would tell myself before the image appeared. Amanda would prompt me to use one of two phrases - "I will disable them with pain" or "I will not kill them." Occasionally, Amanda would ask me to use both phrases during my pre-image preparation.

Now you may think that this would be a rather straightforward and easy process, but you'd be wrong. While I was now fully aware of my abilities, that self-knowledge didn't exist when I was visualizing and feeling the heinous and often painful acts that the images produced. It was like being raped and assaulted 10 times a day. Fortunately, Dr. Winsted and Amanda recognized the stress involved. At the end of each day, I would meet with Dr. Ledbrinker for a debriefing. This session was meant to assess if I had suffered any emotional damage and presumably to treat any lingering psychic insults.

It was grueling. As much as I respected Dr. Ledbrinker's capabilities, I didn't for one minute believe that our debriefing sessions could identify or prevent the potential long-term consequences of the daily barrage of abuse I experienced. Even if it was all "just in my head." I feared it would be like the consequences of repeated concussions. Eventually, after enough of them, my behavior and moods would become erratic, and my thoughts would be all scrambled. I'd be the first teenage girl admitted to one of those locked memory care places like where my grandfather lived. Or should I say existed, which seemed a more accurate description. There I'd be, sitting amongst a group of elderly strangers, perpetually confused. Occasionally visited by other strangers who insisted they were my sister, mother, or my father.

Dr. Winsted and Amanda celebrated my 90% success rate on the first day, but I didn't. I was worried that four more days of this might kill me. Dr. Ledbrinker's debriefing had been only marginally successful in clearing my head. Still, I was far from what Dr. Winsted liked to refer to as "my baseline." By which, I think she meant back to what was normal for me.

When I got back to the dorm, I couldn't take a long enough shower or soap and scrub myself down enough to wash the disgust off that was clinging to me. The thing that ultimately saved me was hanging around my neck. Heather's butterfly pendant reminded me of why I had to endure this torture. Why I needed to endure this curse so that my gift could contribute to the elimination of the evil and exploitation perpetrated on children. Heather had suffered a far greater sacrifice. So had Madison Miles. And Amber Lane, Misty, and even my mother were all still living with the horrors they had experienced. I didn't even want to speculate on the hundreds, thousands, or millions of at-risk children I didn't even know about and couldn't hope to protect.

I didn't sleep the night after that first-day gauntlet of perversions I had heard about and then, unfortunately, had to sample for the sake of science. It didn't make me a very receptive study subject on Day 2. As Amanda started connecting me to the monitoring equipment, she saw the bags under my eyes. She probably sensed the contempt I was feeling for the process. She paused and went off-script.

"You don't have to do this, Aja. We can postpone it, or we can cancel it altogether."

Amanda had always been good about letting me know I had ultimate control over my participation in the assessment process. On previous occasions, I had consistently declined the option not to proceed. This time, however, was different. I was seriously considering accepting the opportunity to postpone or cancel it.

"What will happen if I postpone or cancel it?" I asked, wanting to know the consequences of my decision.

"Postponing it would probably just delay when you join the Peace Sign Killer case. I'm not sure what would happen if you cancel it. That would be likely up to Special Agent Halvorsen and his superiors."

I was torn. I didn't like any of my options. As I was turning my options over repeatedly in my head, I felt a tickle in my chest, like a small electrical charge. I thought it might be one of the electrodes Amanda had connected to me to monitor my vitals during the assessment. But then I realized the real source. It was coming from my pendant. I picked it up, and the tickle transferred from my chest to my fingers. I couldn't believe anything other than this was Heather's way of trying to communicate with me. Not only did I know what she was saying, but all uncertainty about what I should do disappeared.

"No, I want to continue. Let's go. The sooner I do this, the sooner I'm done," I said.

Releasing the butterfly pendant, which fell lightly to its place on my chest. It gave me one last tickle as if Heather was thanking me for my decision to persevere.

Fueled by Heather's communication, I was able to get through Day 2, seemingly unscathed. I was able to eat dinner and then have a fitful night's sleep despite the 10 nightmares I had endured that day. When I woke up, I felt the tingle in my chest again. Heather was preemptively giving me the motivation to continue.

So it was for the rest of the week. I would endure the day's horrors, and between Dr. Ledbrinker's debriefings and Heather's periodic tickles of encouragement, I would recover and gather the motivation to do it all again. I experienced a deep sense of relief after Day 5, thinking I had finally completed the grueling assessment process. When Amanda told me about the next two days of assessment over the weekend, I was shocked. Why I believed the assessment was only going to be a Monday thru Friday thing, I don't know, but I was wrong. Instead, I would be spending the weekend doing the same type of test, but under very different conditions. On Saturday, before testing my abilities, I would take a standard dose of the pain medication, as I had after I broke my nose. On Sunday, they intended to evaluate my performance when I was at varying levels of alcohol impairment.

I had completely forgotten about this aspect of my assessment, and I didn't need Dr. Ledbrinker to help me understand why. When Amanda mentioned the pain medication, I felt the overwhelming guilt over Heather's death all over again. Dr. Ledbrinker and I had talked about the suppression and repression of feelings in our sessions. This was an episode in my life that generated feelings that I clearly didn't want to remember and relive. The only good thing about taking the pain pills, I hoped, was that perhaps they would blunt the emotional pain I would undoubtedly be feeling. And as for following this up with drinking alcohol on Sunday, I guess I would find out what it was like to drown one's sorrows.

Saturday came, and my assessment session went by very quickly. This was because I slept through 6 of the 8 hours of testing. I had taken a standard dose of pain medication and commenced the same test routine as the previous five days. Amanda would tell me about what crime had been committed and prompt me on which phrase to use. Then I'd repeat the phrase to myself before the image would appear, and Amanda would record my experience and the impact on the mannequin. This went along as usual until I woke up, and Amanda informed me I had fallen asleep in the middle of a test, and I was done for the day.

"We're not going to do any more tests?" I asked, thinking I had just fallen asleep in the middle of one test.

"It's 4pm, Aja. You slept for 6 hours. Dr. Ledbrinker is waiting to meet with you."

"What? Really? Why didn't you wake me up?"

"We didn't want to. We continued to run the tests while you were asleep. We wanted to see if any of the images would wake you up or if you had any impact on the criminals while you were asleep."

"Oh, I guess that makes sense," I replied, still wondering where the time had gone.

"Do you need me to help you get to Dr. Ledbrinker's office?"

"No, I think I'm good," I replied, pulling myself out of the chair and standing up, still a bit groggy.

"You sure?" Amanda asked with a look of concern.

"Well, maybe you should walk me over there, just in case."

My session with Dr. Ledbrinker was very brief, as my recollection of the few experiences I had before falling asleep was a bit foggy. I managed to have dinner before returning to my room and promptly fall asleep, still suffering some of the after-effects from the pain medication. If you haven't figured it out by now, I was very opioid- and alcohol-naïve, so when I had one or the other, they seemed to have a more intense effect on me.

Sunday's assessment session was very similar to Saturday's. Only this time, white wine was the culprit. Amanda had given me the option of beer, whiskey, or wine. I chose white wine, which is the only form of alcohol I had any experience with. If you can call the small amount of wine, my mother allowed on occasion as experience. This time, Amanda employed a breathalyzer to record my blood alcohol level before each test. Otherwise, everything else was the same, except that I felt like I was having a lot more fun as the morning wore on. How I could find any of what Amanda was telling me as humorous, I don't know, but I remember laughing a lot. This time I woke up with a splitting headache and queasiness in my stomach. Fortunately, Amanda was prepared, and as I started to apparently turn green, she produced a catch-bucket. I obliged by promptly depositing the contents of my stomach into it. Amanda tended to me until my hangover had somewhat subsided, and I was blowing at a blood alcohol level below .08.

We bypassed meeting with Dr. Ledbrinker, and since my stomach was protesting at the mere thought of food, Amanda escorted me to my dorm. Once again, I was in bed early, and I awoke 10 hours later, much refreshed but famished.

After my morning routine, I grabbed breakfast at the chow hall. Anxious for my meeting to learn about the results of my 7-day assessment. Just enduring the gauntlet of the most depraved and evil human behavior that one could imagine was amazing to me in itself. But realizing that I had the power to put a stop to it filled me with a sense of mission and a confidence that I had previously never experienced. Perhaps most importantly, Heather had shown that she had a way of communicating with me from whatever dimension she now existed.

I walked into the conference room, and it was apparent that I was joining a meeting between Trig, Dr. Winsted, Dr. Ledbrinker, and Amanda that was already in progress. They assured me I wasn't late but that I was just joining their usual Monday morning meeting. Transitioning from whatever they had been discussing before, Dr. Winsted summarized the results of my assessment.

"From a scientific perspective, you improved your ability to control the intensity of your response from 80% to 90%, achieving the proper intensity in 45 of 50 cases. The most reliable pre-image preparation phrase was "I will disable them with pain," where you achieved a perfect 100%. "I will not kill them" was the least reliable at 80%, and using both phrases achieved a 90% reliability. This, I might add, was on the tests not involving the use of pain medication or alcohol consumption."

"That's great," Trig responded enthusiastically. "Good work, Aja!"

"I would caution that performance in a laboratory setting is very different than performing in the real world," Dr. Winsted prefaced. Throwing a bucket of ice water over Trig's enthusiastic response. "We can't be certain she will perform as well in the field."

"I understand, Dr. Winsted. Good point but still very encouraging results," Trig countered.

"Yes, I would agree, encouraging but as yet untested," she responded, showing the restraint of a true scientist or that of a pain in the ass stick in the mud. I couldn't decide which.

"How did she perform on the assessment during her altered states of consciousness?" Trig asked.

"Dismally," Dr. Winsted replied bluntly. "While her abilities were intact briefly in both trials, 30 minutes after taking the pain medication and when she reached a .08 blood alcohol level, her performance diminished rapidly. In both trials, she eventually fell asleep, and during those times, none of the projected images produced a response. In short, the reliability of her abilities is dependent upon full and clear consciousness."

Dr. Winsted's cold and clinical response was like a dagger in my heart. I knew now that I was right to blame myself for Heather's death. It was devastating to know that because I sought comfort for my minor pain, Heather had endured much greater pain and paid for my selfishness with her life. I felt myself crumbling from the inside out. If two things hadn't occurred, I probably would have descended into an abyss more profound than the one that had caused me to swallow the fistful of pills that nearly ended me. First, Dr. Ledbrinker, who was sitting beside me, placed her hand on mine and gave me a reassuring look. Next, I felt my butterfly pendant vibrate. A tear or two dropped from my eyes, but I managed to hold it together as Trig forged ahead.

"OK, I need to get your assessment on whether it's safe for Aja and any perpetrators we may encounter if I include her in the Peace Sign Killer case," Trig said.

"I am supportive of Aja being assigned to the case on one

condition," Dr. Winsted announced. "The most important thing we learned during our assessment was that Aja could not control the intensity of her response once she started experiencing remote viewing. We don't have the luxury of knowing when she will encounter someone who may trigger her. Therefore, I recommend that she get in the habit of frequently repeating the phrase that best moderates her response while she's in the field."

"That makes sense," Trig replied. "Aja, is that something you think you can do?"

"Sure, but what's frequent? Three times a day? Every hour? Every 15 minutes?"

"I don't want to be prescriptive," Dr. Winsted replied. "I think it depends on the circumstances and their likelihood of triggering you. Say it to yourself at least a few times a day. More often, when you think you're in an environment where it's more likely, you could run into someone or something that could trigger your remote viewing."

Dr. Winsted's response reminded me of one aspect of my powers that we had not tested during my assessment. I was hesitant to raise this now, thinking that it might delay my field assignment in favor of engaging me in additional assessment sessions. I decided to risk it.

"In the past, I've received signals from different environments I've been in. I called it my uneasiness meter. I think it was based on the prevalence of unsavory characters in a particular location. I could use that to gauge how frequently to repeat the phrase."

Dr. Winsted looked at me somewhat skeptically, but then her face softened.

"That's something we should study further, but I don't want to delay your assignment. Go ahead and use that ability as a gauge, and when you return from your assignment, we can figure out how to study it."

"OK, we have Dr. Winsted's support. What do you think, Leslie?" Trig asked, which made me wonder if he slipped in using Dr. Ledbrinker's first name or if their relationship was more than just professional. If his casual use of her first name concerned or upset her, she was a master at hiding it.

"I think she's ready, Trig," she replied, also skipping the formality of his title and last name. "Aja's ability to deal with the stress of multiple signals over a short period improved through the week. It was almost like she flipped a switch on Day 2, and from there on out, she was better able to weather the assessment process."

I hadn't told Dr. Ledbrinker, or anyone for that matter, about how I was receiving messages from the dead. It was Heather who flipped that switch, not me.

"Good. And Amanda? You spent the most time with Aja during this process. What's your opinion about putting her in the field?"

"I have no reservations, Special Agent Halvorsen. Aja has more strength and resiliency than I could imagine, and I wouldn't be surprised if her powers evolve and get refined even further over time. I, like Dr. Ledbrinker, saw a change in Aja on Day 2. I'm anxious to see how she does in the field. I think we have a real superstar in our midst," she concluded, not aware that she had used the nickname my father had christened me with when I was just a child.

"It's unanimous then," Trig announced, winking at me in what I took was his agreement with and acknowledgment of Amanda's use of my nickname. "Congratulations, Aja! You're officially cleared to join me in the hunt for the Peace Sign Killer."

I felt a great sense of relief and thanked all of them profusely. Little did I know that the stress I had experienced in a study setting would pale in comparison to what it would be like in the field. Now it was for real. Now, if my powers failed, someone might get hurt or die. And that someone would not be the perpetrator, but either the victim, Trig, or me.

CHAPTER 35

Peace Like a River

T rig and I shoved off from base after breakfast on Tuesday toward our first destination – Waterfront Park, the site where Madison Miles's body was found. Traffic made the 45-mile trip a slow go as we had to circumnavigate the DC metro area toward the northeast suburb of Bladensburg, MD. Crossing the Anacostia River and turning onto Annapolis Road from Bladensburg Road, I spied a tall and prominent tan and pink concrete cross. Trig must have been rereading my mind because he spoke before I could ask my question.

"That's the Peace Cross. It's a memorial to World War I veterans."

"Is that why he chose this area?" I asked, making a link between the Peace Cross and the Peace Sign Killer's signature.

"You're quick," he replied, glancing at me with admiration. "But no. That's not a connection we have been able to make yet with his other sites. However, you're thinking like a true field agent. Good job, superstar."

"Thanks," I replied, proud of myself but starting to feel butterflies in my stomach as I knew we were nearing the park. I started to prompt myself with my "I will disable them with pain" mantra.

"The memorial has one of my favorite quotes," Trig added as we turned right onto Kenilworth Avenue. "The right is more precious than peace. We shall fight for the things we have always carried nearest our hearts. To such a task, we dedicate our lives."

"That's cool," I said, sounding more like a teenager than I had intended. "Who said that?"

"President Woodrow Wilson," Trig replied as we turned into the Waterfront Park's parking lot.

A sense of foreboding prevented me from responding, and my stomach was doing flip-flops. Trig sensed my discomfort.

"Is this triggering anything?" he asked.

"Yeah, I feel like I'm going to puke," I replied.

"Good time to leave the car then," he responded as he pulled into a parking space, opened his door, and stepped out.

I followed suit. Standing up and breathing in the fresh air helped my queasiness some but not entirely. As Trig was already striding with determination down a walkway towards the river, I had no choice but to follow and hope the contents of my stomach remained in place. As I took a couple of uncertain steps, a tingle in my chest from my pendant reminded me that Heather was watching over me and urging me on. I kept silently repeating my mantra and finally caught up to Trig, who clearly had a destination in mind.

"Have you been here before?" I asked.

"Yes, but not with my secret weapon," he replied, turning to look at me. "Are you feeling alright?"

"I'll survive," I said, although, with each step I took, I felt an odd sensation of getting heavier and more sluggish, almost like I was slogging through mud. Despite being in the best physical condition of my life, I felt winded and tired.

We arrived at a bridge, and as we started to cross it, I recognized the area at the other end of the bridge. Suddenly,

Trig was no longer with me, and the day became night, and I was running across the bridge. When I reached the end of the bridge, someone grabbed me, picked me off the ground, and carried me off the trail and down an embankment. I couldn't make out who he was as he was carrying me from behind. One of his arms was wrapped around my chest, pinning both my arms. His other hand, which was gloved, clamped over my mouth and nose. I couldn't breathe, and I tried kicking him, but I needed oxygen and felt myself losing consciousness. Before it went black, I could feel him pulling at my clothing, and I shivered as cool night air hit my exposed skin. Then I saw Trig in a blinding light with a concerned look on his face.

"Aja, are you alright?" Trig was saying, but I was unable to respond, still feeling somewhere in between where I had been and where I now was.

When I finally and fully rejoined Trig, I was sitting on the bridge, looking up at him as he crouched beside me.

"What happened?" he asked.

"I became Madison," I replied. "I was running across the bridge, and he grabbed me."

I told him the entire sequence of events, which I knew lacked sufficient detail to aid our search for him.

"Do you think you can continue on across to where she was found? Maybe you'll see more," he said hopefully.

"Yeah, I think I can do that," I replied as he helped me up.

We walked across the bridge and down the embankment. Stopping at a place that now looked like a memorial to Madison with crosses, flower bouquets, teddy bears, and such. It was sad, but unfortunately, my proximity to the place of her assault and death did not spur any new visions.

As Trig and I walked back across the bridge towards the parking lot, he started to ask me questions.

"When he picked you up, where was your head in relation

to his?"

"He was holding my head against the crook of his neck and his right shoulder."

"And when you tried to kick him, where were your feet hitting him on his body?"

"I'm not sure, but I think I may have kicked one of his knees."

"What was he wearing? Could you tell?"

"No, but in my previous vision, when I saw Madison's picture in her cheerleading outfit, he was dressed in dark clothing. I think he was wearing a hoodie because I couldn't see his face."

"So he was wearing dark clothing and is likely at least 6 feet tall."

"Not much to go on," I replied.

"But more than we had before. It rules out about 79% of men, assuming our perp is from the U.S."

"How do you know that?" I asked.

"Because only 21% of U.S. men are 6 feet tall or taller. Even if we're off by an inch, and he's 5 foot 11 inches tall, we still eliminate two-thirds of the male population."

"Huh," I responded, impressed by his off-the-top-of-his-head knowledge of the distribution of male heights. "What if I said it was a woman that grabbed me?"

"Oh, then we'd rule out 99% of women. Only 1% of women in the U.S. are 6 feet tall or taller."

"And what percentage of women are shorter than me?" I asked, now just interested for my own edification.

"You're 5 feet tall, right?"

"Right."

"Then, you're in the bottom decile."

"Meaning?"

"Meaning that about 1 in 10 women in the U.S. are your height or shorter."

"Huh, interesting," I said as he smiled at me.

"You'll learn lots of these seemingly mundane things the more time you spend in the field. Before you know it, you too can impress your friends at a cocktail party," he said. "Of course, only after you become old enough to drink," he added, smiling.

"Maybe I'll just try out for Jeopardy instead."

"There you go. That would be much better for your liver and potentially your bank account. You said he had a glove on the hand that was covering your nose and mouth. Do you remember what color it was or what material it was made of?"

"It was a dark color. Not leather. Maybe cotton."

"Did you smell anything while his hand was over your mouth and nose?"

"I don't recall smelling anything. Why?"

"You said you blacked out. Certain anesthetic inhalants have distinct smells – some pungent, others sweet."

"Hmm, as I said, I don't remember smelling anything."

"OK, good work. We learned he is about 6 feet tall, wears dark-colored clothing and cotton gloves. Ready for our next destination?" he asked as we got into the car.

"Sure. Where does Amber live?"

"Ellicott City, just outside of Baltimore. They're expecting us for lunch."

I was initially excited about having the chance to meet with Amber and her mother, under obviously much better circumstances than the first time. That is until I began to wonder if seeing them would trigger an episode, just as approaching the site where Madison was attacked had. The last thing I wanted to do is freak Amber or her mother out by going into some trance-like state.

I was beginning to understand how my assessment in the lab could not replicate the unpredictability of the real world. I had no clue as to how I would react to seeing them. It also made me wonder if I could control whether a stimulus even initiated my signal. I knew taking pain pills or drinking alcohol could stop my signals, but could I stop them just by telling myself not to receive signals? It seemed to make sense. If I could control the intensity of my response to signals by self-regulated, pre-stimulus suggestion, couldn't I do the same with whether I had the signals? Were my powers something I could turn on and shut off? Or were they immutable as long as my consciousness level was not altered in some way? And even if I could shut them off completely, would I want to? Could I live with myself if I shut them off and later learned I had done so at the expense of a little girl like Amber? Or at my expense, for that matter? These are the questions that tormented me on our 45-minute drive to Amber's house.

Trig drove through quaint Old Ellicott City with its colorful two and three-story buildings. The flood-prone, upscale mill town looked almost hewn out of the granite hillside. Winding our way out of downtown to the outskirts, we arrived at a newish townhome development where Amber and her mother lived. Amber's mother must have been watching for our arrival as she came out of the house and met us in the driveway. I wasn't prepared for the emotional welcome she gave me as I stepped out of the car, and she immediately hugged me.

"I've waited so long to be able to thank you, Aja," she said, her voice cracking and tremulous. While I couldn't see them, I imagined tears must have been streaming down her cheeks.

I didn't know what to say, and it didn't appear she was going to release me from her embrace until I spoke.

"I, I, I wish I could have done more," I stammered as she continued to hold me, and I could feel a lump rising in my throat and tears brim my eyes.

"You saved my baby's life, Aja," she said, releasing her embrace, her eyes meeting mine while she held me at arm's length with both hands gripping my shoulders. "If not for you, she wouldn't be here. I'm sorry, I didn't mean to get this emotional."

I reassured her that I didn't mind, and she moved to greet Trig with a hug, albeit briefer and with less intensity.

"Good to finally meet you, Special Agent Halvorsen," she said formally.

"You can call me, Trig, Mrs. Lane."

"In that case, call me Cynthia," Amber's mother replied. "Come on in, I just put lunch on the table. Amber is a little shy. I think you may need to go up and coax her to come down, Aja," she said as we entered through the front door.

"Me?" I asked incredulously. "Why would she listen to me?"

"Oh, you have no idea how she idolizes you, Aja. She'll be shy because she knows that there's a man here with you. She still has some residual fear of males she doesn't know. She's working through it, but it's going to take some time. You, on the other hand, endeared yourself to my daughter. You'll see."

I ascended the stairs, still feeling a bit uncomfortable being the one to persuade Amber to join us for lunch. No sleuthing skills were required when I reached the upstairs landing and saw the jungle animal alphabet nameplate on Amber's door down the hall. I knocked gently.

"Amber? This is Aja, can I" before I had a chance to finish my sentence, Amber opened her door and jumped into my arms, wrapping her arms and legs around me. If I thought Amber's mother had let her hug linger a bit long, Amber's felt like an eternity. I didn't mind. I could hear her crying softly into my shoulder. She didn't say a word and didn't have to. I could feel the pain she was letting go of as she clung to me like a remora to a shark. And like that odd symbiotic relationship, I felt like her connection to me was helping expel my pain and the guilt that was tormenting me. Not just the pain and guilt over not stopping Amber's attacker sooner, but also failing to protect Heather. Amber's whimpers subsided, and she asked a simple question.

"Do you want to see my room?"

"I'd love to," I said, causing Amber to unhook her legs from around my waist, prompting me to bend slightly until her feet found the floor, and she released her arms from around my neck.

Grabbing my hand, she directed me into her pink palace that screamed the haven of a 7-year old girly girl. Pink walls, pink curtains, and a furry pink bedspread were complimented by a sheer princess canopy draping down from the ceiling along the sides of the head of the bed. More pillows and stuffed animals than I could count occupied the bed. Chunky-lettered words stood in brightly colored bookshelves and floating wall shelves, encouraging Amber to live, laugh, love, and other in-spirational expressions. In one corner was a reading nook, complete with a canopy and a pit of oversized pillows. On an-other wall was a desk with bins equipped with an assortment of arts and craft supplies.

But what really caught my attention in Amber's room were the drawings and paintings that Amber had done. Presumably, at her creation station, that all had a common theme. Pictures of me, often with images of her. There were at least ten pic-tures, and they were not just hastily taped to her walls. Her artwork was affixed to the walls in a kaleidoscope of colored frames geometrically-arrayed throughout the room. Amber, and her mother, I suspected, had taken great care to treat these pieces as if Amber was an artistic savant. I could tell just by the look on Amber's face as I approached one of her drawings that they held a lofty and reverent place for her. The quality of Amber's artwork seemed pretty typical for a 7-year old, somewhat crude and basic. The content of the pieces, however, told a stark and painful reality. As I went from image to image, Amber provided an explanation.

"That's you talking to my mom and dad," she said as I looked at the picture.

"Oh yeah, what are we talking about?" I asked.

"You're telling my dad to be nice and come back and live with us," she replied.

That was more than I had expected to hear, and consequently, I didn't dare ask her to elaborate. Instead, I moved to the next picture.

"What's this one about?" I asked, looking at Amber holding my hand as we looked at something resembling a dog in a cage.

"You convinced my mom to let me have a dog, and we're buying him," she replied.

Now I was starting to get concerned. It's one thing to be thankful for someone saving your life, but it's quite another to see them as your savior for all things broken in your life. I just hoped the remaining pictures painted a different story.

The next drawing looked like a picture of me, but without the scar on my right cheek.

"This is a picture of you after God heals your face for all the good things you did. You believe in God, don't you?" she asked.

My relationship with God was a bit more complicated than I wished to elaborate on with Amber. Religion or God hadn't played a significant role in my life. Still, I didn't want to burst any of Amber's bubbles in the first minutes of our relationship. I sensed her fragility, and the last thing I wanted to do was disappoint or break her.

"Yes, of course," I replied, which was somewhere between a

lie and a flagrant overstatement. I immediately began worrying about karma and the punishment God may impose on me. Somehow, lying or exaggerating to a child seemed far worse than doing so to an adult.

"How did you get that?" Amber asked, pointing to my star-shaped scar.

"I was dropped when I was a baby," I replied, hoping she'd be satisfied without a detailed explanation.

"Did your dad drop you?" she asked and then added, "My dad twisted my arm once and broke it. He also gave me a bloody lip once. He always seemed to be hurting mom or me by accident."

"No, my dad didn't drop me. It was someone at the hospital when I was born," I replied. Feeling completely overwhelmed and inadequate in the face of the incredible physical and emotional wounds Amber had obviously suffered. I couldn't take anymore and fortunately found an elegant way out of Amber's art gallery.

"Say, I almost forgot, your mom wants us to go down for lunch. Wanna piggyback ride?"

Amber's eyes lit up, and then her face darkened.

"What about the man down there?" she asked, visibly frightened just by the thought.

"Oh, his name is Trig. He's my boss, and he's really nice. You'll like him. Now, hop on."

Amber's face softened, and her eyes regained their flash of excitement. She hopped onto my back, wrapping her arms around my neck and her legs around my waist.

"Hold on," I said and galloped out of her room and down the stairs to gales of little girl laughter. It was a welcome and joyous noise after having endured the darkness and despair framed on Amber's walls.

Joining Trig and Amber's mother seated at a dining table

just off the kitchen, Amber's grip around my neck only became tighter. Her mother and I had to reassure Amber several times before she agreed to release me. Only then did she slide into a chair she had requested be moved next to mine and further away from Trig. As Amber cowered next to me, trying not to make eye contact with Trig, her mother prompted.

"Amber, can you say hello to Special Agent Halvorsen?" causing Amber to bury her head further into my arm.

With no sign that Amber was going to cooperate with her mother's request, Trig interjected.

"That's alright, Cynthia. When Amber feels comfortable enough to speak to me, I can give her the award Aja and I brought with us."

That was effective in bringing Amber out of her shell. Even though I had no idea what he was talking about. She peeked around my arm and responded.

"Hi Mr. Halvorsen," she said shyly.

"Hi, Amber. It's an honor to meet such a brave young lady," he replied, pulling a long, narrow box from inside his suitcoat. Seeing the box, Amber warmed to him even more and risked releasing the death-grip she had on my arm.

"Aja and I would like you to have this award," Trig continued, holding the box out towards her.

It took all the bravery she could muster, but she leaned forward and grasped the other end of the box.

"Thank you, Mr. Halvorsen. And thank you, Aja," she said, looking up at me. "Can I open it?" she asked, her eyes imploring me for permission.

I shot Trig a glance, and he gave an affirmative nod.

"Go ahead," I replied to Amber's excitement.

Her little hands pulled at the top of the box, unfamiliar with the spring-loaded jewelry box mechanism similar to the necklace box that Heather's mother had given me. I reached over and helped her open it. Inside was a silver-plated FBI pendant with a blue background with "Department of Justice" around the top and "Federal Bureau of Investigation" around the bottom and 13 stars encircling the scales of justice, and a red and white banner with the words Fidelity Bravery and Integrity written beneath. Engraved on the back of the pendant was Amber's name. I was moved almost as much as Amber was.

"Can I put it on?" Amber asked excitedly.

"To make it official," Trig responded, "it's customary for the most senior FBI official to place the award around the recipients' neck. Will you allow me to do the honors?" he asked.

To my surprise, Amber agreed immediately and got up from the table and carried the opened box like some fragile and precious possession around the table to where Trig sat. Getting up and taking the box from Amber's hands, he removed the necklace, unlatched the lobster-claw clasp, and in his most official tone, spoke the following words:

"On behalf of the United States Department of Justice and in recognition of uncommon bravery in the face of adversity, I hereby confer upon Amber Lane, this FBI medallion. May you wear it in good health and happiness," completing the act of clasping the necklace and extending his hand for a congratulatory handshake.

But Amber had other ideas and, instead of shaking his hand, leaped into his arms and gave him the biggest hug she could muster. Then she returned to my side of the table. I looked at Trig with admiration as Amber gave me a hug. He had magically transformed her from a scared and sullen little girl into an ecstatic and proud one. Meanwhile, Amber's mother had been tearfully recording the entire event on her phone. This led me to believe that Trig must have tipped her off about this event ahead of time.

From there, lunch proceeded comfortably. Amber even moved her chair back to its respective place, equidistant between Trig and me. Amber couldn't stop smiling or looking at the FBI medallion. Nor could she stop talking about all manner of subjects from school to TV programs and music she liked. But it was a petting farm and amusement park in the area that she was particularly interested in and lobbied for us to take her to after lunch. Her mother was obviously delighted with the change in her daughter's mood. She confided in us when Amber wasn't in earshot that this was the first time she had seen her daughter happy and confident. The little girl she remembered from before the attack.

Despite Amber's pleas to go to the petting farm after lunch, we had to disappoint her. Before she allowed us to leave, she made me promise I would come back and take her there. If my promise was not enough, Trig augmented my promise. Telling Amber, he was ordering me to do so just as soon as my field assignment was completed. Convinced that I would be back, she gave us both hugs. Amber's mother also gave us hugs and whispered in my ear her gratitude for our having returned her daughter to her.

Amber and her mother stood in the driveway, waving as we drove away. They were still waving when we turned the corner, and they disappeared from our view. Tears welled up, and I looked out the side window, not wanting Trig to notice. I should have known my efforts to hide my emotions couldn't fool his sixth sense.

"If you don't stop that, I'm going to cry too."

I turned towards him as a tear fell down my cheek, following the rivulets of my star-shaped scar before proceeding down towards my chin.

"How could anyone hurt such an innocent child?" I asked tearfully. "She's damaged for life. You should see the pictures on her bedroom wall. And her father physically abused her too," I exclaimed, wiping tears from my face with the palms of my hands.

"Yes, but you give her hope, Aja."

"Hope? How?"

"Didn't you see how she idolizes you? How she hangs on your every word?"

"Yes, but how does that help? I can't be there to save her all the time."

"She doesn't want you to save her. She wants to be like you. Yes, she's been damaged, and those scars may never go away, but she's holding on to the one true and good thing in her life – you."

"How do you know all this?"

"I've been talking with her mother over the last few weeks in anticipation of our visit. Amber, and her mother, are in counseling. You're right. Amber's father was very abusive. It's what made Cynthia divorce him six months ago and move here. Amber's obsession with you may have been a dysfunctional avoidance mechanism at first. However, now her therapist believes she's trying to assimilate your strengths to deal with the emotional and physical abuse she's been subjected to."

"Really?"

"Yes, really. Didn't you see how her whole demeanor changed when she realized she could be like you?"

"You mean when you gave her that medal."

"Yes."

"But how long will that last?"

"You ask difficult questions, Aja. I don't know. All I know is that we did a good thing today for a little girl and her mother. We rescued both from the end of their rope."

I knew he was right, but I also couldn't help feeling like our visit had been like throwing a drop of water on a raging fire.

As we turned onto the freeway heading north, my mind struggled to let go of the thought of Amber sitting in her bedroom amidst those pictures. I was conflicted about not completing the full tour of her artwork. Part of me wished I had, and part of me was thankful I didn't. Just as when I first saw Amber's terrified eyes in my vision of her attack, I now couldn't stop seeing the frightening need and the hunger in them. I had to force myself out of my head. I asked a stupid question of Trig, hoping it would generate a conversation that didn't involve Amber Lane.

"Are we driving to New Jersey now?"

"Yep. Your mother is expecting us for dinner."

"You're kidding."

"Nope. I'm serious as a heart attack. And you'll be sleeping in your own bed tonight."

"And tomorrow?" I asked.

"Tomorrow, we take the next step in bringing the Peace Sign Killer to justice."

I knew what that meant. It meant I would be visiting the site of Heather's assault and murder. Nothing about that thought was settling. While it was only the early afternoon, I felt exhausted from the day's visits and the emotional storms they produced. It was at these times that I wished I had a more normal life. Why couldn't I just be a typical 17-year old girl whose worst crisis of the day was unruly hair? I tried to clear my mind for the 4-hour drive and must have fallen asleep because I woke up when my butterfly pendant tickled me, and we were just a few miles from my home.

CHAPTER 36

Home Is Where the Hard Is

Still a bit foggy from my long nap, I thought I was dreaming when Trig and I pulled up in front of the house, and both my parents and Misty appeared at the door to greet us. I couldn't even remember the last time the four of us had been together.

I know being home was supposed to feel wonderful, but it only felt weird. Like I was meeting my family for the first time. Absent the habitual patterns that most families fall into, I had no reference for our family. It had been at least 10 years since the last time we were all together. The fact that I couldn't even pull up one memory of that time made it feel like we had never been together. While I had been with my parents for a few days for Heather's funeral, that didn't seem to count. I was a totally different person then, despite it only being a few months ago. Ironically, it was the smell of what could only be my Mom's lasagna that made me feel welcome. Mom always made lasagna for special occasions. That I remembered.

We convened around the dining room table, and except for the comfort of the meal, I felt like a spectator. Trig and Dad talked animatedly about old times while Misty regaled us on the ups and downs of college life. Mom even chimed in with some stories from the hospital. What could I contribute to the discussion? The totality of my life experiences all seemed to be classified information about disgustingly depraved individuals preying on children. Or maybe I could finally fess up to the truth about my relationship with Heather. How would those be for party-killers? I couldn't even join the celebration and accept my Dad's invitation to have a glass of wine. I feared to do so, may risk compromising my powers for what was in store tomorrow.

How I wished I had some inane and harmless stories that I could share. Why did my life have to be filled with things no one wanted to think about, let alone hear? Why were my powers, or abilities, as Dr. Winsted called them, specific only to sexual abuse and exploitation of children? Why couldn't they be for something as important but more socially acceptable to talk about? More heroic, that wouldn't make people cringe. A cause everyone could get behind that wasn't as messy and unseemly as the crimes I could detect and sometimes prevent. Oh, sure, people cared about the sins I could identify. Literally, everyone, except the sick fucks that perpetrated the crimes, would gladly wave a magic wand to eliminate crimes against children. Still, no one wanted to talk or think about them.

Our dinner, as Italian feasts are apt to do, extended deep into the evening. There were as many empty bottles of wine as there were people around the table, and since I hadn't had a drop, let's just say I watched the progression as words became more slurred. Stories became more animated but less cohesive. It didn't seem to matter to them. They all looked and acted very happy. I, on the other hand, got increasingly frustrated. If I couldn't even fit in with my own family, how would I ever fit in outside of it?

The party finally broke up, and I padded off to bed. I was tired, but as usual, overthinking things, unable to fall asleep. A soft knock on my bedroom door surprised me. Then I heard my Dad's voice.

"You still up, superstar?" he asked, the words slightly muffled by the door.

"Come on in, Dad," I replied.

He came in and sat at the edge of my bed. Looking at me in a way that seemed to register a combination of concern and pride. I was about to ask him what was wrong, but he beat me to the punch.

"I know it's difficult for you, Aja. I just want to let you know that it gets better."

"What gets better?" I asked, not sure what he was referring to.

"The feeling of being alone. The feeling of being so different from others that you're not part of their world. Like everyone is living, and you're just watching."

Perhaps I shouldn't have been surprised that my Dad could see right through me, but I was. He had only spent a few days in the last 10 years with me, but he seemed to know me better than I knew myself.

"How is it going to get better, Dad? I can't even talk about what I do or what my abilities are. My whole life is consumed by the most disgusting excuses for humanity and the fucked up things they do."

"You will find your way, Aja. Everyone's path to fitting in is different, so I can't tell you exactly how or when it will happen. But I know it will happen."

"But how can you be so sure? You've hardly been here over the last 10 years?" I said a little more accusatorily than I had intended.

"I'm sorry for that, Aja, but that doesn't mean I don't know you. Why do you think I'm sitting here right now?"

I didn't answer him. Not because I thought his question was rhetorical. Because I was shocked that he had somehow diagnosed what was going on in my head while he had been yukking it up with Trig at dinner. He continued on when it was apparent I wasn't going to respond.

"I'm here because I know you. I know what you're feeling. I felt similarly when I was in training. Not that I have the powers you do, but when you join the FBI, CIA, NSA, it doesn't matter. You become a different person, and it takes a while to acclimate, find your niche."

I started to cry and couldn't respond. He began to stroke my hair and continued talking.

"I know you lost more than just a friend when you lost Heather," he said and stopped waiting for my reaction.

I looked at him through my tears and only managed two words.

"I did," I wailed and sat up to bury my head in his chest.

He held me for a long time as I cried, not saying a word. He didn't have to. I felt the power of our connection. A connection that we had always had despite time or distance. Then he said words that magically began to heal me.

"Being different doesn't make you unlovable, quite the opposite. Don't you think that's what Heather would be telling you if she was sitting here right now? Being true to who you are is what ultimately led to the happiness and love you found with Heather. Right?"

"Yes," I replied tentatively.

"The pain associated with finding peace of mind and comfort, whether it be in a relationship or in finding your place in this crazy world, is a necessary prerequisite. Without pain, you'd never truly know pleasure. Eventually, you learn not to force things. Be the best you, you can be, and the rest will follow. Achieving peace of mind and finding love and acceptance is a natural process, not a manufactured one. Try too hard to fit in or make someone something they're not, fails every time."

I didn't recall my Dad being so wise and philosophical. Of course, what Dad has deep philosophical conversations with their daughter when they're 7 years old or younger? I suddenly realized that I had unfairly and inaccurately based my perception of my Dad's intelligence on the one and only thing I knew. He had mistakenly identified a cluster of stars as Asia Minor instead of Ursa Minor. As I was pondering his sage advice, he continued.

"Your love for Heather is not lost, Aja. It will always be there. Even when you fall in love with someone else. And you will."

"Thanks, Dad," I said, giving him a hug. "I needed to hear that."

"I know you did, superstar."

As his arms enfolded me in a long embrace, I began to wonder why he always called me that.

"Dad?"

"Yes, he said, continuing to hug me.

"Why do you call me superstar?"

"That's kinda a long story," he said as we released our embrace.

"I've got time," I said, smiling.

"I guess now is as good as time as any," he said. "I gave you that nickname when you were 5 years old. Your mother and I took you and Misty to the zoo. At one of the exhibits, a guy who was standing next to us paid us a compliment."

"What did he say?"

"He said something like what a beautiful family you have, I can't remember exactly. Maybe he said, beautiful daughters. Something like that."

"Creepy," I replied.

"Well, my mother and I didn't think so at the time. He

seemed like just a nice guy. But when he moved on, you said to me that he was a very bad man. That I remember distinctly because I couldn't understand why you would think that."

"I did?"

"Yes, you did. And you said it in such a serious way that I began to watch him. As a matter of fact, I left the two of you with your mother and began to follow him."

"Why?"

"I guess I was suspicious as to why you said that and wanted to see what he did next. And I'm glad I did."

"Why?"

"Because as I watched him, it looked like he was more interested in children than animals. When he approached a young girl who must have been about Misty's age. That's when I went on full alert. For some reason, she was alone. I kept expecting that her parents would arrive, but they never did. I could tell he was talking to her, and after a little while, she took the guy's hand, and he started walking away with her towards the building that housed snakes and other reptiles."

"And she went with him? Willingly?"

"Yes, and you'll understand why soon. The snake and reptile building lights were purposely kept dim. I don't know if they did that to make it scarier or if it had something to do with the environment reptiles prefer. In any case, visibility in the building is reduced, and there are several dark corners, which is where he was leading her."

I didn't like where this story was going and could almost guess what my father would say next.

"I stopped him before he could do anything. He tried to run, but I tackled him and held him while others called zoo security. To make a long story short, she had become separated from her parents and two younger siblings. She went willingly with him because he claimed he had seen her parents and siblings in the reptile building. Ultimately, security held him, and the police arrived. He was a registered sex offender with a long, sordid history. So you had been right all along. He was a very bad man."

"Wow, I don't even remember that."

"Why would you? And I'm glad you didn't have to know about it. But from that moment on, I knew you were even more special than I already thought. Thus, the nickname, superstar."

"Did her parents ever show up?"

"Yes, they did. And they were so thankful I had intervened. It was pretty clear by the younger sibling's behavior that the little girls' parents had their hands full. They were running all over the place. I had never been a fan of those kid leashes you sometimes see parents using, but if there was ever a case for using them, those two kids were it."

I laughed. I knew exactly what he was talking about, and like him, I had always felt a certain disgust towards parents that leashed their children.

"Thanks, Dad. I guess I had my powers even back then."

"I guess you did. And that little girl was your first save."

That hadn't occurred to me, and realizing it now made re-fueled my sense of purpose. I would have to remember that story for the next time I held a pity party for myself about being different and not fitting in.

My Dad kissed me on my scar and tucked me in. I felt like I was 7 years old again.

"You better get some sleep. You have a big day tomorrow."

"I love you, Dad."

"I love you too, Aja," he smiled, getting up from my bed.

I think I was asleep by the time he exited my room because the next thing I remember was waking up the following day to the smell of bacon.

I got ready and went down to find Trig and my family exactly where I had left them the night before, except now for breakfast. I could tell that I felt much better than they did, especially my Mom and Misty, who both looked a little green from the previous evening's wine fest. They picked at their food reluctantly while I dug right in with full helpings of eggs, breakfast potatoes, bacon, toast, orange juice, and coffee.

"How do you stay so tiny eating like that?" Misty asked, sounding more than slightly jealous.

Misty had filled out maybe a little too much than she wished at college. I wasn't used to Misty being jealous of my body. It had always been the other way around.

"I run a lot," I said simply as I shoveled a forkful of eggs into my mouth. I also knew that since Misty turned 21, and perhaps even before that, she had developed a taste for beer. I could only assume that beer hadn't contributed favorably to her figure. However, I certainly wasn't going to throw that in her face.

"God, I wish I could run. I tried once, but it made my back hurt," Misty exclaimed, exasperated. "I just look at food, and it seems to go right to my hips."

"I hear swimming is a good, low-impact way to burn calories," I replied, trying to be helpful.

"Maybe I'll try that," Misty said, but I could tell she didn't mean it. Sisters seem to develop an innate way of communicating that goes well beyond words. Misty may have said she'd try swimming, but everything else about her was screaming, "Are you kidding me? I wouldn't be caught dead in a swimsuit with this body!"

I polished off my breakfast, and Trig asked if I was ready to go. With my Dad's encouraging words still bouncing around in my head and having had a good night's sleep, I replied affirmatively.

"Will we see you again this evening?" my mother asked.

"I wish we could but, no," Trig replied. "We have to go to New York, and then it's on to Connecticut tomorrow."

My mother knew enough not to ask about our trip, even though I knew it was her nature to want to know every detail. Goodbyes were a little weepier than I anticipated. Unlike most kids my age who were only too happy to get out of their parent's home and out on their own, I had a very different perspective. Since the age of 7, I had experienced the sequential subtraction of family members from my life and from under this roof. First, my father mysteriously disappears. Then Misty not so mysteriously goes to college. And now I have left home. I never felt I had enough time with my Dad. Misty was my closest companion and confidant until one day, she traipses off to college. And my mother? I had to leave the house and plumb the dark regions of my subconscious with Dr. Ledbrinker before I finally understood her and appreciated who she was and what she meant to me. But now, I didn't have the luxury of spending time with her to reconcile and enjoy our relationship. None of this seemed fair. Don't get me wrong, I appreciated that Trig let me spend 12 hours with my family. Still, in the larger scheme of things, it was a drop in the bucket and felt totally insufficient.

Our first destination of the day was only a few miles from my home. As we made our way, I began to wonder if I would ultimately regret that I had consumed such a large breakfast. It was early October, and in addition to some of the trees signaling the season, there was that unmistakable chill and scent in the air that screamed autumn. Everything looked familiar to me, and we passed places that triggered memories of times I had shared with Heather. The more normal kind of memories, not the paranormal ones. We stopped in a little turnout parking area, next to a trail that Heather and I had run on many times. Its path wound circuitously through a wooded area, traversing a stream for part of the way, which ultimately led down to a lake if you took a left at the fork where the trail split. But today, Trig and I took the right fork. What Heather and I called the high road because the trail gradually climbed a hillside. Then splitting yet again with the left fork continuing along the ridge and the right fork climbing a steep ascent and cresting the hill returning you to civilization. If Woodside Acres apartment could be called civilization.

We hadn't walked very far up the high road trail when Heather's butterfly pendant started to tingle, and Trig stopped.

"Are you doing alright?" he asked.

"Yeah, why?" I replied.

"We're close, and we have to leave the trail now. I just wanted to make sure you're OK."

Which I took him to mean not experiencing any signals or visions. I hadn't told anyone about how the butterfly pendant communicated with me, and I wasn't about to divulge that now. There was something about keeping that secret that made it feel special, like Heather and I still had a part of our relationship that was only for us and no one else.

"I'm good," I said.

He looked at me as if judging my honesty.

"I am, really," I said emphatically and promptly started repeating my silent mantra to only cause pain.

Apparently convinced, he stepped off the trail to the right and slalomed ahead between several trees and zig-zagging around dense thickets and undergrowth. I was surprised that there was no evidence of a footpath that would have presumably been created when the police and coroner's office personnel had made their way to the scene. About 25 yards in, Trig stopped and looked at me.

"Anything?"

"No. Did it happen here?" I asked, looking around but not getting any signals whatsoever.

"No, it didn't happen here. I tell you what, why don't you lead the way."

I looked at him quizzically.

"Is this some kind of test?" I asked.

"Kind of. I'll tell you if you pass the site," he replied while stepping behind me to allow me to proceed.

I looked ahead briefly before proceeding, and for some reason, felt we were not heading in the right direction. I turned around, facing Trig.

"What's the matter?" he said.

"You're in my way. We need to go the other way," I said, stepping around him and retracing our steps.

As I made my way back to the trail, my pendant vibrated, confirming I was heading in the right direction. I repeated my mantra several times in earnest. Pausing briefly on the trail, I glanced at Trig, whose face was a mask of neutrality. I felt a pull and waded into the underbrush to the left of the path, beyond several trees that stood like sentries guarding the entrance to a fortress. Just past the trees, my pendant and a barely distinguishable footpath signaled I was nearing my target. The slight downhill grade eventually leveled off to a stand of trees that looked like an amphitheater surrounding a clearing. Thickets and other prickly underbrush temporarily gave way to a small grassy area. Stepping into this area made my pendant vibrate wildly. I stopped and scanned the verdant area that was too beautiful for the horrors that had transpired there. I made a few more tentative steps, and a Monarch butterfly flitted past my nose, compelling me to stop. As I watched its erratic flight path, I followed the urge to extend my arm. I held out my index finger from my clenched fist like I expected the butterfly to land on me like some pet parakeet. I felt

Trig behind me, but he remained silent. The butterfly danced around us and, to my surprise, landed on my finger, opening and closing its' wings slowly. The last thing I heard from Trig was his sudden inhalation like he was as shocked as I that the butterfly had landed on me.

It was dark and cold, and the only thing I could see beyond the tops of the circle of trees were stars. I was naked and cold, and for some reason, I couldn't move. My head, arms, and legs felt pinned to the ground. I heard someone muttering and groaning nearby but couldn't move my head to look at the source. Opening and closing my eyes a few times did nothing to change my predicament, so I stared at the stars and realized that I was looking at Ursa Minor. But as soon as I made that discovery and before the irony even registered, he was on top of me. A hooded and blurry face blocked my view of the stars. He sounded like some wild animal gyrating on top of me. He must have been raping me, but for some reason, I felt nothing. Nothing but fear. That all changed when I saw the glint of metal rise above his head and plunge into me just below my left shoulder. The searing pain caused me to scream, muffled by his hand, which was now over my mouth and nose. My vision cleared just as the knife was descending again. I caught a glimpse of his face before I was blinded by pain and a geyser of blood that sprang from his second puncture. I tried desperately to clear my vision, not believing who it was that I thought I had seen. I needed confirmation. I needed to see him again. A series of quick, deep stabs to my belly felt like I was being cut in half. His hand wasn't over my mouth anymore, but all I could manage was a gurgle and a couple of choking coughs as blood filled my throat. I felt myself fading, and the stars started spinning, interrupted by the last thing I saw before all went dark. And then I knew who it was and wished that I had not used my mantra.

CHAPTER 37

You Can't Choose Your Kinfolk

I woke up and had to squint to shield my eyes from the sunlight. I wasn't laying in the green space amongst the trees but on the trail with Trig next to me, wearing a look of grave concern.

"Are you alright, Aja?" he asked, his voice seeming to come from miles away despite our close proximity.

"I don't know," I thought I replied, but judging from Trig's response, I must not have said it or said it too softly for him to hear.

"Aja, are you alright?" he asked again loudly and with greater urgency. His voice was now sounding closer.

I nodded and moved to get up, but he gently put his hand on my shoulder and prevented me from doing so.

"Not so fast, Aja. Just stay down. You still look like you're in la-la land."

"How did I get here?" I asked, hoping that my question would register a response this time.

"I carried you. You looked like you were having a seizure. I have emergency medical personnel on the way to check you out."

My eyes must have registered the same grave concern I saw

in his eyes when I first came to because he immediately acted to try to reassure me.

"I don't want you to worry," he said, putting my hand in his. "The EMTs should be here soon. How are you feeling?"

"I'm fine, I think, but I won't really know until I get up. How long was I out?"

"About 5 minutes and you're staying put until the EMTs get here. Keep talking. What happened?"

"I started to have my vision shortly after that butterfly landed on my finger," I began, but Trig immediately interrupted me.

"Wait," Trig replied. "A butterfly?"

"Yeah, the Monarch butterfly. You were right there behind me when it happened. Didn't you see it?"

"No, I didn't see it. The only thing that happened when you extended your hand was you passed out and fell backward. I thought you were pointing at something in the trees. Good thing I was behind you because I caught you just before your head hit the ground."

"Huh, well, I saw a butterfly, and it landed on my finger," I replied, Continuing to tell him about how I felt paralyzed on the ground and couldn't feel anything the hooded figure was doing to me until he stabbed me repeatedly.

"I started choking on my blood and coughing in spasms, and then I saw who he was, and that was the last thing I remember."

"You saw and recognized him?"

"Yes, he looked like my Uncle Phil," I replied. "My mother's brother. But now that I'm thinking about that, it doesn't make any sense. My Mom told me he had moved to California. Maybe I just saw his face because I know he raped Misty when she was 12," I said. Analyzing my vision as if it was a dream filled with symbolism rather than an accurate account of what had happened to Heather.

"Have you ever seen Uncle Phil's face in your other remote viewing experiences?" Trig asked.

"Well, no, but," I started to say but then paused, unable to complete the thought.

"Well, we will have to check it out. Maybe Uncle Phil moved back?" Trig posited as we both heard people approaching from down the trail.

Moments later, two EMTs rounded a bend in the trail, and seeing us, double-timed it up the slight grade to where we were. The female EMT crouched down beside me, and Trig briefed her on what he had witnessed as the male EMT opened a medical bag behind her. After Trig's account and introducing me, the female EMT took charge.

"Hi, Aja. My name is Lacy. My partner is Jason. We're going to check your vitals, but how are you feeling now?"

"Hi, Lacy. I'm feeling fine. I just wish I could get up."

"OK, good. Let me take those vitals, and then maybe we'll have you sit up," she replied as Jason handed her something, and she attached a clip-like device to the end of my index finger.

"Pulse ox 93%, pulse 58," she called out moments later while Jason presumably documented it as he was scribbling something on a clipboard. Jason handed Lacy another device which she promptly pointed at my forehead.

"Temp 36 point 8," she called out, which startled me sufficiently that she noticed. "That's normal," she said to me. "We record temperature in Celsius, not Fahrenheit," she explained.

Lacy then shielded my eyes from the sun with one hand while she shined a penlight into my eyes and then removed it quickly. She looked like an orchestra conductor the way she wielded the penlight.

"Pupils equal, round and reactive," she announced as Jason

religiously documented.

"Good, now do you think you could sit up?" she asked.

"I thought you'd never ask," I said facetiously. Lacy chuckled momentarily. Then she went back to professional mode and wrapped a blood pressure cuff around my arm and applied a stethoscope to the elbow crease of my arm just below the cuff.

"115 over 71," Lacy called out while tearing the cuff from my arm.

"I bet you're a runner," Lacy said out of the blue.

"Yeah, how did you know?"

"Your vitals are typical of female athletes that do a lot of aerobic exercises."

"So, does that mean I can get up now?" I said impatiently.

"Not quite yet. Before we get you up, are you feeling any pain or discomfort anywhere?"

"No."

"No dizziness, no headaches?"

"No."

"What about pain in your arms, chest, or legs?"

"No."

"OK, let's get you up then. But can you keep a hand on her?" she asked Trig. "I want to retake a few of her vitals while she's standing up."

Trig obliged and held my left arm lightly as Lacy took and called out my vitals again to Jason.

"OK, you look good to go, Aja."

"Thanks, Lacy."

"My pleasure. I'm glad you're alright," she replied, touching my arm where Trig had been holding it.

Lacy and Jason packed up and started their descent down the trail while Trig and I hung back.

"What are we going to do now?" I asked.

"I think we need to talk to your mother."

I was afraid he was going to say that, and the look on my face must have telegraphed my concern.

"Let me guess, she doesn't know he raped Misty."

"No, she doesn't."

"Then we probably need to talk to Misty first, but I don't want to delay. It's already been a few weeks since Madison's attack and murder. I want to stop him before he strikes again."

"There might be a more expedient way to dispense with Uncle Phil," I said, my face communicating my sinister intentions.

"You're not suggesting what I think you're suggesting?" Trig replied.

I'm sure my silence communicated that I wasn't just suggesting it. I desperately wanted to dispense with that murderous pervert, and if anyone was going to commission him to Hell, it was me that wanted to send him there.

"OK, don't even answer that. It's tempting, but what if you're wrong? What if it's not him, and you only saw his face as an artifact of your sister's traumatic experiences like you said?"

"He should fry in Hell regardless of whether he's the Peace Sign Killer or not," I replied.

"That may be the case, but I can't be a party to that."

"You wouldn't be. I forgot to use my magical phrase. Whoops!" I said sarcastically. "It would be on me, not you," I reasoned.

"Not true, Aja. As your mentor in the field, I'm responsible for you. And besides, now that you've suggested it, there's no plausible deniability on my part. I would know you intended to do it, and it would haunt me forever, particularly if it turns out he wasn't the Peace Sign Killer. I tell you what, let's drive up to New Paltz and check out that site. It's only an hour and a half drive."

"OK,: I said, and we started down the path back to the car. Along the way, I wondered if Trig was truly expecting me to rehearse my mantra to confirm the killer's identity as Uncle Phil. Or if he was doing this to allow me an opportunity to not rehearse and send Uncle Phil to his eternal inferno. I thought it best not to voice my confusion, knowing I had some time before my next command performance.

Trig turned onto Highway 87 north and began to brief me on the Peace Sign Killer's assault in the riverside, college town of New Paltz, New York.

"The killer's modus operandi for this attack was very different than his others. Although, where the victim's body was found will look very much like where we found Madison by a bridge along a river in a wildlife sanctuary. Instead of lying in wait for his victim, in this case, we think he picked up a 13-year old girl named Maria Vega, who had run away from home and was hitchhiking."

"Weren't there any cameras where he picked her up?" I asked, knowing that the ubiquitous use of security cameras in many cities often assisted in investigating and cracking cases.

"Unfortunately, no. Where Maria lived was outside of town. There aren't any cameras between there and where she was hitchhiking. One woman saw her hitchhiking but didn't think much of it, as the college kids are always bumming for rides. In any case, she didn't see who picked her up."

"Do we know why she was running away?"

"She had a fight with her mother. Pretty typical story. She wanted to go to a party, and her mother wouldn't let her."

"Where was the party? Did she ever get there?"

"The party wasn't on that evening. It was on the upcoming weekend. But you've obviously been paying attention in class," Trig replied, smiling.

"So, what's the theory of how she got from his car to the riverbank?"

"The theory is that he picked her up, offered her alcohol, which he had laced with GHB. Then he took her to the sanctuary and raped and killed her. Maria had traces of GHB in her system and a blood alcohol level of 0.15."

"He had GHB and alcohol with him when he picked her up?"

"Tools of the trade for scumbags like him, I'm sure."

"Yeah, but then he must have intended to make this one different than his previous attacks."

"That's not uncommon. The perp gets emboldened by getting away with it and thinks he's invulnerable and gets creative."

"Do you think he may have cruised some clubs in town before picking Maria up?"

"He may have intended to, but Maria's time of death around 9pm makes it unlikely. Targeting young adults would have also been a big departure for him. His victims have all been petite teens. And as we know now, he's gone back to his usual M.O."

Exiting off the freeway at New Paltz, Trig asked me if I wanted to grab lunch.

"Maybe after visiting the site would be better," I replied, conscious that my stomach was starting to do flip-flops.

Two things struck me as we drove down Main street. The first being an orange and turquoise two-fingered peace sign mural on the side of a building, followed shortly after that with a sign announcing the turn towards Peace Park.

"I know what you're thinking," Trig said. "I thought the same thing. Why the sanctuary instead of Peace Park?"

I looked at Trig, unsurprised. I was getting used to him being on the same wavelength as me.

"And?' I prompted, knowing he was anxious to supply the answer.

"And Peace Park is small and too close to residences. Although it does have a little wooden bridge that spans a small creek. We now think the peace sign thing is just a red herring."

"A red herring?" I asked, wondering what fish had to do with the case.

"Oh, I see I've landed upon a reference with which my superstar is unfamiliar. A red herring is a clue that is designed to mislead or distract you. It's like a MacGuffin in a book or a movie where a character adds suspense but only draws your attention away from the real killer. The reality is most communities in America have some memorial, monument, mural, park, or plaque dedicated to peace. It's not a distinguishing enough clue to serve any useful purpose."

"So you don't think the killer is trying to make a statement?"

"Oh, he's making a statement alright, but it's not about peace," Trig said emphatically. "Listen, the generation that grew up when the peace sign was prominent is now between the age of 60 and 80. Therefore, not the generation our guy is from," he said, as he turned right, in the opposite direction to Peace Park.

"Now, Aja. I want you to recite your phrase, and it's not good enough to say it to yourself. I have to hear it."

"You don't trust me?" I asked.

"I trust you. I just need to be able to testify that I heard you use it if, for some reason, it doesn't work. Call it protection for both of us."

I proceeded to follow his instructions.

"I will disable him with pain," I recited.

"Again," Trig prompted.

"I will disable him with pain."

"Good. Once more."

"I will disable him with pain."

"Alright, the entrance to the sanctuary is coming up."

I couldn't help but wonder if Trig had me recite my safe phrase out loud three times as cover should I happen to begin reciting "I will kill him" afterward? Did he really want me to kill him without coming out and saying it? And would it even work if I did say it? I was confused but decided not to try using the fatal phrase.

Unlike my previous vision, when the butterfly had landed on my finger and I had morphed into Heather, this time, I was only a spectator. I saw Maria, a petite Puerto Rican beauty with light brown caramel-colored skin. She was stumbling along the path with Uncle Phil at her side, his arm around her, keeping her upright. He hadn't even bothered to wear his customary dark clothing and hooded jacket. She was clearly compromised, and as they approached the bridge, he started to peel off her clothing. She was so out of it that she didn't know or care what he was doing. Now naked, Maria was lying vulnerably on a grassy bank by the bridge, easy prey for Uncle Phil. As he mounted her and raised the knife I recognized from my previous vision, I woke up and saw Trig's face, looking at me with that same grave look of concern. This time I spoke first.

"It's him," I said.

"You saw Uncle Phil again?" Trig replied, asking for confirmation.

"Yes. No doubt. He wasn't even dressed in dark clothing."

"Are you OK?"

"Would you be if you just witnessed what he did to her?" I said, recognizing that I was shaking uncontrollably.

"No, I guess not. Is there anything I can do?"

"Just give me a minute."

"Take as long as you need. No rush."

The transition back from my remote viewing to reality was always a bit gradual. This time was no different and maybe even a bit slower as my mind wouldn't let go of Maria and her last moments. All because she chose to run away from home in response to not gaining her mother's approval to go to a party. Why couldn't Maria have asked some other time? Why couldn't her mother have said, "let me think about it"? Any of several responses other than "No" would have probably saved Maria's life that night. Instead, a beautiful young girl was brutally raped and murdered, and it was my Uncle, my mother's brother, who did it. I felt responsible, and my punishment was to have to watch it and have it haunt me, probably for the rest of my life.

"Can we go back to New Jersey now? I'm ready to tell my Mom and find that sonofabitch."

"What about talking to Misty first?" Trig asked.

"She'll just have to deal with it. I don't want to wait any longer. If I have to go to another crime scene where he's raped and killed some poor, innocent little girl, I'm gonna," I paused, realizing what I was about to say.

"You're gonna what?"

"Let's just go, alright?" I said as tears came out of nowhere. But these weren't sad tears. They were angry tears. I felt a fury like never before. If I could have punched someone, I would have. Why did I have to see things after the fact? After it was too late?

When Trig asked me if I was going to be alright a couple

of minutes later, I think the expression on my face scared him. He said, "Never mind," and turned his attention back to the road. He didn't say another word as he sped out of that tiny burg in the direction of my home. Meanwhile, I fumed in the passenger seat, hating almost everything about the situation and my life.

CHAPTER 38

Peace Be With You

T he uneasy silence as we drove back to New Jersey was broken when my phone rang. I was still angry and probably wouldn't have answered it if it hadn't been my Mom calling.

"Hi, Mom," I said unenthusiastically.

"Aja, your Uncle Phil's in the hospital," she blurted out tearfully. "They say he's not expected to live."

"Really?" I said more brightly than I intended, but I don't think that in my mother's current frame of mind, she even heard me, let alone detected the joy in my response.

"He's in a hospital in Virginia of all places. I don't know what he's doing there, but your father and I are catching a flight. It may be too late by the time we get there."

"What happened to him?" I asked, looking at Trig, who now looked as curious as I was.

"They said they didn't know exactly but that it appeared like his organs were all starting to shut down. He was in excruciating pain, and they had to put him into a medically-induced coma. We have to go. Keep Uncle Phil in your thoughts, and I'll call you when I know more."

Before I could respond, she had hung up. I could see Trig

waiting with restless anticipation.

"Uncle Phil's in a hospital in Virginia. His organs are failing, and they don't expect him to live. My Mom and Dad are flying there."

Trig didn't have to say a word. His face said it all.

"I didn't do it. I promise."

"You didn't recite anything after I had you say your phrase?"

"No," I said emphatically.

"Did you think about it?" he asked.

He had me, and he knew he had me.

"Well, I did think about it, but I decided not to say it," I replied.

"OK, I guess I can't blame you. If I were in your shoes, I probably would have done the same thing."

"What do we do now?"

"Well, we still have to collect evidence that he's our killer. We can't just go on your word. Did your Mom say where he was in Virginia?"

"No."

"What's Uncle Phil's last name?"

"Chelios."

"That should help us find him. What is Chelios? Italian?" Trig asked.

"I don't know. I guess I always thought of her as a Minor, which is English."

"I think it's probably Italian," Trig replied. "That would certainly explain your Mediterranean look and why your mother's lasagna is so good."

"Mediterranean look? What's that?"

"You have a tan complexion, dark eyes, and dark hair. Those are typical of people from Italy, which I assume you know is on the Mediterranean Sea. It's also the only way I can reference your appearance without getting in trouble with Human Resources. They tend to frown upon colleagues making comments about a person's appearance, especially when that person is a beautiful young woman. Which, of course, I would never ever think to say to you."

That made me laugh, and just like that, the anger and guilt that had made my mood so ugly on the first leg of our return trip disintegrated. Trig had a way of doing that, even if, in this case, it did test the bounds of Human Resource dictates.

As Trig got on the phone with someone to track down where Uncle Phil was being hospitalized, I decided to call Misty. I realized that my Mom hadn't said anything about Misty on the call. I would have been surprised if Misty had agreed to join my parents to visit Uncle Phil. I was more worried about the histrionics that may have transpired between Misty and my Mom if she had refused to go.

"Aja, thank God, I was just about to call you," Misty answered, sounding relieved.

"How are you doing?"

"Oh, I'm delighted about Uncle Phil. I just wish it had happened to him 10 years ago. But Mom is completely out of control. She threw such a fit when I told her I wasn't going."

"That's why I called. I figured that wouldn't go over well."

"That's an understatement. Where are you? Are you coming back here?" Misty asked, which sounded more like a plea than a question.

"We're on the road near Newburgh. Probably about 30 minutes out. I think we're going to stop and see you," I said, looking at Trig, who confirmed my assumption with a nod of his head even though he was still on his call. "Yes, we're stopping there."

"Oh, good."

"We'll see you soon, OK."

"Alright. Hurry," Misty replied.

Trig's call ended shortly after I hung up with Misty, and he briefed me on what he had learned.

"He's in a hospital in Richmond. Let's go talk to Misty. Your parents are booked on the 1:25pm flight from Newark, so they should be about to board. They probably won't get to the hospital until 3:30 at the earliest."

"You learned all that on your call?"

"Oh, that and much more. You'd be surprised how much information we have on people."

"What else did you learn?"

"I learned that Uncle Phil never lived in California."

"He didn't?"

"No. He's lived in a suburb of Richmond called Short Pump for the last 8 years. How's that for the name of a hometown?"

"Disgustingly graphic when you pair it with Uncle Phil, I'm afraid."

"Surprisingly, up until a week ago, his record was spotless except for a couple of speeding tickets."

"What happened a week ago?"

"A 16-year old Asian girl named Lucy Chen filed a complaint against him. She claims he was stalking her at a mall in Short Pump. Security detained him briefly, and the police got involved and filed the complaint. Mall video confirmed that he appeared to be following her. He claimed it was a coincidence and that he just happened to be going to the same stores to shop for his niece's birthday present. They didn't have any reason to hold him, so he was released with a warning."

"I guess Lucy Chen won't have to worry about him anymore," I said.

"Yes, but that complaint, paired with our suspicions of him as the Peace Sign Killer, maybe just enough to get a warrant to search his home. After we talk with Misty, I'll call and see if we can get a warrant."

My stomach growled noticeably.

"Is that your stomach protesting searching Uncle Phil's home, or are you just hungry?"

"Hungry. I hope there's some food at the house."

"We could pick something up," Trig offered.

"No, I want to get there. Misty sounded a bit desperate."

Fifteen minutes later, we pulled into the driveway, and Misty came running out of the house as if shot from a cannon. I wasn't clear of the passenger door before she wrapped me in a bear hug.

"I'm so glad you're back."

"Me, too," I croaked as she was squeezing the air out of me.

Finally, releasing me, Misty babbled a mile a minute.

"I didn't know what to do while I was waiting for you. I made you both lunch. I hope you're hungry. It's leftovers from last night. I hope you don't mind," she rattled away.

"Misty, relax," I said. "We're here now, and we're both hungry. Thank you."

Misty let out a big sigh.

"OK, OK, I'm sorry," she blurted, taking a deep breath and letting it out to calm herself. "I'm a little worked up."

"Ya think?" I exclaimed sarcastically.

As I opened the front door, the smell of garlic hit me, making me feel like I, with my so-called Mediterranean look, was walking into an Italian restaurant. My stomach growled again, and Trig didn't waste any time in asking Misty if he could help serve lunch. As we dined, Misty gave us a blow-by-blow of her skirmish with Mom over not going with them to see Uncle Phil. Misty had used what she thought was an elegant, adequate, and truthful excuse about needing to get back to college. She hadn't counted on Mom pulling out the "family-is-more-important" card. Mid-story, Misty paused to ask me a question.

"Does he know about, ya know, that thing that happened?" she asked me, realizing too late that she had started a story she wasn't sure she wanted to complete with Trig in the room.

"He knows," I said. Which predictably caused Misty to feel like I betrayed her. I quickly added, "We're investigating other crimes that Uncle Phil may have committed. He needed to know."

Misty's expression went from hurt to shock.

"You're shitting me."

"I shit you not."

"What else has he done?"

I looked at Trig, not sure how much I could say. He obliged by taking over the conversation.

"Misty, your Uncle Phil may have been involved in a series of assaults on young girls. What we need to talk to you about is strictly confidential, and you must not talk to anyone about what we discuss here. Do you understand?"

"I understand," Misty replied.

"Not even your Mom and Dad," Trig added.

"OK. I get it," she said, making the universal gesture of zipping her lips, locking them, and throwing away the key.

"We think Uncle Phil may be the serial rapist that has assaulted and killed at least 7 young girls across the Northeast U.S. over the last two years."

"How do you know that?"

"I'm not at liberty to discuss that with you, but evidence suggests that he may be the individual code-named "the Peace Sign Killer."

Misty's face went pale, and she had to put a hand on the table to steady herself in her chair.

"Are you alright, Misty?" I asked, placing a hand on her shoulder.

"No. I'm not," she replied, putting her other hand on me as if she was about to faint.

We waited a moment until Misty regained her bearings. When she did, she looked at me like she knew something big. Something she couldn't hold in any longer.

"I have a birthmark that looks like the two-finger peace sign," she exclaimed.

"You do? Where?" I replied, confused because I had seen Misty in various stages of undress my whole life and had never seen a birthmark.

"By my," she blushed, turning to me and shielding the side of her face from Trig as she mouthed the word "vagina."

"Oh, there," I said, the location of which I'm sure Trig had already figured out given the production Misty had made out of communicating it to me.

"That's why Mom and Dad gave me the middle name, "Peace."

"I didn't know that," I said, surprised.

"Yeah, well, I don't use it unless an official form calls for it. It's embarrassing."

I suddenly realized that I wasn't the only one in the family that had issues with their given name. Somehow, knowing that made me feel even closer to Misty than I already was. Trig broke in, returning the conversation to Uncle Phil.

"Did Uncle Phil know you had that birthmark? Did he see it?"

"Yes," Misty replied sheepishly. "It was disgusting. He would secretly give me the peace sign when he visited and would smile in his creepy little way. It made me want to puke."

"Perhaps it's not a red herring?" I said to Trig.

"Red herring?" Misty said, looking confused.

"Ah, you and I can discuss that later, Aja. It's nothing, Misty, just FBI investigative lingo."

Misty seemed to buy that. I suddenly realized that Trig was trying to protect Misty from the fact that Uncle Phil, in a sick way, was either paying homage to her or trying to relive his experiences with her through each of his victims. He was right. Misty didn't need to bear the burden of her Uncle's crimes.

"So Misty, how did things end with Mom?"

"Well, I was within an eyelash of blurting out that Uncle Phil had raped me when Mom fired her final salvo and tried to guilt me for being so selfish. When that didn't work, she stormed off, threw some clothes in a bag, and left with Dad for the airport. Her last words to me were, we're not done here, young lady. I've never seen her so pissed."

"You did the right thing, Misty. She's devastated enough without knowing that about her brother," I replied, wondering if there would ever be a good time for Misty to tell her.

"I think we better hit the road, Aja. We have a lot of work ahead of us," Trig interjected.

"Do you have to go so soon?" Misty pouted.

"I'm afraid so. Duty calls," I replied, giving her a hug. "When do you go back to college?"

"Tomorrow," she frowned.

"I'll be in touch, OK?" I said, feeling guilty about leaving her like this.

"OK, love you, sis," she said, walking us to the door.

"Love you too," I replied, giving her a hug.

Trig followed and also gave Misty a hug. He whispered something in her ear, and her face went from a frown to a smile.

"So, what magical thing did you say to Misty?" I asked as he pulled the car out of the driveway.

"I just thanked her for being brave and telling us about what I'm sure were very painful memories."

"That's it? That's all you had to say to make her smile?"

"You'd be surprised how just acknowledging a person's pain can provide some relief."

"Now, you sound like Dr. Ledbrinker."

He smiled, and while he didn't say anything in response, I could tell by his face and his lingering smile that I had struck a chord.

"Oh my God, you're seeing her, aren't you?" I exclaimed excitedly.

"No, I'm not in therapy with Dr. Ledbrinker," he countered, trying unsuccessfully to wipe the smile from his face.

"I didn't mean that type of seeing. You know what I was asking. You're dating her, aren't you?"

"Don't you think we should be talking about what our next steps are to close the Peace Sign Killer case?"

"Yes, as soon as you fess up," I smiled.

"You're incorrigible."

"Is that another one of your words for young and beautiful?"

"Hardly."

"Well, are you?"

"Am I what?"

"Seeing her?"

"None of your business."

"So you are seeing her. Good. I like her, and I think you make a good couple. Now that that's settled, what are our next steps with Uncle Phil."

Trig looked at me with an expression of amused defeat.

"I get a warrant to search Uncle Phil's home, and we hop a plane to Richmond."

"What about the car?"

"We leave it at the airport."

"And how do we get around when we get to Richmond?"

"The agency will have a car waiting for us there."

"Are you getting tired of my questions?"

"Questions no. You, maybe?" he said, smiling.

"Well, if it's any consolation, I think you're very brave, and I know being my supervisor can be very painful."

"Touche," he said as we broke into laughter.

Nothing about our investigation or what we had to do next was in the least bit humorous. Still, our ability to share a light-hearted moment together gave us a much-needed respite. Without it, the depravity in this world could make one very discouraged, if not hopelessly cynical about the human race. I had almost lost myself to the deep, dark places in my mind once before, and I never wanted to get lost there again.

CHAPTER 39

Too Close for Comfort

As Trig and I were boarding the plane for Richmond, I received a call from my Mom. Except when I answered, all I could hear was her wailing in the background.

"Hi, Aja. Your Uncle Phil died before we got here," my Dad said, causing a crescendo in my mother's howling sobs.

I couldn't say anything in response, and my Dad misread my silence.

"I know this is a shock. We don't know anything yet. Your mother's beside herself, as I'm sure you can hear. I just thought you should know."

"Thanks, Dad. Hug Mom for me," I managed to say, genuinely sad for her, but quite the opposite for Uncle Phil.

"I will. Could you do me a favor and tell Misty? I have to console your mother. We'll be in touch later, OK?"

"OK, Dad. I love you."

"Love you too, superstar."

I hung up, and Trig had already deduced the news I had received.

"I'm guessing we can't count on a confession from Uncle

Phil."

"No, I pretty much made sure of that. I'm sorry."

"Hopefully, we won't need his confession after we search his home."

I spent part of the 90-minute flight hoping my dispensing with Uncle Phil didn't compromise our ability to prove he was the Peace Sign Killer. I was more worried about how we would break the news to my already distraught mother.

As Trig had said, the FBI had a car available for us when we arrived in Richmond. What I hadn't expected was that the car came with another FBI agent trained in the collection of forensic evidence. The three of us made the 30-minute drive to Short Pump and Uncle Phil's apartment complex. The Leasing Manager let us into Uncle Phil's unit after she read the warrant.

To the casual observer, Uncle Phil's living room, dining area, and kitchen appeared like any you would find in an average person's abode. It was when we dug a little deeper that things got not just out of the ordinary but sickeningly creepy and gruesome. Flicking on the light switch in his bedroom bathed the room in a dim reddish glow. In one corner stood what could only be described as a shrine to my sister. Complete with articles of her clothing, posters with peace signs, and pictures of Misty. Some of her naked and likely taken when he raped her, and other more recent pictures that I recognized that he must have gleaned from her social media page. We also found photo albums. One which appeared reserved for his Peace Sign Killer conquests with nauseating before and after photos. After seeing the pictures of his first victim, I excused myself and stepped outside the room, and waited for them to finish. It wasn't that I couldn't stand viewing the pictures. I just didn't want them to trigger my remote viewing. I also didn't want to see the pictures he took of Heather. When Trig emerged, he told me that the other photo albums were filled with images of girls that he had a fascination for or may have been stalking. The most recent photos they found were of Lucy Chen at the mall.

But it was what we found in the freezer compartment of his refrigerator that held the most damning evidence. Stored in a ziplock freezer bag and ironically located next to a package of chicken fingers were the so-called souvenir digits he had removed from each of his victims. I was surprised and impressed by the forensic expert's foresight when he produced a cooler from the trunk of the car, complete with dry ice with which to preserve and transport the grisly evidence.

I thought things couldn't get more shocking than what we had already found when Trig pulled me aside and encouraged me to look in a photo album he had in his gloved hand.

"What's in it? I don't want to look at it if it has pictures of Heather."

"It doesn't. I promise."

"Really, I think I've seen enough. Do I have to?"

"I think you need to see these."

Donning gloves, I opened the album tentatively, not enthused about the prospect of seeing more sickening photos of young girls. What I saw instead was much worse. Inside were pictures of me. Pictures from when I was a baby on up, cataloging my life at every age. Even those years when I thought Uncle Phil was in California. With each flip of a page, my stomach turned a little more. When I got to pictures of me at high school gymnastics meets, I stopped and looked at Trig. I had first thought that maybe my mother had sent him the pictures, but then I remembered that Mom never attended my meets. The only explanation was that he had been there.

"I can't believe this. I think I've seen enough."

"Go on. There's more."

"Do I have to?"

"Trust me."

I continued flipping pages, stopping when I arrived at a picture of me running with Heather. It looked like it had been taken near where he had subsequently raped and killed Heather. I looked at Trig, unable to speak, with an expression that I'm sure conveyed the agony I was feeling and my desire not to continue.

"Go on," he prompted.

There was a picture of me with Travis at dinner and after dinner when Travis kissed me. The last few photos in the album were of me running on the Quantico trail. I shut the album. Uncle Phil had been stalking me. I looked at Trig again, not sure what to say.

"He was targeting you," Trig said.

"How do you know?" I replied.

"We found a diary that documents all of his plans. He was meticulous about how he identified his victims. All but Maria Vega in New Paltz, who, as we know, he stumbled upon."

"If he was targeting me, then he was going to meet his end eventually," I said confidently.

"Yes, I suppose you're right," Trig said robotically with a mile-long gaze that made me think his mind was elsewhere.

"Are you OK?" I asked.

"Me? Yes, yes, I'm fine. This is all just so," he paused, seemingly unable to finish his sentence.

"Disturbing?" I offered.

"Yes, disturbing," he confirmed.

"So, what do we do now?" I asked.

"Other than filing my report, we don't have much to do at this point. I'll get a team in here to make sure all the evidence is collected. The agency will assign a team to thoroughly dig into it to make sure there aren't other victims. The agency will also assign someone to notify the families of the victims once we know the full story."

"So, my Mom will find out?"

"Probably. There's no record of him ever marrying or having kids, so the agency will notify Uncle Phil's parents or his siblings if his parents aren't alive."

"My mom's parents died in an automobile accident when I was a baby. She's the only family he has. Had," I said, correcting myself.

"Then, she'll be the one the agency contacts."

"Shouldn't I tell her instead of some person she doesn't know from the agency?"

"No. It's better that you don't for two reasons. First, you took an oath to keep your involvement in cases confidential. We have you do that because it protects you. Second, hearing the message from a stranger is actually better for your mother and for your relationship with her. You don't want the emotion of that news something she associates with you."

"What about Misty? Should she tell Mom about what he did to her before she finds out the full story?"

"That's up to Misty? Unfortunately, there aren't any easier answers when it comes to these types of cases."

"I'm gathering that. So, we say nothing and just go on our merry way? That seems so, so," I paused, trying to find the right word.

"Callous?" Trig offered.

"Yeah, that's it, callous."

"Or you can look at it from the perspective of all the young girls you saved from that monster."

"Yeah, it's kinda hard for me to appreciate that when I failed to protect the one person who I loved and couldn't live without."

"That's why when we go back to the Academy, you'll debrief with Dr. Ledbrinker, Dr. Winsted, and Amanda. They'll help you work through all of this. It's not easy, but at least you have access to them. When I was a newbie, we didn't have all these resources designed to help us cope with the fallout of our work. Our resources had names like Jack Daniels, Budweiser, Crown Royal, Patron, and Bacardi."

"So, my field assignment is over?"

"Correction. Your first field assignment is over. There will be more if you want more."

I wasn't exactly sure how to answer that. Part of me wanted to, and part of me didn't.

"I guess I'll discuss that with my support team since you're not offering me access to those other old-school resources you mentioned."

"Well, your age aside, your assessment results when you drank wine didn't seem to do you any favors."

"Oh, don't remind me. Just thinking about it gives me a headache."

"Ready to go back to base, Schultz?"

"Whatever you say, Colonel Klink."

When I first heard that I was going to get a field assignment, I couldn't have been more excited. I spent lots of time in the weeks before the mission, imagining what it would be like. Now, as we boarded a plane to return to base, and I had completed my first assignment, it was nothing like what I had imagined. It had been more personal than I had expected, and even though we solved the case and "got our man," it didn't feel like a victory in any sense.

I had initially been happy and motivated to potentially bring Heather's killer to justice. Still, in so doing, the case hit closer to home than even Trig, and I had anticipated. I couldn't help but feel like my family was in shambles, and it would only get worse when my mother ultimately learned the truth about her brother. Worst of all, I had to swallow this and couldn't even talk about it with my family. I was anxious to speak with Dr. Ledbrinker. Because with each passing moment, drowning myself in Jack Daniels, even though I had never touched the stuff, was starting to sound pretty inviting.

CHAPTER 40

My Metamorphosis

B eing back on base felt oddly more like home than my home in New Jersey. Trig and I had arrived in the late evening, and I had gone straight to bed. I was able to sleep in until mid-morning and took my time getting ready for the day. I wasn't scheduled to see Dr. Ledbrinker until mid-afternoon. My debriefing with Dr. Winsted and Amanda was not until the following day. It was lunchtime before I emerged from my room and made my way to the chow hall.

I was pleasantly surprised when a number of my class-mates welcomed me back as I went through the food line. After filling my tray, I saw someone sitting in what I con-sidered "my booth." I couldn't see who it was as they had their back to me, so I started scanning the room for another place to sit. Seeing a small table available near the back, I navigated my way there. Just as I was about to take my seat, a familiar voice called to me.

"Aja, over here."

When I looked up, I saw Travis waving to me from my booth. He was the last person I had expected to see. I quickly traversed my way back.

"I hope you don't mind me sitting in your booth," he said, getting up out of the booth as I approached.

I couldn't help but smile. He was always the gentleman.

"Not at all. It's great to see you. When did you get back?" I asked, putting my tray down.

"Last week," he replied as he took a step in my direction and held out his arms.

Normally, I wasn't one for PDA, but I felt a pull and found myself stepping towards him until our arms encircled each other in a hug.

"I missed you," he whispered in my ear.

"I missed you too," I replied, surprised at how easily my response had fallen from my lips. Not to mention how exhilarating it felt to have his arms around me.

"I thought you weren't going to come back," I said as we slid into our respective sides of the booth.

"We decided to sell the family store. So, taking over my father's business and my dream to become the hardware mogul of Barron County, Wisconsin, was shattered," he laughed. "I was never cut out for that kind of work. Luckily, Special Agent Halvorsen let me rejoin the program. He had to pull a few strings. Where have you been? I was worried when I got here and didn't see you."

"I joined Trig, I mean Special Agent Halvorsen, in the field to work on a case. Kinda like a dry-run to see how I would do."

"Wow! That's great. And how was it?"

It was a difficult question for me to answer. Yesterday I had complained to Trig about not being able to talk to anyone about what I do for a living. Now here I sat with someone I could talk to, someone genuinely interested in what I had to say, yet I was uncertain how to respond. Wasn't that just like me? Uniquely able to focus on and see the clouds within every silver lining.

"It wasn't like I imagined. It was harder than I expected. I'm still kinda processing it all." I answered honestly, wishing I could have responded more positively and enthusiastically.

"Well, it's impressive that you got the opportunity so soon. The rest of us can only hope to get that chance after our training."

"Thanks, but I don't feel all that fortunate at the moment. As I said, I have a lot to think about."

"You're not thinking about quitting, are you?"

"I don't know, Travis. I guess I'm a bit confused by it all. I'm sorry I'm such a downer."

"You're not a downer. I hear what you're saying. You've been through a lot, and you need some time to put it into perspective."

"Thanks, I'm glad you understand."

The rest of our lunch conversation focused on Travis and the pain and suffering of losing his father. And in the aftermath trying to maintain the family business while consoling his distraught mother. Not to mention the disappointment of thinking he would never realize his dream to become an FBI agent.

"Hey, I have to get to class, but would you like to go out tonight?" Travis asked.

His question had an unexpectedly positive impact on my otherwise confused and conflicted feelings.

"I'd love to," I replied in an uncharacteristically spontaneous and over-zealous manner.

"Tony's at 6pm?" he proposed.

"What? You miss your girlfriend, Lydia?"

"No," he laughed. "I miss you. How about we take my car? I'll meet you outside the dorm?"

"It's a date."

We got up out of the booth, disposed of our trays, and exited the chow hall to the hallway, which led to Travis' class.

As I didn't have anywhere else to be, I walked with him. I was feeling something akin to separation anxiety as we arrived at the door of his classroom. He must have felt it, too, because he lingered outside the door as classmates filtered by us.

"6 pm can't come quick enough," he said, his eyes meeting mine with an intensity that sent a pleasant shiver through me.

I couldn't respond except to hug him. He reciprocated, and I had to tear myself away before succumbing to an even more embarrassing display in front of our classmates.

As I walked away thinking we had avoided discovery, he entered the classroom. I heard a collective chorus of "woo Travis" from those who had witnessed our embrace. It almost felt like I was back in high school, where everyone made your business, their business. But it also felt kinda good. I can't lie.

I had a couple of hours to kill before my session with Dr. Ledbrinker. Despite all the conflicted feelings that I had suffered the previous day about my role with the FBI, what occupied my mind presently was something I hadn't thought was in doubt, my sexual orientation. Why did everything in my life have to be up in the air all at once? Couldn't I have one thing that I could count on? One thing that was stable and consistent in my life? Even my so-called powers of clairvoyance and my Active Denial System were unpredictable. I was one month away from the so-called age of majority, and the only thing I had to show for it was that the majority of my life was a fricking mess.

By the time I was to go to Dr. Ledbrinker's office, I was pacing furiously in my room like some caged animal. My butterfly pendant, formerly a source of salvation and comfort, buzzed at the height of my distress. I had no idea whether it was Heather trying to reassure me, warn me, encourage me, express displeasure with me, or what. In short, it just contributed to the chaos formerly known as my peace of mind, as fragile as that peace may have been.

When I walked into Dr. Ledbrinker's office, my usual poker face must have betrayed me.

"Tell me what's wrong, Aja," she said, abandoning her usual non-directive therapy approach.

"It would be easier and faster to tell you what's not wrong," I replied sarcastically.

"And that would get you exactly nowhere, so start at the beginning. What's bothering you?"

"I don't want to have these powers anymore. I just want to shut them off and be normal." I blurted out.

"Have you practiced shutting them off?" she asked.

"No!" I yelled emphatically, annoyed by her unexpected question. I was expecting she'd say something like, my powers make me special, and there is no such thing as normal, and if there were, normal would be boring.

"Why not?" she asked, which only made me feel like she was bating me.

"Because I can't," I blurted, feeling myself getting angry.

"How do you know?"

"Because I've always had them. This isn't helping. You're not helping," I rattled off and felt tears joining my anger.

"Then help yourself. Haven't you learned to control your response to your visions through practice? Didn't your ability to detect all the registered sex offenders in that neighborhood in Alexandria improve through practice? You probably can learn to turn your powers on and off. You just haven't practiced and learned how yet."

I realized she was right. I also realized that turning my powers on and off wasn't the real issue.

"That's not what's really bothering me."

"Then what is?"

"What's bothering me is that when I truly needed my

powers to work, they didn't," I sobbed.

Dr. Ledbrinker sat silently. When my tears subsided and I regained my ability to talk, I told her about what happened when I visited the site of Heather's assault and death. How I had passed Trig's test of finding where it had happened. How the butterfly had landed on my finger. How I had become Heather in my vision and relived the horror of her assault.

"Heather died because I failed her, and because of that, nothing else seems to matter. I can't even appreciate that I helped solve the Peace Sign Killer case. It's just going to destroy my mother when she finds out. And I can't even talk to her about it."

"What if Heather died so that you could live to save others? And what if I told you that you saved Heather and Misty multiple times from his attempts to rape and kill them? Would that change your perspective?"

"What are you talking about?"

Dr. Ledbrinker produced a worn booklet, "This."

"What is it?"

"It's your Uncle Phil's rape and murder diary. He tried many times to abduct Misty while she's been at college. He was thwarted every time by acute pain. The same pain he had felt when he tried to rape your sister after she moved into your bedroom."

"And Heather?"

"You saved her many times too. It's all in here. Heather would have died that day even if you hadn't taken that pain medication. He had a gun with him that he intended to use. When he didn't feel the usual pain as she approached, he reverted to his usual M.O."

"So, because I took the pain medication, Heather suffered a slow and horrific death."

"And you'd be dead right now if you hadn't."

"Why do you say that?"

"Because Trig put you on the Peace Sign Killer case due to your connection to it. He knew you would be motivated to bring Heather's killer to justice. If Heather had died in a manner that didn't connect her to the Peace Sign Killer, you wouldn't have been assigned to the case. It wouldn't even have been an FBI case, just a random shooting for the local police to solve. Thus, you wouldn't have identified and dispensed with Uncle Phil as you did. Instead, he would have shot and killed you on one of your Quantico Trail runs. It's all outlined here. You saw the pictures, didn't you? He was picking out his spot."

I nodded as the clouds of my confusion and ambivalence began to part. Giving way to the clarity and the purpose that had first fueled my desire to accept Trig's invitation to join the FBI. I realized that things had to happen the way they did for me to stop Uncle Phil's reign of terror. The existential crisis that I walked in with died in Dr. Ledbrinker's office, and I left feeling like the weight of the world had been lifted from me.

On the way back to the dorm, I knew that Trig must have read the diary when he found it and realized how fortuitous it was that he assigned me to the case. No wonder he seemed so distracted yesterday when he told me about it. He must have known that the information it contained would be best conveyed to me through Dr. Ledbrinker.

I had a little over an hour to get ready for my dinner date with Travis. Standing under the warm spray of the showerhead, I lingered, letting the water bombard my body, cleansing me not only literally but figuratively. The water rolled down my body and fell like a waterfall from my long tresses. My concerns washing down the drain along with the water. Freeing me and making me feel lighter. Drying my hair, putting on my make-up, and even finding the clothes I wanted to wear wasn't fraught with the doubt and debate about how I looked as it had before my first date with Travis. I put on a white scoop top, my favorite jeans, and accessorized simply with my ever-present silver butterfly pendant necklace. I actually liked what I saw in the mirror. This wasn't necessarily a function of any significant change in my actual physical appearance but a more profound and more fundamental metamorphosis. Something inside me had changed. That it corresponded to turning 18 in a few weeks felt more coincidental than developmental.

Travis was waiting for me out front when I exited the dorm. It felt natural when he greeted me with a hug. As we made our way to his car, he talked excitedly about acing a test in one of his classes. The gentleman that he was, he opened the passenger-side door, and I slipped into the seat, meeting his smile with mine before he closed the door. Lydia wasn't working that evening, or maybe she no longer worked there. It didn't matter. Travis and I were too enthralled in our own little world to notice one way or the other.

After dinner, not ready to call it a night, we drove west, ending up at Shenandoah National Park. A few miles into the park on Skyline Drive, we pulled over at an overlook. It was a cold, clear, crisp evening, and neither of us had worn jackets. It didn't matter. The stars were bright, and we searched the sky for Scutum, my namesake constellation. Failing, we settled for gazing at Ursa Minor. Travis wrapped his arms around me and kissed my scar as he had on our first date. Our lips met, and we shared our first real kiss.

This time when I felt the tingle of my butterfly pendant, I didn't question Heather's message. I knew she was with me and telling me to carry on.

EPILOGUE

My mother wouldn't learn the truth about her brother until shortly after returning home. She and my father had stayed in Richmond for a couple of days to make arrangements to have Uncle Phil cremated and to put his affairs in order. Fortunately, all the damning evidence in Uncle Phil's apartment had been removed, and what was left wasn't of interest to her. She made arrangements for a service to pick up what was left in his apartment and have it donated to charity.

Those first few days after Mom and Dad's return were hell, from what Misty told me. My mother refused to talk to Misty, and the urn with Uncle Phil's ashes, now prominently displayed on a shelf in the living room, haunted her. It wasn't until the FBI agent arrived and broke the news to my mother that a healing process between Mom and Misty began. Mom was understandably devastated. Not only about the awful truth about her brother but also about Misty's fear of telling her about all the incidents of abuse she had endured from Uncle Phil and others. My mother and Misty achieved something of a breakthrough when my Mom took Uncle Phil's urn off the shelf and asked Misty how she wanted to dispose of it. Misty initially thought about flushing his ashes down the toilet. Ultimately deciding that he belonged in the landfill amongst all the other trash. She took great pleasure in heaving the urn into the path of a bulldozer that was busily crushing and burying the refuse and other discarded junk.

The families of Uncle Phil's victims were notified of his death. Eventually, the media grabbed onto what they thought was the story. One newspaper headline captured the media bias best: "Karma, Not the Cops, Kills Serial Rapist and Murderer." The storylines all focused on how it took a rare medical condition to kill Uncle Phil. Casting aspersions on the ineptitude of the police and the FBI in bringing him to justice and failing to protect the nation's youths from abuse and exploitation. I would have been angry about these stories if Trig hadn't forewarned me that the media frequently gets the facts wrong. Local law enforcement agencies were often compelled to share information or try to correct the press. The FBI, on the other hand, was more reticent about doing so. Especially in this case, given my unique and perhaps controversial abilities.

My father stopped by to see me before shipping out to wherever the CIA was sending him. He met with Trig, Travis, and me for lunch in the chow hall. I was a nervous wreck, but I needn't have been. Travis and my dad hit it off famously. Before my dad left, he handed me a small package, which was for my birthday, only a week away. He embarrassed me further by making me open it. Blushing, I unwrapped the present and opened the box to find two marquise-cut diamond earrings.

"Shaped like Scutum, the constellation I named you after," he said, smiling.

"You knew?" I asked, surprised.

"Yeah, but I never wanted to admit my error to your mother, so I just went with it. I knew you'd figure it out eventually."

"I love them. Thanks, Dad," I replied.

"You're welcome. Happy Birthday, Superstar."

As my Dad got up to go, I got up and hugged him.

"When will I see you again?"

"I don't know, but maybe Special Agent Halvorsen here can figure out how we can work together on one of your next cases."

I looked at Trig, my facial expression communicating my desire for an immediate and favorable response from him.

"I might just be able to arrange that, Sergeant Schultz," he replied.

I couldn't restrain myself from hugging him in response.

Meanwhile, Travis shook my dad's hand.

"Nice to meet you, sir."

"Take good care of Aja."

"I will, sir. Although I think she's pretty good at taking care of herself."

"That she is, Travis. That she is."

A week later, Travis and I celebrated my 18th birthday and Thanksgiving together. Normally, my mother would have wanted to host a get-together, but Misty was back at college, and my mother was understandably not in a festive mood. I was surprised when Travis took me to a romantic dinner and overnight stay at a beautiful old bed and breakfast in Fredericksburg. I wore my diamond earrings, my butterfly pendant, a little black dress, and killer black patent-leather pumps. I felt like a real woman - smart, beautiful, confident, respected, purposeful, and loved.

It hadn't been easy getting here, and I was certain there would be setbacks, but I no longer felt cursed. I was blessed with a gift, and I was going to use it.

* * *

Thank you for reading *Aja Minor: Gifted or Cursed*, the first book in the Aja Minor series. Enter link below into browser to purchase the next book in the series – *Aja Minor: Fountain of Youth*.

https://readerlinks.com/l/1350820

ACKNOWLEDGEMENT

One of the defining moments in my life occurred when I was in college and did a 4-week internship at a program for children who suffered from emotional and behavioral disorders. One child, in particular, tugged at my heartstrings. Christy was autistic, and she would sit alone in a corner and silently rock back and forth. The counselors discouraged me from trying to "reach" her, given the short time I would be there. That only motivated me. Every day I would make a point of sitting with Christy, even though it didn't appear that she noticed or cared that I was there. In the last week of my internship, I was pushing a child on a swing and felt little arms wrap themselves around my leg. When I looked down, Christy was hugging my leg and motioning for me to push her on the swing. I tearfully obliged, and the counselors were astounded. It was the first time Christy had ever taken the initiative to interact with anyone at the program.

Fueled by this experience, I subsequently went on to get a Master's degree in psychotherapy and counseling. I worked for years with children and adolescents in a variety of mental health and substance abuse facilities. Many of the children I worked with had suffered from emotional, physical, and sexual abuse. I was fired from one position when I reported a complaint of abuse to my supervisor. It turned out that my supervisor, along with the staff member I reported, had both been abusing the adolescent clients. Ultimately, they were terminated, and I subsequently received letters from the adolescents in the program thanking me for my actions in getting them removed.

I am dedicating this book not only to the children and adolescents I had the honor to help through their challenges but to all people who suffered abuse or exploitation as children. Sadly, there are almost daily reminders in the news about sexual abuse and exploitation. My fictional heroines' powers aside, it's a scourge that can't magically be identified and eliminated.

I will be donating a portion of the proceeds from this book to the National Center for Missing & Exploited Children, which was established in 1984 to help find missing children, reduce child sexual exploitation, and prevent child victimization.

BOOKS BY THIS AUTHOR

Table For Four: A Medical Thriller Series Book 1

A blockbuster Alzheimer's cure. A murder and unexplained deaths. Two aggrieved parties meet by chance. Will they expose the truth, or die trying?

Dying To Recall: A Medical Thriller Series Book 2

A suicide, a break-in, an ominous warning. Is it a coincidence? Or have Jackie and Curt unleashed the wrath of vengeful pharmaceutical executives?

Memory's Hope: A Medical Thriller Series Book 3

The case against AlzCura intensifies until the FDA's shocking response to the data. Will the guilty parties walk, or will they be brought to justice?

Aja Minor: Gifted Or Cursed: A Psychic Crime Thriller Series Book 1

Aja has disturbing powers. She feels cursed, but the FBI thinks otherwise. Will she stop a serial rapist and killer or become his next victim?

Aja Minor: Fountain Of Youth: A Psychic Crime Thriller Series Book 2

Aja Minor goes undercover. The target, an international child trafficking ring. When her cover is blown, the mission and her life are in jeopardy.

Aja Minor: Predatorville: A Psychic Crime Thriller Series Book 3

Solving a surge in assaults and missing children is Aja Minor's next test. But when the hunter becomes the hunted, will she get out of Predatorville alive?

Old Lady Ketchel's Revenge: The Slaughter Minnesota Horror Series Book 1

No one truly escapes their childhood unscathed. Especially if you grew up in Slaughter, Minnesota, in the 1960s and crossed Old Lady Ketchel's path.

Hagatha Ketchel Unhinged: The Slaughter Minnesota Horror Series Book 2

Twenty-four years in an asylum is enough time to really lose your mind. And arouse one to unleash the dark and vengeful thoughts residing therein.

Hagatha's Century Of Terror: The Slaughter Minnesota Horror Series Book 3

What does a crazy old lady in Slaughter, Minnesota, need on her 100th birthday? Sweet revenge, of course.

Loving You From My Grave: A Wholesome Inspirational Romance

He ran from his past. She's held captive by hers. Could love set them free, bridge their differences in age and race, and survive death?

Little Bird On My Balcony: Selected Poems

A collection of poems that speak to the love, loss, longing, and levity of navigating young adulthood.

Adilynn's Lullaby: Poems Of Love & Loss

A collection of poems about love and loss that provide hope and inspiration during some of life's most difficult times.

ABOUT CHRIS BLIERSBACH

 Chris Bliersbach is originally from St. Paul, Minnesota, and now lives in Henderson, Nevada.

Follow him on Amazon, Facebook, Goodreads or join his mailing list at cmbliersbach@gmail.com

Made in United States
North Haven, CT
13 May 2024

52429348R10195